EVERLASTIN' LOVERS

"Damn you, Lachlan, you make me crazy, sometimes! I told you I want you in my life. What more do you want to hear? That I want you in my bed?" Beth sucked in a breath to calm her nerves. "Okay, I do. Want you in my bed, I mean."

Expressionless, Lachlan ran a hand over the top of his sodden hair. "Are you sayin' you want me back in bed, lass, or in *any* bed wi' you?"

A strangled laugh escaped her before she gripped the remains of the front of his shirt. Lifting on tiptoes immersed in mud, she calmly stated, "If you don't kiss me now, I'm going to bury you where you stand."

"You've graduated from threatenin' my monhood to the whole o' me, eh?"

"Lachlan . . ."

He released a throaty laugh and exuberantly threw his arms around her. She looked up, her lips parted in invitation. Sweetened by the rain, his mouth moved languidly over hers, second by second becoming more demanding until she ached with familiar desire. In life or death, he owned a part of her no other man could claim.

HOPE EVERLASTIN'

MICKEE MADDEN

Pinnacle Books
Kensington Publishing Corp.
http://www.pinnaclebooks.com

PINNACLE BOOKS are published by

Kensington Publishing Corp.
850 Third Avenue
New York, NY 10022

First Printing: July, 1999
10 9 8 7 6 5 4 3 2 1

Printed in the United States of America

DEDICATION

For Steve and our children Gwen, Buddy and Brehan, and our grandchildren Eric Brandon and Dameon Michael. Aunt Donna. Steven and Mary, and their children Ashley and Patrick. Matt and Grace, and their children Erik, Kahl, and Alby. Gerri and Anna.

Sandy, mentioned first in this list because she loves to whine, Marsha, Rosella, Guy and my son, Steven, Jr. for critiquing me through another book. Thank you!

Denise Little.

Donna Kater, Heather Moon, Cindy Stapleton, Trisha Mitchner, Kathleen (Meeka) Lombardo, Kim Fried, Angie Wheat and Betty Cimarolli. Just because.

Special thanks to my editor, Carin, and everyone else at Kensington for their talent, patience and support.

Also, my heart-felt thanks to the readers, especially those whose inspiring letters keep me pounding at the keyboard with new purpose.

Last but not least, Lachlan, who's of the belief there can never be too much written about him.

GLOSSARY

abou'/about
afore/before
anither/another
aught/anything
bahookie/buttocks
canna/cannot
corbie/crow
daith/death
dee/die
deil/devil
dinna/don't
dule/sorrow
efter/after
faither/father
fegs/damn
ither/other
mak/make
mairrit/married
mither/mother
na canny/unnatural
no'/not
nocht/nothing
o'/of
ou'/out
shouldna/shouldn't
tak/take
tha'/that
thegither/together
tis/it is
trow/to believe
twas/it was
verra/very
wae/woe
wasna/wasn't
weel/well
wha'/what
willna/will not
winna/won't
wi'/with
wouldna/wouldn't

Lachlan Baird
13/2/1811–24/3/1844
Aberdeen, Scotland

On a storm-driven night at three minutes before midnight, Ciarda MacLachlan Baird gave birth to her fourth and last son, Lachlan Iain MacLachlan Baird. In front of dying embers at the hearth, she'd suffered her labor alone while her husband and sons attended to the business of completing a merchant ship across town. She was a woman accustomed to a solitary existence. From the time her sons could walk and talk, they became solely Guin's, their father's, to mold into his future partners. His heirs. She ceased being their mother; was instead the woman who cooked and cleaned for them. By the third son, she expected no more from her family. Ever. Until this night.

From the instant Ciarda had conceived this child she'd known he would be different, and had feared his birth more than she had feared anything in her life. No longer, though. Not only did he bear the dark red hair of her forefathers, but she sensed through something more powerful than maternal instinct, that he would always be *her* son, one whose destiny had yet to be written.

In the years to come, Ciarda cherished Lachlan above all else. It saddened her to watch him struggle for his father's attention and approval, and to prove himself worthy of participating in the family business, something his brothers, for whatever reasons, were bitterly against. Lachlan was younger than Angus by seven years, Gavin by ten, and Patrick by twelve. By the time he had a fair idea of what his father's business entailed, his brothers were gradually taking over.

Lachlan was never one to settle for the odd jobs meted out to him by the older Baird males. He was blessed with a sharp, inquisitive mind and a talent for succeeding at whatever he applied himself to. His mother had once told him his brothers felt somewhat threatened by his ability to learn and adapt. She always encouraged him to experience life and all it had to offer, often telling him that the world did not revolve around the Baird business nor the dictates of his father and brothers, and that of all her sons, *he* alone was a true MacLachlan.

Unlike his siblings, Lachlan was a dreamer. As a boy he had an imaginary friend named Onora, who he believed was his guardian angel. She often told him in his dreams that the world was his to explore. Told him that as long as he kept his mind open to all possibilities, the secrets of life would offer themselves to him. During his formative years, he seldom did anything without consulting her first. He respected her wisdom and trusted her to watch over him.

In between working odd jobs for his father and brothers, Lachlan met a Frenchman named Millard Barluc, a moderately known swordsman at the time. He'd taken a fancy to seven-year-old Lachlan and was pleased by the boy's request to satisfy his curiosity about the history of the sword. Soon, he began teaching Lachlan swordplay, which two years later led to Lachlan taking fencing lessons from another Frenchman, Charles LaForte, a friend of Barluc's. The training he received from both mentors helped him to develop irrevocable confidence and self-esteem, and taught him to discipline his growing impatience with his father and brothers.

When Lachlan was twenty, his maternal grandfather died. Lachlan took it harder than even his mother. It was then that Barluc told Lachlan and his parents that he was planning to enter a swordsmen's tournament which would span most of Western Europe during the next two years. He wanted Lachlan to go with him. Ciarda didn't want her youngest son to leave, but Guin insisted it was time Lachlan was cut free of her apron strings. Lachlan went with Barluc, but only because of his father's propensity to take out his displeasure of his son on Ciarda.

Lachlan made good use of the tournament circuit during the ensuing two years. He competed and won more often than not against contestants in his category, then turned his small winnings into a sizeable fortune through various gambling endeavors during their travels. Barluc would shake his head in wonder at Lachlan's good luck at cards and dice. Would shake his head and laugh when Lachlan bested gypsies at their own games. *The Lucky Baird,* he called Lachlan. The nickname spread across Western Europe, and usually greeted Lachlan when he and Barluc arrived at a new city. Wielding steel or gaming, he met each challenge with a grin and an attitude of that win or lose, life was a grand experience.

Lachlan didn't spend all of his time competing and gambling. He also took every opportunity to mingle with merchants, seamen, dockmen and the owners of shipping companies, accumulating an *inside* understanding of what happened after a ship was built and claimed by its owner. He studied comparative building techniques of other countries and, during the tournament's stay in Italy, learned the art of Italian molding. His insatiable craving for knowledge and outgoing personality made it easy for him to approach strangers and gather information. Whether his friends and acquaintances called him "The Crazy Scot" or "The Lucky Baird," he was duly accorded the respect he earned.

However, the man Lachlan had become still could not sway his father and brothers' opinions of him.

When he returned to Aberdeen, he was grief-stricken to discover that his mother had died eight months prior. No one had made any attempt to let him know. His resentment for his father and brothers grew tenfold, for they refused to tell him how his mother had died. Months later, a family acquaintance, Giles Towne, finally spoke up while sharing a lager with Lachlan at a local pub. Ciarda had broken her neck during a fall down the staircase in her home. According to Towne it had been a terrible accident. During the man's conversation, though, strange images flashed through Lachlan's mind. Of his parents arguing about him at the top of the wide staircase. Of Guin shoving Ciarda in a fit of rage. He could hear his mother's bones breaking as she tumbled down the wide steps. Could *hear* her silence when she sprawled onto the first floor landing, where she remained motionless and pale while her husband remained atop the staircase, his hands balled into fists at his sides.

Lachlan never again questioned her premature death, but he would always harbor an aching void in that part of his heart that was hers alone.

Guin Baird had retired shortly after his wife's death, and remained a recluse in the family home. The business was in dire tax arrears, and was on the verge of closing. Lachlan obtained a shrewd barrister to draw him up a contract with his father and brothers. In exchange for investing a portion of the fortune he had amassed into the company, he would own fifty-one percent of the business. Resentfully, they signed the document, but not before warning Lachlan the maneuver was considered a blow against the "family." Regardless, Lachlan took over the reins. During the next ten years, despite his brothers fighting his decisions at every turn, *Baird Ships* excelled, from cargo ships to schooners.

Lachlan worked with the builders, teaching them all

he'd learned from the craftsmen in France, Italy, and Germany. The demand for luxury ships was especially on the rise, and the contracts for schooners the business received were almost more than the employees could build within the allotted time. Somehow, deadlines were always met, and the company expanded year after year.

Still, the older Bairds looked upon Lachlan as an outsider. Once, when Lachlan was twenty-seven, his brother Angus had commented that Lachlan would always be a MacLachlan. He'd said this disparagingly, as if their MacLachlan lineage were something to shun. Granted, Angus, Gavin, and Patrick had their father's fair coloring, light brown eyes, and light brown hair, while Lachlan bore his mother's dark auburn hair and near-black eyes. He was taller and more broad-shouldered. His features were more chiseled than rounded like theirs. But coloring, bone structure and size should not have been enough to cause their refusal to accept him. No matter how often or how forcefully he demanded to know the basis for their animosity, his brothers remained smugly reticent.

With his father barely able to look *at* him and not *through* him as he had all of Lachlan's life, Lachlan decided at thirty to sell his share of the business to his brothers, and for an exorbitant sum, at that. One that he felt would justify the others ridding themselves of him forever. As an added bonus to leaving, all of his mother's belongings were given to him, including the relics and furniture she'd brought into the marriage. It was as if his father and brothers wanted all trace of her stripped from the house. Stripped from their lives. Wealthier now than the Baird men collectively, he moved to the lowlands, where he eventually built Baird House.

He returned to Aberdeen only to find himself a proper Highland bride, then returned to his estate with Tessa Aiken and her brother, full of dreams for their future.

That same year, his still bride-in-name-only, and Robert Ingliss—who he discovered was her lover, not her brother—murdered Lachlan and walled him up in the tower of the Victorian mansion. It should have been the end of "The Lucky Baird." Instead, it was only the beginning.

And only upon his death did his true destiny finally become engraved into the annals of time. . . .

HERE THE DEVIL LIES
LACHLAN IAIN BAIRD
13/2/1811 - ?/1844

CHAPTER ONE

With the advent of night, the temperature dropped to the high thirties in Crossmichael, Scotland. Roan Ingliss and Lachlan Baird sat on separate crates in the carriage house, briskly rubbing their hands within the heat emanating from the wood stove. Two lanterns provided them with adequate visibility. Their dinner basket had been emptied two hours earlier, and lay at Roan's feet.

The previous night, Lachlan, Roan, and Winston Connery had gotten into a brawl at Shortby's Pub in town. Their women, fed up with the "Scotch" taking precedence over them, had strongly suggested the men move into the carriage house for a time. No one was more to blame than Lachlan, himself.

He hadn't taken his reemergence into life all that well. No, that was an understatement. In truth, he was more afraid of life than he had been of death. His reluctance to face his new responsibilities had caused a rift between him and Beth, and had somehow started a war of wills between the other men and women residing at Baird House. Thus far, only Winston had mustered up the nerve to face his love, Deliah. That morning, he'd gone back into the main house and hadn't been seen since. Either Deliah had turned him into the "nubby toad" she'd threatened to on a few occasions, or—

" 'Tis a fair wager he's snuggled up wi' her," said Lachlan a bit testily. "As we should be wi' *our* women."

Roan grunted. He rapidly ran his hands up and down his face, then raked his fingers through the unruly loose curls of his light brown hair. "If you remind me once more o' our sorry predicament, I'll throttle you, Lannie."

An amused glint shone in Lachlan eyes as his gaze swung to Roan's profile. "Jaggy o' heart, are we?"

Again Roan grunted.

Silence companioned them for a time, then Lachlan released a long, woeful sigh. "I keep thinkin' abou' my children." He shivered, snugged deeper into the blanket draped about his shoulders, and leaned closer to the stove. "How did you react when you first learned you were goin' to be a faither?"

Roan stared off into space for a moment, then said, "Stunned. Adaina and I had already decided to separate. I thought she was tryin' to spite me at first—for no' bein' the husband she wanted. I didn't even believe her till she started to show."

"Efter Jamey was born?" Lachlan asked softly.

A fond smile wove its way through the tension in Roan's face. "The instant I laid my sorry eyes on him—" His voice broke and he cleared his throat. "I was never prouder or happier. He was such a wonder, and brought more joy to my life—for wha' little time he had on this earth. I've often wondered wha' he would look like now. Whether he would think me a good faither, or the loser his mither thought me."

"I didna mean to open the wound."

Roan gave a nod. "I know you didn't." He shook his head as he plucked absently at a loose wool fiber along the edge of the blanket covering his shoulders. "When you lose someone, Lannie, you can't shake from your mind the wha' ifs or the regrets. Every cruel word and deed eats at you till you think you'll go mad, even though you know tha' person is beyond you redeemin' your worth to them."

"I've only ever lost myself," Lachlan said with a comical lilt to his tone. "And in the grand scheme o' life, 'twas but a wee loss, I'm sorry to say."

His eyes twinkling as he regarded Lachlan, Roan chuckled, "You're incorrigible."

"Tha' I am. Roan, why is it the womon carries the child and suffers givin' birth, but 'tis the mon who feels threatened?"

"Maybe it has to do wi' the financial responsibility o' havin' children. Tha' and the emotional commitment it taks to bein' a parent. Women seemed to be blessed wi' an incredible ability to adapt. Look at Laura. A career womon never really wantin' children, and she inherits three rowdy nephews. Aye, she panicked at first, but her maternal instincts were quick to surface. Not sure how I would have coped if I'd found myself in her position. Wha' hurts like hell is knowin' she could raise those lads just fine withou' me."

"I dinna agree wi' tha', my friend. Laura needs you as much as the boys do. Dinna sell yourself short."

"Ah, maybe so. I'm just in the dumps, so Kevin says."

Lachlan frowned thoughtfully, then said, "I've been thinkin' abou' my faither. He was never around much, and for tha' I was grateful. He had a mean streak up his back tha' was as wide as his arse."

A grin tugged at Roan's mouth. "Quite an image you paint."

"Aye. We had no love for one anither. Love, understandin', and security . . . that's wha' a parent is abou'. My faither was a terrible role model, and I spent wha' I had o' my life tryin' no' to be anythin' like him. I was determined to be kind where he was cruel, and strong where he was weak, which is why I canna understand why I withdrew like I did from Beth and the twins. I've never backed off from a challenge, Roan, and yet their wee faces filled me wi' such terror, I got lost in fears o' inadequacy. I was more afraid o' disappointin' them than o' abandonin' them."

"Was?" Roan asked softly, delighted that Lachlan was finally coming around.

Lachlan nodded. "Aye, I've come to my senses." He gushed a breath in vexation. "Little wonder Beth is furious, eh? She's left no choice but to fall into the role o' parent, while I tak to sulkin' and Scotch. I'm goin' to have a deil o' a time undoin' *this* mess, I am."

"Are you still plannin' to approach her in the morn?"

Lachlan released a strangled laugh. "Aye, but I wish I could don armor first. She has a fine temper, and I wouldna change tha' for all the Scotch in the land." He sighed deeply. "But I've never been such a fool afore, nor seen her so angry and hurt."

To Lachlan's amazement, Roan began to laugh, its deep rich sound filling the carriage house.

"Have you gone daft, mon?"

Roan's mirth wound down. "Sorry. I got this image o' Beth comin' at you wi' a fryin' pan."

"You *are* daft," Lachlan grumbled.

"No. Wha' really struck me funny was seein' in my mind Laura doin' the same to me. Women may be called the weaker sex, but you and I know differently."

"Aye," Lachlan chortled, and clapped Roan on the shoulder. "A fryin' pan my thick skull could tak, but I wouldna put it past my Beth to do me a more serious deed." He grimaced and grew quiet for a few moments. "I've too many swords and the like in the house." He sighed again. "Aye, 'tis a mess, for sure."

Roan stood and stretched the small of his back. "I've got to step ou' back and relieve my bladder. Don't soak up all the heat while I'm gone."

Lachlan gave a brief nod, then braced his elbows on his thighs and watched Roan go out the back door.

The night air made Roan grimace as he walked toward the white picket fence separating the property. He was about to unzip his fly when he detected voices. After a moment, he pinpointed the general location and realized he was hearing segments of a heated argument. Dashing back to the open door, he shouted, "Lannie, something's goin' on in the field!"

Lachlan appeared at the threshhold. He followed Roan to the fence, where he, too, heard voices drifting in from the clearing beyond the woods, the area of his supposed resting place.

The two men entered the woods, oblivious to the cold, their concentration focused on keeping afoot on the slick ground. Before they exited the wooded area, two beams of light could be seen bobbing beneath the bare branches of the solitary oak in the center of the field. Both men stopped to weigh the situation, then looked at each other.

"Why would someone be messin' around the graves?" Roan asked, his heart hammering inside his chest.

Lachlan lit into another run, taking the lead, fury fueling his momentum.

Near the ancient oak, Roan and Lachlan found three men struggling on the ground. One of them, younger than the others, seemed to be fighting off the other two, his fists sailing and guttural Gaelic curses abounding. The older men appeared to be attempting to hold down the third. As Lachlan and Roan slid to a stop, one of the older men raised his flashlight in a gesture that indicated he intended to bring it down on the younger man's head.

Lachlan grabbed the man's lifted arm. Ignoring his yelp of surprise, Lachlan yanked him off the younger man, leaving Roan to handle the second. While Roan was trying to separate the fist-driving pair, Lachlan's captive unexpectedly elbowed him in the midriff, then shoved him. Lachlan pitched backward and struck the ground, while his assailant ran toward the road bordering the side of the property.

Dazed, Lachlan had sat up before he realized there was something odd about the ground beneath him. It was soft dirt, not packed snow or ice. From the corner of his eye, he saw something erect a scant half an arm's reach away. Horrified, he found himself gawking at his headstone.

He was sitting atop the partially excavated depression of his own grave.

With a howl, he bolted to his feet, in time to witness the second old man swing his flashlight at Roan. The blow caught Roan just above his right temple, and he fell to his side, disoriented and unable to stop the man from taking off after his partner.

Panting, the younger man rolled onto his knees and gingerly helped Roan to sit up. Lachlan stepped out of the two-foot deep depression and loomed behind the remaining stranger, his hands fisted at his sides.

"Get your paughty hands off him!" Lachlan warned, not touching the stranger for fear he would beat him to a pulp.

"I had no part in this but to try to stop them," the young man said testily.

Lachlan's hands swooped downward. In his right he clutched the collar of the man's jacket, in the other, one of the flashlights. Both he lifted with equal ease. Whirling around, he deftly slammed the man against the broad trunk of the oak and cinched his free hand across his throat.

Focusing the beam of the flashlight on the man's face, Lachlan snarled, "Wha' are you doin' on this property, diggin' up my grave?"

"Your—" Despite the harsh light, his blue eyes widened. Then he squinted and gripped the wrist of Lachlan's hand in a futile attempt to move the beam from his face.

"Answer me!"

Roan got to his feet and unsteadily stood at Lachlan's side.

"I found them diggin'. Afore I had a chance to say a word, they turned on me."

"You just happened to be here, eh?" Lachlan asked heatedly, and tightened his grip.

"Aye!" the man gasped.

"Let him go," said Roan. "Lannie, the ither two wouldn't have run like they did if they weren't the culprits."

"How do I know they didna merely turn on one o' their own?"

The young man's eyes pleaded with Roan to reason on his behalf with Lachlan, but before Roan could say another word, Lachlan released him and stepped back.

Massaging his throat, the young man nodded in gratitude, his wary gaze on Lachlan.

"Wha' the hell?" Roan murmured, using the second flashlight to inspect the disturbed ground. Two shovels lay on the opposite side of the grave.

"Grave robbin' is a grievous offense," Lachlan gritted out, his gaze raking over the stranger.

The young man straightened. He was as tall as Lachlan but slender in build and approximately in his mid-twenties. His long, wavy hair was unkempt and hung a good three inches past his shoulders. High cheekbones. A prominent jawline with a deeply cleft chin. Blood trickled from the left nostril of his straight nose.

"Sir, I may be withou' a home or a place to sleep, but a grave robber I am no'. On my honor, I was walkin' the road and saw the lights. I thought myself fortunate to find anyone ou' so late, and only trespassed to ask if perhaps they had a place I could sleep for the night. I didna know wha' was goin' on till I saw these markers and those men diggin' up the ground."

Lachlan tilted up his chin and eyed the man with blatant cynicism. "Just walkin' along the road, were you?"

"Aye. Lookin' for a place to sleep the night."

Roan and Lachlan exchanged dubious glances, then both focused on the stranger.

"What's your name?" asked Roan.

"Reith, sir."

"Where are you from?" asked Lachlan, coldly.

"Originally from this area, sir. I've been away some time

and, as you can see, I be a wee down on my luck. For the past two days I've been tryin' to find a job in town."

"Wha' kind o' work do you do?" asked Roan.

"I'll put my hands to anythin', sir, but I be best workin' land. Gardenin' and prunin'. I'm willin' to work for room and board."

"Are you now?" said Lachlan suspiciously.

"Aye, sir, on my honor. I've really no use for money. A place to lay my head and food in my stomach is all I need."

Lachlan ran the beam down the man's length, and grimaced. "You're dressed like a ragged tinker, mon. Have you no pride?"

"Pride?" A tinge of indignation tainted Reith's voice. "Sir, I have more'n my fair measure o' pride, but 'tis never brought me nocht but shame and grief. All I own be on my back, and I be as glad to have it as you in your fancy shirt."

Roan grinned despite the throbbing pain in his head. "Damn me, but I like his spirit."

Lachlan continued to scowl into the young man's face. "Do you know who I am, laddie?"

"Lannie," Roan warned, which Lachlan impatiently flagged off with a hand.

Reith jerked in surprise at the question, then gave Lachlan a serious looking over. "No, sir. Should I?"

"Lachlan Baird."

Genuine puzzlement masked the man's face. "Are ye someone o' importance?"

With a somewhat sardonic grin, Lachlan pointed to the disturbed ground. "Prior to a few weeks ago, tha' was *my* grave."

A smile of uncertainty twitched on Reith's mouth. "You're a . . . *ghost,* sir?"

"I'm a born again pain in the arse."

Roan rolled his eyes heavenward and clenched his teeth against a groan.

"Weel, laddie, wha' have you to say to tha'?"

Reith blew out a breath, glanced at the grave, then closed

one eye and searched Lachlan's face with the other. "I've seen my fair measure o' wonders, so I guess I say welcome back, Mr. Baird."

A glint of wry amusement awakened in Lachlan's eyes. "Are you no' sorry you set foot on my land, then?"

"Only for the beatin'," Reith said in earnest. "I *need* to work, sir."

"For your room and board?"

Reith nodded.

Lachlan glanced at Roan, who shrugged and said, "There's soon to be plenty o' work around here."

"Tell me, laddie, where is your family?" asked Lachlan, suspicion still lacing his tone.

Reith lowered his head. "My wife asked me to leave."

"You're mairrit?"

The blue eyes lifted. "Aye, Mr. Baird."

"Why did she ask you to leave?"

"In truth?" Reith croaked.

"Always," said Lachlan curtly.

"I shamed her. Shamed my clan."

"Och, and you expect *us* to trust you?" Lachlan exclaimed.

"I be no longer tha' immature fool," Reith said. His gaze shifted to Roan, then back to Lachlan. "Sir, have ye never erred and wished ye could turn back time to right your wrongs?"

Lachlan and Roan exchanged dubious glances and shifted uneasily.

"All right," said Lachlan, scratching his nape. He glanced at Roan, who nodded in confirmation as if divining Lachlan's thoughts, then frowned at Reith. "Tonight, you'll have to share your lodgin' wi' us. But wi' luck, come morn, our women will be forgivin' *our* . . . errin' . . . then you can have the carriage house to yourself. Room and board you'll have, but also a fair wage."

"That's verra generous, sir."

Lachlan scowled formidably. "Step ou' o' line, and you'll answer to me."

"I'll do ye and the land proud."

Roan knelt at the edge of the grave and scooped up a handful of the rich dirt. He considered its weight and texture, then spread his fingers and watched it fall back to the earth. "You don't have any idea wha' they were lookin' for?" he asked Reith.

"I overheard the men talkin' afore they realized I was here. One o' them said if they found the graves empty, they would have their proof."

"Proof o' wha'?" Roan clipped, standing and facing the younger man, his hands on his hips. It wasn't his intention to appear intimidating to the stranger, but his stomach was knotted with something he couldn't quite define, and he was anxious to get away from the graves.

Reith didn't answer right away. His shrewd gaze was fixed on Roan's face as if reading his thoughts, or at the least, pondering the cause of Roan's sudden testiness. Finally, he said, "Physical proof. That be the term I heard. I thought it be a strange thing to say, but even stranger when the ither man said somethin' about the scam already bein' the hottest story o' the decade. Photographs o' empty graves would be worth a wee fortune."

"Scam," Roan murmured, his bleak gaze shifting to Lachlan's now blanched face. A memory flashed vividly through his mind. "Shortby's. Good God Almighty! There was a mon sittin at the counter wi' a camera!"

"Och, aye, the flashin'!" Lachlan exclaimed. "Fegs, wha' have I done?"

"Dinna panic," Roan rasped, his hands held up in a pleading manner. "Those bastards didna get their bloody photos, thanks to young Reith, here. No, no need to panic. I'm sure we'll come up wi' a plan to prevent this from happenin' again."

"Do you now?" Lachlan asked with a scowl. "How abou' if I lie in my grave and wait for the next corbie to come along? A weel-timed *boo* might solve *all* our bloody problems, aye?"

"At the least," said Roan humorously, "the intruder would shit his breeks."

"I dinna think so," said Reith cryptically, pointing.

Roan and Lachlan looked in the direction of the manor. The sky between it and the carriage house was unnaturally lit up. Horns and voices rent the night.

"No," Lachlan murmured, swaying on his feet like a drunkard. "Canna be so. Tell me it canna be so!"

This time Roan took the lead, Lachlan and Reith closely following as they ran across the field and into the woods. They stopped and hunkered within a patch of high brush situated between the houses. From this position, they could see a horde of men and women, some with varying camera equipment, others with professional lighting systems. There were shouts for the occupants of the main house to come out and answer questions, and heated demands for a response to the accusations of fraud regarding the supposed hauntings of Baird House.

A media blitz had arrived.

"Reith," said Lachlan, "go into the carriage house and stay ou' o' sight."

"But, sir—"

"Do as I say!"

Without hesitation, the young man stayed low to the ground and made his way to the back door.

Lachlan met Roan's troubled gaze and rasped, "My God, wha' have we done?"

"*We?*" Roan rasped. Hadn't Lachlan accepted the blame at the graves?

Lachlan Baird's convoluted existence had never been more complicated than it was now. He watched the media frenzy unfolding a short distance away, his horror deepening with each passing second, and his fevered mind scrambling to come up with a simple way to unravel the havoc he'd inadvertently brought upon the estate and its occupants.

He inwardly winced, shriveled from the inside out at the thought of Beth's reaction. She'd already relegated him to the carriage house, temporarily barring him from seeing her and their two week old twins. Not that he could blame her. He *had* been an ass of late. Nothing she wouldn't forgive after a while. But *this?* She blamed their problems on his liking for Scotch. How anyone could hold a wee libation responsible for a man's stupidity was beyond him. Granted, he'd been in his cups more than he should since their return, but he had a damn good reason.

Didn't he?

Crouched behind the hedge, Lachlan looked askance at Roan when he gave his arm a squeeze, as if to warn him not to make a sound or move. He didn't need coaching in that respect. He planned to stay very quiet and very still . . . unless Winston or one of the women—or, God forbid! one of Laura's nephews—opened the door to confront the reporters.

He squeezed his eyes shut a moment, then opened them and glared at the noisy trespassers not more than twenty feet away. Every shouted accusation of fraud made his hands repeatedly clench.

Fraud against whom?

Crossmichael?

The county?

All of Scotland?

Mentally groaning, he cursed his now former pride in being the renowned ghost of Baird House—*worldwide.* Over the long, long decades, many articles and stories had been written about his murder and his sometimes very deliberate, ostentatious shenanigans to verify his spectral existence. He couldn't count all the psychic investigators who had visited the mansion over the years, most of whom had believed it their duty to send the "restless spirit" to his final resting place.

The reporters had been equally guilty of underestimating him. While a few came with the sincere hope of seeing The Lucky Baird, himself, there were countless numbers who had mocked his existence and strived to prove him an elaborate hoax. He'd toyed with psychics and reporters alike, using them to dull the edge of his boredom. Back then, it never occurred to him a time would come when he would regret the publicity he'd milked out of his murder. Now it was all coming back to haunt him.

Wouldn't the reporters just love to sink their career-sharpened fangs into this story! He could well imagine the bold headlines:

GHOSTLY DUO ONCE AGAIN BONA FIDE FLESH AND BLOOD MORTALS!

TWINS! HEAVENLY CONCEPTION OR DEVILISH DECEPTION?

His stomach churned as he wondered if Beth had been pregnant before she died. Being dead himself, he hadn't thought precaution necessary.

Yesterday, an innocent visit to Shortby's had resulted in a brawl with several of the regular patrons. What bloody bad luck that one man'd had a camera. And now, if the media storming his property was any indication, Baird House was about to make the news again.

This time, Lachlan wasn't of a mind to play with them. It was no longer a game. His immaturity in accepting his new life paled in significance to the fact that he now knew he had to cease being Lachlan Baird. For the sake of Beth and their children, he had to lose his identity, and that terrified him. Everything he'd done in his prior existences had been for naught, and he had no one to blame but himself.

Gulping back a burning sensation in his throat, he shifted his gaze to Roan's profile. The man's face was like an open book, every line telling the story of his thoughts. Lachlan knew that for his sake, Roan was trying his mightiest not to appear panicked or resentful, but it was there in his gaunt features and the way he searched Lachlan's eyes as if desperate to understand how Lachlan could have been so careless to announce his identity at Shortby's. Roan was right, but there was no going back. The damage was done and Lachlan didn't have a clue as to how to defuse the situation.

Wiping his brow with the back of a hand, Roan began, "No matter wha' happens—"

Lachlan's head shot around and his eyes widened in shock, effectively cutting off Roan's intended warning. One of the male reporters was reaching out for Braussaw, the stuffed peacock sitting atop the partially melted snowman that Roan, Laura and the boys had put together a few days earlier. With a howl of outrage, he bolted from his hiding place, leaving Roan behind to dumbfoundedly watch after him. Just as the reporter's hand was about to touch Braussaw's tail, Lachlan slugged the man to the ground. He pulled the peacock into his arms protectively, cradling it against his chest as he was besieged by other reporters. Harsh lights blinded him. Shouted questions flew at him like an onslaught of bullets. He turned his back to the crowd closing in on three sides, but turned again when he heard Roan bellowing for the trespassers to get off the property. Microphones and glaring lights were thrust in Roan's face, which he batted aside again and again with increasing belligerence.

Panting, Lachlan tried to clear his mind. He'd really done it this time, but he couldn't have allowed an outsider to touch Braussaw. He at least owed the defunct bird *that* much. But in rescuing a dead peacock, he'd gotten Roan and himself into deeper trouble, and something told him, an insidious voice laughing in the back of his mind at his rashness, that this time, he was in over his head.

A piercing, clanging sound rang out, then again and again until the reporters moved away from Lachlan and Roan and shuffled closer to the carriage house like a swarm of bees preparing for an attack. One alarmed glance from Roan prompted the two men to push through the jostling group, whose voices were rapidly crescendoing in another verbal assault. The portable location lights blinded Lachlan as he led Roan to where Winston's car was parked in front of the carriage house. His first thought had been that Reith had caused the ruckus to draw attention away from him, but it was Winston casually holding a hubcap in one hand and a tire iron in the other.

Winston again clanged the implements, eliciting immediate silence from the onlookers.

Vapored breaths rose into the night sky. Lachlan settled himself to Winston's right, Roan to Lachlan's right. Winston passed a knowing grin their way, then leveled a peeved look on the media, who were so quiet and still, the situation was almost laughable.

Clutching Braussaw's stiff body against him, Lachlan muttered out the side of his mouth to Winston, "Any ither grand ideas?"

Winston cocked one black eyebrow, a lopsided grin suggesting he did in fact have a plan. Then the eyebrow lowered and his grin vanished when a blond woman in her thirties stepped forward. Dressed in a three-quarter length beige wool coat, black boots, and a black knitted tam pulled down on one side of her head, she clutched a small tape recorder in one leather-gloved hand.

"Are you Lachlan Baird?" she asked dispassionately, her eyes on Lachlan both accusatory and cynical.

A painful tightness manifested in Lachlan's chest, and his throat closed off. He cast the main house a remorseful look, his mind scrambling for something to say that would end this nightmare, but not a viable thought formulated. Nonetheless, he opened his mouth in the hopes *something* would roll off his tongue. Preferably, something that wouldn't cook their carcasses any more than his antics already had.

"I . . ." The single syllable sounded inordinately deep. He sucked in a roar of breath and was about to make the plunge when Winston laughed, completely disorienting him.

"I detect a slight New York accent," Winston said to the blonde reporter.

"Marette Cambridge, New York Times," she said, her intense blue gaze riveted on Winston now. "I've come a long way for this story." She cast Lachlan a disgruntled glance. "For an obvious hoax, it seems."

Questions erupted from the mass. Winston lifted the hubcap and tire iron in a threatening manner. When silence prevailed again for several seconds, he lowered his attention-getters and smiled ruefully at the crowd. He glanced at Lachlan and Roan with a look that warned them to let him handle the matter. Then he frowned as he turned his attention back to the reporters.

"The trouble in this electronic world o' ours," he began amicably, "is that rumor spreads faster than the speed o' light." He bowed his head graciously to the blonde. "It's a shame the one responsible for releasin' the information on the newswire didn't bother to verify his story."

A tall, bushy-haired man pushed forward and held out a large microphone inches from Winston's face. "A man claiming to be *the* Lachlan Baird of Baird House was reported to have started a brawl at a local pub," he charged in an accent of German origin.

Without thinking, Lachlan boasted, "Aye, but my monhood was insulted!"

"Lachlan," Winston warned, shooting the laird a scowl.

The German went on excitedly, "The same *ghost* Lachlan Baird, I witnessed perform the alleged miracle last Christmas Eve?"

"Alleged!" Lachlan fumed.

"You dinna look much like a ghost now!" accused a man with a Highland accent. "Wha' did it cost to perpetrate *tha'* hoax?"

"O' all the bloody—"

Winston nonchalantly flagged the tire iron in front of Lachlan's face, cutting him off. Then, with a long sigh of impatience, he addressed the media. "Ladies and gentleman, I introduce Horatio Lachlan Baird." Ignoring Lachlan's startled grunt, he went on, "Cousin many times removed of the original laird of Baird House."

Murmurs passed among the media, while Lachlan inwardly groaned, *Horatio? I wouldna name a stuffed bird Horatio!*

"Mr. Baird arrived two weeks ago at the request of Baird House's new owner, Mr. Roan Ingliss. Mr. Ingliss is plannin' to open his home as a retreat, and asked Mr. Baird, who—" He gestured to Lachlan. "—as you can see, bears a remarkable likeness to the now departed Lachlan Baird."

Skepticism appeared on some of the faces across from him. Others were peeved. A few were even more curious than before.

Winston gave an elaborate shrug. "*This* Mr. Baird has been rehearsin' for the grand opening, which Mr. Ingliss hopes will be sometime this summer."

Roan nodded stiltedly.

"Mr. Baird has been studyin' the original laird's background, mannerisms and dress, to perform as the laird, himself, durin' the grand openin'.

"Yes, ladies and gentlemen, we *did* go to Shortby's, and *yes,* a brawl ensued. Mr. Baird's declaration that he was Lachlan Baird of Baird House, was no' a lie, and it certainly wasn't his intention to imply he was the *deceased* laird. Had he been given the opportunity he would have explained. When we left Shortby's, we had no idea his presence in Crossmichael would cause such a stir."

Another man, young, dark-haired, shoved his microphone toward Winston. "Am I mistaken, or are you Detective Winston Connery?"

"I am. Efter the exhaustin' conclusion o' the Phantom case, I needed to get away. Mr. Ingliss was kind enough to offer me a room here durin' my holiday."

A woman in her late fifties called from the center of the group, "Is Agnes Ingliss's spirit still present in the house?"

"My aunt just recently passed over," said Roan, emboldened by the brilliant coverup Winston had initiated. "Baird House is now free o' ghosts, but the magic and serenity o' the place remains. And I would like to add at this time, it would be greatly appreciated in the future if the media would no' jump to conclusions in regard to anyone or anythin' connected to this estate. I plan to marry soon and raise a family here. I'll no' stand for the press or anyone else trespassin' on a whim. You'll find me verra accessible to answerin' your bloody questions, but as equally hostile if my privacy is mistreated."

For what seemed an eternity to Lachlan, a myriad of questions were asked about Roan's plans for the estate and Winston's experiences on the Phantom case. Lachlan remained gratefully silent, vaguely listening, wishing he could escape before someone demanded a response from him. He was now feeling the chill of the night seeping into his bones. He was also overly conscious of hugging the bird, but he couldn't bring himself to release it. The feathered solidity against his chest gave him comfort, as if the bird helped to lessen the pounding of Lachlan's heart. He was sure that if the media could hear its wild, erratic beat, they would deem his willing reticence the fear it was.

In truth, he was sick with fear. What if Beth had emerged from the house? Could Winston have explained away her *remarkable resemblance* to Beth Staples, as easily? Perhaps the press could accept the story of *Horatio* Lachlan Baird, but he doubted if a Baird with a duplicate of Beth would even fool a blind person. Winston had temporarily given them a reprieve. It certainly wouldn't last long, though.

As if compelled by some inner voice, he looked across the sea of faces, many of which were blotted out by what few lights remained trained on him and his companions, and spied a woman at the back of the reporters. She stood behind another woman's shoulder. He could only see her nose, eyes, and a portion of her brow. A hood covered her hair. She stared at him with eerie directness, unblinking, as if she were reading his thoughts and held him in contempt of the charade his silence was validating. He stared back at her with all the calm he could muster. Although she was four bodies away from him, he thought there was something familiar about her eyes, but he was too rattled to concentrate.

A male voice commented that he didn't remember the

new oak as having been there Christmas Eve, and panic lanced Lachlan's heart. He saw the mysterious eyes still watching him, and his panic deepened until he was sure he would burst with need to escape the crowd, the night, and the woman's scrutiny.

His nose detected a potent whiff of smoke. Looking over his shoulder at the carriage house, he muttered, "Excuse me," then passed Roan and went into the building, where he found his new employee sitting on a crate in front of the wood stove. Blue eyes looked up at him through the lantern light, eyes betraying Reith's concern for what was going on outside. Pulling up one of the other crates, Lachlan sat, placed Braussaw on the floor, then ran his hands wearily down his stubbled face. Reith remained quiet and placed the lantern at his feet further away from the peacock. He waited a time longer before clearing his throat and asking in a hushed tone, "Be ye the *true* laird?"

Lachlan eyed him peevishly. It was on the tip of his tongue to continue the lie, but there was something about the lad that told him it wasn't necessary. He nodded while planting his hands on his thighs, and again flexing the stiff muscles in his back.

A hint of a smile appeared on Reith's generous mouth as he braced the underpart of his forearms on his thighs, and linked together the fingers of his hands. "I heard ye spoken o' in town," he said, again keeping his voice low.

Lachlan frowned. "Regardin' the brawl at Shortby's?"

"Aye, and more, sir." Reith sighed deeply. "Three days back, I was sittin' by the loch and heard a womon and two men talkin'. From wha' I gathered, one o' the men was visitin' from Edinburgh, and the ither mon and womon were braggin' abou' Crossmichael's esteemed ghost. I thought them a wee bent in the mind, talkin' o' ghosts as they were, but I listened nonetheless.

"Sir, earlier, ou' in the field . . . I thought *ye* more'n a wee bent in the mind when you said twas *your* grave wha' was bein' desecrated by those men. My apologies."

Lachlan chuckled tiredly. "Weel, laddie, tis no' every

day you happen across a beleaguered lot as we here at Baird House."

"No, sir. Sir?"

Lachlan looked expectantly into the earnest blue eyes.

"Ye can trust me."

Smiling with appreciation, Lachlan nodded. "Tis the damndest thing, laddie, but I know I can." He frowned thoughtfully at the young man. "You should let your wife know where you are."

"I will."

Lachlan focused on Reith's hands and nodded. "Dinna mak my mistakes. Get your priorities in order, and dinna let anythin' sway you from them."

"My faither used to say, 'If ye be lookin' into the past, your head isna on straight'."

Lachlan chuffed a low laugh and nodded in agreement. "Sounds like a verra wise mon, your faither."

"He is," said Reith sadly. "I've been a disappointment to him a verra long time." He looked into Lachlan's eyes and smiled halfheartedly. "But I be workin' on redeemin' myself."

"I'm sure you are. You strike me as bein' an intelligent, compassionate mon. Whatever happened in the past, shouldna cloud your future. Time has a way o' healin' wrongs. For those o' us who are prone to mishap—bloody hell, let's call it wha' it is, *trouble*—time can seem like a long sentence. So I say to you wha' I've been tellin' myself, never give up the struggle to do right. Especially to do right by your loved ones."

Reith's gaze drifted off to one side. "Be all women complicated?" He looked at Lachlan. "Or is it we males be inordinately dense when it comes to wha' they want or need?"

Gesturing his hopelessness with a shrug, Lachlan said, "Somethin' atween the two, I think. Maybe if we—"

Lachlan bit back his words when the door opened. Roan and Winston walked in, the former dragging the last crate to Reith's right, while Winston crouched to Lachlan's left.

"They're finally leavin'," said Roan, his tone deep with fatigue and strain.

Lachlan noted Winston staring at Reith and introduced them, briefly describing what had happened in the field.

"Ye did a fine job ou' there, sir," Reith told Winston, with a respectful bob of his head.

"Fine?" Lachlan breathed, then clapped Winston on the shoulder. "You saved our arses, you did." He noticed Winston cast a wary look in Reith's direction, and added with a chuckle, "The lad knows the truth."

Winston nodded, but it was obvious he wasn't pleased with Lachlan bringing the young man into his confidence.

"The women must be furious wi' us," Roan moaned.

"They weren't too happy when I left," said Winston, his gaze remaining fixed on Reith for a moment longer. "I suggest the three o' us face them and try to explain what's goin' on."

Lachlan grimaced. "Beth'll tie my testicles in a knot when she hears. Fegs, mon, canna we wait till morn? She's always a wee sluggish efter awakenin'. Her reflexes are slower."

"Coward," said Roan.

"Bloody right I am," said Lachlan, exasperated. "You both know as weel as I, *I'm* responsible for this mess. Beth will no let me soon forget it, either."

"Come on," Winston said as he rose.

Roan stood, but Lachlan vigorously rubbed his palms on his face before rising to his feet. He passed Reith's upturned face a harried look, then asked, "Are you hungry or thirsty?"

"No, sir. Just tired."

Lachlan heaved a ragged breath. "I'm likely to be back afore long. If there is to be anither miracle this night, I'll be stayin' in the main house, but I'll see you in the morn wi' breakfast. Do you prefer tea or coffee?"

"Coffee, if ye please." Reith stood and wiped his palms on the ragged material covering his thighs. "Chin up, sir."

He smiled timorously. "I'll be hopin' no' to hear your footfalls anytime soon."

Lachlan glanced down at the peacock "Tak care o' Braussaw for me. He's a paughty one, but deservin' respect."

"Aye, sir," said Reith, lifting the bird into his arms.

He watched the trio leave, Winston in the lead, Lachlan shuffling along at the rear. Moments after the door closed, Braussaw sprang to life and struggled in Reith's gentle grasp.

"Wha' have we here, now?" he laughed low. His eyes sparkling with a shimmer of tears, he stared at the door and murmured tremulously, "I so missed this land."

CHAPTER TWO

Laura was pacing at the foot of the staircase when Winston led the men into the house. She froze for a moment, her eyes appearing too large in her shocky face as she watched them approach. Winston stopped a short distance from her, but Roan continued on until he was an arm's length away. He fumbled for the right words to break the silence between them, but before he could speak, she flung her arms around his neck and hugged him almost painfully.

"You sonofabitch," she wept, quaking against him as he enveloped her in his arms.

"I'm sorry, Laura," he whispered achingly, hugging her as if to never let her go. "Are you all right?"

Loosening her hold on his neck, she eased back enough to tearfully stare into his light brown eyes. "All right?" she asked in a hoarse tone. "I thought that mob was going to hang you!"

He told her everything that had happened from the men in the field to Winston's quick wit in covering Lachlan's return. She listened as if dazed. When he stopped, she squirmed until he allowed her to step away, then she backed up to the foot of the stairs, her gaze studying each of the men.

Finally, unable to stand her silence, Roan asked, "Did the lads wake up?"

She nodded and gulped. "Deliah's with them, trying to calm them down."

Stepping forward, Lachlan scowled self-consciously. "Where's my Beth?"

Laura shook her head. "Don't try to talk to her right now. Lachlan, she's scared, and angrier than I've ever seen anyone."

With a guttural sound, Lachlan headed up the staircase.

"For God sake, Lannie!" Roan exclaimed.

Lachlan stopped and looked down at the anxious faces. "I willna let anither night go by withou' her!" he exclaimed, then stormed up the stairs.

By the time he was halfway down the third floor hall, his pace slowed and his resolve faltered. His heart drummed against his chest and a sickening sensation of pressure filled his head. He paused at the door to the master suite for a long moment. Something tickled his left temple, distracting him. He gave the area a swipe with a hand, and was surprised to realize his brow had broken out in a cold sweat, some of which was trickling down the sides of his face.

Steady, Lannie, he told himself, then rolled his eyes heavenward with a mute groan.

Steady or not, if he entered the master suite, Beth was surely to lose what little restraint she had left on her temper. But if he walked away, he knew the gap between them would only continue to open wider and wider, until it would be nigh impossible for them to find their way back to each other. She might be hurt, angry, and disappointed in him, but he didn't doubt her love or its depths. He'd go to hell and back for her. If she didn't know that, she was about to, temper or no.

He started to rap on the door, then jerked his hand away and stared down at the crystal knob. It occurred to him that, to make a stand, it would be best he acted the part right off. Her lover. Her love. Her man, and the man of their family. With this bit of fortitude bracing his spine, he boldly turned the knob and walked into the room, but he couldn't help his gaze cutting about, in search of her lunging at him. He closed the door softly behind him and stepped further into the embracing familiarity of his old suite. The bedcovers were turned back, and the hearth was ablaze with warmth. There were no other lights on and, although he squinted to see every corner of the room, he couldn't locate her. His gaze lingered on the circular display of swords on the wall to the left of his portrait. A chill coursed through him. Ignoring it, he went to the foot of the bed, wondering where she could be at this time of night.

The door opened. Beth walked in and closed it behind her. Her head down, shoulders slumped, and her gait slow as if she were beyond tired, she progressed toward him. She slipped out of her bathrobe by the time she reached the side of the bed, and haphazardly dropped it on the floor.

A pulse of exhilaration thrummed through every part of Lachlan. He felt as he had that first day when she'd arrived last July. For two years prior, his only connection with her had been through the portrait her friend Carlene had painted. The portrait which still hung above the fireplace in the parlor. Back then, he had somehow managed to link with her mind, getting to know her through her thoughts and experiencing her emotions. He had thought he knew everything about her by the time she arrived. He'd been wrong. Meeting the physical woman had exceeded all his expectations. The mindlinks hadn't revealed the way her blue eyes gleamed like multi-faceted sapphires when she was passionate or angry, or became as fathomless as the deep blue sea when she was troubled. The mindlinks hadn't connected him to the scent of her, or the way she shuffled her shoulders and gave a toss of her curly, light brown hair when she was frustrated. Her softness. The sound of her voice. Her quick wit. The curves of her body—

Lachlan gripped one of the walnut posts at the foot of the bed when she placed her hands at the small of her back and languidly stretched. Her full breasts strained against the pale blue linen of her nightgown. The thin strap on her right shoulder slipped over the smooth curvature. That small movement struck Lachlan as being more sensual than anything he'd ever beheld. Beth had never considered herself beautiful. He did. Every line and plane of her body was perfection, made him long to touch her more than he'd longed for anything in his enduring existences.

He realized he hadn't been given another chance at life on a whim. Whatever had brought him back hadn't really considered *him* the worthy factor. It was *Beth*. Beth and their children. He didn't understand how or why he knew this now so undeniably, but it was so clear, so absolute, he didn't question the knowing. Perhaps his life, his future did hold some measure of importance, but *she* was his connection to whatever fate held in store for him. Had the *knowing* been in his subconscious when they'd been brought back? Embedded deeply in his mind, trying to surface through the maze of confusion, and initializing those fears and insecurities that had driven him to turn away from her and the twins?

Some things still didn't make sense, but in time the pieces would come together.

Beth lowered one knee onto the mattress. She sighed and was about to finish climbing into bed when her head shot around and her eyes widened on him. A breath became trapped in his throat. God, she was beautiful! Her lips were parted, and her hair a wild mane of curls surrounding the face that always left him breathless and lightheaded, even when he hadn't had the corporeal equipment to actually *feel* anything at all.

She remained frozen, one bent leg on the bed. Lachlan's gaze fell on the drooped strap of her nightgown, and he swallowed past the tightness forming in his throat. He couldn't summon up saliva to alleviate the dryness in his mouth. His first attempt to speak came out as a croak, then he cleared his throat, once, twice, and threw all of his willpower into saying her name.

"Beth."

Her breathing became shallow and her eyes narrowed. "Get out."

Lachlan glanced at the door, then at her and shook his head. "You have to listen to me."

"I don't have to anything," she said in a low, warning tone. She stiffly pointed to the door, her eyes remaining intensely fixed on him. "Get out. And don't come back."

Lachlan locked his teeth against an immediate response. *This* time he wouldn't walk away. *This* time she would listen, even if he had to sit on her.

"Beth-lass—"

He jerked back as a pillow came swiftly toward him. It struck him with enough force to compel him back a step. The second blow swiftly followed, then another and another. He was astounded by the ferocity of her attack, and astounded that he could do no more than hold up his arms to protect his face. Through the staticlike roar in his ears, he could dimly make out bits and pieces of words. *"Bastard."* A garble of sounds, then *"Irresponsible jerk."* Louder static, piercing his eardrums. *"Not"* (something) *"gullible."*

"Beth!" he gasped, his head reeling. He blindly reached out, gripped softness and gave it a hard tug. A guttural cry startled him. His vision cleared to find a pillow clutched in one hand and he dropped it to the floor. He was conscious of a blur of movement, then of a jab to his midriff. He looked down and released a chuff of disbelief when he realized the cause of his discomfort was the point of a poker. On the other end, Beth's fury-filled eyes dared him to move.

At least she hadn't gone for one of the swords.

Lachlan's patience lost to burgeoning anger. He regarded the poker, then her, his black eyebrows drawing down into a stormy scowl. "Tis one thing, Beth, to order me ou' o' my bed, my bedroom, my home . . . anither to hold a weapon against me." He drew in a ragged breath. "Put it down."

"Who were those men trying to dig up our graves?" she asked through clenched teeth. When he didn't answer right away, she jerked her head in the direction of the door. "I saw them through one of the nursery windows. I *saw* them trying to *exhume* us! Why? *Damn you,* answer me!"

Drawing back his shoulders, he replied, "They wanted to verify I was in the ground."

Her chin quivered and a mist of tears formed in her eyes. "Why?"

"Beth—"

"Why?"

Lachlan closed his eyes a moment, then forced himself to look at her. "At Shortby's . . ." He shook his head, unable to finish.

He winced when she prodded him with the poker, and looked down at it resentfully before continuing, "I told some men my name. I didna know there was a reporter in the room. Beth—"

"What else did you tell them?" she asked achingly, a tear spilling down her ashen face. "That I'm back, too? That we have a son and daughter, conceived in the after-life?" Her voice ended on an almost shrill note, making him flinch.

"No," he said miserably. "Only my name. 'Twas enough, though."

"I'll bet it was. I-ah, opened the window and listened. I heard what those reporters were shouting. Do you have any idea what your goddamn jaunt to Shortby's has cost us? Not just you and me, but our children?"

Lachlan rolled his eyes heavenward and shrugged with resignation. "I know it was reckless o' me, but Winston came up wi' a story, and it seems to have satisfied the press."

She stared at him expectantly.

"He told them Roan was plannin' to turn the estate into a retreat this summer. Tha' I'm *Horatio* Lachlan Baird, a distant relation, here to play the former laird durin' the grand openin'."

"It's just a coincidence you look exactly like him, right?" she sneered, jabbing him again. "Something tells me that story won't work as far as I'm concerned. But that's okay, Lachlan." She nodded more than necessary. "That's okay. At least *you're* protected, right?"

"Beth—"

"Shut up!" Her nostrils flared, and it was obvious she was barely in control of her anger. "I'll be more than happy to *buy* myself another identity, and more than happy to take myself and *my* children as far away from here as possible."

Lachlan's blood turned to ice water. "I once told you I would never let you leave me. Tha' hasna changed, lass."

"Hasn't it?" she asked bitterly, trembling, tears falling in abandon down her cheeks. She laughed, a pathetic little sound that unnerved him more than her hostility. "Maybe in the mid-eighteen hundreds, women put up with egotistical windbags, but you're in *my* time now. Having a penis doesn't give you the right to tell any woman what to do, or what she can or can't think! So get it through your thick skull, I *am* leaving, and there isn't a *bloody* thing you can do to stop me."

"I can." He planted his hands on his hips. "And I will."

"No." Something between a smile and a grimace flashed across her mouth. "You're going to leave this room and stay away from me. If you came through into this life with even a smidgen of common sense, you'll tell yourself you know you and I are finished!"

Lachlan stepped back on one foot and snatched the poker iron from her grasp, then harshly flung it to the floor. Beth stood paralyzed, staring at her extended hands as if disbelieving he could have disarmed her with such speed and such ease.

"I may be a wee behind the times, *grádh mo chridhe*—"

"Speak English!"

"Grádh mo chridhe, love o' my heart, and tha' you are. But right now I'm resistin' a powerful urge to shake some sense into you! 'Tis no' womonly to wield a weapon on a mon, no' unless her virtue or her life is bein' compromised. I bloody weel *dare* you to stand there and tell me I have compromised you in *any* way!"

Beth's fists clenched at her sides and she shook violently. For but an instant, he thought he glimpsed a man's visage with chilling pale eyes, flash in front of her face. The semi-transparent features were grotesquely carved with rage, almost demonic. Then her tirade began, and the memory of it temporarily slipped from his mind.

"You tricked me into coming here. You knew I was dying and you didn't even have the decency to tell me before it happened! But you made sure you seduced me first, didn't you? Oh, yeah. The *great* Lachlan Baird used all his wit and charm to coax a virgin into his bed, just so *he* could have everlasting companionship!"

"Enough! If you remember, Beth, *you* were my first as weel!"

"When I think back on how gullible I was, I want to puke! I hate—" Her voice cracked, but she forced the words, *"hate* you for every lie and stunt you've pulled since the moment I first laid eyes on you!"

Lachlan chewed on his lower lip for a time. He couldn't remember when he'd been angrier or more hurt by mere words. If she had opened his wrist, or had pierced his heart, he knew the pain would have been tolerable in comparison to what he was suffering now.

"Are you done ventin' your indignation at havin' fallin' in love with such a reprobate?" he asked tightly.

A masculine, rattling sound emanated from her throat, shocking him. His head reared back with neck-wrenching force when her left fist smashed into his jawline. Searing pain shot up his jaw and exploded inside his head. If he didn't know better, he would have sworn the blow had been dealt by a man larger than himself. Something else was wrong. Before his mind could focus on it, her fists began to pound against his chest.

He tried to justify her actions, but couldn't. This was not mere anger. She was out of control, and his own temper had surfaced as a shield against her assault. She shoved him, released a low cry and whirled to run in the direction of the door. With a growled, *"Ach!"* he bounded after her, reaching her before she could grab the doorknob.

Fueled by a raw primordial need to overpower her, he swung her thrashing form up into his arms and carried her to the bed. He was beyond feeling the sting of her hands striking him. Beyond caring that his superior strength and size only served to enhance her rage. He tossed her onto the bedcovers. Before he was fully on his knees atop the mattress, she gripped the front of his shirt, rammed her bare feet against his abdomen, and yanked. The linen ripped vertically, the tear seeming to echo in the room. She cast off him, nearly toppling him over the edge of the mattress, then scrambled to her hands and knees and made a valiant effort to get off the far side of the bed.

Lachlan lunged. He only intended to stop her from eluding him, but beneath the strength of his fingers one of the straps of her nightgown ripped away from the back. With a cry of outrage, she whirled, swinging her arms, and knocked him across the top of his head with the back of a hand. He grunted as he wound his arms about her middle and wrestled her toward the center of the mattress. Releasing a stream of curses that made his ears turn crimson, she kicked, slapped, punched and did her best to bite him. The latter he escaped by only a hairsbreadth, most of the time. He kept one side of his face pressed to the area between her shoulder blades, and one arm snugly about her middle. With his free hand he grappled with her left arm, the elbow of which repeatedly jabbed his rib cage. Once he anchored both arms—

He released a howl of surprise when her teeth sank

into his raised forearm. Wrenching free, he swung her facedown onto the bed.

"Damn you!" she cried, kicking him with her heels as he straddled her backside. She attempted to buck him off, then buried her face into the covers and screamed. The muffled release finally quieted her. She turned her head, panting, straining to see him.

"Get off me!"

"Have I your word you'll no' raise anither hand to me?" he asked harshly, his breathing also labored, his body quaking with the force of holding back the larger portion of his anger.

After a laden pause, she said, "Yes!"

Without hesitation, Lachlan swung himself to her right. He no sooner sat beside her than she flipped over and made a valiant bid to drive her left knee into his chest. He blocked the blow with the same forearm she'd bitten. Then, with a swift, fluid motion born of vexation he straddled her abdomen, his large hands pinning her wrists to the mattress above her head. Breaths wheezed from him. She was flushed and gasping, the mounds of her breasts rising and falling, straining against the thin material as if to burst free at any moment.

"You have to let me go eventually," she panted, glaring at him. "And when you do, I swear I'll . . ."

"Wha'?" he taunted, lowering himself until his face was inches from hers. He could feel her warm breath fan his neck, face, and the area now bared by the torn shirt. "What's left, Beth?"

"Your manhood," she rasped. Her eyes flashed. "With that jeweled dirk, I'll cut off your—"

Her threat became garbled when his mouth covered hers, crushing the inner lining of her lips against her clenched teeth. She relentlessly bucked and squirmed beneath him until, after what seemed like an exhausting eternity, her struggles grew weaker. Lachlan lessened the pressure of his mouth. He hadn't intended the action to be construed as a kiss, only a means to stop her threat of castrating him. The idea that she was angry enough to *think* it, let alone carry it out, horrified him. He'd give up his life again before he would allow her close enough to tamper with what nature had bestowed upon him.

Fatigue robbing his temper of fire, he eased up his head and wearily peered into her eyes. She was still angry, but also spent of fight.

"Is this wha' you truly want, Beth-lass?"

"Yes," she said breathlessly.

His head dropped for a brief time, then he forced himself to climb off her, then the bed. He headed for the door, saying over his shoulder, "I'll no' bother you again."

He closed the door behind him as he entered the hall, missing her choked, "That's not what I meant."

Lachlan's hand remained on the knob to the closed door when he spied Deliah and Winston standing in the doorway to the nursery. He stiffened with hostility, an instinctual response to the argument he was sure would come. Although Deliah's eyes were soft with compassion, Winston's held an unmistakable glint of reproach, and Lachlan was reasonably sure he'd already choked down his quota of guilt for the day.

Releasing the doorknob, he brusquely headed past them, but stopped when Deliah touched his arm. He drew in a deep breath and faced her, then sighed, "I've a hole for a brain, I know."

She smiled sympathetically and whispered, "I be sorry, Lachlan."

"Sorry for wha'?"

Her head lowered as if she were ashamed. "For no' tellin' ye the truth afore I brought ye and Beth back."

Puzzled, Lachlan looked into Winston's pale gray-green eyes, then placed a crooked finger beneath Deliah's dimpled chin and lifted her face to his view. " 'Tis no fault o' yours."

Tears rapidly sprang into her eyes and her chin quivered. "Aye, I be responsible. I didna tell ye because I wasna sure *when* the return would happen, and I didna want ye and Beth to be anxious durin' the waitin'."

Fondly, Lachlan smiled, then bestowed a kiss on her brow. "Deliah-lass," he said, searching her despondent eyes, "dinna you think 'tis time I paid my dues for all the trouble I've caused? I'm a foolish mon, I grant. I need to face *my* responsibilities."

"Lachlan . . ." Winston paused and frowned. "Don't be so hard on yourself."

"No' ready to hang me yet, eh?' " Lachlan asked wryly.

Winston chuckled low. "No' yet." He sobered, placed an arm about Deliah's shoulders, then frowned again. "Tha' was a nasty argument you had wi' Beth."

This time Lachlan lowered his head. "Aye. But no more. I'll keep my distance till we can figure ou' where we go from here." He looked up and beyond the couple, to where the crib was located halfway across the room. "Are the bairns asleep?"

Deliah nodded. "Do ye want to see them?"

Shaking his head, he turned to leave. "No' yet," he said, and headed for the staircase.

He kept his mind blank during the descent. Turning left at the bottom of the stairs, he walked toward the doors and was nearly to them before he saw three small bodies blocking his exit. He slowed to a stop and regarded their upturned faces. Alby was teary-eyed, Kahl frowning, and Kevin as angry as a riled hornet.

"Where you going?" asked Kahl, his reddish blond hair tousled, his eyes laden with sleep. "It's raining hard out there."

Lachlan glanced at the double doors and murmured, "Is it?"

"Why do you havta do so many stupid things?" Kevin asked harshly. His brothers gave him a shocked look, but he ignored them and went on, "If you was my size, you'd get your butt swatted and spend some serious time staring at the walls of your bedroom."

Lachlan didn't want to grin, but one ticked at the right

corner of his mouth as he crouched, resting his buttocks on the heels of his boots. "For absolute sure, I would. 'Tis lucky I'm just a stupid mon, aye?"

"You're not stupid!" Alby cried, then flung himself into Lachlan's arms, winding his own about Lachlan's broad neck. "Don't say you're stupid!"

"Oh, lad," Lachlan crooned, relishing the warmth of the boy's body, "I promise no' to again."

Sniffling, Alby released his death-grip and backed off enough to look into Lachlan's eyes. "It's the boogeyman making everybody so cranky."

"You dinna say? Hmmm. Then we should send him packin' right soon, shouldna we?"

Alby nodded vigorously. From behind him, Kahl said in a soft voice, "We got scared when we heard Beth yelling at you."

Lachlan opened his left arm and Kahl immediately stepped into it. But Kevin held back, his blue eyes stormy with accusation until Lachlan cast him a pleading look for forgiveness. Then it was three boys he was hugging, and three warm bodies hugging him in return. He kissed each on the cheek, then vowed, "You have my word, it willna happen again."

"For honest?" Alby asked in a quivering tone.

Nodding, Lachlan said, "You know how when you're scared, weird things come ou' o' your mouth and you canna stop them?"

Again Alby nodded vigorously, while his siblings regarded Lachlan as if seriously mulling over his words.

"Weel, your Aunt Beth has a fine temper, she has, and she's no' afraid to let me know when I displease—"

"You mean piss her off," Kevin interjected, to which Lachlan comically flinched.

"Aye, and tha', too. Which reminds me, there's a young mon now stayin' at the carriage house. He's the new groundskeeper. Would it be too much to ask you three to have mercy on him and no' give him the deil's due?"

Kahl laughed, then nodded along with his brothers.

It suddenly struck Lachlan that one day he would be talking to *his* children like this, holding *their* bodies in the crook of his arms. His heart leapt with joy, but then as quickly sank into a murky hollow of depression when he realized Beth could easily prevent his children being raised around him. One voice in his head told him to challenge her rights if she tried. But another more logical voice told him he would go along with whatever she decided, no matter what it cost him emotionally.

Standing, he gestured toward the staircase. "Long past your bedtime, laddies."

"Aw," Kevin began, but instantly quieted when Lachlan arched an eyebrow. "Okay."

"Straight to bed," Lachlan said with a hint of a smile. "No stoppin' along the way to have you a wee mischief."

Kevin led his brothers to and up the stairs. As soon as they were out of sight, Lachlan walked into the night. It was indeed raining. Large, icy drops of water pounded the earth in a lament of spring's arrival. They stung his exposed skin and the coldness seeped into the marrow of his bones, but by the time he made it to the field, he was too numb to feel much of anything except the sorrow weighing heavily on him. He didn't see the dark-clad figure slipping through the opened bulkhead and into the basement. He didn't hear the curses growled in condemnation of his unappreciated stroll through the backyard. He only knew he needed to be alone. To think. To try to understand how he could have gotten so angry at Beth. To perhaps even pray for some guidance before he unintentionally brought about another disaster, like setting the planet on fire.

Beth tensed when she heard a soft rap, then her door opening. She wasn't sure if she was glad it wasn't Lachlan or not, but she nonetheless gestured for Deliah to join her by the window. Rain pattered loudly against the panes. Coldness seeped through the glass, and her skin was broken out in gooseflesh. The night was relatively dark, barely enough light for her to make out Lachlan's figure emerging beyond the far end of the wooded area. He was going to the old oak. To the graves. Why? Why put himself through that kind of torment?

She mentally cursed his stubbornness, then found herself choked up with regret and self-loathing.

Yes, she'd been angry with him, but not so angry that it justified her assaulting him as she had. What amazed her was how he'd taken so much of it before utilizing his superior size and strength against her. She was more frightened about their futures than upset about the reporters, although the exposure meant they couldn't stay at Baird House, not without someone spotting her on the grounds.

So why strike out at him like a bloodthirsty shrew?

What had brought on that instantaneous eruption of heat inside her when she realized he was in the room?

It was almost as if something had gotten inside her and taken over her body and mind. Or was she just trying to give her temper an excuse, when there really wasn't one to be had?

"The babes be still asleep," said Deliah, coming to stand to Beth's right. Her bright blue eyes looked into the night, and she frowned thoughtfully. "When do they begin to sleep the night through?"

Beth sighed. "I have no idea. I was an only child, and was never around babies or toddlers. That makes me about as ignorant as a rock."

Deliah smiled, then blurted, "I have pledged to marry Winston."

"What?" With a low squeal, Beth threw her arms around the smaller woman and hugged her. Then she eased back, her face glowing with happiness. "Congratulations! When did this happen?"

A dark blush stole into Deliah's cheeks. "Afore, durin', and efter all three times we made love today."

Beth also blushed. "Three times?"

"I wanted more, but alas, he pooped ou' on me, silly mon."

Impulsively, Beth again hugged the slender woman. Tears spilled from her eyes as she released her and faced the window. "I'm so happy for you, Deliah."

"Aye, I know. 'Twould mak me happier, though, to see ye a wee happy for yourself."

Beth cast her a harried glance. "I don't see that happening in the near future. God, Deliah, I pounded on him! Bit him. Kicked him." She lowered her voice. "I threatened to castrate him with that damn dirk."

Deliah smiled ruefully. " 'Tis no surprise now why the poor mon didna want to remain in the house."

Although Deliah's tone was light, almost playful, her words cut into Beth's conscience. "This isn't right, Deliah. I shouldn't be in here feeling miserable, and he out there—God, he has to be freezing without a coat! Why has he gone to the graves? Is he some kind of masochist or what?"

"Today be March twenty-third, the day o' his dyin' so long ago."

Stunned, Beth turned to face Deliah. "He was murdered on March twenty-third?"

"Aye. I dinna think he realizes the date. Subconsciously, mayhaps."

"Tessa drove the dirk into his heart, and I threatened—Oh, *God,*" Beth ended on a groan. "I didn't know! His headstone only has the year!"

"I wasna aware myself till Winston and I started talkin' abou' a date to marry. Now I wonder. . . ."

"What?" Beth asked anxiously.

Deliah gave a weary lift of her shoulders. " 'Tis no' for me to mak excuses for him, but . . . the timin' o' your return couldna have been worse, aye? So close to his death date, I mean. I be no expert on the ways o' the human mind, but 'tis a fair guess his subconscious is dwellin' on that night." She forlornly gazed through the window. "Now he be ou' there, cold and alone, as was he tha' night when he was moved into the tower. I should no' have interfered wi' his passin' on, Beth, but I couldna stop myself."

Trembling with an onslaught of tears, Beth could say nothing.

"No word nor action," Deliah said softly, placing a hand on Beth's shoulder, "should put asunder a love wha' transcends time and space, and this world and anither."

Beth shook her head miserably.

"I know ye fairly weel, Beth. It no' be in your heart to isolate yourself from him." Deliah sighed. "I must return to Winston, but it saddens me to leave ye alone at this time."

"What do I say to him?" Beth asked, placing her fingertips against the cold panes.

"Tha' would be up to ye. 'Twould be a blessin' upon this house and all it has stood for, though, if we all were to lie within our lovers' arms, and ward off the cold wi' the heat o' our bodies."

Beth nervously moistened her lower lip with the tip of her tongue. "I don't think I could keep myself together if he turned me away, Deliah."

The Faerie princess released a scoffing chuff. "Do ye really believe he would?"

"I . . . don't know."

"I tell ye he willna. The babes be asleep. I promise to listen for them while *ye* give this date a new meanin' for your mon. Dinna be afraid. Aye, our Lachlan has his faults, but would ye really have him change?"

Beth laughed a bit unsteadily. "No. No! Not one iota! He can be so infuriating, but it's—I must be nuts—what I first loved about him." She glanced at the door, at Deliah, then lit into a run. "See you in the morning!"

CHAPTER THREE

Barefoot and only wearing her torn nightgown, Beth dashed into the night. She was soaked before she rounded the house, and numb by the time she reached the woods. Nonetheless, she hastened along the path to the field, thoughts of Lachlan's arms enveloping her all that kept her going.

The field seemed unusually long, the oak inordinately far. She slowed her pace when she was close enough to see that he was on his knees in front of her headstone, then arced slightly to her right until she could see his fingertips touching the engraved lettering on the granite. She stood not more than five feet from him, lapping at the wetness on her lips. The rain tasted sweet and somehow reviving. Shudders coursed through her, but she didn't care. Soon. . . .

"When there is too much to forgive, wha' does tha' leave a mon to do?" he said in a low, husky voice. "I canna live withou' you, Beth, nor can I die. I've no way to know how to mak up for the wrongs."

Beth slowly positioned herself on the opposite side of her headstone, where she could only see the back of his bent head. She realized he was praying and waited a few moments until the cold became too unbearable, and thoughts of snuggling beside him in a warm bed gave her the courage to break the silence.

"March twenty-third, eighteen forty-three—" His head shot up and his fathomless dark eyes looked at her as if he were seeing a ghost. "—a heartless bride took her husband's life and had her lover wall him up in the tower."

A hearty preternatural breeze, laden with pellets of rain, swept around Beth. She caught her breath at its frigid caress. Sepulchral voices rose from the ground, whispering in her ears, but she couldn't decipher the words. For a moment she feared something would erupt from the earth and carry Lachlan and her back into their graves. Anything was possible. They both existed as testimony to the unexplainable, the unbelievable, and knew firsthand how fragile was mortality.

The breeze melted into the night, carrying away with it the voices and a large part of her anxiousness. Rain poured from the infinite sky, through the canopy of still-barren branches above them. Sweeping back the hair wetly plastered across her face, she told herself her life wouldn't end if Lachlan rejected her. She would leave the relationship with a hole in her heart, but she would survive. The twins would fill a vast portion of her life. Right now, all she could do was to try to mollify what had happened in the bedroom. She couldn't explain the extent of her anger, but she *could* tell him that she loved him above all else.

"On March twenty-third, nineteen ninety-five," she forced herself to go on, "another heartless lover drove this same man into the cold of a rainy night."

She stepped closer to the stone and gripped its top. A breath lodged in her throat when Lachlan slowly rose to his feet, still staring at her as though disbelieving she were real. Usually he wasn't so quiet or still. It was unnerving and she almost wished she hadn't left the house.

"Are you hoping to die of pneumonia out here, is that it?" she asked. Shivering, she hugged herself with her arms.

"It just won't do, Lachlan. I can't allow you to deny your children their father."

He stepped to one side of the headstone, his boots making sucking sounds in the mud.

Gulping, Beth pressed on, "Okay, so I'm not that unselfish! I'm here because I want you."

In the semi-darkness, she saw his right eyebrow arch in a challenge.

Releasing a sparing breath, she cast a forlorn look in the direction of the mansion. She was cold and tired, and her stomach was tied in knots. The twins would be waking at any time to be fed. And Lachlan was milking her discomfort for all it was worth. Making her squirm. Waiting for her to swallow a fat, old corbie and *say* what he wanted to hear, not her feeble attempt to skirt around an outright apology.

"I'm sorry," she finally said in a small voice, peering at him from beneath her soaked eyelashes.

He stepped directly in front of her, leaving little space between them. Heat replaced the chill in her body as she blinkingly stared at his chest. The wet, blue material of his torn shirt clung to the muscular contours, making her needy to touch him.

Damn the chemistry between them!

Her head barely reached his chin. From the moment they had met last summer, his height, barrel chest, and broad shoulders had felled her inhibitions. He was so powerful, so masculine, so magnetic that she could no more resist wanting him than she could resist breathing.

"Sorry for wha'?" he asked, his deep voice husky.

Sorry for what? she fumed. She didn't expect him to forgive and forget in a matter of minutes, but was it necessary for him to make this so grueling?

Without thought, she openhandedly whacked him on the chest and sputtered, "For ever coming to this *damn* country—" She gasped, then straightened back her shoulders and looked into his eyes with what she hoped was a semblance of remorse. "For hitting you. Okay . . . for hitting you *and* running off at the mouth."

His silence squeezed her heart and she released a shuddering breath. "Damn you, Lachlan, you make me crazy, sometimes! I told you I want you in my life. What more do you want to hear? That I want you in m-my bed?" She sucked in a breath to calm her nerves. "Okay. O . . . kay, I do. Want you in my bed, I mean."

Expressionless, Lachlan ran a hand over the top of his sodden hair. "Are you sayin' you want me back in *my* bed, lass, or in *any* bed *wi'* you?"

A strangled chuff of laughter escaped her before she gripped the remains of the front of his shirt. Lifting on toes immersed in mud, she calmly stated, "If you don't kiss me now, I'm going to bury you where you stand."

"You've graduated from threatenin' my monhood to the whole o' me, eh?"

"Lachlan. . . ."

He released a throaty laugh and exuberantly threw his arms around her, molding her shivering form against him. His possessive embrace elicited a sigh from her and she laid one side of her face against his chest. The cold wetness of him was barely felt as she listened to his heart. The beat was strong, as inspirational as a symphony in a park on a warm summer's day. When they'd made love in the past he didn't have a heartbeat, only a life pulse that she now knew had been a gift from Deliah.

"I canna kiss you wi' your head down," he whispered.

Beth instantly looked up, her lips parted in invitation. Her fingers kneaded the small of his back as his head lowered with teasing slowness. But when his mouth covered hers, she found the long hours of the past two weeks worth the wait. Sweetened by the rain, his mouth moved languidly over hers, second by second becoming more demanding until she was so completely lost in love that she had no concept of the weather nor their location. She ached with familiar desire. It heated her blood and made her pulse quicken. In life or death, he owned a part of her no other man could claim.

Ending the kiss abruptly, Lachlan tilted back his head and, breathing heavily, allowed the rain to splat against his face. Beth watched him for a moment, then placed her right hand against his cheek. He looked down at her, wonderment enhancing his handsome visage. His mouth quirked with a grin as he slowly shook his head.

"We're soaked, my Beth. I can think of a less no canny place to mak love to you."

"Can you?"

"Aye, darlin'." He winced comically. "I'm abou' to break through my breeks for want o' you."

"Sounds serious," she said with a wicked little grin. She shuddered and released a mewl of appreciation when his arms again enveloped her. Although he was as wet and as cold as she, being in his arms afforded her psychological warmth. He gave her a hearty squeeze, then scooped her up in his arms and gave her neck a teasing nibble as he settled her against him.

With a laugh, she linked her arms about his neck. "You can't carry me to the house. Not in this mud."

"Right now, my love, I could fly you to our room on wings o' love."

Beth released a long, dreamy sigh. "I love it when you get poetic."

Grinning, Lachlan started off toward the house, his boots heavily plopping in the mud, its thickness slowing his usual gait. To keep her in the mood for what he hoped would be a long night of making love, he began to sing in baritone, *Tell Me How To Woo Thee,* by Graham of Gartmore.

"If doughty deeds my lady please,
Right soon I'll mount my steed:
And strong his arm, and fast his seat,
Tha' bears from me the meed.
I'll wear thy colors at my brow,
Thy picture in my heart;

And he tha' bends no' to thine eye,
Shall rue it to his smart."

He paused to blink into the stinging rain and softly blow at the moisture on his lips. Then he continued:

"Then tell me how to woo thee, love,
Oh tell me how to woo thee.
For thy dear sake, no care I'll take,
Though never anither trow me—"

Lachlan grunted as his feet went out from under him. His butt hit the boggy ground and a splattering of mud and water sprayed up around them. He managed to retain his hold on Beth, but nearly released her when she began to laugh. Its rich sound filled the night, drowning out the drumming rudiments of raindrops striking solid objects. Within seconds, her infectious laughter caught him up in its throes. He cradled her against him, rocking back and forth, his own deep laughter harmonizing with hers. Next he knew, they were rolling on the cushiony ground, kissing, clinging to one another as one entity. The past and future held no meaning to them. Only the moment existed, and it was as sweet as the rain diluting most of the sodden earth covering them.

Finally, exhausted and too cold to frolic any longer, Lachlan scrambled to his feet, nearly falling twice, and helped Beth to hers. As best they could, they ran across the rest of the field, through the woods, around the house, and through both sets of double doors. When the last was closed behind them, Beth threw her arms up and laughingly glanced over Lachlan, then herself. She shivered violently and her teeth chattered, but she couldn't remember a time when she'd been happier. Lachlan looked like a drowned, long-haired hamster, his dark eyes peering at her between strands of hair matted to his face by rain and shifting globs of mud. She knew she didn't look any better, but didn't care. To prove this, she flung herself into his arms and kissed him. He tasted of rain and moist earth, and his lips were as cold as her own. No matter. Life was better than it had ever been, and not a word of complaint would pass her lips, not even if she shivered through the floor like a drill through rock.

"Och!" cried a voice, startlinq them apart. Deliah rushed toward them with two blankets. Passing each of them one, she placed her hands on her hips, her round eyes sparkling with joy. "I canna say I be sorry to see ye in each ither's arms, but tak heart, my friends, no' to catch your death from the cold."

Breathing heavily, Beth haphazardly rubbed one end of her blanket over her face and hair. "I n-need a hot b-bath-"

Smiling, Deliah dealt Lachlan a knowing look, one which prompted him to arch an eyebrow. "Weel, 'tis seems your lucky night," she beamed. "Ye will find a hot tub awaitin' ye in your room."

Eyes wide, Beth look at Lachlan, then swung her gaze to Deliah. "Have the twins—"

"They be sleepin' as soundly as an oak."

With a low laugh of glee, Beth planted a wet kiss on Deliah's cheek, took Lachlan by the hand, and hastily led him to the third floor. She stopped to verify that the babies were asleep. They didn't so much as stir while she stood at the side of the crib, staring at them with the same love and pride she always felt when near them. Her perfect children. Their world was so uncomplicated, and she silently promised them she would do her best to always keep it that way.

She heaved a breath of contentment, then turned to rejoin Lachlan in the hall, but found him standing to her left. He stared at the infants in abject wonder, and a shiver of delight passed through her. Their gazes met. His Adam's apple jerked as he gulped, then he swallowed again as he leaned a little closer to have a better look at them. The gaslight fixture on the wall lent a soft glow to the room, enough to make the babies' features clearly visible. When he straightened back, blinking hard and worrying his lower lip, Beth knew he was fighting back a compulsion to touch them. Although she had counted the long days for that to happen, now wasn't the right time. They were cold and wet and—

Again she took his hand and led him out of the nursery. She spared a look at the wet, muddy mess they'd tracked on the wood floor, then partially closed the door. Lachlan took the lead into the master bedroom, past the fully stoked fireplace and into the bathroom. Once she was inside, standing near the steaming tub of water, he closed the door and turned in time to see her deposit her blanket on the floor.

His chest went tight and he shook with expectation. Steam rose and curled between them. The gaslight was turned down low enough to lend the bathroom a romantic, seductive atmosphere. His erection strained against the tightness of his breeches. He desperately wanted to strip out of his clothes, but her wide eyes were regarding him a bit shyly. She repeatedly lapped at the moisture on her lips, her tongue making slow sweeps along the ridges. His swollen penis spasmed as he imagined himself entering the warmth of her, burying himself into the blissful tightness of her. He gazed down her length, noting every enticing curve her clinging gown displayed, lingering on the dark patch visible between her legs. When he again met her eyes, he read uncertainty in them. Her hands went to her abdomen. She looked down at them and shifted from one foot to the other.

"I-ah," she began unsteadily, her voice lower and huskier than usual, "have changed somewhat." She peered up at him and managed a weak smile. "Giving birth. . . ."

Lachlan's gaze briefly lowered to the placement of her hands. He dropped his blanket off to the side, then stepped up to her and tenderly framed her face with his large hands. "You will always be my sun, my moon, my sky, and my earth, Beth. You are more beautiful and desirable now than when we first met." He kissed her lightly, then pressed his brow to hers and sighed deeply. "Two babies or twelve, you will always be my womon, and I'll never love nor lust for no ither."

He sighed again, drew back his head, and looked deeply into her eyes. "I've been a fool, but a fool who loves you more'n any mon has ever loved. I want you so, my blood and my brain is afire, but I dinna want to rush you into makin' love if you're no' ready."

"I was born ready for you," she said breathlessly.

"I wasna thinkin' afore. You had the bairns mere weeks ago. Beth . . . your body needs to heal."

"It already has. Deliah made me a douche—"

"A wha'?"

"It's something you insert—"

"Och!" He felt the skin of his face grow hot. "I dinna think I want to hear this."

Beth gave an exasperated roll of her eyes. "Okay, no details. But I am healed. Inside and out. There's no need for you to worry."

He blinked in surprise. "So why are we standin' in our wet clothes?"

A mischievous grin spread across her mouth and brightened her blue eyes. Lachlan stepped back, leaning against the sink while he struggled to pull off one of his boots. He kept his gaze on Beth as she shimmied out of her nightgown, pulling it over her head. A breath caught in his throat. She stood naked in front of him, her clasped hands now resting in front of her pubes, her gaze watching him closely for a reaction. He could only gulp and manage a one-sided grin, all the while jerking on the boot until it finally slipped off his foot. The second boot took less time—whether this was due to his heightened eagerness, he didn't know or care. He peeled out of his socks and tossed them at the window, where they landed and draped on the sill. Standing, he whipped off his shirt over his head, heaved his chest as he drew in a deep breath, then flung the tattered material behind the far side of the toilet. His fingers went to the buttons on the front of his breeches.

His hands trembled so fiercely, he held them out at his sides and shook them as if to relieve their stiffness.

"Let me," said Beth. Stepping up to him, her gaze never wavering from the dark depths of his eyes, she calmly unfastened the five small buttons. She lightly nibbled on his lower lip while she eased his breeches and thick worsted undergarment down his hips and thighs.

Lachlan gripped her wrists to stop her. His erection freed, it throbbed against her nakedness, throbbed for another kind of release. Worming her right hand free, she wrapped her fingers around his length, stroked, gently stroked, then brushed the head across her smooth abdomen. Lachlan shuddered with the strain it took to maintain control. His muscles bunched, twitched, and he released a low groan when she again swept the sensitized underpart across her skin.

"Beth!" he gasped.

The room was steamy and growing hotter by the second.

"I want you in my mouth," she said in a low, raspy tone.

Lachlan's eyes widened in disbelief. They had both been virgins when he'd taken her to his bed last summer. He'd pleasured her in that special way to ease the first entry, as Millard Barluc had told him more than a century and a half ago. Barluc had also told him of how a woman could take a man into her mouth, but it had been Lachlan's understanding that only prostitutes performed that duty. And as often as Barluc had teasingly offered to pay for Lachlan to experience that pleasure, Lachlan could never bring himself to do anything that intimate with a woman he didn't first love.

"Have I shocked you?"

"Aye," he replied, quivering with anticipation.

She studied the wariness in his eyes for a long moment. "Carlene used to fill me in on all her exploits. And whenever I reacted as you are now, she would call me a prude and tell me there wasn't anything wrong in giving a man pleasure."

Lachlan stiltedly nodded. He stared at the enticing poutiness of her lips and wondered how it would feel to have them embrace him. The thought nearly made him spill his seed. He held back with all his willpower, trembling with the strain, his heart hammering wildly behind his chest.

Beth caressed his nose with hers; then sank to her knees, her hands trailing down his chest during her descent. He rolled his eyes heavenward, but closed them when she helped him to step out of the remains of his clothing. A second more passed. Hoarse breaths pumped in and out of his lungs, then became trapped in his throat when something warm and soft encompassed the end of his cock. He spasmed almost painfully when her tongue stroked him, the texture both maddening and intoxicating. Every flick of her tongue or slide of her mouth, made him jerk in sheer pleasure. It wasn't quite as gratifying as being inside her, but it was a damn good bit of foreplay in his opinion.

His testicles became rock-hard. He realized he couldn't hold on much longer, and he was put off at the idea of his seed spilling into her mouth. With a guttural, "Beth!" he gripped her arms and pulled her onto her feet. She looked at him, dazed, as if believing he wasn't pleased with her actions. "You're so grand!" he gasped, wound his arms around her and kissed her deeply, passionately.

He was reaching a point of mindlessness, need outweighing his determination to hold on until they could attain gratification together. Ending the kiss, he hugged her, burying his face into one side of her wet, curly hair.

"Fegs, lass," he groaned, "if we dinna slow down—"

"Now," she said, her tone strained, tight.

Lachlan looked into her eyes, unsure of her meaning.

"Don't worry about me."

"Lass?" he probed with uncertainty.

She reached down and curled her fingers around him.

"Fegs," he breathed.

He positioned her against the sink, lifted her left leg and supported it with a hand. She strained on the tiptoes of her right foot to give him better leverage. The instant he slid inside her, fierce shudders swelled through him. Her arms wrapped around his neck and she kissed him. Sounds of pleasure rattled in her throat as he made precise thrusts, still determined to pleasure her before he went over the edge. But then Beth began to take control, moving to sheath as much of him as possible. Lachlan was titillated by her boldness, further aroused by the fact she was no longer that shy young woman who'd had so little confidence in herself when she'd first arrived at the house. His thrusts grew gradually more forceful each time she groaned in a way that told him this was what she wanted. He kept himself focused on *her* needs, *her* pleasure and, somehow, managed to overcome his body's urgency to release itself.

Beth broke the kiss. Panting hard, she tilted back her head, giving him access to the graceful lines of her throat. He ran his lips and the tip of his tongue along her jawline, then down her neck. She quivered in his hold. Her fingers kneaded his nape, sometimes roughly, urging him on. On. On.

"Oh God, Lachlan!" she gasped, and squeezed her eyes shut. "Oh God. You feel so . . . *good.*"

"Look at me."

She did so immediately.

They stared into each other's eyes as sensations built layer upon layer within their heated bodies. Her eyes widened amidst an expression of sheer wonder, while his were black with passion, his features taut, jaw clenched. A sound of startlement escaped her. Lachlan growled deep in his chest as his own orgasm coursed through him. They clung to each other, riding the storm of sensations, shuddering, quaking, gasping in the throes of their love-making's offerings.

For long seconds afterward, they remained embraced. Sweat mingled with the residual mud clinging to their skin.

Releasing a long breath, Lachlan planted a brief kiss on her lips, then peered adoringly into her eyes. "You have spent me, lass. I've no' the strength to move, let alone climb into the tub."

"No?" She grinned as she traced a finger along his lower lip. "If you're planning to sleep beside me tonight, then I suggest you get into that tub with me."

He playfully arched his eyebrows. "You do, eh?"

She nodded, her eyes bright with laughter.

"Efter you," he said, stepping back and giving her a partial bow at the waist.

Beth lowered herself into the water. It was still surprisingly hot, but not enough to be uncomfortable. Deliah had added bubble bath. The remains of the iridescent bubbles swirled around her as she settled frontward, making room for Lachlan to sit behind her, his bent legs to each side of her. When he rested his arms and the back of his head along the porcelain rim, she nestled into him, her head using his chest for a pillow.

They were contentedly silent for a time, then Lachlan said, " 'Tis a sin to feel this bloody good."

Beth smiled and absently caressed the back of his thighs. "I'll wash your hair if you wash mine."

"Right now?"

It was almost a groan, and she chuckled. "The sooner done, the sooner we can go to bed."

The muscles in his thighs tightened. "Bed, eh? No' to sleep, I hope."

"I thought you were exhausted."

"I'm resilient," he chuckled. He turned her face to him and bent his head to kiss her mouth. "Especially when it comes to lovin' my womon." He straightened back. "Beth, we need to marry soon. For our sakes and the babes."

"*Need* to?" she asked stiffly.

"Aye."

She turned enough to look him in the eye. "We don't have to do anything. Lachlan, lovers don't always marry, these days."

He scowled. "No? Weel, I'm an *auld-farrant* mon wi' an *auld-farrant* attitude."

"A what attitude?"

"Auld—" He frowned thoughtfully, then carefully pronounced, "Old-fashioned."

"Ah."

"Had I my druthers, we would have mairrit afore I first made love to you."

Beth locked her teeth, then dipped her hair into the water. She briskly scrubbed her scalp with her fingertips, then combed the strands with her fingers. Lachlan watched her in silence, the scowl again intact, his thoughts grim. She took an inordinately long time to rinse the muck out of her hair, but he knew she was doing this to make him think over what he'd said. She could take a week, but he wouldn't change his mind. The more he learned about this century, the less he liked. What kind of society didn't encourage marriage? Or was this merely *her* opinion of nuptials?

She finally sat up and flipped her hair behind her, spraying him in the process.

"Beth, are you no' willin' to marry me? Is tha' it?"

Without looking at him she said, "I don't recall you asking me."

He thought about this and his scowl darkened. "Beth, will you marry me?"

"Yes," she said simply, scooping water into her hands and splashing it against her face.

"Yes?" he asked hesitantly.

She turned and shot him an amused look. "Aye."

His face broke out in a broad grin. "You like to mak me squirm, dinna you?"

She grinned, nodding.

With a laugh, he wound his arms about her and brought her against his chest. "You wee, wanton tease."

"Wee, am I? I'm certainly big enough to keep you in line!"

"Aye," he said contentedly. "You're more womon than the likes o' me deserve—but I'll no' decline your offer to mak an honest mon o' me."

"*My* offer?" she chortled.

He nodded, grinning from ear to ear, his eyes lit with mischief.

"You're incorrigible."

"Insatiable, too. Comes from you bein' so devastatingly sexy, love. Maks a mon think o' nocht but havin' you twenty-four hours a day."

"I would be bowlegged in no time."

He laughed. "All the easier to slip atween your soft thighs," he said in a mock wolfish tone. To his delight, her face turned crimson and she looked away. "Is my soon-to-be-bride blushin'? Efter me havin' you at the sink, just moments ago?"

She cleared her throat. "I remember *me* having *you* at the sink."

"Do you now?" He coiled his arms snugly around her. "Weel, the truth is, I dinna care who had who, as long as we have each other thegither."

"Have each other thegither," she murmured, then looked at him. "Does that make sense? Each other thegither, I mean."

He shrugged his broad shoulders. "Does to me."

"Hmmm. Oops. I hear little voices coming from the nursery."

Lachlan cocked an ear. "You're right. But I dinna think little voices could be heard from there."

She stood and stepped out of the tub. Lachlan watched her rinse her breasts at the sink, then pad out of the bathroom.

With a grin, he sank beneath the bubbleless, murky water.

In one part of the cellar, Wade Cuttstone—a.k.a. the Phantom—glared at the flame flickering on the two-inch stub of a candle on the table in front of him. He was cold and hungry, both of which magnified his hatred of his dank solitude. His life had somehow become overly complicated. At every corner, his mission met with bizarre twists and turns. He couldn't count the times he'd nearly gotten his hands on Laura Bennett. Tonight, he'd been about to leave the closet in the nursery when all hell had broken loose. He'd gotten outside via several of the passages to the first floor, and had nearly been seen by reporters. What had brought them to Baird House? Why were they shouting accusations of "fraud"? It all had something to do with a ghost, but he hadn't encountered one. With his superior mental abilities, he would know if a ghost existed within this house. Within the town, for that matter, although he hadn't picked up on that winged woman. Now *she* was a surprise. He still hadn't fully grasped her purpose. Was she a queen begetter? Was *she* the one leading the human women astray, creating the future generations who would destroy the planet with their chemicals and overpopulation?

His ice blue eyes narrowed as he gripped the handle of a jeweled dirk and jabbed the sharp point into his right palm. He didn't wince at the pain, nor pay attention to the rivulets of blood oozing from the wound. His gaze remained locked on the squirming flame, as if staring at it hard enough would afford him the answers he sought.

Perhaps the Guardian was testing him. Why else would he have been seen by that runny-nosed brat in the backyard, then confronted by none other than the esteemed detective, Winston Connery, himself? The boy and the man should have died that night, but the winged wonder had intervened. He would have to repay her for that bit of folly. Her wings would make an interesting conversation piece on his wall in the parlor of his small flat. Of course, no one would ever see them. He had no family, and had never bothered to acquire friends. In his line of work, no one could be trusted.

And then there was this third woman, called Beth. A begetter of twins. She'd tapped into him tonight. No warning. She was suddenly there, draining his energy, and it had taken all of his willpower to telesend his outrage to her in warning for her to cease her invasion. And that man, Lachlan. He was another threat, although not as serious a one as the woman. This man didn't possess the attention span to traipse through the psychic channels for very long at a time.

A thought occurred to Cuttstone and he stopped mutilating his palm. Grinning, he laid the dirk on the table and leaned closer to the flame.

Perhaps the woman and man were allies, sent by the Guardian to aid him in his unending quest. Since their arrival, static clogged most of the psychic airways. Connery had been cut off from mentally locating him, cut off from picking up trace impressions of his presence.

Allies.

How far would they be willing to go to help him to rid the world of Laura Bennet and her future offspring, and the winged queen of the infestents?

If only the Guardian would stop sending him cryptic messages.

A cold draft swept through his hideaway, extinguishing the flame and plunging him into pitch darkness. He remained motionless, not even blinking, mentally scrambling to remember if he had thought or said anything that could have offended the Guardian.

CHAPTER FOUR

Except for an occasional crackle or pop from the fireplace, quietude mantled the house like an old, faithful security blanket. The rain had stopped. Lachlan's eyelids drooped more from contentment than fatigue as he watched Beth nurse their son. With his back braced against one of the decorative walnut foot posts, his sleeping daughter cradled against his bare chest, he wondered if life could get any better than what he had now. In one respect, it was a little scary. He had more to lose. In the past, all that could be taken from him was his life and his estate. In death, though, he had managed to hold on to not only his belongings, but also a semblance of life.

His gaze shifted to regard his daughter. Pale peach fuzz covered an otherwise pink head. Blond eyelashes and eyebrows. Her nose was barely bigger than his thumbnail, her mouth a darker pink and pouty. She was a tiny replica of her mother, with one hand poking out of the pink blanket, the gracefully spread fingers twitching against one rounded cheek. She had been the one to awaken and exercise her lungs to be fed. Surprisingly, the boy had slept through the ruckus.

When their daughter had her fill of mother's milk, Beth had asked Lachlan to hold the squirming bundle. He'd panicked at first, then hesitantly nodded. Now, with the baby's warmth against his chest and bare arms, he couldn't believe he'd ever been afraid to touch his children. It felt amazingly natural to hold his daughter, as if he'd done it a hundred times.

Straightening his right leg, he looked up when Beth chuckled and commented, "Are you trying to entice me into jumping your bones again before your son's belly is full?"

He frowned at first, then glanced down at himself when her gaze pointedly flicked to his leg. For a moment longer, he puzzled her remark, then dawning brought a deep blush to his cheeks. Before Beth had handed him the baby, he'd haphazardly draped one corner of the top quilt across his lap. His bent left knee was visible and most of the right leg. Now he looked as if he were posing, but in truth, he wasn't. With her second chuckle, he peered at her with a mischievous glint in his eyes. There she sat with their son attached to her left nipple, only the top of his dark head visible behind the sheet she had draped over her right shoulder to hide her nakedness from Lachlan. With her damp hair a mass of curls framing her face, and her round eyes sparkling with happiness, he had never seen her look more beautiful or desirable.

"Darlin', 'twouldna be proper for our daughter's faither to—ah—come up, so to speak, while he's holdin' her. So I say to you, love o' my life, tarry no' wi' our son's feedin'. The sooner they're both fed and snug back in the crib, the sooner you and I get back to the business o' lovin'."

"You forgot one thing."

He considered her lighthearted manner with a tad of wariness. "Oh?"

"Their diapers will need changing before they return to the crib."

A blank look fell over Lachlan's face as he glanced down

at his daughter, then up again at Beth. "I dinna do diapers. That's a womon's task."

"The rules have changed a wee since your time."

His eyebrows shot up. "Some changes are no' for the better."

Beth playfully wrinkled her nose at him. "You haven't lived till a baby wee-wees on you."

With a grimace, Lachlan cast each infant a dubious look. "I've lived more'n most."

"Now, now, darling, you only *think* you have."

"I have," he insisted.

Beth shook her head and flashed him a teasing grin. "Trust me. Changing diapers is a character builder."

"Some would say I've enough character."

Beth sighed with theatrical martyrdom. "Fine. I'll do the messy ones."

"Messy ones?" He grimaced again, then made a feeble attempt to appear brightened by his decision. "All right, lass. We're parents thegither, through the good and . . . no'-so-good."

"And?"

He wrinkled his nose at her. "I'll do my fair share, and no' a whimper you'll hear from me."

She smiled, her features soft and radiant with love. "I've missed you," she whispered, one hand smoothing the tiny head at her breast.

"And I, you," replied Lachlan. He became pensively silent for a moment, then regarded her with such sadness, concern leapt into her eyes. "Beth, I canna say *enough* how sorry I am for my behavior these past weeks."

"It's in the past."

He nodded, glanced down at his daughter, and smiled. His jaw still ached from Beth's blow earlier, a reminder of how close they'd come to letting their anger wipe out all the love they had for one another. But he didn't want to think about that now. Instead, he met the somewhat anxious look in Beth's eyes and said, "We have to name them."

The infant in her arms stopped suckling. He was asleep,

and she studied his face for a time, her expression dreamy. There was no doubt in her mind he would grow up to resemble his father. Unlike his sister's fuzzy pate, he had a mop of thick dark hair, almost black with fiery highlights. He pursed his lips and she looked up at Lachlan and smiled.

"You choose the names."

Lachlan was both startled and gladdened by her words. He'd always wanted a daughter named— "Weel," he began hesitantly, then worried his lower lip for a time. " 'Twould be best if we combined the names we most fancy."

"Let's start with our daughter. Does a name jump out at you when you look at her?"

Lachlan grinned. "Beth."

Beth wrinkled her nose. "One in the family is enough. My mother's name was Rita Elizabeth. She never liked Rita, and wanted to be called Beth, but her mother insisted on her proper first name. I would rather not use Rita, so what about your mother's name?"

She knew by his intake of breath that this was what he was hoping for.

"Her name was Ciarda." Ke-ar-da.

Beth slowly pronounced it, then nodded. "It's beautiful."

"She was a beautiful womon. I adored her. I remember bein' wi' her in the afterlife. Do you?"

"No. Sometimes I get flashbacks, but most of them I can't make any sense of. I do remember my parents and Borgie. I think I remember Carlene and David."

"Me, too. Vaguely." He frowned. "My mither tried to tell me somethin', but I canna remember why she didna carry it through."

"What was she like?"

Lachlan wistfully looked heavenward, then lowered his gaze to Beth. "I have her hair and eyes. My brithers all took efter our faither. By the time I was born, my brithers were workin' wi' him, so it was mostly my mither and me at home. She was a compassionate, lovin' womon, Beth. Sometimes, I can still hear her laughter, like sweet bells ringin' in a distance. She had a bonny voice, she did, and often sang to me, even efter I reached my teens. Never did I hear her raise her voice in anger. For it all, though, she was the most lonely, saddest person I've ever known."

"In what way?"

Lachlan gave a gentle shrug. "I dinna think she really loved my faither. He was a difficult mon, and seldom at home. I have all her journals in the attic. Never read them, though. Too painful, and I guess I've always been a wee fearful of learnin' just how miserable she was in her mairrage."

"At least she had you," Beth said softly.

He nodded, then sighed. "I could have been a better son."

"We all think we could have been better children or better parents. That's human nature."

He nodded again. "So, lass, wha' do you think o' the name Ciarda Elizabeth?"

"You don't have to use my name."

"Aye, we do. Ciarda Elizabeth MacLachlan Baird."

Beth softly chuckled. "That's a mouthful."

"But a fine name."

"I agree. Then Ciarda Elizabeth MacLachlan Baird, it is. Now, what about our son?"

"May I hold him, Beth?"

"Thought you'd never ask."

Lachlan reverently kissed his daughter's brow, then scooted across the mattress. He positioned himself next to Beth, his back to the headboard. With great care, so as not to awaken either baby, Beth first passed their son into the waiting crook of Lachlan's arm, then took their daughter into her own. Lachlan was quiet for a time, the fingertips of one hand tenderly brushing the mass of hair on the boy's crown. When he looked at Beth, tears misted his eyes, magnifying the pride glowing in the dark depths.

"They're both so grand, Beth."

She nodded, unable to speak for her throat was tight with emotion.

"Wha' was your faither's name?" he asked her.

Beth swallowed hard before answering. "Jonathan. But your son is going to be the spitting image of you. He needs a Scottish name."

"My poor wee bairn," Lachlan cooed with mock sympathy. "Look like your faither, will you?"

Beth chuckled. "As if that doesn't thrill you."

"Aye, I'm a vain, sorry mon," he beamed at her. "A Scottish name, eh? Certainly no' efter my faither."

A chill gripped his spine, then coursed through him as a zephyrous sound passed through his skull. He shuddered and blinked, feeling as though someone walked over his grave, but he knew no one had, at least, not right then.

"What's wrong?"

Lachlan didn't answer right away. When he finally spoke, a name rolled off his tongue. "Broc Laochailan."

"What?"

" 'Tis *neònach.*"

"What did you just say?" she asked humorously.

He looked bewilderingly at her, then jiggled his head. "*Neònach.* Strange. Strange tha' his name came to me so forcefully."

"Who is he?"

"A many times great-uncle on my mither's side, born mid-eighteenth century." Lachlan frowned as tidbits of information rose to the fore of his mind. He couldn't recall his mother or grandfather imparting the facts, but they were there in his memory as if just released from a well deep inside his subconscious.

"Lachlan?" Beth asked softly, concern lacing her tone. "What's wrong?"

He gave in to a mild shudder and managed a wan smile. "Old age, love."

She grinned, but it faded when he frowned again.

" 'Tis *orra,* Beth. I canna shake a feelin' tha' . . . ."

"Of what?"

"Weel, tha' I should know more abou' him. For the life o' me, I canna understand why I even thought o' him now."

"Was he an important figure in your clan's history?"

Lachlan released a breath through pursed lips, his expressive eyebrows forming a lazy, reclining S above his dark eyes. "No' really. He was a crofter, as was his faither, brither and cousin. For centuries, Beth, a clansman crofter paid his rent in fightin' service, but efter Culloden warrin' became a thing o' the past. Many o' the Highland Chieftains demanded money, but the crofters had none, so the chiefs, enamored wi' greed, took to removin' the crofters and sellin' or leasin' their lands to the English and Lowland Scot sheep farmers."

"That's terrible."

"Aye. Weel, Broc wasna happy abou' it. His family had fought long and hard for their land, and he wasna abou' to leave withou' a wee fight o' his own.

"There was an old mon called Mad Fergus who was so old, it was said no one remembered his birth. He told o' treasures hidden on the Isle O' Lewis. No one had ever taken his stories seriously, but Broc was desperate enough to listen to anythin'. Wi' his younger brither, Niall, anither mon from the clan, and two Campbells, he set off to the isle. Three months later he returned wi' a small fortune, but he was alone. The ithers had died. He never said how or why."

"No one ever found out what happened?"

Lachlan shook his head. "He turned the treasure over to his cousin, Lethan, who he trusted to divide it among those who still held their land. He told Lethan he was returnin' to the isle. Alone. No one was to follow him."

"Was he after more treasure?"

"Aye, and he claimed he had unfinished business there."

Beth shivered. "He never returned, did he?"

"No. And despite wha' was offered in rent, the chieftain sold the land ou' from under Broc's immediate clan. Broc's parents, grievin' the loss o' their sons, moved to Edinburgh. Lethan took his wife, two sons and daughter, and two male second cousins, to the isle. They used wha' remained o' the treasure to build a tavern and inn near Caloway, close to the Callanish Standin' Stones. Twas where my mither was eventually born, and where my grandfaither died."

"What are the Callanish Standing Stones?"

Lachlan's face brightened. "I only saw them once, but I'll never forget them. Spooky and grand, they are. Next to Stonehenge, they're the most famous megaliths in all o' Britain."

"I would love to see them."

"Aye," he said wistfully. "I wouldna mind seein' them again. I wonder if . . ."

Silence befell the room for a time, during which Beth expectantly watched Lachlan's dreamy expression. When she could no longer bear the wait, she prompted, "What do you wonder?"

He looked at her a bit puzzled, then grinned. "Weel, darlin', I wonder if I would still feel the *tinglin'* there, as I did when I was a lad."

Beth's mouth gaped open, then shut. "The tingling?"

He nodded, glanced down at his son and sighed wistfully before looking into Beth's eyes. "You see, my grandfaither harbored a passionate hatred for my faither. She was the first in his family to marry outside the MacLachlan clan, and he refused to visit my mither in her home in Aberdeen. So, once every few years, my mither would travel to Lewis to visit wi' her family. My faither wouldna allow my brithers to go, but didna mind her leavin'.

"I was six when she took me to the inn. O' course my faither didna mind me goin'. Truth be, he was glad to be rid o' me. Probably as glad as was I to be away from him.

"Twas a hard journey, Beth, but my mither never complained." Again he fell silent for a time. "She was a wonderful womon. Bonny as a Highland summer day, strong-willed, and as kind as any womon ever born to this earth.

"Anyway, the inn was grand. We stayed for two weeks,

and I didna want to leave my cousins. The night afore we were to tak the coach back, I ran off and found myself at the stones. 'Twas rainin', and the marshland there was covered wi' water, over my ankles. I was never so scared as when I first saw those loomin' stones, Beth. In the Highlands the sun doesna set in the summer, but hovers along the horizon. 'Tis called the gloamin'. The rain was warm, but I was cold, like some malevolent thing was inside me. I'm no' sure, scared as I was, why I ventured further among the megaliths. It was as if somethin' compelled me, Beth, and I couldna mak myself turn away from them. The whole time I was there I experienced a tinglin' sensation. It vibrated through me. No' exactly an unpleasant feelin'. Almost . . . comfortin'. I dinna know how else to explain it.

"Sometime later, my grandfaither came for me. He told me the *knowin'* had brought me to the stones, but didna elaborate on wha' tha' was supposed to mean. He was like tha', my grandfaither.

"When he took me back to the inn I was shocked to see my mither's face. She was so pale, Beth. Pale and terrified, and she hugged me as if she'd been afraid I wouldna return to her. She made me promise never to return to the stones and, although I did visit my grandfaither from time to time on my own, I never went near them."

"Weren't you curious why she was so afraid of them?"

He shrugged slightly. "Aye, but I couldna break my word to her, could I? But I dinna think visitin' them now would go against my promise."

"No," Beth said thoughtfully. "I think her fear stemmed more from your age. Why was she afraid of the stones, though?"

"I dinna know. Everyone I knew back then are all gone. I wonder if the inn still stands, and if my mither's clan still lives there."

"When the weather gets better, we could visit and find out."

Lachlan's eyes widened. "You really wouldna mind?"

"You have my curiosity piqued. Besides, it's part of your heritage. Except for your death, Lachlan, do you realize this is the first time you've talked about your past? I really don't know much about your history."

He told her everything. Beth quietly listened, digesting the information and analyzing the man he'd become. By the time he was through, she felt as if she did know his mother, and admired the loving woman she'd been, despite her hard, lonely life. Although Lachlan had not spoken of his father or brothers with even a hint of bitterness, their treatment of him irked her. Were they alive, she would give them a piece of her mind, not that anything *she* would have to say would faze the likes of them.

"Beth, have I upset you?"

"What? Oh . . . no." She sighed and offered him a tender smile. "I was just thinking how sad it was for you and your mother to be treated like outcasts."

Lachlan's eyebrows shrugged. "Sadder for her. Actually, I canna complain. My faither and brithers gave me the gumption to fend for myself. If I hadna left Aberdeen I wouldna have died here, and certainly wouldna have met you." He grinned his most charming, boyish grin. "And your century would have been denied my presence. *Och!* Scary thought, is it no'?"

She frowned slightly, then said, "You once told me you and your brothers took over the business after your father died."

"Ah, weel, he was no' actually dead. He became a recluse. I'm no' sure when he actually died, or my brithers, either."

He was surprised he'd told Beth so much of his childhood, when in fact he hadn't thought about it since his death. His anger then had been directed toward Tessa and Robert, their betrayal far worse than anything his father or brothers could have perpetrated. He hadn't told Beth about his guardian angel, Ornora, especially since she'd deserted him after his murder. Besides, although Beth seemed to accept death and faeries without too much trouble, he thought perhaps his childhood secret playmate might be a measure too much. And he had avoided telling her about Broc's connection to the dirk. For some reason he couldn't even begin to fathom, the name was very important to him right now, and he didn't want to risk souring Beth against it.

"Weel, love, wha' do you think o' namin' our son efter my ancestor?"

"Broc Laochailan." She nodded, grinning. "I like it."

Pain inexplicably pierced Lachlan's temples, making him wince. Before he could stop himself, he corrected, "Broc Laochailan Jonathan MacLachlan Baird."

Beth laughed. "My God! Isn't that a bit much?"

"No," he said, seriously gazing into her eyes. The pain had vanished as quickly as it had come. " 'Tis a grand name. A name befittin' the mon our son will become."

"Okay." She reached out and lovingly caressed Lachlan's cheek. "Have I told you lately how much I love you?"

Blissful warmth spread through him as he breathlessly said, "I love you, too, my bonny Beth. And once we put the bairns back in their crib, I'll show you just how much."

Roan was lifted through layers of sleep when his mind registered an enticing floral scent. He opened his eyes to darkness. Immediately, he was aware of cold air on his face. The fire in the hearth had died out, but from the neck down he was warm, partially due to the covers, and a greater part due to Laura's body. Her head lay on the hollow of his right shoulder, her bare right arm and leg draped across him. Her blond hair lay across his throat, the floral-scented shampoo she'd borrowed from Beth filling his nostrils. His body hardened in response to her scent and proximity, and he rolled his eyes in contemplation of awakening her.

They'd only been together a few months, but he felt as if she had always been a part of his adult life. His short marriage to Adaina seemed but a distant memory, although his son remained clearly fixed in his mind. Both had died in a fire two years prior. Until Laura and her nephews entered his life, he'd unknowingly been on a path of self-destruction, living each day with reckless disregard for the future—in truth, dreading the possibility of living too much longer with the burden of guilt he'd carried over the death of his son. Jamie had only been three years old, and should have been with his father at the park. But Roan had forgotten. By the time he arrived at the house, the inferno had been impenetrable, his ex-wife and son at the window moments before the flames had taken them.

But life went on. Laura had taught him that.

Moaning low, he shifted onto his side and pressed his lips to her brow. In the darkness, he heard her sigh contentedly. He waited, but she didn't move or make another sound.

Should he wake her? They'd made love only a while ago, a rushed bit of pleasure, thanks to the lads. He was far from having even a portion of his fill of her—if it was possible to ever have enough of her body or her mind.

In the mid-nineteenth century, they'd been the lovers who had cold-bloodedly murdered Lachlan, her husband. They'd later married and had nine children. Their marriage had been miserable, their children eager to leave home as soon as possible. Fate had brought back Tessa and Robert. Reincarnation had given them a chance to resolve the past, as Laura and Roan.

Laura rolled onto her back. Roan eased his arm from beneath her and started to position himself on top of her, until his hand bumped a solid object. A grunt followed, an unmistakable sound that could only be Kahl. Gingerly, grimacing all the while, he reached over a little farther, then more until his hand had encountered all three of the small shapes alongside Laura.

When had the lads sneaked into bed with them?

Damn me, he mentally groaned.

His desire for Laura fled on wings of hopelessness and

frustration. He eased off his side of the mattress, stood, and stretched the small of his back. A rueful scowl masked his face as he pictured the boys snuggled beneath the covers.

A rumbling in his stomach interrupted his mental grumblings. Padding barefoot across the cold floor he went out the door and into the hall, dressed in pajama bottoms. Cold air rose gooseflesh on his exposed skin. Ignoring his discomfort, he went down the staircase to the first floor, where, instead of going down the secondary hallway to the kitchen, a niggling impulse directed him to the parlor. He didn't stop to question why he was taking this route, not until he was passing through the parlor and sensed someone else was in the room. His first thought was that another burglar or reporter had gotten into the house. Anger formed a ball of fire behind his breast as his gaze searched the darkness.

Then a low voice said, "Roan, I be at the window."

Releasing a breath, he made his way across the room. He was nearly on top of her before he could make out her form sitting on the window seat. He sat beside her. She was sitting on one leg, her face turned to the window, a blanket draped over her shoulders. He didn't need to see her face clearly to determine she was troubled by something.

"Want me to build a fire?"

"I be warm enough."

"Deliah, you're voice sounds a wee shaky."

She sighed, a woeful sound. "I be no' feelin' too weel."

He reached out and placed the back of a hand to her brow. "You dinna have a fever."

"Faeries never get ill, so I be a wee frightened, Roan. I canna tell Winston. I dinna want him worryin' abou' me."

"He loves you," said Roan with a low chuckle. "O' course he'll worry abou' you."

"Worried abou' wha'?" asked a voice in the darkness.

"Lannie, we're by the window," said Roan. "Deliah's feelin' a wee jaggy. No fever, though."

"Fegs," Lachlan muttered. "I'll light two o' the lamps."

In the dark, Lachlan took a box of wooden matches from the fireplace mantel. He retraced his steps toward the hall, stopping before he reached the threshhold. He struck one sulfur tip along a coarse strip on the box, then turned the key at the base of the wall light fixture to the right of the door. With this lamp lit, he went to the one to the right of the sideboard, which was positioned about seven feet away from the nearest window. Soft light graced most of the room, awarding them adequate visibility. He placed the box on the sideboard and walked to where Deliah and Roan were sitting.

"Canna sleep?" Roan asked him, then glanced at Lachlan's naked legs, visible beneath his knee-length robe. He released a choked laugh and looked into Lachlan's face with wide eyes. "I thought at first you were wearin' fur leggin's, mon!"

Lachlan peered down at the dark hair covering his legs, wiggled his bare toes, then cast Roan a look of chagrin. Deliah's wan smile drew his attention to her.

"Ye havena seen my Winston's legs, have ye?" she said with a glimmer of humor in her blue eyes.

"Never mind our legs," Lachlan grumbled, and gently placed the back of a hand to her brow, then her left cheek. "No fever, 'tis true, but you're pale, lass. Have you been eatin' properly? The body canna sustain itself on love alone, you know."

She blushed and lowered her gaze for a moment. Lachlan's stomach rumbled loudly and she looked up, her eyebrows arched in amusement.

"Aye, I'm hungry." Lachlan grinned apologetically; then glanced at Roan. "And you?"

"Starvin'."

Deliah clamped a hand over her mouth. She paled even more, then her face became flushed and her eyes dulled. Moments later, she lowered the hand and swallowed almost convulsively. She shuddered and stated, "I dinna like tha' feelin'."

"Describe it," said Roan.

She thought over her response before answering. " 'Tis like my insides are tryin' to escape my mouth."

"You're nauseated?"

"If tha' be it, aye," she said weakly "Ither times, I feel like a leaf caught up in a swirlin' breeze, and darkness winks around me. 'Tis so frightenin'. I canna understand wha' be wrong." Tears welled up in her eyes as she looked into Lachlan's face, which had darkened with concern. "Lachlan, wha' be it like to die?"

"Deliah!" Roan choked in shock.

She burst into wretched sobs and buried her face in her hands, her slender form quaking beneath the blanket.

Roan glanced helplessly at Lachlan. "I'll get Winston."

Lachlan nodded, although Deliah adamantly shook her head. Roan immediately dashed across the room and into the hall. Lachlan swept Deliah up into his arms and carried her to the sofa, where he sat with her on his lap and cradled in his arms.

"Hush, lass," he said softly. He adjusted the blanket to better cover her nakedness, then snugged her closer against the warmth of his body. "You're no' dyin'. Fate wouldna be so cruel to bless us wi' you, only to tak you away so soon."

"It took you," she wept against his shoulder.

"Fegs, lass, but fate had ither plans for me. I was always meant to be wi' my Beth, as you are meant to be wi' Winston. I know this to be true. Know it as surely as I can know anythin'."

Her weeping ebbed some, and he went on, "Everythin' tha' happens in an individual's life, Deliah, happens for a reason. If you hadna been trapped in the root, and I hadna built this grand house on top o' you, how different would have been my death, eh? Beth would have died in the States. Laura and Roan would have never met, and God only knows wha' would have happened to the lads. You brought us all thegither. Withou' you, Deliah lass, Baird

House would be just anither old house, wi' no' a lick o' magic to grace her walls."

Sniffing, she tilted back her head and looked into his eyes. "But wha' if this fate doesna think me useful anymore?"

He chuffed a laugh. "Fate is more the paths we choose in life."

"But 'tis wrong o' me to exist in your world."

His eyebrows jerked upward. "Is it now? *Fegs,* girl, wha' o' me? I'm a century and a half off kilter!"

She chuckled. "Aye, we be both ou' o' our elements here."

"No. You and I belong where we belong, which is in the here and the now."

Two breathless men ran into the room, Roan flushed, Winston's face the color of ash. Roan sat on the settee to the sofa's right, while Winston hesitantly seated himself on the edge of the sofa next to Lachlan. Deliah looked at Winston through watery, troubled eyes, her chin quivering, one side of her face pressed against Lachlan's shoulder.

"I didna want ye to know," she told Winston tremulously.

Winston was at a loss for words. His breathing was erratic, his eyes dulled with worry. After a few seconds, he released a gust of breath and raked the fingers of one hand through his tousled hair.

"You haven't eaten since late this morn—yesterday morn," he corrected, glancing at his watch. It was just after 2:00 A.M.

"I havena felt weel for some time," she said, fresh tears brimming her eyes.

Lachlan stiffened and stared off into space. His body tingled almost uncomfortably, and his brain felt afire.

"How long?" Winston asked her.

"More 'n a week. I be sorry to worry ye."

"Never mind me!" He cast Lachlan and Roan a look of helplessness, not noticing the former's eerie, frozen state.

"We can't tak her to a doctor. Bloody hell, if she is sick, wha' do we do?"

"Dinna panic," Roan muttered, then briskly rubbed his palms up and down his face. "Wait," he said, lowering his hands, "you're psychic. Canna you mentally determine wha's wrong wi' her?"

Winston eagerly took her left hand between his own. He breathed hard in concentration, moments later pressing the back of her fingers to his brow. " 'Please, God, help me," he pleaded in a tight, strained tone, but the harder he tried to scan her, the colder became his brain. When a full minute passed and no information awarded his attempts to screen her condition, he jerked back, his face ravaged with bitterness. "Nothin'," he bit out, kneading her hand. "My mind's meetin' wi' a wall!"

Lachlan drew in a sharp breath, blinked, then grinned a bit dazedly. *"Uirisg,"* he said, staring down at Deliah's upturned face. He saw puzzlement flash across her expression, and repeated the Gaelic word.

"Wha'?" asked Roan and Winston in unison.

"No," she murmured. " 'Tis a myth, a legend among faeries. It canna be."

"Wha'?" both men asked in unison again. They glanced at each other with frowns, then focused on Lachlan and Deliah.

"Wha' can't be?" asked Winston testily.

Deliah sat up, her eyes locked with Lachlan's, a wondrous expression glowing on her face. "No, but I wish it be so wi' all my heart."

"If someone doesn't tell me wha' the bloody hell is goin' on, my liver will burst through my ears!" Winston cried.

Lachlan passed him a comically chiding look, then grinned at Deliah. "Weel, lass, your wish is true enough."

Wide-eyed, she stared at Winston, who couldn't decide whether she looked horrified or ecstatic. Her gaze unwavering, as if looking into Winston's soul, she asked Lachlan, "How can ye believe this?"

"I just know."

" 'Tis a myth," she said dreamily.

Roan jumped to his feet, scowling at Lachlan. "Wha's this *uirisg?*"

"A joinin' o' God and nature," Lachlan laughed, and hugged Deliah.

She remained in a dazed state, inwardly screening herself. Yes, it was there. Inside her. As real as anything she had ever encountered.

"Lannie," Roan growled, his nerves raw with concern, "there isna anythin' funny abou' the lass bein' sick!"

Lachlan put on an air of affront. "Weel, me laddies, if you knew your Gaelic like a good Scot should—"

"Please," Winston pleaded in a hoarse whisper of a tone, his eyes imploring Lachlan to tell what he knew of her condition. He didn't ask himself how the man could know something about Deliah his psychic ability couldn't even glean. Nothing mattered but finding out what was wrong with her.

"Weel," Lachlan said loftily, his black eyes lit with merriment, "it seems Baird House will be blessed wi' the verra first *uirisg,* which maks me wonder if the magic isna all from our Deliah, here." He paused to further build the suspense, knowing damn well what he was doing was a form of torture. But his news was too grand to simply blurt out.

Deliah's gaze cut to him. She looked more beautiful than he'd ever seen her. Radiant. Glowing with such happiness that its warmth seeped into his own body. He somehow knew she was now aware of her condition.

"Lannie!" Roan practically shouted.

" 'Tis for Deliah to announce," Lachlan said, nodding at her.

Her brilliant blue eyes searched Roan's strained features, then Winston's. "A *uirisg* be the offspring o' a mortal and a faerie."

Roan blinked repeatedly in confusion. Winston stared blankly into her face, his black eyebrows drawn down, but not in a frown or a scowl.

"O' course, a *uirisg* be but legend and myth," she went on, her tone airy, playful. "So I no' be sure wha' to call wha' I be carryin' inside me. I think mayhaps a . . . *baby.*"

The word hung in the air as silence encompassed the room for a time. Then Winston slid off the sofa and plopped hard on his butt on the floor, his gaze never leaving Deliah's face. Roan sat back on the settee, astonishment youthening his visage. He could do no more than stare at Deliah, his mouth agape, his heart pounding wildly behind his chest.

Winston's heartbeat was also hammering away, seemingly in his throat, cutting off his oxygen.

"Are ye no' pleased?" she asked him, a hint of nervousness in her tone.

"Baby?" he whispered. "How? When? Tonight—I mean, yesterday?" His face brightened. "Two weeks ago, when we first made love! You're experiencin' mornin' sickness!"

" 'Tis no' only in the morn," she sighed. "But, aye. When first ye and I joined, we created a life. I dinna know why nature has granted me this, Winston, but I be verra happy abou' it. Are ye?"

Unsteady, he rose to his feet. She, too, stood with Lachlan's help, clutching the blanket about her, her round eyes searching Winston's face for an indication of his acceptance of becoming a father.

"Winston, are ye?" she asked again, a tremor in her tone.

In response, he pulled her into his arms and kissed her. A moment later, gripping her upper arms to steady her, he looked into her eyes like a man unable to express the depths of his own happiness. "Aye," he rasped. He nodded. "Aye! But I thought faeries couldn't have babies. Deliah, can you give birth withou' damagin' yourself?"

"Aye, I can," she said breathlessly, smiling. "The knowin' be strong, I swear. We're goin' to have a son, Winston. A prince born atween our worlds. A link atween the kingdoms of all faeries and all mortals."

Lachlan stood, frowning thoughtfully. "Deliah, wha' do you mean by the *'knowin'*?"

She looked over her shoulder at him. "The *knowin'* o' past, present and future. It be stronger in you than in Winston and me. Twas no' my own *knowin'*wha' discovered my baby. Twas *you* passin' it through to me, Lachlan."

"Damn me," Roan muttered, still befuddled by the news of Deliah's pregnancy.

"No, Roan," she beamed. "We be none damned, but blessed. 'Twas no magic o' mine wha' gave us this child, Winston. It be somethin' I dinna understand, but be so verra grateful to."

"Why couldn't I sense our son?" Winston asked.

"Mayhaps because I told you I couldna bear children," she replied, and kissed him lightly on the mouth.

He shrugged. "Could be." He released a breath. "A son." Sitting on the sofa, he coaxed her to sit next to him. His left arm went about her shoulders and he pulled her close. He grinned up at Roan and Lachlan, a grin that held an element of uncertainty. Although he was excited at the prospect of becoming a parent, he couldn't help but wonder what the future had in store for Deliah and him. "Weel, laddies," he said, perfectly imitating Lachlan's voice, " 'twould be fittin' to celebrate, eh?"

"No Scotch," Deliah said in a small voice.

"Food," Winston quipped.

Deliah grimaced. "I canna stand the word, let alone be thinkin' o' puttin' a morsel in my mouth."

"Lannie and I will scrounge up somethin'," Roan said. "Anythin' in particular you fancyin', Winston?"

"Surprise me."

Roan led a reticent Lachlan into the kitchen, where he lit a lantern positioned on the island counter. Whistling merrily, he went to the ice box, standing off to one side once the door was opened, to permit the light to illuminate the antique appliance's interior. "Ah, we have eggs, part o' the roast we had the ither night. Cheese—*ach!*" He removed a bowl and closed the door. "Be still my heart," he chortled, placing the bowl on the table, leaning over and inhaling its contents. "Mealie puddin'. Thought it was all gone."

He lifted one of the thick sausages, made of oatmeal, suet, onions and seasoning. "Fried, these will banish the empty bellyaches."

Lachlan's silence caught his notice. He looked up to see him standing at the far end of the island counter, staring off into space.

"Lannie, what's wrong?"

A moment later, Lachlan's dark eyes swerved to regard Roan forlornly. "This *knowin'*."

"I dinna know wha' shook me up more," Roan said, chuckling. "Deliah's pregnancy, or her sayin' you're psychic. O' course, I canna imagine a mon returnin' from the dead withou' havin' a few perks." He sobered when Lachlan remained as still as a statue. "Lannie? Is there somethin' you kept from Deliah? The pregnancy canna harm her, can it?"

"No. She, Winston and the bairn will live a long life here."

Lachlan's monotone caused gooseflesh to spread across Roan's arms. He approached him, almost warily, a sinking feeling of dread in his stomach. "Then what's wrong?"

Sighing, Lachlan hooked one hand on his nape. "I can see you, Laura, the lads, and Winston's family here, but no' me and mine."

"Wha' do you mean?" Roan released a sound caught between a choke and a laugh. "This will always be your home. Damn me, but you're no' still thinkin' I want you away from here, are you?"

" 'Tis no' abou' us, Roan. I just canna see Beth, the twins and I here much longer."

"I dinna understand."

"We don't belong here anymore."

"Lannie, this is *your* home! I'll no' let you leave it."

"There's changes comin'. I dinna know exactly wha',

but they are in the makin', and there's nocht we can do to avoid them."

"Go where?" Roan asked angrily, although he was more stricken than angry at the idea of them leaving the estate. "Let me tell you somethin', and I want you to listen verra carefully. Lannie, I dinna fully understand this bond you and I share, but it damn near killed me when you passed over. I thought the emptiness I carry for my son was painful, but it didna compare to the ache your absence brought me. I know it sounds daft, but I'm tellin' you the truth.

"Winston told me you and I are still linked, but he didna know why," Roan went on. "Unfinished business, I guess, although for the life o' me, I canna imagine wha' more could be atween us."

Roan's throat tightened. "I panic when I think o' you no' bein' here. It's like a part o' me goes wi' you."

Distressed by Roan's declaration, Lachlan sighed wearily. " 'Tis guilt. Let it go."

"Guilt abou' wha'? Aye, there are times I feel there's somethin' I need to tell you, but I dinna know wha' it is. But 'tis no' guilt. We've reckoned our past."

Lachlan shrugged. "I believe we have, too, but I've sensed guilt in you since tha' first morn you came to this house." He smiled a little at the memory. "You were a brazen mon, if ever I saw one. Demandin' no' only employment from me, but a fair wage."

Roan's tension waned and a tenuous grin appeared on his mouth. "You scared the bejesus ou' o' me when you appeared. Tha' seems like eons ago."

"Aye. Look, 'tis best we say no more abou' this, especially in front o' the ithers. When I know what's to come, I promise to tell you. Till then, dinna dwell on what's to be. We all have our paths to travel, and travel them we must."

"Maybe this feelin' you have is a result of the media gettin' wind o' your return."

"Could be."

"But Winston—"

"Aye," Lachlan said softly, and placed a hand on Roan's

shoulder. "Aye, he came up wi' a good cover. For *me.* Mayhaps 'tis knowin' Beth canna be so easily explained away tha' has had me thinkin' o' leavin'. No mayhaps abou' it. 'Tis tha', true enough."

"We'll find a way—"

"Roan." Lachlan scowled into the man's face. "I'm sorry I burdened you wi' this."

"We're friends. It would be a harsher burden if I thought you couldna confide in me."

"Spoken like the laird o' Baird House," Lachlan said proudly. "So," he added, stepping back and casting the bowl a look of longing. "Fry them, are you?"

Roan eyed the sausages and nodded. "Aye, but . . ." He looked at Lachlan, his head tilted in a thoughtful manner. "Some fried potatoes and chunks o' cheese."

"Coffee."

A genuine grin spread across Roan's rugged face. "Aren't we a sorry lot, eatin' in the middle o' the night."

"A hungry lot," said Lachlan.

Lachlan moved around the counter and took down one of the cast iron skillets dangling from a ceiling rack. "I'll dice, you cook. Agreed?"

"You're on. But you mak the coffee. Mine tastes like mud."

"Now tha' you mention it . . ."

Roan struck an indignant pose. "Are you mockin' my cookin' again, mon?"

"Me?" Lachlan waved a hand theatrically. "My brain and my heart appreciates your kitchen talents, but your coffee hits my stomach like a deil in a fit o' temper."

Roan shrugged off the insult.

CHAPTER FIVE

Three hours sleep was all Lachlan could manage. He'd been tired enough after the last feeding and changing of the twins, but an inexplicable restlessness had prevented him from falling into a deep sleep. At the crack of dawn, he was wide awake and went down to the first floor, where he ambled through the rooms, imbibing the quiet and stillness of the house. He found himself comparing the ambiance of the place as it was now to how he'd perceived it during the long decades of his other life. Back then, he'd taken it all for granted. Dawns and dusks were merely the passing of days. Now, each signaled a new chapter in what he hoped would be a long life. The house seemed larger in his corporeal existence. Larger and quieter and a great deal more solid. He knew the latter didn't make any sense, but he nonetheless was more aware of the walls, floors, and ceilings, of their colors and smells and the occasional sounds. He loved every square inch of the place. It was a part of him—or, him of it. The idea of leaving his home unnerved him, but only a little. For a reason he couldn't bring to full understanding, he was more afraid of remaining. He belonged within these walls, and yet he didn't. The estate was his past and present, but instinctively he knew it would not be his future.

The *knowing*. If only he understood the concept or could figure out what he was supposed to do with it. Knowing what? He'd determined Deliah's pregnancy. How, he didn't know. Enlightenment had simply come to him.

Grandfather Rory had told him as a lad he had the gift. Did that mean the old man had the *knowing*, too? Wouldn't it take his grandfather having the *knowing* to know Lachlan possessed it?

Lachlan went into the kitchen and browsed through the icebox. He wasn't really hungry, not after the meal Roan had put together a few hours earlier, but he decided to fix Reith something. Although it was early, he figured the young man would wake up ravenous. Besides, Lachlan wanted some company, and he was relatively sure Reith wouldn't mind being hauled out of bed.

He cooked eggs and what remained of the mealie pudding, reheated the leftover fried potatoes, made a pot of coffee, and lastly cut a thick slab of bread and slathered it with jam. It all went on a platter, which he topped with a silver cover. Platter, two cups, coffeepot, a fork and knife, and a linen napkin were all placed on a silver serving tray. He was about to lift the tray when he glanced at the pepper grinder on the island counter. Without asking himself why he felt compelled to take it along, he entered the secondary hall with Reith's breakfast.

Drizzle met him when he exited the last set of doors. The air was cool, but by no means as chilly as it had been since his return. Only patches of snow remained. Despite the dampness, he could smell the freshness of spring.

He wore his favorite black boots, a clean pair of black breeks, and a wool, full-sleeved shirt of forest green. His hair was queued at the nape with a thin, black leather cord, and he was cleanly shaven. The sky was pale gray. To some it would be a dreary morning, but he paid it no mind. A few of the peafowl strutted around the yard, glancing his way as he advanced toward the carriage house.

He greeted the birds with a grin and a "Good morn," but wondered if they knew him in his physical state. They, of course, were familiar with the ghost Lachlan. The feathered creatures must wonder at his change—if they could reason, that was. They were certainly curious about his presence, although they didn't seem uneasy or perturbed in the least. But then, the peafowl of Baird House were famous for being brazen and protective of their sanctuary. Several had cried out the advent of dawn even before he'd noticed the sky lightening.

The front door to the carriage house was open. Entering the building, Lachlan squinted in the semidarkness to where the cot was situated. He could see no sign of Reith, but he did hear him. Placing the tray on the cot, he went to the open rear door, where he found the young man crouched a few feet away, amid seven peafowl. He was stroking the head of one brown peahen and talking softly to her. It was unusual for the birds to trust strangers, but it was obvious Reith had a winning manner with more than people. Lachlan observed him for a short time, then cleared his throat to get Reith's attention. Bright turquoise blue eyes swung around to him, and a smile appeared in greeting.

"Good morn, Mr. Baird. Up a wee early, are ye no'?"

"I could say the same for you." Lachlan nodded toward the birds. "I see you've won their admiration."

The young man laughed as he stood. "Some o' them kept me company durin' most o' the night. They be a curious lot."

"Tha' they are. I brought you breakfast. 'Tis inside. You should eat afore it gets cold."

Reith's eyes lit up hungrily and he followed Lachlan to the cot, where he sat on one end, watching as Lachlan removed the plate cover and laid it aside.

"I couldna remember if you wanted coffee or tea," said Lachlan apologetically.

Inhaling through his nostrils, Reith grinned appreciatively. "Coffee, sir. I thank ye for this grand breakfast."

"Everyone in the house is still asleep. I brought ou' an extra cup. Mind if I stay and have coffee wi' you?"

Reith's eyes widened in surprise. "Sir, 'twould be a pleasure to have your company. Have ye eaten?"

With a crooked grin, Lachlan eased the tray closer to Reith, then sat, placing the food between them. "A few hours ago. Roan made the mealie puddin'. The mon can cook, I'll certainly give him his due."

"Have some, sir. I dinna feel right abou'—"

"Dig in," Lachlan chided, and filled the cups with steaming coffee.

Reith stared down at the platter a moment longer, his nostrils twitching, then he took the pepper grinder and zealously coated all the food with the seasoning. Lachlan had never seen anyone use so much pepper. Sipping his coffee, he watched with amusement as Reith set the platter on his lap and eagerly forked some of the fried potatoes into his mouth.

"Did you sleep weel?"

Reith nodded and swallowed. "The mattress be verra soft." He lifted a portion of fried egg, but paused to pass Lachlan a mischievous glance. "I tak it ye and your lady have worked ou' your problems."

"Aye. She's a forgivin' lass."

Reith chewed the egg morsel, nodding. After swallowing, he rolled his eyes and smiled at Lachlan. "This be verra good."

Lachlan continued to sip his coffee. It struck him that the young man's speech was very similar to Deliah's, but he didn't comment on it. Instead, he watched Reith make short work of the meal. When the runny egg yolks had been sopped up with chunks of bread and the plate was left without a speck of food, Reith released a sigh of contentment, then lifted his own cup to his lips .

"You've a good appetite," said Lachlan. "I can fix you more."

" 'Tis kind o' ye, sir, but I've had my fill. Thank ye."

With a grin, Lachlan nodded. "You're welcome." He

dug into a small watch pocket in the front of his breeks and removed a wad of Scottish bills. "Here, from Roan and me. 'Tis a hundred pounds to buy you some decent clothes."

Reith looked both startled and chagrined. "I prefer to first earn my wage."

"Dinna be thickheaded abou' this, laddie. 'Tis no' much, but 'twill get you started. From wha' Roan tells me, this money willna go far in these times, but I refuse to see you work withou' warm clothes on your back, and proper footwear."

Reith hesitated before reluctantly taking the money. He stared down at it, frowning, looking almost as if he would burst into tears at any moment.

"Laddie," Lachlan said softly, " 'tis no' charity. Swallow your pride."

"Sir, I told ye I have no pride left."

The raspy, despondent tone jerked on Lachlan's heart-strings. He liked this young man, and sensed a deep-rooted sorrow in him. Reith lifted his cup to his mouth, the hand trembling slightly, certainly enough for Lachlan to notice. His other hand was fisted around the money, too tightly, in the laird's opinion.

"Are you thinkin' o' your wife?" asked Lachlan. "Is she in need o' money?"

He looked at Lachlan through an expression of wonder. "Ye are a generous mon, sir. No, I wasna thinkin' o' my wife, nor does she need money. In her own right, she be verra wealthy."

The information surprised Lachlan. "Then why are you roamin' the countryside like a mon destitute?"

A small smile appeared on the man's handsome face. "O' my own makin', I can assure ye. Ye see, sir, no' too long ago I was o' the opinion the world owed me a mighty big favor. I had it all, but I was so self-centered, I couldna see my way clear o' wantin' and demandin'."

"Wha' changed?"

Reith's shoulders moved in a semblance of a shrug. "I discovered I love my wife."

A laugh escaped Lachlan before he could stop it. Then he sobered and frowned at Reith. "You didna love her afore?"

"No. Twas an arranged mairrage, and I resented her. To say I was cruel to her would be softenin' the truth o' it."

"So . . . now you love her, but she doesna love you?"

Reith smiled sadly. "She loves me. More 'n she should."

"I'm confused."

"Aye, sir, I'm sure ye are. 'Tis a tangled mess, for sure, but I know in my heart she'll come around."

"And if she doesna?"

The blue eyes earnestly searched Lachlan's face. "I willna accept a future withou' her. If need be, I'll storm our home and mak her see reason, but only efter she's had time to miss me."

Lachlan's eyebrows arched dubiously. "Weel, if she has *half* the temper o' my Beth, laddie, I suggest you don armor."

Reith laughed softly. "I dinna think armor will spare me much."

"Aye, tis the wounds to the heart tha' hurt the most."

Reith nodded.

"Weel, tha' aside, tak the money and go into town this morn. If this weather is the same around ten, I'll ask Roan or Winston to drive you."

"I dinna mind walkin'. Have ye thought where I'm to start on the grounds?"

"Settle in for a few days," said Lachlan. "No' much you can do wi' the rain."

"It doesna bother me. The rhododendron hedge had quite a few broked branches. Should I start prunin' them?"

Lachlan chuckled. The young man even said the single syllable word "broked" as did Deliah: Bro-ked "As you will. We're no' slave drivers. I know you'll do your work.

You dinna have to prove yourself to me or Roan. We want you to be comfortable."

"I am, but I need to work, sir. There's also a section o' the northeast field tha' needs a bit o' trenchin' to keep the rains from poolin'. It wouldna tak much to route the water to the hedges. They tak a good measure o' waterin', and trenchwork would be useful in the summer, especially if I can rig a pump to the old weel ou' there."

"There's a pump in the loft," said Lachlan, glancing upward. "I dinna know how weel it works."

"I'll mak do." A frown marred Reith's brow. "Sir, did ye say no one else was up in the house?"

"Aye, why?"

"There was a womon at the back o' the house, earlier. I didna approach her. Didna think it was my place."

"Wha' did she look like?"

Reith sighed. "She had an umbrella. I couldna see her face, but she was wearin' a long red coat, and black boots." He paused and arched one eyebrow. "I tak it she isna a member o' the household."

"No. Ou' back, you say?"

"Tha' was awhile ago. She went around the far side o' the house . . . abou' a half hour afore ye came."

Lachlan stood. "I'm goin' to check the grounds. She could be anither reporter. For her sake, I hope no'."

"I'll go wi' ye."

"Stay here and finish your coffee. Your clothes are already damp. I dinna want you catchin' your death."

"Sir—" Reith fell silent when Lachlan placed his cup on the tray, then stormed out the back door.

Lachlan's blood was simmering as he walked through the strip of yard between the back of the house and the woods. At one point he could see the field clearly, but didn't spy anyone traipsing around the area. His narrowed gaze searched the woods. There weren't many trees with wide trunks, especially trees large enough to conceal a long red coat. It irked him that a reporter could be still snooping around. Who else could she be? He wasn't in the mood to deal with any more questions or accusations, but he was less inclined to permit a stranger to trespass on his land.

Coming to the covered stoop, he stopped short and scowled at two large black suitcases. An inward chill passed beneath his skin as he questioned the relevance of someone leaving them behind. Many of the reporters had been from out of the area—from out of the country. Had one of them decided to pry into the lives of the Baird House residents one more time before moving on?

Gritting his teeth so hard a muscle ticked along his jawline, he lit into a run to the far end of the house. Just as he rounded the corner, he glimpsed a flash of bright red material disappear around the next corner. Without thought as to what would happen once he caught up with the woman, he ran after her. He came around to the front of the house and staggered to a stop. She was no more than seven feet away. All he could see of her beneath the rim of the black umbrella was the coat and boots. She didn't appear to be in a rush, but rather was taking her time, as though lost. He knew she wasn't though. She was glancing through the windows to see what she could beyond the panes. She stopped at each of the three dining room windows, peering in, then moving on. Lachlan's nostrils flared, and he breathed heavily to combat the anger knotting inside him. Was she so brazen *because* she was a woman, and didn't fear coming face-to-face with one of the occupants?

Next he knew, Lachlan yanked the umbrella from her grasp and tossed it aside. He ignored her gasp of alarm and pinned her to the bricks between two of the windows, one forearm planted across her covered collarbones to keep her secured.

"Where the bloody hell do you think you're goin'?" he asked harshly, his face inches from her own. All he could see were eyes widened with fear amidst an ashen face.

Her mouth opened, then closed. Lachlan stepped back, dropping his arm as if contact with her sickened him. His gaze raked over her contemptuously. She was tall for a woman, at least five-foot ten. Her hair was hidden beneath the hood of her coat, and she clutched an oversized purse against her chest, as if expecting him to snatch it from her grasp. She was around Beth's age, he guesstimated, her pale skin almost translucent.

Then her eyes registered in his fevered brain. They were overly enhanced with thick black mascara, black liner, and gray and moss-green shadow. He recognized those eyes. Their shrewd, pale amber depths had unabashedly watched him during the media onslaught the previous night. There was an edge of hardness in her features which rankled him. She was a beautiful woman, but he sensed she lacked the emotional attributes he most loved in women. There was nothing kind or patient in her character. The porcelain skin and classical bone structure of her face was but a mask to conceal a devious, cunning mind.

"Who are you?" he bit out.

She swallowed so hard that he could hear it. Lowering the purse until it hung from the thick strap draped on her right shoulder, she unzipped the top compartment and began to anxiously rummage through the contents.

"Dinna bother showin' me a press badge," he clipped, placing his balled hands on his hips. "It doesna give you license to invade our privacy."

She snorted a disgruntled sound, then hastily removed a pack of Marlboro cigarettes and a blue lighter, from her purse. Lachlan scowled as he watched her place a cigarette between her lips, light the end, and inhale deeply before returning the items to the purse and zippering it closed. She took another drag and released it slowly while staring into his eyes. Her fear of him had passed and was replaced with an air of haughty tolerance.

"I'm surprised you recognize me," she said, smiling in a manner that was wholly mocking. "I must say, you were a good deal more passive last night."

"You are a bloody reporter," he accused.

"I wasn't here last night—or now—in that capacity. If

you recall, I didn't ask questions, and I didn't have a mike or a recorder with me. I'm only guilty of bad timing."

Her accent made him grimace. It held a bastardized hint of the Queen's English to it, but he was relatively sure she wasn't British.

He caught a whiff of the smoke her pursed lips emitted, and wrinkled his nose disdainfully as he eyed the cigarette. He had never seen a woman smoke. It certainly contributed to her less feminine mannerisms.

"Sir, is everythin' all right here?"

Lachlan turned his head to see Reith approaching to his right. The young man's gaze was on the woman. It was obvious he was displeased to see her, also not impressed by her somewhat garish appearance. Lachlan glanced at her in time to see her red-colored mouth twist in a parody of a grin.

"Nothing lacking with the males around here," she chuckled unpleasantly. "At least with the packaging." She cocked a penciled eyebrow and looked Lachlan up and down. "You're definitely the brooding type, but real easy on the eyes." Taking another drag of the cigarette, she scandalously perused Reith. "And you, honey, are sweet looking enough to eat."

Reith's face turned beet-red with embarrassment, while Lachlan's reddened with indignation. "Laddie, go on. I'll tak care o' her."

Reith hesitated, then turned and hastened in the direction of the carriage house.

The woman laughed, her singsong tone falling short of sounding sincere. "Even his ass is cute!

"Is tha' your luggage on the back stoop?" Lachlan asked curtly, too repulsed by her to hide the fact.

Her disconcerting eyes regarded him for a time. She took another deep drag, dropped the cigarette and crushed it beneath the toe of a boot, then sighed with regal impatience when she again met his gaze. "If you are planning to co-host the grand opening of this place, I suggest you work on your attitude. Growl at prospective tourists the way you've been growling at me, and you'll have children, women and men alike pissing in their pants as they run for the nearest exit."

Lachlan winced. "I'll escort you to your luggage and *off* the property. I suggest you go on your way and dinna ever return."

She released a nasty little chuckle. "You may look like the former laird, but you don't have any say around here." She reached out and patted his cheek with a cold hand. "You have to be careful you don't take the role-playing too seriously." She stepped closer, planting her mouth mere inches from his, her eyes lit with a challenge for him to abandon his ground. "Besides, from what I know of that bastard, a dirk in the heart was the least he deserved."

Lachlan stiffened. A breath lodged in his throat, and his heart hammered at his chest.

With an isolated index finger, the woman traced his lower lip. He wanted to distance himself from her, but he refused to cow to her seductively intimidating ploy to unnerve him.

"Did you know that your ancestor got off playing to the media?" She chuckled. "Never to me personally, I regret, although I don't think I would have been too impressed by his antics. Men will be boys, even in death, and the late, great Lachlan Baird was a mischievous little devil, wasn't he?"

When Lachlan remained silent, she grinned knowingly and cupped her hands around the curvature of his shoulders. "Cat got your tongue?" Her gaze flitted across the breadth of his chest and shoulders before returning to stare deeply into his eyes. "I wonder if the inglorious ex-laird had your build. I've seen pictures of his portrait, and you do look like him. But was he as tall and as broad-shouldered as you? Is that why poor Viola Cooke had the hots for him, and Miss Stables was willing to come here and die to remain with him?" She seemed to gauge Lachlan's silence for a moment, then asked, "Was he a good lover in death? Are *you* a good lover in the flesh?"

She arched her eyebrows at his continued silence. "I don't know, big guy. I think I would bed you even if you were the worst lover on the continent. Especially if you wore a kilt, without trews, of course." She sighed wistfully. "I'm a pushover when it comes to big shoulders, and yours are . . . *big*, Horatio. Big and solid."

Before Lachlan could react to the repulsion he felt at her words, she clapped her hands to each side of his face and planted a hard kiss on his mouth. He gripped her arms and finally shoved her away, his face dark and stormy, his brain floating in a sea of fire. But before he could give her a piece of his mind, he noticed two small faces pressed in the center window. Alby and Kevin's eyes were wide, and their mouths agape. To his further chagrin, the woman glanced over her shoulder at the boys and clapped her hands in delight.

"Oh, this is too precious!" she laughed. "I certainly hope you're not married, Horatio. I wouldn't want the little woman—"

"To what?" interrupted a husky voice from Lachlan's left. "Pull your hair out by the roots?"

To Lachlan's horror, Beth, clad in a bathrobe and slippers, came to stand next to him, her fiery glare fixed on the stranger. Her hair was in wild disarray, lending her ill mood a more sinister edge.

"Beth," Lachlan said between clenched teeth, "get inside."

The stranger's expression lost its humorous glow, paling and becoming taut with disbelief. She backed into the house, her gaze riveted on Beth, labored breaths channeling through her nostrils.

"Screw it," Beth said heatedly, passing Lachlan a look that could quiet gale-force winds. To the woman, she said, "Would you care to explain why you were lip-locked with him?"

"My, God . . . it's true," the stranger murmured sickly, her gaze pinging between Beth and Lachlan. "I didn't know." Parting her lips, she sucked in a ragged breath.

"You both returned." She blinked as if struck by a thought, then looked horrified at Lachlan and swiped the back of a hand across her mouth. "I *kissed* a *dead* man! I'm gonna puke!" She clamped a hand over her mouth and gagged, but the hand fell away when another voice, deep and cutting, intruded on the scene.

"Still up to your old theatrics."

Lachlan and Beth's heads shot around to see Roan ambling toward them. Barefoot, dressed in jeans and a blue shirt left unbuttoned down the front, he wore an expression of thinly veiled anger. Lachlan gave a start and looked into the woman's eyes. Finally, the reason for their familiarity hit home.

"Roan. Nice to see you," she said flippantly.

"I canna say the same." Roan stopped next to Beth and folded his arms against his chest. "Wha' do you want here, Taryn?"

"You know her?" Beth asked.

Roan nodded grimly. "She's my kid sister. And by the looks o' her, the parents spared her the rod."

"Still as charming as ever," Taryn Ingliss said to her brother. "I didn't expect you to welcome me with open arms, but siccing your resident spooks on me is low, even for you."

Roan exchanged a smug grin with Lachlan and Beth before responding to her comment. "Haven't you heard, little sister, there are no more ghosts at Baird House? Lannie and Beth are as alive as you, only they have hearts, no' the stone you have wedged behind your breast."

"Your sister," Lachlan murmured, grimacing.

"Aye." Roan frowned at her. "I dinna remember okayin' your visit."

"I didn't think I needed your permission," she said airily. "I arrived last night, but ended up in the middle of a media feeding. I stayed at a B&B in town, but I was anxious to see you."

"Why?"

"Why?" A sour laugh ejected from her throat. "You're

my brother, that's why! I haven't seen you for damn near twenty years!"

"It's been twenty-one years, but who's countin'."

Exasperated, she looked at each of the angry faces in front of her. "Fine! I should have waited for a goddamn invite! But I'm here. Are you going to invite me inside, or chuck my ass off the property?"

"Chuck—"

Lachlan cut Roan off. "Fegs, mon, she's your kin."

"Damn me if she is," Roan said with a scowl. "She was born a brat, and has obviously grown into a shrew. Trust me, Lannie, you dinna want her around. She's trouble."

"Thanks," Taryn said dryly, but a slight tremor was in her tone. "I'll just get my bags and get the hell out of here."

"No," said Beth, peeved. She was torn between going for the woman's throat and chalking up the whole incident to bad taste and worse timing. "She's here. I suggest we all calm down and get a grip. The boys don't need to see us acting like a pack of adolescents."

Roan glared at his sister. "I know her. She wants somethin'. She didna come all the way from Rhode Island because she needed a siblin' fix."

Three pair of eyes fixed on Taryn. After a moment of trying to ward off her deepening sense of futility, she sighed and gestured placatingly. "Even before the story of Lachlan's return hit the newswire in the States, I had planned to visit. I uncovered some information, Roan. Information that warranted more than a letter."

"Information abou' wha'?" Roan asked coldly.

Taryn gave an exasperated roll of her eyes. "Family history stuff."

"I know all I need to abou' the family."

A pained expression softened her features. "Do you?" She sighed and gave a shake of her head. "Then tell me, Roan, how do you feel about Robert Baird?"

Roan frowned, while Lachlan asked, "Who is Robert Baird?"

The pale amber eyes searched each of the faces before she replied, "The bastard son of Guin Baird. You're probably more familiar with his legal name." She grinned tauntingly. "Robert Ingliss."

An insidious swell rose up from inside Roan's gut, something not unlike bubbling tar, immersing his vital organs and brain in its searing thick blanket. His vision and hearing clicked off. Images sparked his memories of a time he longed to forget, memories not belonging to the man he was now, but the man he had been in the nineteenth century. He slammed each file shut as it opened and reopened. Denial was all that kept him sane, and he clung to it like a man whose life depended on clinging to a piece of flotsam out in the middle of a turbulent sea. Before Laura and the boys had entered his life, he would have gladly given in to the cold embrace of death. Life could be unbearably painful and unforgiving. The loss of his son had taken away his will to fight for anything. Originally, he'd even come to Baird House to challenge the then Ingliss–hating Lachlan Baird—not in hopes of freeing his Aunt Aggie from the ghost's tyrannical demands, but of provoking the powers of the unknown to end his misery.

Some people believed reincarnation allowed troubled souls to return to atone for the wrongs done in a past existence. How many times would Robert's soul be cast into another body before his crimes were forgiven? A conscience swayed by greed was a conscience damned to unrelenting torment. Whatever the name or physical appearance, the soul shared by Robert and Roan could not escape the avenging sword of its guilt.

Five hours later, Roan remained lost within the thick mire of his shame. Although he had yet to confront the inner demons his sister's revelation had loosed, he was little more than a zombie. He remained blind and deaf to everyone around him. He couldn't remember how he'd gotten back into the house, or what had gone on since. Deep in his subconscious he knew he would have to face the others and listen to what Taryn had to say. But for as long as possible, he needed this nothingness, and would remain lost within its infinite realm until forced to leave.

Now and then, little spurts of awareness intruded. He knew he was in the bar, elbows braced on the counter and staring at a shot glass of Scotch. He knew he was hungry and thirsty. He knew the ache plaguing him was his bladder seeking relief. He also knew there was a fly in the room because it kept buzzing in one ear then the other, and occasionally brushing against his eyelashes, forcing him to blink. To swat the insect would take more energy than he was willing to expend. Besides, movement could wrench him from the realm of the lost, which he wasn't yet ready to leave.

The fly careened off his right eyeball and he jerked upright. Blinking hard, he tried to will himself to ignore the trappings of his sense, but the buzzing, which was now in his left ear and growing louder and more persistent, was more than he could bear. But before he could raise a hand to bat at the nuisance, a voice penetrated the thinning layers of his stupor.

"Don't hurt her!"

He reacted as if someone had doused him with ice water. His head shot around and he stared at Kahl, whose pale, freckled face dominated his vision. Disoriented, he wondered what the boy was doing in the bar. He should have locked the door. Of course he hadn't. That would have been the *responsible* thing to do, and Roan wasn't always a cautious man.

Something whizzed past his line of vision, again startling him. His right hand shot up at the same moment a tiny figure perched on his nose. He froze in shocked realization. The fly was Deliah, no more than three-quarters of an inch tall.

"She's only trying to help," said Kahl . "Don't hurt her."

His eyes crossed in a vain attempt to focus clearly on her, Roan laid his palms on the counter. She cast off his nose, circled three times a short distance away, then suddenly assumed a human size on the opposite side of the counter. Standing five-foot-six inches, her ankle-length hair concealing her nakedness, she scoldingly eyed Roan. She lifted the shot glass and regarded the golden liquid for a moment before it and the glass vanished into thin air. Her magnificent blue and gold wings fluttered at her back, the light in the room enhancing their iridescent webbing. While she and Roan continued their visual show-down, Kahl retrieved her dress from the floor and held it out to her. Reluctantly, she tore her gaze from Roan's and looked down at the boy with a loving smile.

"He be one o' the livin' now," she told Kahl, her tone light and deceptively calm. "Tell the ithers we'll be along in a while."

Roan's gaze crept to Kahl. The resentment in the boy's eyes made him cringe.

"I don't like it when you make Aunt Laura cry," the boy said angrily, his small shoulders trembling.

"Why is she cryin'?" asked Roan, still a bit dazed.

"Cause you wouldn't talk to her! If you hate us so much—"

Roan dashed from behind the counter and swept Kahl up into his arms and hugged him so forcefully, the boy yelped with surprise. He rolled his misted eyes to the heavens, relishing the paternal warmth spreading through him. "How can you think I could ever hate you?" he choked, then lessened his hold and smoothed a hand over the back of Kahl's strawberry-blond head. "God, Kahl, you lads and your aunt are my life."

A sob escaped Kahl. Roan eased him back enough to look into his hazel eyes. "I'm sorry I frightened you. I love you, Kahl. Dinna ever doubt tha'. I dinna care if you unravel every sweater and tear into strips every piece o' clothin' in this house, I'll love you."

Mention of unraveling sweaters brought a hint of a grin to Kahl's mouth. "You mean it?"

"Wi' all my heart."

"About shredding the clothes?" the boy asked impishly.

Roan didn't hesitate. "Aye, lad, although I hope you show us poor adults a wee compassion in tha' respect. But, if demolishin' our clothes puts a smile on your face, then do it."

"Naw. I was just testin' you. It would be too gross if you all walked around naked." Kahl looked at Deliah, who had retracted her wings and had just finished donning the dress, and he blushed. "Except Deliah. I like it when she lets her wings out."

Roan smiled in gratitude at her. "Aye, we're fortunate to have our own faerie princess." He lowered Kahl to the floor, but not before planting a kiss on his cheek. "Tell the ithers we winna be long, okay?"

"Okay." Kahl's eyes searched Roan's a moment, then he wiggled an isolated finger in a gesture for Roan to bend over. When he did, Kahl flung his arms about his neck and gave him a quick hug. Then the boy opened the door and ran from the room.

Roan straightened with a wondrous look on his face.

"Ye be a lucky mon to have the love o' those children," Deliah said softly.

Roan nodded, then stepped up to her, his eyes downcast in shame. "I must apologize, Deliah."

"For makin' me act the part o' a pesky fly?"

He grinned. "Tha' and more." He searched her delicate features for a moment. "How are you feelin' this morn?"

"Verra good. Winston said the *knowin'* o' my condition might ease the symptoms and my fears, and tha' it has."

Gently, Roan drew her into his arms. "Ah, lass, I am happy for you. Have you any idea how precious you are to us all?"

"Ye be my family," she said contentedly, then tilted back her head and peered into his eyes. "Tis why I worry so when I know ye be hurtin' in the heart. Roan, ye must trust the mon ye are. And ye must trust those who love ye to stand by ye, no matter wha'."

Stepping away, Roan raked the fingers of one hand through his hair. He couldn't bring himself to look at her.

His eyes ached to tear, but he held back the need with all his willpower. To tell her that he feared what Taryn knew was to admit there was more to Robert than he wanted to remember. But her next words told him she was already aware of what was tormenting him from the darkest recesses of his subconscious.

"I dinna trust your sister. She doesna have your heart, Roan, and she speaks no' wi' a light o' whole truth in her words."

Roan forced himself to meet her troubled gaze. "You know wha' happened ou' side?"

She nodded. "She hasna said anythin' more regardin' your family history, but she has—and I be verra gracious in my words, Roan—manipulated Lachlan and Beth into tellin' her abou' their return. She doesna know my origins, but she watches me too closely. I think she be aware I am more'n I appear on the surface."

"I dinna trust her, either," Roan said.

"There is somethin' more ye need to know."

Roan frowned as dread formed a knot inside his stomach.

"I glimpsed her thinkin' o' the dirk."

"The MacLachlan dirk?"

"Aye. She wants it."

"Wha' on earth for?"

Deliah shrugged. "Somethin' abou' a project she be researchin'. Wha' concerns me is, I canna locate the dirk. I know it be in the house. I sense its vibrations."

"Vibrations?"

"Aye, Roan. Most times 'tis barely perceivable, but 'tis there, nonetheless."

"Wha' kind o' project could she be workin' on tha' could possibly have anythin' to do wi' tha' damn weapon?"

"Roan, your sister be a reporter."

This shocked him more than hearing of Taryn's interest in the dirk.

"She be hard to probe, but tha' much and this abou' her I be certain: she be here for a story, and I believe she be ruthless enough to go to any lengths to get wha' she wants."

"Verra perceptive o' you," said Roan dryly. "She was always demandin' her own way. She could do no wrong, accordin' to my parents."

"This, too, ye must know," Deliah went on. "She be envious o' ye and this estate, but she does love ye."

"From wha' I've deduced from her meager letters over the years, I dinna think she's capable o' lovin' anyone."

"Aye, her heart be hard, but I sense she be more lost than gone."

"Wha' do you mean by 'more lost than gone'?"

A secretive smile appeared on Deliah's face. "Weel, we shall see. Three paths await her. One will lead her back to her home. Two ithers will tak her into anither realm, where she will find love, or she will find death."

Roan paled and gave in to a shudder. "Anither realm? The grayness?"

She shook her head. "I can say no more. She must choose her path. Ye canna help her."

"She may be a royal pain in the ass, Deliah, but she is my sister!"

"Ah," she said wistfully, her bright eyes sparkling. "Here now stands the brither I knew ye to be."

"Humans are verra capable o' lovin' and hatin' the same person," he grumbled.

"Do ye truly hate her?"

With a hangdog expression, he muttered, "I guess no'."

"I will tak the lads to the nursery and watch them and the babies. Keep Winston wi' ye, Roan. He knows wha' I have told ye. If she be hidin' more, he will know."

Roan heaved a ragged breath. "I dinna know if I can hold up to wha' Taryn has to say."

"Aye, ye can, because ye be a strong mon, Roan. But if ye feel your knees gettin' weak, think o' me sittin' on your nose."

He laughed at this. "I'll keep tha' in mind."

CHAPTER SIX

Taryn Eilionoir Ingliss wasn't happy about being the center of attention in the library at Baird House, although she was confident enough about her acting abilities to know the others viewed her as being cool, calm, and unperturbedly collected. Sitting on one corner of the sofa, an arm across its back and one leg crossed over the other, she represented the "Queen of the Paparazzis," a title her editor at *The Investigator* magazine had given her three years prior. She had been dubbed that because of her ruthlessness in obtaining photographs of reluctant celebrities, and later had added journalism to her accomplishments, using her fertile imagination to embellish the story behind the photographs. She'd been approached by competitive rag magazines, but no one would give her the creative freedom Dan Whitecomb did. Now and then she freelanced, especially with her writing, often taking one of their older space alien or hairy-creatures-in-the-woods stories and rewriting them with a new slant on the supposed sightings. The Loch Ness monster was always a favorite.

Ironically, it'd been a light conversation at a Christmas Eve party two years ago that had brought about her latest obsession. Dan's wife, Julia, had commented on the current fad of Scottish movies and books, and had asked Taryn about her background. It was the first time Taryn realized she didn't know that much about her heritage. She was six when her parents had moved to Providence, Rhode Island, and she considered herself an American. She'd never had any interest in anything Scottish, until she remembered her parents had a set of journals hidden away in a locked cedar chest in their bedroom. She remembered finding the journals in a box shortly after their move to the States and asking her mother if she could color in them. Brusquely, her mother had said they were very old, and Taryn watched her lock them in the chest. Until the party, she hadn't given them another thought. And until she'd read them she'd had no idea of the incredible story of her own ancestry. She wasn't through investigating the past. The dirk was the key to unlocking all the secrets.

The others in the room grew more restless by the minute. She inwardly gloated at her ability to camouflage this meaner streak in her personality. An unsettled audience was one easily swayed to playing the game according to her rules. She was here on a give-and-take mission. Her brother's less than cordial welcoming had smarted a little, but when he found out she'd left with the dirk, he would probably disown her, anyway. Such was the price of obsessions. They didn't keep her warm on winter nights or ease the occasional itch of sexual need, but they kept her mind as sharp as a honed knife, and she wouldn't trade any of it for a man. Well . . . maybe she would detour for a bit of time with a man like Lachlan. During the past five hours, she'd barely been able to keep her eyes off him. He made her tingle in places that hadn't shown life for some time. Fours years, to be exact. Maybe she was due for another fling. The possibility of it happening with *him* made her mouth water. Now that she knew he was alive again, she regretted wiping off the taste of him from her lips.

Beth Stables was a problem, though. She hadn't left the laird's side except to feed the twins. Imagine that. Twins from the womb of the departed-returned. Dan's ulcer would petrify if she wrote this up. Somehow, she figured telling him she'd had an affair with Nessie would ring truer to him. Whatever. She didn't plan to expose the duo's secret. Robert Baird and Broc MacLachlan were her targets. She would resurrect their long-dead carcasses through her reports. Fame awaited them in the annals of the bizarre and the unknown. The world, especially the female populace, would have a fantasy love-affair with them through her planned series. More so, Broc. Thus far, he was the hero of the two, but she still had a great deal to investigate on his background. For all she knew, he probably had more skeletons in the closet than not.

She would have to be careful about how she wrote up Robert. After all, he was her direct ancestor, and her parents were going to pitch a fit when she deliberately exposed the Baird/Ingliss entanglement. But a good writer could make a reader weep for a villain, even one embroiled in betrayal and murder. By the time she finished writing Robert's history, he would stir passion in women's hearts and understanding for what he'd done.

She withdrew from her reverie and locked eyes with Winston. Realizing his intense stare meant he was delving into her thoughts, she paled and stiffened her spine. Roan, Laura, Beth, and Lachlan didn't pose a threat. Not even the sickeningly sweet Deliah, although something about that woman made Taryn damn uneasy. But ol' Winston was another matter. A psychic in the group made it more difficult for her to hide information.

"Taryn," Roan clipped, scowling at her.

He stood with an arm braced on one end of the fireplace mantel, Laura next to him. Beth and Lachlan sat on the window seat. Winston was seated on the opposite end of the sofa, right ankle resting atop the left knee, his gaze unwavering and his expression guarded.

"Yes, my room is very comfortable," she said sarcastically to her brother. "Thank you for asking."

Roan rolled his eyes in exasperation. "Spare me the theatrics."

She grinned, but there was nothing pleasant about it. "By the way, Mom and Dad send their love."

Roan's jawline clenched.

"Okay," she sighed, casting each of the others a weary glance. "Pardon my bitchiness, but I wasn't expecting to have to spill my guts in front of an audience."

"Think o' them as *my* family," Roan said.

"I'm your family."

He crossed to the coffee table and sat on it facing her. "No, you're a dim memory," he countered, his tone holding more sadness than bitterness. "I know that's no' your fault, Taryn, but you canna show up efter all these years and expect me to welcome you wi' open arms."

"I never expect anything from anyone," she said airily.

"You're a reporter."

His blunt statement took her aback. She glanced accusingly at Winston, who arched his eyebrows and offered a hint of a smile.

"Paparazzi slash reporter. So what?" she challenged, peevishly meeting Roan's gaze. "A girl has to make a living, doesn't she?"

"Among a pool of sharks?"

She chuffed a laugh. "We're not all sharks."

"No? Havena met a reporter yet I would trust wi' my garbage."

She winced. "Ouch. Well, big brother, I'm not into garbage. And before you start flinging accusations, I have *no* intention of reporting a word about the Baird/Stables miracle."

"Did you say Sta*bles?*" asked Beth.

"That is your name, isn't it?"

Beth drew in a deep breath through her nostrils. "Actually, it's Staples."

After a moment, Taryn released a burst of laughter. "That explains it."

"Explains what?" Beth asked.

"Why I couldn't get information on your background. It came across the newswire that Beth *Stables* of Kennewick, Washington, had died at the Baird Estate and then returned to haunt the walls alongside her lover, the nefarious laird himself."

Lachlan grunted at this.

"Why were you checking into my background?" Beth asked.

"You were a hot story for a while." Taryn was pensively quiet for a few moments. "Do you have any relatives who know of your death?"

Beth shook her head.

"Hmm. Then it's possible no one in the States really knows it's you who died."

The thought brightened Beth's features. "Wouldn't a death certificate have been filed here and the American Embassy notified?"

Lachlan's expressive eyebrows drew down in a frown. "Viola Cooke took care o' the details. I know Beth's passport and paperwork are still in the armoire. There was an autopsy, but Miss Cooke brought Beth's body back here in a casket. I dinna know wha' ither information she gave to the police."

"Which means there's a possibility my bank was never contacted about my death," Beth murmured.

"Why is tha' important?" asked Roan.

"My mother's will had everything put in a trust for me. The taxes on the house and the monthly bills are all paid through a lawyer. So this could mean my house and trust are still intact. I just hope the neighbors are still feeding my cat."

"I can look into it," said Winston. "Use my association with the agency to screen whatever information the police have on their files."

"Watchit," Taryn grinned wryly at Winston. "You're divulging plans in front of the enemy."

"Are you?"

Roan's soft tone put a chink in her sarcasm. "No. I told

you, I won't reveal anything about their return or the twins."

"So wha' is your interest—and dinna tell me it's me."

"Oh, Roan," she sighed, "you never change, do you? You were a self-righteous prig when we were kids, and you're a bigger one now. For your information, I *do* think of you, and often." She briefly lowered her gaze. "Mom and Dad are getting on in years, and you and I only have two cousins and one aunt left. Then it's the end of the Ingliss line—unless you and Laura decide to have children."

"I'll bet my last Scotch you dinna give a damn how much o' the family remains," Roan said, again no bitterness in his tone. "You see, Taryn, these folks here, they dinna judge me, and they're here for me no matter wha' happens."

"Your family, I know," she said coolly.

"Right. They could tell me the sky was pink, and I would believe them. But you, lass . . . we're more strangers than anythin' else."

"As you said, that's not my fault."

"Aye. Is there no Scottish left in you, Taryn?"

"I've spent the past twenty-one years in the States. Dammit, what do you expect, Roan? No, I don't have your accent, and I tend to be American blunt and American crude when cornered. That doesn't make me any less your sister!"

"I wasna talkin' abou' *your* accent or your crude behavior ou' side the house. Wha' I'm referrin' to is the coldness I see in your eyes. You were a bonny brat as a girl, wi' eyes tha' sparked life when you were up to no good. Wha' I see now is a stranger who looks at me as if measurin' me for a kist."

"A what?"

"Coffin," he replied impatiently, disappointed that she had lost her knowledge of the lowland Scottish language.

"Thanks."

Taryn considered telling them all to go to hell in a

handbasket, but decided it would only make her "mission" more difficult. Her original plan had been to cozy up to Roan, play the kid sister to the hilt, then disclose what she'd uncovered with all the emotional fanfare she could muster. But alas, she was left no choice but to expose the family skeletons with the bluntness of an anvil.

"Perhaps I take after Robert Baird," she said, glancing down at her manicured fingernails with their dark red polish.

She looked up in time to see her brother wince as if in pain. It occurred to her she should feel something for him, something kinful, but he was only a larger version of the jerk she remembered.

"You keep referrin' to this Robert Baird," Lachlan said with an air of boredom. "Wha' I find most intriguin' was your comment abou' this man's legal name bein' Ingliss."

Taryn eyed him through an unreadable expression. God, he was a lot of man. She'd bet a month's wages he was hung like a horse. He was too damn masculine for his own good. So . . . virile. So . . . nineteenth century. So . . .

Forcing herself to withdraw from that runaway train of thought, she focused her attention on her brother. She was a bit surprised to see how gaunt his features had become. He looked older, somehow. For the first time, she realized how tense he was. Did he already know?

"Do you remember Papa Ailbert?"

"Vaguely remember hearin' abou' him," said Roan wearily. "Faither's great grandfaither, wasna he?"

She nodded. "He published six short stories in his heyday. Guess I inherited the writing bug from him. Anyway, he was also a ritualistic journal keeper. Ever read any of them?"

The question was delivered with an air of lightness, but Roan's eyes narrowed on her.

"No. Why?"

"Papa Ailbert was also a historian of sorts, especially when it came to the family." She sighed and flicked a glance at her fingernails again. "After reading his journals,

I couldn't help but wonder if he wasn't actually trying to unburden his soul, poor man."

"Get on wi' it, Taryn."

The way Roan rolled the R in her name caused a delightful thrill to pass through her, and she realized just how hard her parents had worked to get rid of their accents.

Collecting her thoughts, she said, "Anyway, he came to this house at the turn of the century."

"Baird House? Why?"

Roan's clipped tone gave her pause. "To interview Tessa Ingliss. It didn't go too well. She ended up demanding he leave and never return."

Laura jerked as if she'd been pinched. Staring off into space, she stated in a monotone, "He came to the house with accusations that Robert's father had masterminded the Baird-Aiken marriage."

"How could you possibly know about that?" Taryn rasped, her eyes wide. She looked at Roan and accused, "So you *do* know about Guin Baird!"

Lachlan shot to his feet, his face darkened with hostility. "Wha' has *my* faither to do wi' Robert Ingliss?"

Taryn felt as if she'd been thrust into the heart of a tornado. The room was so thick with tension it clung to her skin. Her gazed volleyed between Lachlan and her brother, who rose to his feet like a man afflicted with arthritis. His face was shockingly pale and taut. It alarmed her to see him like this, but she couldn't bring herself to offer him a kind word, let alone reach out to him.

Although her throat had partially closed off, she managed to go on. "Papa Ailbert was summoned to the deathbed of a distant uncle, who told him he had to pass on a secret before he died. It was—"

Roan/Robert cut her off, his voice strained and hardly sounding like his own. "I couldna stand the guilt. A few months efter Tessa and I mairrit, I couldna look at her no more withou' thinkin' o' wha' I'd done."

"What are you talking about?" Taryn asked, believing her brother had lost his mind.

"Be quiet, lass," Lachlan warned her. "Leave him be till he's finished."

As if in a daze, Roan/Robert went on, "I went to see Uncle George, my mither's brither. He'd never approved o' me, but he was always there when I needed him." A sour laugh rattled in his throat. "And I *really* needed his advice at tha' time."

Roan/Robert looked across the room and stared bleakly into Lachlan's dark eyes. He knew from the laird's rigid bearing that the man was in pain, the anticipation of what was to come evident in the gaunt lines of his face. The memories were freed from Roan's subconscious. Now he understood the bond that had kept his soul tied to Lachlan.

"My mither was a wild girl," said Roan/Robert.

"Roan!" Taryn cried, outraged that he could say such a thing about their mother. She didn't realize Robert was talking through her brother.

"Haud yer wheesht!" Lachlan barked at Taryn.

As if unaware of the interruption, Roan/Robert continued, "Her parents couldna control her. She had an affair wi' a mairrit mon, and eventually gave birth to his son. Her faither refused to have anymore to do wi' her. He demanded she no' use the family's name on her bastard, but she defied him still, instead, adding anither S to the end o' it.

"My faither visited now and then. He was a cruel mon, but my mither loved him. I heard wit my own ears his promise to wed her. Said he despised his wife and couldna go on pretendin' he had any feelings left for her."

Taryn wanted to shout at him, to tell him to stop ranting and acting so insane, but her insides were cold and she couldn't stop shaking. Something was happening that she didn't understand. Intermittently, she could almost swear she could see a translucent face appearing in front of her brother's when he spoke, flicking on and off like a spectral mask.

"But he didna marry her. When I was thirteen, he came to the house. My mither was cryin' she was so angry wi' him. It was the first time I heard her raise her voice to him, or defy his wishes. She demanded he leave his wife. My mither told him she had given up her family for him, and *her* son deserved to know his half-brithers." He sneered the next words. "She told him she would tell Missy Ciarda the truth."

Lachlan murmured a prayer in Gaelic, and Roan's features became lax as the spectral mask became more defined.

Only the spectral mouth moved as Robert said, "She never did. Passed away two years later o' a stomach ailment.

"I went to live wi' Uncle George. He wasna happy abou' it. He had his own family, and money was scarce. One time, no' long efter I moved in, he told me I had four half-brithers who were livin' like royalty. He resented them all, and said he was o' a mind to expose the Bairds' secrets and let the mighty Guin get a taste o' his own medicine.

"When next I saw my faither, I was twenty-four. He came to the textile mill where I worked wi' my love, Tessa Aiken. He took me to an isolated park, where we sat on the grass and he told me he needed my help. Said he was desperate for my help. His youngest son wi' his wife had returned to Aberdeen to choose a bride. He said this son, Lachlan, had tried to ruin the family business. Had taken most o' their fortune, includin' wha' he had put aside for me.

"I was enraged by all I heard. Enraged enough to mak this so-called brither pay for denyin' me wha' was rightfully mine. My faither told me o' a plan and, although I didna believe Tessa and I could carry it through, I *needed* to try."

Roan/Robert's bleak expression became enhanced with torment. He stared at Lachlan, his shoulders slumped. "Years afore, I'd told Tessa my faither had died when I was verra young. All she knew abou' the plan was tha' this mon, Lachlan, had wronged my family. Twas why she went along wi' it. She never knew my faither had asked me to . . . murder my brither."

"She drove the dirk into my heart," Lachlan accused.

"We were in love," Laura murmured, although it was Tessa speaking through her. "So poor, love wasna enough. I knew Robbie couldna pull off killin' Lachlan. Despite everythin', he liked him. I think he . . . respected him. But it wasna Robbie tha' Lachlan wanted to bed. I couldna stand the thought o' any man touchin' me but Robbie, so I . . . I took the initiative to spare him." Her hardened gaze cut to Lachlan. "But you couldna just *die,* could you? I drove tha' blade straight into your heart, but you held on, tormentin' Robbie even efter your death!"

"Tessa!" Roan/Robert growled.

Taryn wanted to run from the room, but she knew her legs wouldn't support her. They were all insane! Worse yet, it was contagious! Now she was seeing a superimposed image on Laura's face. It was translucent, yet blond ringlets at the sides of the face and icy blue eyes were clearly visible.

"You had everythin' handed to you your entire life," Laura/Tessa said scathingly to Lachlan. "You betrayed your faither and brithers, and nearly destroyed everythin' your faither built. Why should I feel sorry for the likes o' you? You thought you could *buy* a wife!

"Aye . . . I hated you. *Aye* . . . it felt *bloody* good plungin' tha' dirk into your miserable heart!" Breaths roared in and out of her lungs. "I would do it again for Robbie! For *me!*"

A whimper escaped Laura and she swayed, then gripped the mantel and steadied herself. The ghostly image vanished. Eyes wide with horror, she stared at Lachlan. "That wasn't me!" she cried. "Lachlan, I couldn't stop her!"

" 'Tis no' your fault, Laura," said Lachlan. He glanced down at Beth's stricken face, then sat beside her and draped an arm about her shoulders. "Are you feelin' jaggy, Beth?"

She stiltedly shook her head, her gaze riveted on Roan. "Go on."

Roan/Robert appeared dazed. Lachlan watched him for

a moment, stood, then approached him until they were within arm's reach of each other.

"Robbie—" Lachlan had to clear his throat in order to go on. "Was the money, the life-style, worth killin' me for?"

The light brown eyes of both Roan and Robert stared with stricken solemnity into Lachlan's face. A single tear fell unchecked down the flesh cheek, and Roan swayed.

"For the rest o' my life, I couldna close my eyes withou' seein' your eyes those last seconds as I walled you up in the tower. If only you had been angry at me . . . at the injustice and the betrayal. If I could have just seen anger in your eyes, I could have convinced myself wha' we'd done was for the better.

"I told Uncle George wha, I'd done," Robert went on, "and he kept sayin', 'Your own brither. Your own brither.' Like I didna know wha' a monster I was, already. I made him promise you would be properly buried when Tessa and I were gone . . . dead.

"As you know, I was first to die, but I waited for her spirit to leave her body on her death and then hastened her through to the ither side so you couldna keep her here. I denied you even tha' pleasure. Tha' wasna ou' o' spite, though, Lachlan, but for the sake o' your own soul."

Silence domed the room for excruciating minutes. Taryn's skin crawled as she stared apprehensively at the two men. She could no longer believe this was a cruel joke on her brother's part. The drama was too real, the emotional torment of the men more than a seasoned actor could possibly portray with such realism.

"I wrote a full confession and gave it to my uncle," Roan/Robert said dully. "He passed it on to his son, who passed it on to my son Robert when Tessa died. 'Twas Robert who had you buried in the field. 'Twas Robert who exposed his parents' heinous crime, but kept secret my Baird lineage."

"Say the words," said Lachlan, his voice hardly more than a hoarse whisper. "Roan canna be free o' you till you do. I've no fondness for you, Robbie, brither or no', but Roan means a lot to me, and I willna have him bear your *bloody* guilt anither day."

The superimposed image broke up, then returned, the ghostly visage a mask of sorrow and poignant regret.

"Did you die soon efter the wall was sealed? I have to know."

Lachlan's response was a barely perceivable shake of his head. The translucent eyes shut tightly, then opened to reveal such anguish that even Taryn was choked up with tears.

"The takin' o' any life is grievous," said Robert Ingliss, independent now of Roan, his metallic voice softly echoing in the room. "But the takin' o' a mon's life by his own kin can have no forgiveness. Do I regret havin' money to tak care o' my wife and children, and live in this house? No. Do I regret losin' a brither to obtain it all? Aye, I do.

"I inherited our faither's greed, and his black heart. I couldna have carried through wi' wha' I did if I'd been a mon o' honor."

Lachlan looked down at his shiny boots for a few seconds, then looked into the eyes of his past. "Aye, greed was in part your motivation, Robbie, but I know too weel my—*our*—faither's cunnin'. Twas the honorable part o' you who couldna rest durin' your life efter tha' night, nor rest in death." He glanced at Laura. "Tessa protected her body and her love for you in the only way she felt she could." His gaze swerved to Robbie's image. "No' that' I condone her betrayal, for I did love her, Robbie. At least I thought I did, till my Beth came along. I know now tha' wha' I truly felt for Tessa was only infatuation."

Roan/Robert nodded, and a sigh passed Roan's lips. "For Roan, and for the eternal peace I long for, I say to you now wha' should have been spoken long ago. I regret my weaknesses and my lack o' compassion. I regret turnin' on a mon who opened his home to me, and who trusted me to be the mon I claimed to be.

"Forgive me, Lachlan. I pray you forgive me and mine for all we did to you."

A shudder coursed through Lachlan. Tilting back his head, he closed his eyes and locked his teeth. For one hundred and fifty-three years he had nurtured a sickening hollowness in his gut over the betrayal, and now it was gone. He was at last free of its presence. He couldn't understand why, but hearing of his father's betrayal only hurt a little. He'd never expected much from his father, but he had liked Robbie Ingliss before that tragic night.

When he again looked into the translucent eyes, and beyond into Roan's, he realized that the past was very nearly that—gone and no part of his future. Immensely relieved it was over and the truth was out, he said, "I do forgive you, Robbie Ingliss Baird, and I wish you and Tessa peace and happiness in the ither world. Give my regards to our faither," he added wryly. *"Och,* better yet, tell him for me to tak a dive off a high cloud, but no' one over Baird House."

The ghostly lips mouthed a "Thank you," before the spectral features faded away into nothingness.

Roan swayed. Gripping him by the shoulders, Lachlan said calmly, " 'Tis over, Roan. We're both free." He glanced at Laura and corrected, "We *three* free o' the past."

"My stomach's churnin'," Roan said, a sickly pallor to his skin.

" 'Tis unmonly to purge one's innards in the company o' ladies," Lachlan said merrily. He gave Roan's right shoulder a hearty clap. "Roan, my friend! Are you no' feelin' just a wee different, for the better, I mean? Lighter, perhaps?" He laughed and gave Roan a shake. "No more Robbie swirlin' around in your subconscious!"

Roan blinked in bewilderment. "I do feel different."

"Unburdened. No guilt."

Roan nodded, then frowned. "You and Robbie, brithers. No wonder his soul couldna rest."

"Aye."

The frown smoothed out, but returned with more intensity. "How could you bring yourself to forgive him, Lannie?" He grimaced and placed a hand over his hammering heart. "And your faither—*fegs,* the bastard!"

"Roan, I dinna care abou' any o' it no more. It wasna hard to forgive Robbie or Tessa. 'Twas anither time. My mind and my heart belong to the here and the now, and lettin' go was the easiest thing I've ever done. But how are you farin'? You're still a wee pale."

"I'm fine. So there willna be anymore o' these visitations?"

"You're free, laddie."

Roan gulped and glanced at his sister. She was staring at him as if he were a stranger, and it dawned on him that she had no idea about what had transpired. He offered a smile of heartfelt appreciation to Lachlan, then sat on the coffee table and took Taryn's hands into his own. Her skin was like ice, and he readily noted her unease with his touch, but he didn't care.

"Laura and I are the reincarnations of Tessa and Robert," he said with a goofy grin.

"Right," she smirked.

"I'm serious, Taryn."

She looked up at Lachlan. He nodded.

"You're all nuts." Pulling her hands away, she nervously patted the tight French braid at the back of her head. "Ghosts and reincarnation? Have you any idea how ludicrous this all sounds?"

Roan and Lachlan exchanged a conspiratorial glance.

"It'll seem the norm when you've been around here awhile."

"Any more secrets I should know about?" she asked bitterly.

"No," Roan lied quickly, thinking of Deliah.

"Thank God! And here I thought I'd brought you this shocking revelation." Her sarcasm was so strong, Roan had to laugh.

"It shocked the truth ou'. It was the proddin' I needed."

"Wait a minute," she said, holding up her hands. "Does

this mean you and Laura don't have your own souls? I thought the soul and the spirit were the same."

For the first time, Winston spoke up. "They are, in a sense. A soul can be fractured upon leaving the body."

Taryn cast him a disgruntled look, and interjected, "Fractured. Oh, that explains everything. Thank you."

Winston smiled tolerantly. "Please, permit me to finish. Someone living a long time with emotional or physical pain, or an unexpected death in which the person's subconscious hasn't had time to prepare for the departure, can cause fragmentation. Guilt tormented Robert and Tessa for most o' their lives and, when they died, segments o' their souls carried over to Laura and Roan in search of absolution they couldn't grant themselves. But they're whole now. Your brither and Laura can live ou' their lives in peace."

"I have a headache." Taryn rose to her feet. "A major headache. If you all don't mind, I think I'll go to my room and take a *long* nap."

As soon as she was out of the room, Winston's mouth formed a rueful grin. "I can't believe she's your sister."

Roan nodded. "No' to blow my own horn, but we are verra different."

"Blow to your heart's content," Beth said, her tone sickeningly sweet, the smile accompanying it verifying her dislike of the woman. She stepped to Lachlan's side and placed an arm about his middle. "A few days around her, and I may start fantasizing about plunging the dirk into her heart."

Lachlan chuckled and planted a kiss on her flushed cheek. "Retract your claws, lass."

Beth grunted. "If you give her the opportunity to lip-lock with you again, *darling*, you'll wish you were back in the afterlife."

"There is only one pair o' lips for me," he said. Then his attention was drawn to Roan, who was staring at Laura somberly, his brow furrowed in thought.

"Roan?"

Roan swung his gaze to Lachlan.

" 'Tis over," said Lachlan.

With a sigh of despair, Roan shuffled out of the room.

Beth turned to Laura. She'd been appalled when Tessa had gone into her tirade. It had taken all of her willpower to not jump to Lachlan's defense, not to tell the woman that Beth thought her to be a pathetic excuse for a human being. She was glad now she hadn't. Everything that was said had needed saying, but she knew that an aftermath of shame would shadow Laura and Roan for some time to come.

"You okay, Laura?"

The green eyes were dull and the corners of her mouth drooped. With a single nod, she murmured, "I'll be with the boys." Then Laura left the library, as lethargic as Roan had been moments ago.

Beth linked her arms through one of Lachlan's and leaned her head against him. "This has been one helluva a day, already."

"Aye, it has," Lachlan said softly. He asked Winston, "How soon can you find ou' if Beth's death is on record here?"

"First thing in the mornin, if that's all right. I promised Deliah we'd spend this efternoon together." He looked sheepish, and added, "You know."

Grinning, Lachlan nodded, then smacked a palm to his brow. "Fegs, I nearly forgot! I gave Reith some money for clothes. I was supposed to get him a ride to town this morn."

Standing, Winston said, "I hope you're no' askin' me to let you use my car."

Lachlan's expression went deadpan. "Are you insultin' my drivin' skills?"

"Absolutely."

Beth chuckled and winked at Winston. He returned the gesture, then said goodnaturedly to Lachlan, "I saw him earlier at the carriage house. He told me to tell you he'd already gone to town."

Sighing woefully at his forgetfulness, he asked Winston, "Did you spare the lad a grillin'?"

Winston feigned a lot of affront, a hand resting over his heart. "Me? Perish the thought."

"The birds like him."

Lachlan's statement took Winston aback, prompting the laird to explain, "They dinna easily trust strangers."

"Ah." Winston passed a look of amusement to Beth. "Lachlan, then far be it for me to question the wisdom o' a feathered friend."

"Speaking of clothes," Beth piped up, "Deliah could use a wardrobe of her own."

"I know," said Winston. "She's never been off this land. It's time she learned to—" He grinned impishly. "—spread her wings."

Lachlan groaned and gestured for Winston to leave, then drew Beth into his embrace and kissed her.

By dusk the drizzle had abated, but dampness clung oppressively to the air. Laura was lost in her thoughts as she stood staring at the headstone bearing Lachlan's name. She could not shake from her mind Tessa's vicious words, or the hatred that had burst inside Laura like an atom bomb. What a fool she'd been to think she had come to terms with her past life. She couldn't tell Roan the disgust she felt for herself. Couldn't ask him why he had avoided her since leaving the library, because she knew why. As Robert, he had loved a monster, and she couldn't convince herself that a part of that vile woman didn't still exist in herself. It wasn't over. Not by far. The ache in her heart would stay with her for the rest of her life.

With a cry of anguish, she rammed the bottom of one booted foot into the granite. It toppled on impact, causing muddy water to splash along the curvature at the top. If she thought the action would purge her, she was wrong. Self-loathing clamped onto her mind and squeezed unmercifully. She wept from fear of who and what she really was.

From fear that the person she had always thought herself to be was just another lie.

" 'Tis too chilly to be ou' withou' a coat," said a gentle voice from behind her.

She whirled and stared blearily through tears at a handsome young stranger, who proffered a double-knitted, navy blue sweater. His appearance disoriented her, and she stared at the article of clothing as if afraid it would leap out and devour her. The young man closed the distance. She didn't move, only tried to understand why he stepped around her, then draped the wool over her shoulders. When he again stood in front of her, she found herself looking into the most beautiful turquoise eyes she had ever seen. She read compassion in their depths, and a small measure of curiosity.

"I be Reith, ma'am."

"Lachlan hired you," she stated in a husky tone.

He nodded.

Swallowing past the tightness in her throat, she started to look behind her at the fallen stone, but stopped herself.

"The ground be loose from the rain," he said diplomatically. "I'm sure the marker has toppled afore."

"I kicked it." She didn't know why the words spilled past her lips, but she didn't regret telling the truth.

"Aye, I saw. I canna imagine why a lovely womon would feel the need to come ou' in this chill and vent her pain on a cold slab o' granite, but I suggest, ma'am, ye dinna give it anither thought. I'll right it. No one need know ye were here."

She couldn't stop herself from spilling the story of her former life, neither coloring her part in Lachlan's murder, nor softening the abject bitch she had been. The words poured from her as if siphoned from the well of her soul, her sobs hitching her voice now and then. The young man listened with no apparent shock or revulsion. He stood not in judgment of her, but as someone who somehow understood her torment. When at last she finished, she drew up one of the sweater sleeves and buried her face into the coarse yarn. It was minutes later before she felt spent of tears and self-pity, and timidly looked up to see if he was still there. He was, as calm and serene as a summer's morn, his expression kinder than she believed possible under the circumstances.

Laura turned her back to him, but could not bring herself to look upon the headstones. "You must think me a raving lunatic," she said shakily.

"No, ma'am. I think you're a bonny womon wi' a great deal to work through."

"Thank you," she said tremulously.

"Ye be a Yank," he said with a hint of amusement. Then he sobered. "Tha' term isna disrespectful, is it?"

"No. At least, I think it's cute. Americans are called far worse in other parts of the world."

"Ma'am, may I ask how ye came to be here?"

Sighing deeply, raggedly, she turned and offered him a small smile. "My brother lived in St. Ives, England. He died some years ago, and his second wife—my three nephews' stepmother—couldn't handle them. I came not knowing she planned to abandon them." She gestured disparagingly. "Believe me, leaving them in *my* care was equivalent to abandonment! Anyway, due to other bizarre circumstances, we were on our way to the American Consulate in Edinburgh. I'd never driven in this country, or tackled a stick shift, so driving in winter conditions was an accident waiting to happen. I-ah, somehow came up the driveway here and crashed into the oak at the front of the property.

"Fate at its nastiest best, wouldn't you say?" Her voice trembled. "Every time I try to rationalize the chain of events that led me here, I feel as if a jackhammer is going off in my head."

"Ye be where ye should be."

"Am I?" she whispered achingly."

"We all come home."

"Laura?"

Reith turned and Laura's gaze shifted to Roan, who was coming to a stop alongside the new groundskeeper. The young man passed her a look of understanding, then said to Roan, "Ye be wha' she needs."

Roan said nothing, but nodded. He watched Reith head across the field in the direction of the carriage house. When he was long out of hearing range, he shoved his hands in his pants pockets and met Laura's timid gaze.

"I was gettin' worried abou' you."

She looked off to one side and clutched the sweater about her more tightly. "I wouldn't blame you if you wanted me to leave."

"Why would I?"

Her gaze cut to his. "How could Robbie ever love Tessa? She was—" She choked on emotion and had to draw in a breath before completing, "—so evil."

"No, no' evil, love. She was desperate and afraid to live in poverty."

"I *saw* the look on your face when I—*she*—was saying those awful things to Lachlan!"

"Aye, I was shocked, but I understood, Laura." Stepping closer to her, he reached out and tenderly brushed the fingers of one hand against her left cheek. "Havena we done enough to punish ourselves? They're gone, Laura. We're free to be just Laura and Roan, two people who love each other, who have been blessed wi' the love and respect o' some verra exceptional friends."

"We are blessed."

"Aye, and it's time we started actin' like the two people plannin' the everlastin' weddin' o' their lives."

"Wedding?" Warmth blossomed in her cheeks, and the gloom that had dulled her vibrant green irises, became lost beneath a glow of joyous expectation.

"Wha' do you think o' a threesome?"

"What?"

"Lannie and Beth, Deliah and Winston—"

"Roan and Laura," she interjected dreamily. "Wow."

"It would be a helluva grand ceremony," he said, then placed a lingering kiss on her lips. When he lifted his head, he said in a low, raspy tone, "I want you for my wife, Laura Bennett."

"You got me," she laughed. "But may I say one thing?"

"Sure."

"The new groundskeeper . . .?"

"Wha' abou' him?"

"He's gorgeous."

Roan jerked back. "He's a fairly nice-lookin' lad."

"No, he's *gorgeous.* Almost too beautiful to be male."

Roan scrinched up his face in disbelief. "Have I reason to be jealous?"

Laura laughed. "Roan Ingliss, I like my men ruggedly handsome, as broad in the shoulders as a luxury liner, and having sexy brown eyes."

"In case you havena notice," he said, grinning sheepishly, "my eyes are brown."

She flung herself into his arms and kissed him.

Moments ago, she'd thought herself incapable of ever being happy again. Love was like that, though. When you least expected it, it peeked over the darkest horizon and promised a brighter day ahead.

CHAPTER SEVEN

Taryn decided her only allies were Laura Bennett's three obnoxious nephews. They alone sought her company. Their endless chattering and questions gave her a real headache, but she tolerated them because she could be herself around them. They liked her bluntness, and thought her goofy when she refused to handle Wiggles, the household Doberman in the guise of a mouse.

Nice.

The women remained distant whenever she was in the same room. They watched her every move as if expecting her to steal the clothes off their backs.

Nice.

The men weren't much better. Considering their first encounter, Lachlan was surprisingly the most polite, although he was careful about how he answered her questions, which had nothing to do with his death or return. She didn't dare mention that subject. If any one of them thought she was there for an inside story, they would have her either thumbing her way back to the airport or strapped to a dunking stool over Loch Ken.

Despite her dislike for lamb, she politely ate the roast

dinner without a complaint. However, the gathering was fraught with burping contests among the boys. Taryn remained tense throughout the meal, questioning how the other adults could put up with the crudeness. Were the boys her responsibility, she would have sent them to their rooms without supper. Laura had only once told them to stop, then laughed when Kevin released a liquid-sounding burp that made Taryn's stomach do a double flip-flop. Taryn suspected her hosts and hostesses were ignoring the antics because they knew it irked her.

Nice.

But she did survive dinner, and she did manage to keep her chin up when the women practically ignored her in the kitchen during the cleanup. Again she got the impression Deliah was the one she needed to avoid. She couldn't figure out what it was about the "softly spoken" woman that made her skin crawl, and she was usually quick to size up strangers' personalities. Their weaknesses. Their strengths. Not this one, though. Looking into the vibrant blue depths of Deliah's eyes reminded Taryn of a roller coaster ride. Scary. Thrilling. Dangerous. Although Deliah looked years younger than Beth, Laura, and herself, Taryn couldn't shake an inexplicable impression that the woman was the mother hen of the household. Everyone was so solicitous toward her and her "condition." Even the boys. Taryn found it sickening, but kept her opinion to herself.

Now, she was to endure yet another insult.

After the boys were put to bed and Beth had fed the twins and returned downstairs, the adults gathered in the parlor. Taryn, of course, joined them. She was a night owl who usually slept until late morning, and was looking forward to some stimulating conversation with people closer to her own age. But no sooner had she sat on one of the high-back chairs, Roan approached her and told her there were plenty of books in the library to look over until their discussion was through. At first, Taryn could only stare at him in disbelief. Considering what she already knew about the residents under this roof, what else could be deemed secret? Being excluded was right up there with a slap. No, a punch. In the face.

Nice.

When Roan scowled at her, Taryn laughed. It was one of those caustic little laughs that always escaped her whenever her pride got nicked or she was taken by surprise. It was an automatic response, one she'd tried to curb for years. At least she didn't snort, as did Helen Tooley, her editor's secretary.

"You want me to *leave?* Why?"

Roan stared down at her through narrowed eyes, the scowl intact, his mouth set grimly and his hands on his hips. "Family business."

She locked her teeth against a retort. He was baiting her, expecting her to storm out of the room in a snit. She refused to give him an excuse to demand she leave the estate before she was ready to split on her own.

"Fine," she said, forcing lightness in her tone as she rose to her feet. She smiled into his face and offered a nonchalant shrug. "But I don't feel much like reading. Mind if I explore the house?"

Roan glanced at the others. They didn't appear thrilled at the idea of her roaming the halls, but in the end they nodded their assent. Her brother explained which rooms were currently occupied, and she agreed to avoid them.

She headed for the hall door, her step lively, her projected demeanor camouflaging the resentment fermenting in her gut. She closed the door behind her and took a moment to will back the tears pressing at the back of her eyes.

Damn you, Roan! she silently cursed. *You didn't have to humiliate me like that in front of the others!*

Her spine rigid, she climbed the stairs to the second floor.

Her room was directly across from Roan and Laura's, its gold and red tones complementing the French Provincial furnishings. It was a feminine room with lace doilies, a collection of etched perfume bottles and vases, and a massive wall tapestry depicting a French courtyard of a bygone century. The fireplace was her favorite, with its immaculate white rock and white cherub columns supporting a gold-veined marble mantel. The drapes were ruby-red velvet with lace sheers which gently flapped from the breeze coming through the partially opened windows. It was cool in the room, almost chilly, but she preferred fresh air.

She'd left both suitcases opened on the canopy bed. As yet, she hadn't hung up or put away any of her belongings in the drawers. She was superstitious by nature, another flaw she couldn't pluck from her faceted personality. As long as she was prepared to leave at a moment's notice, it wouldn't happen. She'd long ago determined her life was governed not by a god or the planets according to astrology, but by the dictates of Murphy's Law—what could go wrong, would. At least she had the moxie to think her way around obstacles. And a sense of humor, which few people would agree she had. But of course she did. Determination and a thick hide were necessary in her line of work, and if she didn't view the world as one big, revolving joke she would have capitulated years ago to her parents' unrelenting pressure to marry and have a horde of kids.

"One man and noisy brats ain't my style," she said in a singsong manner, and removed a flashlight from the bottom of the largest suitcase. She tested it and, satisfied the wide beam would see her through her exploring, she headed for the attic door on the third floor.

The boys had shown her the attic and the tower, earlier. Although the tower had given her the creeps when Kevin pointed out where Lachlan had been interred by her ancestor, the brief tour of the attic had made her heart rejoice.

When she'd first begun delving into Ailbert's journals, she'd had no real interest in her family's history. She'd heard stories of Lachlan Baird since she was a child. Once, when she was not quite five, she had eavesdropped on a conversation between her mother and her Aunt Aggie. They had gone to Aunt Aggie's for one of their monthly visits. Usually, Taryn enjoyed her aunt's company—

although Cousin Borgie was a bore and a bully—but that day Aggie was in a foul mood. She told Taryn's mother, her sister-in-law, she didn't know how much longer she could work for the laird. The *"deil"*, Aggie called him again and again, as if to brand him a devil gave her perverse pleasure. Taryn had never disbelieved the stories of the ghost harassing her family, but she hadn't taken them all that seriously until this day. For nearly a year later, she had nightmares of a fiendish ghost making her scrub his floors and windows, his green misty body hovering over her as she worked herself to exhaustion. Moving to the U.S. had ended them, and she'd tucked all memory of him away in a dark niche in her subconscious.

Her research had begun with the Ingliss clan, then the Bairds relevant to her ancestry. Only one of Lachlan's full brothers had married and had children. Gavin, who had three sons of his own. In January, she'd had the good fortune to track down two of his living relatives. Margaret Cunningham, and Collin Guin-James Baird. Brother and sister resided in Aberdeen, Margaret in the house where Lachlan had been born. At eighty-two, Margaret was a widow with no children, and a mind as sharp as a sword's edge.

It amazed Taryn how Scottish families kept their histories alive through the telling of stories from one generation to the next. Margaret eagerly spoke of Ciarda and Guin, and all that had befallen the family since those turbulent years. If one could believe the old woman, Guin Baird had been a saint, beyond reproach. She never mentioned—nor did Taryn enlighten her to her own knowledge of—Guin's part in Lachlan's death. Either Margaret didn't know, or chose not to expose that delightful bit of information. She also described Ciarda as a cold, distant woman who preferred to be alone, who only left the house when she traveled to the Isle of Lewis to visit her father. According to Margaret, Ciarda displayed no love for her first three sons. Only Lachlan.

Collin Guin-James Baird was three years younger than

his sister. At one time he had shared the family home with Margaret, but confided to Taryn that she snored so loudly in her sleep, he could not escape the sound in any part of the house. He lived alone in a small cottage, a robust man with thick white hair and light brown eyes that nearly mirrored her own. He had never married, but claimed to have had more than his share of women. To his knowledge, he had fathered no children. He spoke proudly of his Baird heritage, and talked greatly of Guin's accomplishments in the early 1800's. When Taryn asked what he knew of Ciarda, he became sullen and resentful.

"She was a witch," he'd said, his face contorted with contempt. "Her and the whole bloody pack tha' settled on the Isle o' Lewis. Aye, the whole lot o' 'em, evil. Old Lachlan was given his own ceremonial dirk, and you and me know bloody weel the kind o' ceremonies *it* was used for!"

He went on to say how the family's scrapbook remained at the family house. Margaret hadn't mentioned it, but Collin explained that his sister's memory wasn't as clear as his own. To Taryn's delight, he went with her back to Margaret's, where he brought out three large, leather-bound books, then seated himself next to Taryn at the dining room table, and took her on a visual tour of the Baird history through diary excerpts, letters, newspaper articles, and photographs. A lot of the information Taryn found boring, but outwardly she remained enthused. The highlights were the articles written about Ciarda's and Lachlan's deaths. When they came to the latter, Collin slammed a fist on the oak table top and released a squeal of glee.

"Fittin' the bastard should die by tha' cursed dirk!" he'd exclaimed.

He then pulled out a sketch of the dirk. It was one Lachlan, himself, had drawn sometime before he'd left for Europe with Millard Barluc, and it was easy to see why the Baird males at the time had thought the weapon evil. The sketch was detailed, especially the demonic-looking faces on the handle. Taryn had shivered at first glance, but then became fascinated by the possibility that Ciarda could have been a witch.

Everything ever written about Lachlan Baird was contained within the books. The only mention of the history of the dirk was that it had been handed down for generations on a particular side of the MacLachlan clan. When Taryn questioned where the dirk had originated from, Collin had shrugged and stated, "From Broc MacLachlan in the seventeen hundreds. Ciarda, tha' one was reluctant to talk much abou' her ancestry in tha' respect. All she would say was he was a hero, and had vanished on the isle. Her family had located there to honor his memory. Lies, if you ask me. Wha' better place to conduct the deil's work than at those evil stones?"

"What stones?" Taryn had asked.

He had looked at her as if she'd grown two heads. "The Callanish Standin' Stones! Surely you've heard o' them, lass!"

Taryn hadn't.

"Weel, I'll tell you this much, Miss Ingliss. Tha' dirk's a key to the gate o' Hell. One night, my great great-grandfaither, Gavin, overheard his mither talkin' to Lachlan while he slept. *Och,* Lachlan was young, nine or ten, I think, and had been down wi' a fever for several days. Ciarda was sittin' wi' him, talkin' o' this Broc MacLachlan, and wha' due the clan owed him. But wha' shook up my dear Gavin was her tellin' Lachlan she had figured ou' the secret. Aye, she had, and it was the dirk. The dirk was the key to the mystery and the lost souls who couldna leave till—" He made quotation marks with his fingers. "—the dirk was returned to the stones.

"Aye, Gavin told his children and their children, and they their own and so on, o' how she told the sleepin' Lachlan she could no' return the dirk for fear she would be lost there, too, or her son demanded in payment o' Broc's sin. And she asked for her son's forgiveness."

Collin had leaned toward Taryn then, his eyes reflecting

the maniacal workings of his mind. "Now you tell me, does it no' all reek o' witchcraft and the deil, hisself?"

Taryn hadn't responded, but thanked him for his time and returned to her hotel room.

The next morning, with the sketch she'd stolen of the dirk tucked away in her purse, she took a train to Inverness. The following day, she flew to Stornaway, where she'd rented a car. With the directions she'd gotten from the man at the rental office, she drove to the MacLachlans' inn. The three-story building had been formerly called the *Sgeul Inn,* but was translated into the *Astory Inn* at the turn of the century.

It was there she discovered she could learn no more about the dirk's history, and that the remaining eleven family members of the original clan were as tight-lipped as clams. During her five-day stay they watched her when she ate in the dining room, and when she walked around the grounds. She could almost swear they even watched her when she was in her room. If she struck up a conversation with one of the guests, one of them always seemed to be around, listening in. To say they had deemed her a threat from the moment she had signed the register might sound paranoid, but she was convinced it was true.

A threat to whom or what?

On the first floor, there had been a room dedicated to Broc MacLachlan. A shrine. It had given Taryn the willies, made her sick to her stomach every time she tried to cross the threshhold. Directly across from the doorway was a massive portrait of a man in the MacLachlan red and blue tartan, his black hair a wild mane falling nearly to his waist. Although the figure stood larger than life, Taryn couldn't focus on his features, only his black eyes, which gave her the distinct impression they were boring into her with a silent accusation. Accusing her of what, she didn't know.

Taryn had left the inn without having viewed anything stored inside the shrine. She visited the standing stones, a cruciform setting of megaliths which had filled her with such dread, she couldn't stop shaking. Twenty yards from the nearest stone, she couldn't force herself to go closer. It was as if an invisible hand had slapped against her chest and remained there to ward her off.

From Stornaway she flew to Inverness, then to Glasgow that evening. She stayed overnight at the Holiday Inn on Argyle Street, rented a Volkswagen the next morning, and drove to Edinburgh. For the next three weeks she met with various professors at the university, showing them the sketch and asking their opinions of its origin. Although intrigued, they all claimed they had never seen anything quite like it. The last professor suggested she talk to Michael Stoughton, a retired archaeologist and renowned collector of ancient weapons.

It took ten days before Stoughton responded to the messages she'd left at his home and office. He invited her to his home, a two-story, red brick house with white trim. She had expected him to be an affluent man—a collector of ancient weapons, after all—but in fact the house was moderately furnished. He was a man in his sixties with salt and pepper hair, deep-set hazel eyes, a charming smile, and only a hint of an English accent. Over tea, Taryn showed him the sketch.

"The MacLachlan dirk," he had said, a tremor in his tone. His shrewd gaze had lifted to regard Taryn. "What's your interest in this?"

At first, Taryn had considered lying to him, but there was something in his eyes that told her he would see through her if she tried. So, she told him about the connections between the Baird and Ingliss clans, and how Ciarda's father had given the dirk to Lachlan. All the while she spoke, she was keenly observant of the way he repeatedly ran his thumbs over the dirk's handle.

"I remember reading about his murder when the story was released last year on the current happenings at the estate," he had murmured. "This sketch is supposedly of the dirk that killed him?"

Taryn had nodded. He paled then, and shivered. After several moments, he gestured for Taryn to follow him.

He led her to a large room behind pocket doors. The contents had taken her breath away. Not only did Stoughton collect ancient weapons, but armor and small artifacts as well. There was so much to see that she couldn't look at everything as she followed him across the room. At one point, he had commented that this part of the collection was composed of reproductions, which answered her unspoken question as to how he could have these items in a home with no apparent security.

She was wrenched from her preoccupation when she realized he had somehow engaged a hidden wall to open. He led her down a staircase, the end of which opened into an enormous room. Here, he had said, was his true collection.

Taryn had felt as though she had stepped into another world. She couldn't even begin to imagine the value of the pieces. Each weapon was enclosed in glass with soft showcase lights. She didn't dare ask him why they weren't in a museum, for fear she would offend his sensibilities.

Stoughton escorted her to a polished maple desk and instructed her to sit in the only chair in the room. He left her there and returned about a minute later with something in his hand. Sitting on the edge of the desk, he positioned a lighted magnifying glass, mounted to the side of the desk, in front of her, then handed her what appeared to be a gold spearhead approximately four inches long and an inch and a half wide at the base. The tip was sharp, and Stoughton cautioned her not to touch it. At this point, Taryn regarded it without the aid of the magnifying glass.

Stoughton smoothed out the sketch on the desk, the handle pointed downward. "You can't see them with the naked eye," he'd said, indicating the spearhead. "Use the glass."

"Is this really gold?"

He had nodded.

Taryn adjusted the magnifying glass and held the artifact beneath it. It had taken her a moment to find just the right position to make clear the details along the edge of the spearhead, and she jerked back in surprise.

"Gargoyle faces," Stoughton had told her, "not demons."

Taryn couldn't bring herself to look at the spearhead for several seconds, during which her heart seemed lodged in her throat. Then, hesitantly, her hands trembling a bit, she again placed it beneath the glass and forced herself to concentrate on the engravings. Yes, they were faces, each slightly different. Twenty-six, thirteen on each side, and to the naked eye smaller than the head of a pin. Magnified, each face was eerily detailed. Brows and cheekbones differed. The set of the eyes. The mouths. Down the center of both sides of the spearhead were symbols. As if divining her thoughts, Stoughton stated, "Runes. Each side translates to *Family of Karok.*"

"What?"

"That's what it says."

"Where did you get this?"

"It was wedged in a side seam of a trunk my nephew purchased at an estate sale."

Taryn numbly stared at the sketch of the dirk, specifically at the drawn strip of symbols on the blade. "Are these runes, too?"

"Yes," Stoughton said. "It translates to 'Passage Key Karok'."

"What does it mean?"

"I have no idea," Stoughton had said, frowning. "When I first translated the spearhead, I searched through every book I could find on myths of gods and demigods. Nothing. Not even a king or prince who used the gargoyle as a symbol.

"Gargoyles originated in Greece and Rome as water spouts," he went on, as if lecturing a class. "The word descends from the Middle English word *gargule* and the French word *gargouille,* meaning throat, and refers to the gargling sound of water through a spout."

"So gargoyles were never worshiped?"

He shook his head grimly. "Not to my knowledge, which is why finding them engraved on a gold piece is so unusual.

"What are the odds, Miss Ingliss," he'd gone on, his voice monotone, a faraway look in his eyes, "of you and I coming together with two very unique pieces involving gargoyles and runes?"

She had shrugged and shaken her head in bewilderment.

Stoughton picked up the sketch and studied it for a time. "I would like to see what's on the other side of this dirk. Do you know where it is?"

Unwilling to tell him any more than she had, she again shook her head.

"Pity, because I believe something is trying to call both items home."

A chill had clamped onto Taryn's spine. "Home?"

He'd smiled ruefully, and his eyes had taken on a disconcerting look of foreboding. "Why else would our paths have crossed?

"Passage key," he'd murmured. "Most curious. A passage into what, I wonder."

Stoughton's last words continued to haunt Taryn. She'd left his home unshakably convinced of two facts: the dirk was a key, and the secret it held had something to do with the Callanish Standing Stones. Never had an obsession with a story been more deeply rooted in her gut. Whatever it took, she would return to the stones, with the dirk, and learn the secret Ciarda had feared.

As she rummaged through the trunks in the attic, the ache in her back made it feel as though she'd already spent hours bent over them, when in fact not even a half hour had gone by. She kept herself focused and worked as fast as she could move her hands. After the ninth trunk she began to lose heart, and slowed her search until she came across one with the brass initials CM. Now her heart began to race again. A rush of adrenaline restored her energy.

The trunk was locked, but that didn't concern her. Removing one of the bobbypins from her hair, she bit off the cushioning tip and deftly inserted the blunt metal end into the keyhole. Three seconds was all it took for the tumblers to click.

Taryn opened the trunk and positioned the flashlight on the left rear corner, at the crook of the top and bottom. Like a child cut loose in a candy store, she fished through tablecloths and doilies, lace handkerchiefs with CM embroidered in red and blue thread, books and papers. There was a large jewelry box with a stunning collection of necklaces, rings, and bracelets with various precious stones. The pieces were old, in gold or silver, all detailed with Celtic designs, but none of them interested her. She closed the lid and replaced the box inside the trunk, then started glancing through the papers. Receipts, and letters from family and friends. Again, nothing that caught her interest. Most of the books were poetry collections, one was titled *Plato's Notes,* and one, she discovered, was a Bible. She skimmed through the pages of each, saving the Bible for last.

It was a thick and very old book, the thin leather binding handsewn with cords of darker leather, and the contents written in Gaelic. Getting more discouraged by the moment, she carelessly flipped through the pages until she glimpsed a glint of metal in the corner of her right eye. She placed the Bible next to her on the floor and reached into the trunk. Between the folds of one of the handkerchiefs was a gold chain, at the end of which was a locket. The front border was intricately carved with a circle of Celt knots. In the center was CM in Old English letters.

Taryn gingerly ran a thumb over the surface, then opened the locket. Inside were two tiny oval portraits, one of a boy of about three-years-old, the other of possibly the same boy at about age ten.

"Lachlan' " she murmured, then tilted his images into the light for a better look. "You were a cute devil, even then." She chuffed a low laugh. "What secret was your mother hiding, huh? Come on, Lachlan, you can tell me."

With a resigned sigh she peered into the trunk. She placed the locket in her left hand, using the right to prod and squeeze the various other fabric items. Finally, in the front right corner at the bottom, her fingers came across a semi-stiff article. She pulled out a pouch no larger than her palm and closely inspected it.

An icy sensation began in the pit of her stomach and spread through her veins. She couldn't be sure, but the texture felt like coarse hair, black and masterfully woven, the knotted tie cord made from the same material. There was something inside the pouch, but she couldn't bring herself to open it right away. An abysmal sense of foreboding cloaked her, a feeling similar to what she'd experienced when seeing the gargoylian faces on the spearhead, beneath Stoughton's magnifying glass.

Her lips tightly compressed and breathing sparingly through her nostrils, she opened the pouch. She leveled her left palm and tipped the pouch over atop it. A necklace fell out. It wasn't like anything in the jewelry box or anything she'd seen, with two exceptions. The knotted cord was made from what appeared to be the same hair as the pouch, and was attached to the loop of a tear-shaped pendant made of cobalt blue stone. The second similarity was in the tiny carvings in the rock. She didn't need a magnifying glass this time. Gargoyle faces and runes.

A violent shiver coursed through her. She told herself to replace the necklace in the pouch, toss it in the trunk, and forget she had ever seen it. But it was a vital part of the mystery, and she could no more let it go than she could join a convent. Both went against her nature.

Hastily, she crammed the pouch into one cup of her bra, wincing at the feel of the coarse weave against her skin. She righted her V-neck sweater, patted and smoothed the area concealing the pouch to make sure it wouldn't stand out if she encountered someone on her way back to her room, then picked up the Bible and tossed it inside the trunk. She took the flashlight in hand and was about to close the lid when she noticed a corner of paper sticking out from between the front pages of the Bible.

Anticipation quivered through her. She nervously moistened her lower lip by sucking it in, and angled the full beam of light on the intriguing piece. The scalloped edges told her it wasn't one of the pages that had come loose. This was something someone had tucked inside the book. A letter? From Ciarda? To Lachlan?

She eased the paper from between the pages. It was folded in half with such care, the edges were perfectly aligned. She tucked the flashlight between her legs, beam upward, then gingerly unfolded the letter. The handwriting was small and graceful, but to her dismay, the words were in Gaelic.

"Dammit," Taryn muttered. "Fine, I'll just-ah, find someone to translate it after I leave. *Shit.* Gaelic. Good ol' English beneath you, Ciarda? Oh, but don't worry your pretty little skeletal head. It'll take far more than a damn language to discourage me."

Taryn closed the trunk and stood. Again placing the flashlight between her thighs, she carefully tucked the letter into the front of her tailored, brown tweed slacks, then took the light into a hand.

She went rigid at the sound of footsteps on the stairs. Then she heard Roan call, "Taryn, you in the attic?"

Sucking in a deep breath, she went to the top of the staircase and saw him paused halfway up, a questioning eyebrow cocked in her direction. She forced a smile and said lightheartedly, "It's cool up here. Have you ever gone through any of the trunks or boxes?"

"You didna get into any o' that stuff, did you?"

"I peeked in a couple of the trunks," she said merrily, and started down the stairs. He descended ahead of her and waited in the hall. While he closed the door, she looked down at her clothing, then jerked in surprise. "That has to be the cleanest attic I've ever been in. Do you have a housekeeper?"

He issued her an impatient look before shaking his head.

She laughed mockingly. "Don't tell me *you* do housework!"

"The house taks care o' itself."

A blank expression fell over Taryn's face. "You're kidding."

"No. The stuff in the attic belongs to Lannie."

"Okay." She gave an airy shrug. "There's two trunks with some great old clothes up there."

"Aye. Some o' it belonged to his mither."

"What about the rest?"

"Tessa and Robert's children were only allowed to remove their personal belongings when they moved ou'. Everythin' else remained, includin' their parents' things."

"What right did Lachlan have to keep their stuff?" she asked with a hint of bitterness.

"By right tha' it was *his* money they lived on. He could have prevented their children from takin' anythin' but wha' they had on their backs, but he didna, did he?"

"Magnanimous sonofabitch, isn't he," she said flippantly.

"He's tha' and more. I would appreciate it, if you spoke o' him wi' the respect due him, especially when in *his* home."

His scolding brought a crimson color to her cheeks, and she couldn't stop her immediate response. "Why don't you just sacrifice a friggin' lamb to him! Jeee-sus, better yet, one of those goddamn peacocks!"

"I'll see you in the morn," he said stiffly. "Good night."

She glanced at her watch. "It's not even nine o'clock."

"Everyone else has turned in."

She watched him stroll down the hall and disappear down the staircase, then grumbled, "Life in the fast lane, it ain't. But what else can one expect from a house that favors the dead?"

It was the dampness and chill of the night making him so jittery. At least, that's what Stephan Miles kept telling himself. His horn-rimmed glasses kept fogging up. He'd swiped the moisture off with his fingers so many times that the lenses were smudgy and getting more difficult to see through. Without them, though, he was blinder than a bat on a sunny day.

He sat on the cellar bulkhead like a man whose legs had turned to rubber. His three-quarter length black raincoat tented his lean body, making him appear thinner than he actually was. He was twenty-six, but knew he could pass for forty. His dark hair was short-cropped, worn that way because of its tendency to form ringlets when even an inch long. Mediocre blue eyes. High cheekbones, and a chin too pointed for his liking.

Basically, he was a miserable man who detested his job but didn't believe himself suited for anything else—at least, nothing that would pay the bills. His ex-wife remained a nag, and his dog disliked him. He had no real friends, and his boss was on the verge of firing him. And his mother—He didn't want to think about her.

Life in the nineties. What a bitch.

The only other time he'd set foot on this estate was last July, when he'd told the American woman he was interested in buying the place. Right, like he would ever be able to afford anything more than his dinky little flat in London. The fib had gotten him through the doors, although not for long. Something had happened to him while he was talking to the American woman. Something vile had seeped into him and made him vomit green ooze for the rest of that day. It had shaken him up enough to make him terrified of returning, even when he was told about the impending Christmas Eve miracle the ghostly laird had promised the media and people of Crossmichael. His boss had demanded he be there for the story. At the time, Miles hadn't thought any piece of news was worth chancing another attack of green slime.

"So what the bloody hell am I doing here?" he asked himself, glancing apprehensively around at the varying shades of darkness.

He knew the answer. Unless he came up with a sizzling story by the end of the week, he could kiss his job goodbye. Any reporter could be here now and accomplish the same job, probably better. He didn't have any hangups about being a so-so journalist. Some men were born for literary greatness, others, so-sodom.

Good ole Whitney Melcamp. Sonofabitch. He was the editor from hell. What kind of man sent another man on a mission like this? Had Melcamp barfed green slime? *No!* Had *Melcamp* watched his pathetic life flash before his eyes until the throes of the *whatever it was* had spent itself?

Hell no. He laughed at me! Belly-laughed until tears streamed down his flaccid cheeks!

Well, let me tell you Melcamp, ole boy, if the "whatever" gets inside me this time, I'll be sure to puke the green slime right in your face for my troubles!

The mental image of that happening brought a wan smile to his sickly pallor, but did little to heighten his willingness to venture into the house. Nonetheless, he would have to. He needed his next paycheck. He'd already recycled his boxers by wearing them inside out. Another round of use and a *story* would smell *him* coming.

Releasing a burst of breath, he rose to his feet and hastily opened one side of the bulkhead doors. The fathomless darkness that peered up at him made him shudder. He repeatedly told himself that if old Viola Cooke could use this method to listen in and move about the house, he should be able to get past his fears.

One step at a time, he counseled himself, then finally turned on his flashlight and headed down the steep stone steps. He closed the door, pausing momentarily as if afraid he had sealed himself in a tomb, then puffed up his cheeks and moved the light around the room.

As cellars went, this one was pretty clean and organized. His head bobbed in appreciation of this. No cobwebs that he could see. Nothing scurrying about. Not yet.

A few minutes into his unhurried exploration, he began to hum the theme from the *Red Dwarf* series. It helped to quell his unease. He idolized the character of Lister, believing him to be the epitome of a man's man, the ultimate hero and slob *extraordinaire.* Favorite segments of the show flashed across his mindscreen, and he grinned as he searched what turned out to be a vast sectioned-off area of the basement. Sometime later, he detected a rather unpleasant odor. He came across a door and opened it. A foul stench rolled over him from the room beyond, a stench reminding him of body excrement, rotten food, and something else he couldn't begin to analyze.

"Oooo-eee," he rasped, pinching his nostrils closed. Now sounding like a cartoon character, he added, "I've been in garbage dumps that smelled better than this."

He leaned into the room, the beam of the flashlight dancing on the interior walls, then lingering on a table a short distance away.

"What the bloody . . .?"

Releasing his nose, he cautiously stepped to the table. Amid empty pork rind bags and other various food containers was a heap of white sausages.

Not sausages he realized upon a closer inspection. He gagged and clamped a hand over his mouth when the flashlight dipped and he saw a gutted peafowl on the floor by the nearest table leg. His eyes wide with horror, he trained the light back on the table. He now knew the sausages where in fact the bird's intestines. Someone was hiding in this cubbyhole in the cellar, eating whatever they could find. And anyone capable of eating the raw innards of a bird was not someone he wanted to encounter.

Another fact registered. The wicks of three short, black candles were smoldering, as if the flames had been extinguished a short time ago.

Trembling violently, his gorge rising into his throat, his flashlight dangling from a slack hand at his side, he rigidly turned toward the door. Pale gray eyes stared at him from above the flickering flame of a held candle. There was no life in those eyes. No fear or surprise. Certainly no, "Hello. Welcome to my sty."

At first, Stephan Miles felt only a mild punch to his chest. Then twinges of pain—annoying pain—made him look down and slowly raise the beam of the flashlight to the area. He thought it utterly ridiculous to find a knife poking out from his breast, a large hand attached to the handle. The knife was given a twist by the stranger's hand, and Miles' pain turned to searing agony.

Bewildered more than anything else, he looked again into the pale eyes. *Why?* he wanted to ask. *Was this really necessary?*

No words passed his lips. He'd always had a problem with voicing his objections.

The blade again turned inside him, but he looked unwaveringly into those eyes, seeing his stupidity and his own death reflected in them.

What really galled him was knowing the man was enjoying himself. This guy was a killer, and no amateur. A great story in itself. To hell with the green-slime-infesting-ghost. Here he was, faced with a flesh and blood killer, and wasn't it just like freakin' fate to have *him* on the victim side of the story!

The word "Shit" gurgled from his blood-filled throat, and his tunneled vision diminished to pitch darkness. He wasn't aware of falling, or of the blade being wrenched from his flesh before he hit the floor. He was bewildered by the fact he could still think, and believed himself floating within the infinite blackness.

Hello! he called into nothingness. *Hey, asshole, where are you? Just for the record, you just murdered a nice guy! That's right, you bloody shit! A nice guy! Are you going to explain to my mother why I was found with my shorts inside out? Asshole! Couldn't let me die with a little dignity, could you!*

Cuttstone stared apathetically down at the heap at his feet, absently wiping the bloodied blade against the left leg of his pants. A buzzing filled his ears. He ignored it and stepped over the body and stood at the table. The smell of death didn't bother him, nor did the other stenches in the room. He could shut off any of his external senses when they became intrusive.

He was about to place the dirk on the table when he realized it was emitting a pleasant vibration. His fingers flexed almost caressingly around the handle. The blade winked in the meager glow of the candle he held, and he lifted the knife to regard it more closely.

The gleaming, blood-spackled steel rippled like the surface of a pond when a rock is tossed into it. His pulse quickened in anticipation of the Guardian contacting him, and he breathed heavily through his opened mouth. The vibration intensified, pulsing rhythmically. Then came a hum from the knife, its cadence primordial, beckoning, mesmerizing.

Trancelike, Cuttstone cleared off the table with his left forearm, then lowered the knife to the wood surface. The hum grew louder as a blue glowing speck appeared on the border surrounding the runes. Seconds later, the blue glow spread like liquid fire along the entire border, illuminating the runes and making them appear three-dimensional, hovering above the blade.

"I'm here for you," Cuttstone said in a monotone, his unblinking gaze riveted on the runes.

The dirk rose to stand on its steel tip atop the table. It gradually rotated, spinning faster and faster until the dirk appeared to be but a blur of glowing blue mist. The hum crescendoed into a symphony of countless rhythms. Pounding. Beating. Pulsating like the skins of drums under the driving force of hands. Maddening rhythms. Compelling rhythms. Rhythms that deftly wove a spell of encompassment. There was no escaping them. Cuttstone had no will to escape.

The mist spread out, its blue glow turning the squalor of the room into a mystical setting. Cuttstone's head first lolled to one side, then the other. He could see a door appear in the heart of the mist. It was opening, slowly, but nonetheless opening. His heart hammered painfully. A normal man would fear the pain, but he considered it a gift. All that mattered was his belief that the Guardian thought him worthy enough to visit.

When the door fully opened, the aperture expanded until it was large enough for him to lean his head and shoulders through. Beyond, he found more blueness of varying shades. Enchanting splendor. Serene. Infinite.

"I'm here," he said, his voice soft with awe and reverence.

A disembodied face rushed at him, enlarging and halting a few feet from the opening. He couldn't breathe. He couldn't move. To him, the visage was no more hideous than his own. A mere man would have gone into shock and died from terror. Not Cuttstone. He had longed for so many years to look upon the Guardian, and now realized that he had countless times in his life, in more cities than he could remember. This one had a raised, glowing red disfigurement that ran from its right brow, across the left eye, and down half the craggy cheek. Cuttstone accepted it as an identification mark, one that enabled him to recognize *his* Guardian from the others he was now sure existed.

Man called them gargoyles, but he now knew them to be gods.

His personal Guardian roared. Cuttstone's eardrums burst, and he instinctively shrank back as the Guardian's hot breath blasted against his face. The door closed, the mist vanished, and the dirk fell onto its side.

The man known as the Phantom lowered himself onto the chair and dazedly stared off into space. His world was now soundless, and would be for the rest of his life. He didn't question the necessity of this, or resent the blisters forming on his burned face, for he knew he'd waited too long to claim the begetters in this house, and the Guardian had punished him.

Beneath the Callanish Standing Stone on the Isle of Lewis in Scotland, the ground rumbled.

CHAPTER EIGHT

The day began with a light drizzle, but by late morning the sun won out over the clouds. Beth and Lachlan decided to bring the twins outside and, to Roan's delight, asked if the boys could join them. Taryn was still asleep, and Deliah and Winston drove into town to go through the files at the police station.

Whistling, Roan practically danced up the staircase. The boys had finagled their way into his bed again last night. It was so seldom Laura and he had a chance to be alone, he now felt as if he were blessed.

When last he'd seen Laura—about an hour ago—she'd mentioned she was going to make the beds. He knew her routine. She always did the boys' rooms first, then theirs. If his timing was right, and he was sure it was . . . .

A broad grin spread across his face when he opened their door and saw her bent over the bed, tucking in the bottom right corner of the sheets. He eased the door shut and tiptoed behind her. His eyebrows lifted appreciatively as he checked out the roundness of her hips and buttocks beneath his shirt that she wore. She had dressed for breakfast, then bathed after the dishes were done. Obviously, she had decided to make the beds in as little as possible, because she was barefoot, bare-legged and, he hoped, devoid of underwear.

She released a squeal of surprise when he clamped his hands on her hips. She whirled, but stopped short with a laugh when she realized who it was.

"You scared the hell out of me!"

Roan flashed a devious grin and, his hands still on her hips, drew her tightly against the hardness of his body. "Hey, gorgeous. You up to some serious play time?"

Her face brightened, then fell into a look of mild despair. "The boys."

"They're ou' side wi' Lannie and Beth," he said merrily. His fingers kneaded the firmness of her hips and he moved his lower body in a manner that told her what he had in mind. "I've got a wicked hunger for you."

"How wicked?"

His right eyebrow stretched upward as far as he could make it go. "Weel, I really havena had a chance to try to break my three hour record."

"I don't think we have that much time," she chortled.

"We could mak love in double time."

An amused frown creased her brow. "Pray tell, how does 'double time' work?"

In response, he swept her up into his arms and deposited her on the bed. Then, her laughter ringing through the room, he peeled out of his shirt with incredible swiftness, twirled it over his head and gyrated his hips with a quickened rendition of "The Stripper" theme crooning from his throat. Finally, he tossed the shirt across the room and sat on the edge of the mattress. He removed his shoes, socks and pants with record-breaking speed, then stood in his white boxers with his hands on his hips and sang out, "Ta-daaaa."

Laughter brought about a painful stitch in Laura's side. Her arms braced against her middle, she rolled into a fetal position and tried to will back her mirth, but her laughter flowed from her like a waterfall down a mountainside. She could no more cut off her laughter than she could plug up a cascade with a bottle cork.

"Laura?"

Roan soberly glanced about the room, then looked at her pensively. "Lass? I didna think it was tha' funny."

Still she laughed, squeaks intermittently escaping her.

Roan rolled his eyes to the heavens, then climbed on the mattress and turned her onto her back. Tears streaked her flushed face and brightened the emerald green of her eyes. Her laughter finally wound down, but hiccups took over and she giggled after each as if she had no control. Stretching out alongside her, he smiled down at her with the patience of a man deeply in love.

"Are you through?" he chuckled moments later.

She was breathing hard and staring up at the ceiling. "Sorry." Hiccup. Giggle. Groan. "But while you were undressing with the speed of light—" Hiccup. Giggle. A muttered light curse. "I had this image of the Energizer Bunny trying to make love to me, and I wore him out."

"I'm offerin' you this perfect body o' mine, and you're thinkin' abou' a bunny?" he asked with comical disbelief. "Is there a message in this, oı am I bein' a wee obtuse?"

Her eyes sparkled with mischief. "Who told you that you have a perfect body, huh?"

He grimaced sheepishly. "So I'm gettin' a wee paunch."

"No, you're not." Placing a hand on his chest and shoving him onto his back, Laura straddled him and removed the rubber band that held her hair in a ponytail. She shook out the thick mass of pale gold strands, then looked down at him with a seductive smile as her fingertips trailed from his shoulders to his lower rib cage. "There isn't one inch of you I would change, Mr. Ingliss."

"No?"

She playfully ran her fingers through the golden curly hairs on his chest. "No. Even if you did develop a paunch, it would be all the more for me to love."

Roan released a breath through pursed lips. He could

feel his body tightening beneath her rump. Feel himself strain to breach their underwear to slip inside her.

"Are we—" Hiccup. At least they were coming less frequently now. "—anxious to get down to business?" she asked coyly while unbuttoning the shirt she wore.

"Anxious? I'm bloody aroused for the occasion!"

Her slender eyebrows arched and she clucked her tongue. "Don't get me laughing again." She opened the shirt and teasingly lowered it from her shoulders.

Roan's eyes fixed on her firm, naked breasts. His mouth went dry and his nostrils became pinched. "Aye. No laughin'."

She completely removed the shirt with deliberate slowness and dropped it over the side of the bed. "Are you?"

He forced his gaze to look into her eyes. "Am I wha'?"

"Aroused?"

"I'm abou' to catapult you across the room," he said wryly.

She laughed, then she hiccupped and sighed. "It feels good to laugh. Good to be free."

She yelped with laughter when Roan masterfully reversed their positions. She stared up at him with eyes wide and blinking, and her lips parted in surprise.

"My, my, big guy. We *are* in the mood!"

"That's wha' I've been tryin' to tell you," he said with a mock growl. Planting his hands to each side of her shoulders, he leaned toward her, his gaze riveted on her lips. "God, you're a beautiful woman, Laura. Just lookin' at you maks my blood sing."

If Laura had intended to keep up the playful bantering for a time longer, his poignantly spoken words rendered her speechless. She reached up and placed her hands along his jawline and swept her gaze over his face as if recommitting it to memory. Roan felt a little breathless. She was all he had ever wanted, or could possibly ever want in a woman, and he realized that he very much wanted to have a child with her. Of course, that was ridiculous. It wouldn't be fair to Laura to burden her with another responsibility, and Kevin, Kahl, and Alby needed their full attention.

With a sigh, he sought the pouty contours of her mouth and kissed her deeply. He rolled onto his back, at the same time cocooning her within the muscular strength of his arms and legs. His tongue caressed hers, then languidly traced the inside of her lips. A low moan of satisfaction rattled in her throat. His hands slid to the waistline of her cotton panties. Hooking his thumbs in the narrow elastic band, he had started to slip the material down her hips when her fingers gripped his wrists.

"Not so fast," she said with a lazy grin.

She squirmed just enough to prompt him to untangle his legs from hers. Then she sat up and stretched out her arms, relishing the glaze of passion in his eyes and the flush on his face. It was seldom she got the opportunity to explore the boundaries of her sexuality with him. There were always interruptions—mostly the boys—or one of them was so tired by the time they were ready for bed, sleep won out. But now the children were outside with Beth and Lachlan. They were both rested, and glorious sunshine poured through the windows. She wanted this time with him to be special, something that would keep a grin on his face for days to come.

With this in mind, she sensuously combed her fingers through her hair, knowing the uplift of her arms showed her breasts to their best advantage. Roan's hands cupped them with diligent tenderness. The texture of his palms against her nipples sent a delicious thrill through her, and another low moan escaped her. His erection flexed beneath her groin. Smiling contentedly, she trenched her fingers up his chest, then rolled his nipples between her thumbs and forefingers. His eyes closed. A deep breath swelled the powerful contours of his chest.

A more fiery passion ignited low in her abdomen. *Enough teasing,* she told herself. She wanted him inside her. Wanted to climb the spirals of ecstasy in his arms.

She was about to swing her right leg over him when a

movement in the outer corner of her right eye gave her a start. Believing one of the boys had come into the room, she jerked her head around.

A scream ejected from her throat, and she scrambled off Roan, then off the bed, on the far side of the cause of her alarm. Roan bolted into a sitting position. Dazed, his wide eyes spastically searching the room, he rasped, "What? What's wrong?" He was expecting to find one of the boys about, but saw nothing to justify Laura's reaction. With a grunt, he cast her a harried look, then frowned with concern. She stood trembling, her arms folded across her breasts, her face shockingly pale and the green of her eyes overly bright with what appeared to be fear.

Climbing out of the bed, he went to her and gripped her upper arms. Again he was perplexed by her behavior, for she leaned to one side to see around him, but a glance over his shoulder told him there was no one but them in the room.

"Laura, what's wrong?"

"Didn't you see him?" she shrilled, staring into his face as though he'd lost his mind.

"See who?" He scowled. "Did one o' the lads—"

"That *man!*" she cried, pointing to the other side of the bed. "He was standing there, watching us!"

Now Roan stared at her as though all her marbles weren't quite in a row. "There was a mon in this room? Watchin' us, you say?"

"Yes, dammit! He was right there—" She blinked in bewilderment. "He-ah . . . ."

"Wha'?" Roan released a dry chuckle. "Are you playin wi' my mind, lass? Normally, I wouldna care you havin' a wee fun wi' me. But if my memory serves me correctly, were we no' abou' to embark on some hot and heavy sex?"

"I could see through him," she murmured, then swallowed hard enough for him to hear. "But I saw him, Roan. He had this stupid look on his face. You know . . . like he was shocked we were . . . you know."

"He was shocked because we were gettin' down to lovin, eh?" he asked wryly.

"I swear I saw him. When I screamed, he . . . well, he sort of broke apart."

An abrupt laugh escaped Roan. "Damn me, Laura. Wha' did you put in your tea this morn?"

Wounded by his skepticism, she stiffly backed up a step, her bleak gaze studying his face. "I know what I saw. He was wearing a long black raincoat and glasses."

Roan frowned with deepening impatience. Then, with a sigh of resignation, he walked to the other side of the bed and repeatedly swiped a hand through the air as he covered the floor space along the length of the bed. Laura watched him, shaking her head in disbelief. She couldn't decide if he was earnestly trying to determine if something had been there, or was adding further insult to her claim.

"If you're looking for a cold spot," she clipped, "there won't be one."

Roan stopped and placed his hands on his hips, and passed her an exasperated look. "There has to be an explanation."

"Besides me being a hysterical female?" she asked bitterly.

"Laura."

"Don't 'Laura' me! Maybe when Deliah brought Lachlan and Beth back through, another spirit came along for the ride. Who knows! Maybe *hundreds* of them came through, and we're just not aware of them *yet!*"

Roan's face blanched. "Dinna say tha'."

"It could be true." Shuddering, she hugged herself and looked forlornly about the room. "Let's face it, Roan, when it comes to Baird House, *anything* is possible."

Roan sat on the edge of the mattress. The prospect of his home being invaded by unwelcome ghosts made his stomach queasy. "Winston or Deliah should be able to determine if we're under invasion," he said, vainly trying to inflict a hint of humor in his tone. "Maybe even Lannie."

Laura dashed to the closet and removed a pair of jeans and a pale pink sweater.

"What are you doin'?" Roan asked, watching her approach the foot of the bed with the garments in hand.

"Getting dressed."

"Wha' happened to—"

Her eyes flared up with anger. "I'm not in the mood."

With a mischievous grin, Roan stood and opened his arms to her. "Give me a minute or two and I'll change your—"

"No way," she said, pulling up her jeans and fastening them. She hastened to the dresser and removed a bra from the top drawer, saying over her shoulder, "I'm not into being watched while I make love."

"Laura . . . ." His groan trailed off as he watched her quickly don the bra. She returned for the sweater, which she slipped on as though her life depended on her speed. As she tugged the bottom down to her hips, she met his gaze through a worried frown. Silence passed between them for several long seconds, then she brusquely headed for the door.

"I'll be outside."

She left the door open and disappeared into the hall. Again Roan sat on the bed, shaking his head with incredulity. He didn't doubt Laura had seen *something*. Except for the mouse incident when she'd jumped on the dining room chair and shrieked, she wasn't inclined to hysterics. In fact, he told himself, she was one of the strongest women he'd ever known.

"Whoever the hell you are," he muttered, "I dinna think much o' your timin'."

A dreamy smile seemed a permanent fixture on Beth's mouth that morning. From where she sat on a bench in the south garden gazebo, an elbow braced on the latticework railing and her chin atop the crook of the arm, she couldn't imagine ever being happier. Lachlan, a bundled infant in each arm, was introducing them to the peafowl scattered about the yard. The boys were performing acrobatics beneath the bright sunlight. Although the ground was sodden from the melted snow and the rains of the past few days, and the boys were more wet than dry, their singsong laughter filled the air and a large portion of her heart.

Despite all the unprecedented events that had befallen her since first arriving at the estate, there was something about this place she loved. It was more than just the aesthetic splendor and the overall ambiance. Had she been born within the walls of Baird House, she couldn't have been more connected to the land.

Lachlan returned to the gazebo, cooing softly to the babies as he approached Beth. She straightened away from the railing, telling herself it was a little scary to love someone as much as she loved him. Every new day that she looked at him, it was as if her heart and soul went through a rebirth. He was the most exasperating person at times. Also, the most loving. The kindest. Certainly the most unusual. That he loved her and their children, she didn't doubt. That he cherished his home and land was also not in question. However, that he could walk away from Baird House in order to secure a more normal existence for his family troubled her.

During the night, they'd talked some about the possibility of moving to her home in Kennewick, Washington. In one respect, the idea excited her. In many others, she could see pitfalls he couldn't. He'd told her they could visit Baird House whenever they wanted. That was true, but *living* on the estate and *visiting* were not the same. He told her he would not regret any decision they came to, even a move to what he considered to be a foreign country. He *believed* he could cope, but she wasn't so sure. Perhaps she would have gone along with his conviction before he'd told her about his life prior to his death. Before that, she'd thought of him always as a wealthy man who had not known what it was to struggle from one day to another. How wrong she'd been. It was one thing for someone used to luxury to adapt to a lifestyle of budgets, another for an eighteenth century man who had amassed his own fortune to find his way in a strange country, in a time when electronics were the norm of everyday life. Lachlan would never be truly happy unless he could use his brain and brawn to better his existence.

During the meeting last night, Roan had been adamant that if she and Lachlan moved to the States, Lachlan's fortune would go with them. It was sizeable, but not even Lachlan knew how much he was worth. There was over three hundred thousand in Scottish monies, but the gems had yet to be priced, and there were far more than even Roan had known about. Lachlan had invested most of his fortune in precious stones, which were mostly still hidden in various parts of the house. Winston had suggested he take some samples of them to Edinburgh, where he would have a gemologist of his acquaintance appraise them. It was agreed, but later, when Lachlan and Beth had retired to their room, he told her he didn't feel right about taking anything from the house, except for his personal belongings.

" 'Tis no' like I canna build anither fortune," he'd told her with all sincerity, confident of his ability to provide her and his children with what he considered to be a proper way of life.

Beth didn't tell him what present day life was like in the outside world. And she didn't voice her concern with his refusal to wear anything but the clothes he favored. She could just imagine him going on a job interview, dressed like a gentleman pirate minus the gold earring, his swaggering speech and his eighteenth century attitude, and his reaction when asked which computer program he knew. She could hear him say, "Wha' do I need a computer for, mon? I have a brain, dinna I?"

"Beth?"

Lachlan's chuckle of her name wrenched her from her reverie and she found herself staring into the smiling depths of his dark eyes. Her heart skipped a beat, and she felt the heat of a flush in her cheeks. "Sorry. I was daydreaming."

With a sigh, he looked down at each of the babies' sleeping faces. "Do you hear tha', young Broc and Ciarda? Your mither is cravin' my sorry bones again." He looked up at Beth and shook his head. "Shame on you, lass."

Beth laughed and fanned her face with a hand. "Shame on you! I do think of other things besides your body."

"Hmmm." Again he glanced at his children. "And how easily a lie passes her sweet lips."

"You're incorrigible."

His eyes rolled up to study her mischievously. "And a handsome deil, if I say so myself."

She laughed again and focused on the peafowl for a time, then adoringly met his gaze.

He was handsome. His brow was broad and smooth. Black expressive eyebrows and a long, straight nose. Long, thick black eyelashes surrounded eyes that were so dark, only in daylight could the pupils be seen. High cheekbones, and a squarish jawline. Grooves in his cheeks and a cleft in his chin. Chiseled lips, the lower fuller. Unless his hair was touched by sunlight it looked black, but in fact had glossy, dark red highlights. And since their return, he'd lost the paleness of his ghostly pallor. His skin wasn't tanned, but naturally darker than her own.

"Beth, you're lookin' me over like a hungry wolf abou' to pounce on its prey."

A warmer blush suffused her face. "Am I?"

"Aye, you wicked womon."

She released a short sigh, then said nonchalantly, "I love you."

He blinked in surprise. "Wha' brought tha' on?"

"Can't I tell you I love you whenever I like?"

" 'Tis no' like you to just say it."

"Life is about change."

She hadn't meant to sound so cryptic, and knew from his mild frown that her behavior was perplexing him. "Lachlan, may I ask you something?"

"O' course."

"I want a straight answer, okay?"

He nodded.

"Why do you love me?"

His first reaction was astonishment, then he softly laughed and gave a shake of his head. "I canna believe you asked me tha'."

"I'm not questioning your love, really I'm not. I guess what I'm asking is, what do you think makes people fall in love?"

His eyebrows peaked comically.

"Okay," she said with a little smile. "Every time I look at you, I can't help but think how you could have any woman you want, and yet you choose to be with me."

"Beth," he moaned humorously.

"Let me finish." She took Ciarda into her arms, caressed her pink cheek for a moment, then looked into Lachlan's eyes. "I know I'm not homely, but I'm not beautiful, either. I used to be mousy, but now I'm short-tempered, and I'm certainly not knowledgeable enough to wow you with intellectual conversation. So what's the attraction, Lachlan? Why me?"

He blinked once, twice, then blew air out the side of his mouth. "You never fail to amaze me, or insult my character when I least expect it."

"I'm not fishing for compliments, or trying to insult you. I just don't understand."

"Are you fancyin' a wee crazy notion tha' I'll tire o' you?" he asked with a hint of pique.

"I've thought about the possibility."

"Ah." He repositioned Broc into his left arm, then cupped Beth's nape with his right and drew her toward him. His mouth covered hers in a slow, deep kiss. When he ended the kiss, he pressed his brow to hers for a few moments, then straightened back and somberly looked her in the eye. "Beth, I could ask the same o' you. As for me havin' any womon I want, if memory serves me, afore you, the only womon I chose dirked me in the heart." He smiled ruefully. "But I didna choose her because I loved her. I had no mind o' wha' love was abou' then. I only knew she would give me grand babies.

"Beth, I've my share o' intelligence, but you have yours as weel. It disheartens me to hear you think so little o' yourself."

"I'm sorry," she murmured.

Lachlan shook his head in amazement. "You are more'n than most men dare to dream o' havin' in their lives. You *are* beautiful. You have a timeless beauty tha' gives wings to a mon's heart. You're sensitive and carin', and have a way o' lookin' at me tha' maks my knees weaken and a lump to form in my throat.

"I once told you, lass, I wasna capable o' lovin' anyone *but* you. There's no' anither mouth in the whole o' this vast world I want to kiss, or anither body tha' I will ever long to pleasure. So in answer to your question, I love you because you are who you are. You gave life and love to an embittered *bòcain,* ghost, and hope to a mon who, to be honest, doesna deserve you. Wha' created the love atween us, God only knows, but I refuse to question its existence."

He fell silent and Beth stared at him misty-eyed. She was ashamed to have doubted him, and ashamed that she did in fact think herself unworthy of unconditional love.

"Beth," he said softly, "I promise you you'll never regret marryin' me. Were I a mon wi' a wanderin' heart and eye, would I have died a bloody virgin?"

This last wrenched a laugh from her. The twins jerked, startled, but quickly settled back into their cozy realm of sleep.

"Uncle Lannie, watch!" called Kahl.

Beth and Lachlan turned their attention to the boys. Kahl made a valiant attempt to stand on his hands, teetered, then flopped onto his back. Droplets of water sprayed up around him. Soaked to the skin, he gasped, then peals of laughter erupted from him and his brothers joined in. Beth passed Lachlan a grin, then said to the boys, "Change your clothes. It's still chilly out here."

The three ran to the gazebo, bounded up the steps, and stopped in front of their adopted aunt and uncle. His hair dripping wet, cheeks rosy and hazel eyes bright, Kahl swiped a hand under his nose, then exposed his small white teeth in an impish grin.

"I'm not cold. Can't we play some more?"

Lachlan glanced at Beth before saying to the boys, "Change into warmer clothes, laddies, then come back ou'. But you might want to try to stay drier."

"Okay," Alby beamed. He stepped closer and peered down into each of the tiny faces visible within the folds of the blankets. "They sleep a lot."

"Pretty soon," said Beth, "they'll be chasing you."

"Really?" said Kevin, wide-eyed. "When do babies start walking?"

Beth shrugged. "I think about ten months old."

"That's a long time away," Kahl said.

"Yeah," agreed Kevin. "We'll be old by then."

"Laddie," Lachlan began wryly, a twinkle in his eyes, "*I'm* old. 'Tis a fair wager you will all still be lads when the bairns start runnin' abou'. Now scat, and get ou' o' those wet clothes afore you catch cold."

A ponderous expression masked Kahl's face and he asked, "How can you catch a cold?"

"I can catch a ball," said Kevin.

"I can catch a worm," Alby giggled.

"And I can catch your bahookie wi' the sole o' my boot," said Lachlan with mock seriousness.

With a squeal, the boys dashed off in the direction of the house, Kevin in the lead and Alby trailing as they held out their arms like wings and made sounds that were suppose to be that of engines. They didn't stop until Laura came out of the house and met them a few feet from the front door. They briefly spoke to her, then disappeared inside.

"She doesna look happy," Lachlan commented, watching Laura approach the gazebo.

"I hope she's not upset because the boys got so wet."

Lachlan frowned. "No. Somethin's troublin' her."

Beth decided not to question the conviction in his tone, for she also felt a shadow of foreboding pass over her awareness. By the time Laura stepped onto the floor of the gazebo, she was briskly rubbing her arms for warmth. She sat to Beth's right and released a burst of breath, then turned her gaze on the couple with a look that bespoke of uncertainty.

"You look as if you've seen a ghost," Beth said, not thinking about her choice of words.

Laura paled. "I have. Roan thinks I'm crazy, but I know what I saw in our bedroom."

A chuff of a laugh escaped Lachlan before he realized Laura was serious. Sobering, he asked, "A wha' in your room?"

"A man," Laura said with a tremor in her tone. "Short dark hair. Glasses. A black raincoat. I swear I could see him as clearly as I see you both."

Lachlan's face darkened with a scowl. "Perhaps a reporter has gotten into the house."

"I could see *through* him!" Laura exclaimed.

Two pairs of eyes stared blankly at her.

"I know how it sounds, but it's the truth. Roan and I were in bed, about to—" She caught her breath and blushed hotly. "Well, we were in a compromising position when I caught sight of this man in the corner of my eye. He was there for a second or two while I looked straight at him. It wasn't an illusion. He *was* there."

"Oh shit," Beth murmured.

"Is it possible another spirit could have come through with you?"

"Laura, I think we would have known," said Lachlan.

"I agree. And if one had somehow managed to come through, why wait so long to appear?"

Angrily, Laura sputtered, "Do you know how unnerving it is to realize *something* has been watching you when you're naked? I'm so pissed off, I could spit! The sonofabitch seemed to be getting off watching us make love!"

"Roan didna see him?"

Laura made a gesture of futility. "No, but my hero felt the air for the bastard."

Lachlan and Beth chuckled in unison, but regretted it when Laura scowled at them scoldingly. "Look, this may strike you two in the funny bones, but I'm not amused. Beth, how would you like it if you found a stranger watching *you* during an intimate moment?" Before Beth could reply, Laura charged on, "And how would you like it, Lachlan, if a dead man were drooling over Beth?"

"I'd split my spleen," he grumbled.

"So how do we get rid of him?"

"Laura," Lachlan said on an exaggerated sigh. "I was in the business of spookin', remember?"

"How could I forget?" she retorted.

"Weel, now, how would I know how to send a spirit off?"

The green eyes stared at him with a sour accusation. "You think it's amusing, don't you?"

"Laura, be serious," Beth said.

"I am!"

"Fegs, lass, dinna put thoughts in my head or words in my mouth. I dinna know wha' you expect me to do, is all."

Laura became instantly contrite. "I'm sorry. Seeing him has me so damned rattled, I don't know what I'm saying."

" 'Tis all right," said Lachlan kindly. "Laura, soon as Deliah and Winston return, you'll have your answer. If they canna tell us how to handle this, no one can."

"You're right." Laura released a pathetic little laugh. "I guess I thought you two had an inside connection to the afterlife."

"I hope not." Beth grinned, but it vanished when she noticed Lachlan shiver. "What is it?" she asked him.

"I wish I knew. It has happened afore."

"What has?"

"The best I can explain it, 'tis like a wink o' darkness inside me."

Laura's features contorted in a grimace and she shivered. "I'm going to have nightmares."

Lachlan's dark eyes became glazed and riveted on Laura as swift images flashed through his mind, too nebulous for him to decipher. A loud hum from an unknown source filled his ears, and something akin to flames licked along the periphery of his vision. The hum moved into his throat, his chest, then spread into his fingers and toes, numbing him. Through it, he vaguely heard Beth calling his name. He forced himself to concentrate on her, using her as a lifeline to tow himself back to reality. Then again the *wink of darkness* occurred. He experienced an internal *pop,* and was released from the clutches of the spell.

"Lachlan!"

He was startled to see Laura holding Broc. The babies were crying, squirming within the confines of their blankets. He stared down at his empty arms while he tried to release the information nibbling to escape his subconscious.

"Lachlan, you're scaring me," said Beth, her tone husky with concern.

Remember . . . .

He looked up, startled at the sound of his mother's voice caressing the inside of his skull.

"Remember wha'?"

"Hey, Lachlan," said Laura, "What's wrong with you?"

"My mither," he murmured, then scowled and gave a forceful shake of his head, as if to clear his boggy mind. "She wants me to remember somethin'. Wha', I dinna know."

"Your mother's trying to contact you?"

"No, Beth." He sighed wearily. "I think a memory from the itherworld was tryin' to surface. 'Tis gone, though."

The sound of a car coming up the driveway drew their attention away from their immediate concerns. Winston's dark blue Audi parked in front of the carriage house. He climbed out of the car and opened the door for Deliah, then waved to the trio sitting in the gazebo.

Lachlan gestured for the couple to join them. The babies, now quiet, squinted into the shaded light. By the time Deliah and Winston stepped onto the planks of the gazebo, Broc and Ciarda were again sleep. Deliah, her smile as bright as the sunshine when she spied the infants, reached for Ciarda. Beth passed her into Deliah's arms, planting a kiss on the infant's brow before releasing her.

"It has turned out to be a beautiful day, hasn't it?" Winston commented.

Both Beth and Lachlan saw through his guarded front, and Lachlan asked, "Wha' did you find?"

Winston focused on Beth, whose eagerness to hear what he had uncovered was deeply etched in her face. "There isn't a death certificate for Beth on file."

A breath gushed from Beth, and Lachlan grinned with immense relief.

"But how's that possible?" asked Beth. "There was an autopsy performed on me."

"Aye," said Lachlan. "Miss Cooke showed me the report —no' tha' I understood any o' it. She said Beth died of a cerebral hemorrhage."

"There was never an autopsy done on Beth," Winston said. "Nor could I find a single legal document pertaining to her death."

Bewildered, Beth glanced at Lachlan, who met her gaze, then looked at Winston with his eyebrows scrinched down in a scowl. "Beth *was* in the coffin, and I was there when she was put in the ground."

Laura shuddered. "This conversation goes beyond weird and morbid."

"So Deliah and I paid a visit to Phineas Stratton," Winston went on, a rueful glint in his eyes. "Now there's a character straight from the imagination o' Edgar Allen Poe." He sat on the bench across from the others and braced his forearms atop his thighs.

"He be the mortician," said Deliah.

Winston nodded. "And the only one who could have supplied the coffin for Beth."

"Which he denied," Deliah said.

Beth asked, "Why?"

Winston briefly massaged the nape of his neck before replying, "At first, I thought he was tryin' to cover his tracks, wha' wi' buryin' someone withou' goin' through the proper legalities. Needless to say, he was no' only reluctant to talk to us, but resentful. Borderline belligerent. However, Stratton is a mon wi' a burdened conscience, and his mind was verra receptive to my scannin' it."

He sighed like a man too weary to go on, his gaze flitting between Lachlan and Beth before settling on Lachlan. His brow furrowed thoughtfully. He linked his fingers and absently rotated the thumbs for a time, then cleared his throat and asked Lachlan, "Where were you when Beth died?"

Stricken by the question, Lachlan paled significantly. It was a time he would give anything to forget, and it pained him now as much as it had when it had happened last July. "Earlier," he began, his voice hoarse with emotion, "Beth collapsed from one o' her headaches."

"The migraines," Winston inserted.

Lachlan nodded. "I knew she didna have long. We'd argued on the tower, and I had spent most o' my energy. When she collapsed in the hall, 'twas all I could do to carry her to her bed. When she woke up hours later, I was still unable to fully leave the grayness. She ate a sandwich, then went into the parlor, where I sensed she started to have anither attack."

Through a thin mist of tears, Lachlan painfully regarded the strain in Beth's taut features. She couldn't bring herself to meet his gaze, instead, stared down at her lap, where her hands were tightly clasped. Lachlan closed his eyes a moment, gulped back his emotions, then looked at Winston. "She was in so much pain, I didna know wha' else to do except—"

"Please don't tell that part," Beth murmured.

"All right, Beth." To Winston, he said, "Again she collapsed, and I managed to get her to her room. I dinna know how, but I knew she wouldna live till morn, so I contacted Miss Cooke."

"How?" asked Winston.

Lachlan frowned, then gave a light shrug. "I only had to call ou' to her and she always came. Her mither was the same way."

"Go on."

"Weel, she lived in a wee cottage along the loch, so it didna tak her long to come to the house. Mr. Stratton and anither man came wi' her."

"Were you present when Mr. Stratton examined Beth?"

"Winston, I couldna—" Lachlan's voice broke. Willing back the emotional knot in his throat, he shook his head. "I shut myself off. It was the first time I really understood how verra lonely was the grayess, but I desperately needed the solitude."

"Go on," Winston said again.

"I wanted to ask God to please spare her for a wee time longer, but I couldna. I didna want her sufferin' no more, so I didna pray. I didna think at all for a time until Miss Cooke summoned me and told me it was over. Mr. Stratton and his apprentice had taken Beth from the house. I was no' to worry. She would see to it Beth had a proper burial."

Lachlan frowned. Seconds later, it darkened into another scowl. "Her reaction was strange, now tha' I think abou' it," he said in a low voice, as if talking to himself.

"Strange, how?" Winston asked.

Lachlan looked hard at Winston. "I insisted Beth be buried alongside me. Miss Cooke was verra upset and tried to persuade me to reconsider. O' course I wouldna. I was in Miss Cooke's debt. She, her mither and her grandmither, had assisted me in paying the bills on the estate, and 'twas Miss Cooke who had my bones placed in a proper kist in the early nineteen-sixties. But wha' she asked was beyond any debt o' gratitude I felt I owed."

"So she respected your wishes and buried Beth alongside you at the oak," said Winston.

"Aye. Beth's spirit had never left the house. She was in

the grayness for abou' a week. I figured she needed the aloneness to prepare for her new existence."

"Understatement," Beth muttered.

Lachlan nodded in agreement, then asked Winston, "But wha' has all this to do wi' Beth's death no' bein' on record?"

Beth stiffened her spine and looked up. It was impossible not to notice Winston's reluctance to go on, and Deliah's gaze was downcast, pointedly avoiding Beth's. "I need to know what you found out," she said to Winston, her voice surprisingly calm yet forceful.

"All tha' really matters is tha' you're here, now," he said kindly, but she read torment in his eyes, and it chilled her to the marrow of her bones.

"Winston, don't sugar the truth," she demanded. "Nothing drives me crazier! Just tell me what you found out, and don't omit any of the details."

As if he couldn't hold back the information a moment longer, Winston braced himself and stated, "You didn't die o' natural causes, Beth. Viola Cooke smothered you wi' a pillow."

CHAPTER NINE

Deliah nudged Laura with a knee, but the blonde was so stunned by Winston's revelation, it was necessary for Deliah to place a hand on her shoulder and give a firmer nudge. The green eyes swung to stare at Deliah with horrified incredulity.

"It be best if ye and I tak the babes into the house," said the faerie princess.

Nodding dazedly, Laura rose to her feet. For several moments, she was at a loss as to what to do, then focused on the sleeping bundle in Lachlan's arms and held out her own. She realized he was in a state of shock, which helped her to shake off the remains of her stupor. Tenderly, she kissed him on the brow, then eased Broc from his hold. Her tear-filled eyes studied Beth for a moment. She wanted to put her arms around Beth's trembling shoulders and tell her she was there for her, but she couldn't. Instead, she smoothed a hand over the crown of Beth's head, then followed Deliah out of the gazebo and toward the house.

Winston started to get up, stopped himself, then rose to his feet and sat next to Beth. He heard himself release a thready breath. It hadn't been his intention to blurt the information. On the way back from town, he'd thought carefully about how he would tell the couple. Deliah had told him to wait, and he'd responded by telling her he didn't feel right about withholding the truth, even for a few hours.

"I would have known," said Lachlan miserably. Leaning forward, he looked at Winston as though ready to explode with grief. "Dammit, mon, I would have known if somethin' like tha' happened beneath my roof!"

"You were in the grayness, grievin'." Again Winston sighed, a sound that told of his difficulty to continue. But he knew he had to. Despite the grimness of Beth's actual death, it freed her in the present. "Stratton examined Beth and discovered she still had a pulse. Viola pretended to feel faint and asked the apprentice to make her a cup o' tea. As soon as he was out of the room, she took the spare pillow alongside Beth's head and held it over her face."

"Why?" Lachlan cried, jumping to his feet, his hands clenched at his sides.

A mantle of numbness fell over Beth as she looked into Winston's eyes. "She wanted me away from Lachlan."

"That's my guess," said Winston. "She was willing to kill Agnes and sacrifice the boys to win his love."

Lachlan's heart thundered behind his breast as he walked in a circle in the center of the gazebo. "But I brought my Beth to Baird House because I knew she was dyin'," he said, again as if talking to himself.

"You only knew she was goin' to die," Winston corrected, softening his words as best he could. "Lachlan, you couldn't know tha' bringin' her here was wha' would kill her."

"What about my headaches?" Beth asked.

"I've no doubt the migraines were excruciatin'. Beth, you were under a great deal o' stress for years, and the migraines were the result."

"They got worse after I fell down the stairs at my mother's house."

Winston nodded. "I'm sure they did, but again, I believe the stress o' your life brought them on. You came to Scotland hopin' a visit wi' Carlene would bring you peace o' mind, but shortly after you arrived, she left. You were worried about her. Right?"

Numb, Beth managed a weak nod.

"And Beth," Winston went on in a softer, more gentle tone, "at tha' time you were also keepin' the guilt o' your mother's death locked inside you. You didn't allow yourself to resent the years you had lost takin' care o' her."

Winston laid a hand on one of her slumped shoulders. "Human beings are complex machines. Guilt is one o' those emotions tha' erode our gears in such a way, there's no tellin' there's damage till it's almost too late."

"I'm as responsible as Miss Cooke for killin' her."

Beth's head shot up at Lachlan's words. Then she stood and went to him, wrapping her arms tightly about his middle and laying a cheek against his chest. "You weren't responsible. Lachlan, don't ever think that again."

Looking upward with a mute plea for strength, Lachlan wrapped his arms around her shoulders and held her against him. "Aye, I am. I as good as put tha' bloody pillow in her hands!"

Beth began to weep against him. Tears spilled down Lachlan's face, and his lips compressed into a fine, white line.

Now Winston stood, his face pale and taut, his eyes dulled by the helplessness he felt. He was restless, antsy. To still his hands, he slipped them into the pockets of his black trench coat. He wanted to return to the house and put off the rest of what he knew, but a little voice in his head told him to be done with the matter. At the moment, he longed to be in the security of Deliah's arms, in one of their beds, away from the troubles of Baird House and the rest of the world.

He watched the couple cling to one another. Unwittingly, he tapped into their roiling emotions and found himself sinking deeper into a morass of desolation. Of the two, Lachlan was the most stricken. Beth's concern was more for him, her fate at Viola Cooke's hand a far lesser evil than Lachlan's guilt at misjudging the eventual cause of her death.

They were a remarkable pair, Winston told himself. He couldn't imagine them not being together, any more than he could imagine a future without Deliah.

He drew in a deep fortifying breath, and said, "Stratton and Cooke were third cousins. She threatened to implicate him in the murder if he told anyone. He's a bit o' a mouse, this Stratton, and we all now know how aggressive was the prim Miss Cooke. Anyway, he went along wi' her scheme to bury the body—sorry, Beth," he added with an apologetic yet wan grin when she turned her watery eyes on him. "It isn't easy talkin' abou' this."

A hint of a smile appeared on her mouth. "I know, Winston. Viola was a cunning, warped woman." She peered into Lachlan's face. "But I guess I can understand her obsession. Lachlan, she was determined to have you."

She stood on tiptoe and kissed him tentatively on the lips, then brushed her brow against his chin. "You're not responsible for her madness. You brought me here because you loved me." She smiled in earnest as she met his teary gaze. "Had I not come here, I wouldn't have met you and we wouldn't have the twins. I was a miserable, lonely woman in the States. If I don't regret what brought me to this point in my life, you sure as hell better not."

"My Beth," he choked. He snuggled her tighter within the powerful bands of his arms and nestled a cheek against the top of her head. "I dinna deserve you."

"I know." She sighed, then released what sounded like a chuckle.

"The good news is," said Winston, hoping his cheery tone would help to lift their spirits, "Beth's trust fund and home should be intact." The couple's eyes turned to him. Beth was elated. Winston could hear her mind churning with possibilities. But although Lachlan put on an admirable front, his apprehension about leaving Scotland wafted off him in waves Winston easily absorbed.

"Lachlan," Beth said excitedly, "we could go to my home in the States until all this nonsense with the press calms down."

A strained smile ticked along his mouth as he nodded. "Aye. 'Twould probably be best."

Beth's face clouded thoughtfully and she turned to Winston. "He doesn't have any identification, though."

"It's in the works."

"How? He'll need a passport."

"I purchased a camera this mornin' to take his photograph. I also called a man I know in Ayr. He worked for the Shields Agency, but was forced to retire five years ago. One of his many talents is an ability to create worldwide legal documentation. He's done quite a bit o' work wi' the Witness Protection Program in the States, in relocating persons ou' o' tha' country. When I told him abou' your predicament—"

"The truth o' it?" Lachlan gasped.

Winston grinned. "He's an ardent fan o' yours. He was in the hospital for a week last Christmas and was unable to attend your . . ." He made quotation marks in the air. ". . . 'miracle' Christmas, but he has toured your home whenever possible over the years. He said you once complimented him on his mustache."

A knowing grin appeared on Lachlan's face. "Is this mon short and round, wi' white hair?"

"That's him."

Lachlan laughed, then said to Beth, "Fegs, lass, the ends o' this mon's mustache went past his collar bones, no' a hair ou' o' place. I dinna usually speak to the people on the tours, just mostly moaned a wee and flitted in and ou' o' sight to give them a thrill. But when I saw this mon, I had to inquire abou' tha' masterpiece on his face." He flashed Winston a broader grin. "Does he still have it?"

Nodding, Winston said, "It's his pride and joy."

"And he's willin' to help me?"

"Said he was thrilled to help. He's in Dublin, but has to be in Edinburgh tomorrow for another client. We've arranged to meet in the mornin'. I plan to take Deliah along." He grinned. "On a shoppin' spree. Tha' should prove interestin'."

"Aye. So this mon . . . he can really produce the documents tha' quickly?"

Winston bobbed his head in admiration of James Grayson, then glanced at his watch. "Which reminds me, I'd better get on the move. I want to leave for Edinburgh in abou' an hour. Lachlan, do you have the gems you want me to have appraised?"

"They're in a pouch in my room."

Again, Winston checked his watch. "I'll have to take several Polaroids of you, Lachlan, which means you'll have to borrow two or three shirts from Roan."

"What's wrong wi' my own?"

Winston grinned dubiously. "You need to look like a twentieth century mon."

Releasing a woeful sigh, Lachlan nodded with blatant reluctance. "I'll do wha'ever I must."

"Chin up," Beth laughed, and kissed the cleft in that area. Then she looked at Winston and asked, "Is Deliah excited about going to Edinburgh?"

"She's nervous, but I think she'll have fun. Oh, and Lachlan, Reith—"

"Fegs! I forgot to thank you for takin' his breakfast to him this morn."

"No problem. We had a nice chat."

Lachlan grimaced. "Do you still no' trust him?"

With mocking affront, Winston placed a hand over his heart. "Far be it for me to doubt your instincts. He is a likable lad. Almost too polite." He shrugged. "I just wanted you to know the money you gave him was well spent. He opted to purchase clothin' at the secondhand store in town."

"Why secondhand?" Lachlan asked.

"Because, and I quote, 'I prefer the texture o' tried cloth.' Unquote."

"That's cute . . . 'tried cloth'," said Beth. "Actually, I like pre-worn clothes, too. Especially jeans."

"In my day—"

Beth placed a forefinger against Lachlan's lips, silencing him. "I have so much to teach you," she sighed airily, her eyes sparkling with mischief. "And you have *so* much to learn."

Lachlan winced. "One day at a time, lass."

Walking to Lachlan's side, Winston clapped him on the back. "Ready to smile for the camera?"

Lachlan wilted with resignation. "Aye, but as a good friend is fond o' sayin', damn me."

For the next hour it was a scramble to get everything ready for Winston and Deliah's departure. Begrudgingly, Lachlan suffered through four shirt changes and listening to the boys howl with laughter at his attempts to pose with a semblance of dignity for the camera. Beth and Laura found a calf-length skirt of navy blue and a beige sweater smaller than the others for Deliah to wear. Footwear wasn't so easy. In the end, she donned three pairs of thick socks to keep Laura's boots from flopping on her feet.

Everyone made up a short list of what they would like Winston to bring back from the city. Finally, the Audi pulled out of the driveway and out of sight.

"That was almost exhausting," Laura commented as she closed the inner door.

"Can we go out and play?" asked Kahl. He and his brothers were still wound up, their energy level at critical mass.

"Stay in the south yard," Laura said, issuing them a look that warned they had better obey this time. "If I see any of you—"

A bloodcurdling scream rent the air. Everyone in the hall stood frozen with shock until, a moment later, a higher pitched scream followed.

"Taryn!" Lachlan gasped, and was the first to run for

the stairs. He burst into Taryn's bedroom, the other adults and the boys at his heels.

Another scream ejected from the young woman's throat, but it was not the ear-piercing sound that was responsible for the men and boys' paralysis. It was Taryn, herself. She stood atop her pillows at the head of the bed, her eyes wide with horror and gaping at nothingness at the foot of the bed. Her exercised-firmed body was clad in a red satin cami that barely covered her large breasts, and a red satin thong that only just covered her pubic hairs. Unbound, her light brown hair fell nearly to her waist in soft waves, benefit of the plait she'd worn for the past two days.

"H-he was here!" she squealed, her eyes darting from the group back to the foot of the bed. "The sicko was leering at me!"

Her male audience didn't respond to her outburst. They were entranced by her lack of clothing, and her sculptured build. She normally wore clothes that concealed her figure. Gymnastics and weightlifting were her spare time activities, and she worked out mornings and nights to keep in shape. She thought her one flaw was her chest, which was far too large in her opinion. Her waist was nineteen inches, though, her rounded hips lean, and her legs and arms muscular.

"Lachlan!" Beth snapped, forcing his gaping mouth to close by putting the heel of a hand beneath his chin and giving it a shove upward. His teeth clacked as his glazed eyes swung to stare at her as if he didn't recognize who she was.

Her face flushed with anger, Beth pinched his right cheek and smirked with satisfaction when he swore in Gaelic. "Pull your eyeballs back in your head," she warned, and his face turned crimson with realization. To avoid looking at Taryn again, he turned his back to her.

Roan jerked from his stupor and hastily said to the boys, "Ou'! You wanted to go ou' and play—*go!*"

"What a babe!" Kevin gushed, his eyes wide with appreciation for the vision atop the bed. "I want to stay and keep her company."

"Ou'!" Roan fumed, an outstretched arm pointing to the door.

On the way out of the room, Kahl winked at Taryn, then grumbled, "We never get to have any fun."

Alby just quietly left, a bit dazed by all the hoopla. No sooner was he in the hall than Roan closed the door and returned to stand alongside Laura, whose arms were folded against her middle, a look of disapproval riveted on his sister.

"For the love o' God, Taryn," Roan muttered heatedly, "cover yourself."

Taryn's face was ashen, her eyes still wide and glassy with fear. After a moment she glanced down at herself, then cast the remaining group an indignant glare. "Get a life! I wake up to find a freakin' ghost drooling at my bedside, and you're all worried about my state of dress?"

"I think that red satin has gone to your brain," Beth said testily.

"You saw him?" Laura asked Taryn. "Glasses, short hair—"

"Black raincoat," Taryn completed, then jumped down from the bed and stood in front of the blonde. She ignored Lachlan when he turned, glanced at her, and grunted before placing his back to her again. "So you saw him, too?"

Nodding, Laura stated, "I saw him from the corner of my eye when Roan and I were—" She cut herself off and cleared her throat. "Let's just say his timing was lousy."

"Bloody lousy," Roan grumbled. Stepping to the bed, he pulled off the top quilt and draped it over his sister's shoulder. She shucked it off, glaring at him to back off.

"Is she decent yet?" Lachlan asked.

"I'm always decent!" Taryn barked.

Dryly, Beth countered, "That's debatable. Please, put on a robe. At Lachlan's age, I don't know if his heart can take another shock." She roughly patted him on the shoulder and added, "Right, Lannie *old* boy?"

"Aye," he said, in a tone that said he didn't dare contradict her. "But I have a few questions."

"She can hear just fine," Beth fumed.

He sighed, "All right."

"Dammit," Taryn ground out. She flipped open one of the suitcases and removed a short red satin robe. "Satisfied?" she asked Beth with hostility.

Before she could respond, Lachlan turned. His eyebrows peaked and a lopsided grin twitched at one corner of his mouth. Beth looked askance at him, but decided his obvious appreciation of Taryn's build wasn't worth another comment. She turned her attention to Laura, who was frowning.

"This man—"

"Beth, he wasn't a *man!*" Laura interjected. "He was translucent."

"I could see the fireplace through him," Taryn said.

Lachlan and Beth exchanged a look of concern, which Laura misread as skepticism. "Beth, why would I make up seeing a ghost?"

Beth started to speak, faltered, then forced the words out. "How could there be another ghost here? Are you sure you didn't recognize him?"

"No! I've never seen him before!"

"Taryn, what about you?" asked Beth.

She stared peevishly at Beth for a time, then shook her head. "No. Look, I was wide awake and just lying there. Thinking. You know. Debating whether to get up or not. I closed my eyes for maybe a minute or two. When I opened them, he was standing at the side of the bed, *literally* leering down at me."

Lachlan glanced at Roan, who shrugged noncommittally.

"Where exactly was he standin'?" Lachlan asked Taryn.

She pointed to the right side of the bed. "He was there, but then he moved to the foot of the bed. I-I thought I was hallucinating, at first. Then he-ah . . . well, he jumped on the mattress and . . . and then had the nerve to open his arms to me. He stood right there on the foot of the bed, gesturing for me to come closer. All I wanted to do was smack that hideously smirking grin off his face!" She shivered and drew in her shoulders. "I didn't start screaming until he started toward me. Like hell was I going to let a *dead* pervert touch me!"

Lachlan walked along the foot of the bed, then stood where she had first pointed. After a moment, he said to the others, "Someone *was* here."

"No shit, Maynard!" Taryn spat.

"Taryn!"

"Shut up, Roan!" Taryn sucked in a ragged breath, her face nearly the color of her robe. "The last thing I need from you is another lecture."

Roan, his own face mottled with anger, took a step toward his sister. "You're no' too big to put across my knee!"

"Hold it!" Beth boomed. She looked at Roan with dark impatience. "I'm not a big fan of your sister—"

"I love you, too."

Ignoring Taryn's sarcasm, Beth went on, "—but she has every right to be upset. We should be focusing on how this spirit came to be here, and nothing else."

Roan gestured his frustration and released a sigh of resignation. "Fine."

"Stephan Miles," Lachlan said in a monotone. He stared off into space, his expression oddly rapt.

"I've heard that name," Beth murmured. At first, she couldn't remember when or where. Then her expression brightened and she snapped her fingers in the air. "He was the guy who came here last July. Remember, Lachlan? He said he was interested in buying the estate."

A mild frown settled on Lachlan's face.

"You did something to him," Beth said. "Remember? He had green mist coming out of his ears."

"I remember now." Lachlan bobbed his head as he

played the memory through his mind. "A persistent mon. You asked him to leave, and he wouldna budge."

"Green mist?" Roan grimaced.

"Tha' and a wee green slime in his gullet," Lachlan chuckled.

"You mean this guy has died, and his spirit decided to come here?" Laura asked, appalled by the idea.

Lachlan and Beth's gazes locked, while Roan released a scoffing laugh.

"Oh, come on. If everyone who'd ever set foot on this property died and their spirits came here, the livin' would have to move ou' to mak room. Besides, Borgie died shortly efter his fall here, remember. His spirit crossed over."

"Maybe because he was terrified of Lachlan," said Beth.

Roan considered her statement, then nodded reluctantly in agreement.

"Oh, God," Laura groaned, putting a hand to her brow. "I have this terrible image of Baird House becoming *Hotel Layover*. Forget the afterlife. We have the perfect room for you!"

"Well, guess what, guys?" Taryn said in a flippant, singsong tone. "I'm outta here first thing in the morning."

"No' sooner?"

Roan's hateful remark stunned both Laura and Beth, but Taryn merely looked at him with cool hauteur. "It's too late for me to drive to London, or I would be outta here within the hour. Now, if you all wouldn't mind, I'd like to get dressed." She shifted a coy look to Lachlan and said in a sultry tone, "You can stay and watch if you like."

With a grunt of disgust, Roan led Laura from the room. Lachlan looked wide-eyed at Beth and gave a shrug that as much said, "I havena said or done anythin' tha' would give her the idea I would even consider it!"

Beth gestured for him to come around the bed and join her. He passed the amber-eyed woman a harried glance as he walked around the foot of the bed. When he was at Beth's side she calmly said to Taryn, "The boys are more mature than you are."

Smug satisfaction and the hardened gleam in her eyes detracted from Taryn's lovely features. "You really should learn to curb your jealousy. In my experience, men like Lachlan don't appreciate the proverbial leash."

"Taryn," Lachan warned in a low growl.

"I don't think it's so much jealousy, " said Beth. "Your behavior is insulting, Taryn. Not only to your victims, but to yourself. Roan is one of the finest men I have ever known. It's really hard for me to believe you're his sister."

A caustic laugh burst from Taryn, while Beth grew more somber.

"I would have given anything to have had a sibling, which is why it's so sad this animosity exists between you and your brother." Beth linked an arm through one of Lachlan's and dipped her head to the side until it rested against the curvature of his shoulder. "Do yourself a favor, Taryn, and try to mend the rift before you leave."

Taryn's nostrils flared. "Beth, drop dead. Again."

A disparaging sound rattled in Lachlan's throat. Before he could say anything, Beth said lightly to Taryn, "At least you're a consistent pain in the ass."

Although the ghost wasn't seen again the rest of the day, Taryn's presence had everyone but the boys on edge. She griped about the steaks and tattie scones Roan had cooked for dinner, and griped about the fact there was no deck of cards or television in the house. Her penchant to provoke tempers during even the most innocent of conversations wore on the adult's nerves, and their crankiness made the boys willing to go to bed on time, without the usual argument.

Roan and Laura were the first to say they were retiring for the night. Taryn cocked a challenging eyebrow at Beth and Lachlan, daring them to desert her as well. Beth, too tired to care what the woman thought, told Lachlan she was going to feed and change the babies, then go to bed.

"I need to bring Reith his supper," said Lachlan, rising to his feet. "I'll be up in a bit."

Beth cast Taryn a sour look, then kissed Lachlan on the mouth before heading out of the parlor.

As soon as she was out of sight Taryn crossed one leg over the other and quipped with equal sourness, "She's so charming."

"Haud yer wheesht!"

She batted her heavily mascaraed lashes at him and twisted her mouth in a mocking grin. "Did you just swear at me?"

"I told you to hold your noise—or shut up, whichever you best understand."

"You're going to miss me when I'm gone."

A strangled laugh escaped him. "Miss Ingliss, when I say I'm lookin' forward to seein' your backside, I dinna mean 'tis because I fancy it."

Her features clouded with pique. "Not one of you even tried to get to know me, especially that egocentric brother of mine."

Lachlan sadly shook his head "I know there's more to you than you let people see."

She laughed bitterly. "Okay, tell me what."

"Reith—"

"He can wait," she clipped, rising to her feet from the settee and positioning herself close to him. "I want to know what you really think of me. We're alone. You can be honest."

"Can you tak the truth o' it?" he asked calmly.

She smiled coyly, inched closer, and fingered the front of his shirt. Her gaze lingered on his mouth, then lifted to peer at him through her lashes. "I can take anything you're willing to give."

Lachlan's gaze never left her eyes. "I see you as a womon wi' no respect for life, and no dreams beyond gettin' through each day."

She stiffened.

"You want a mon who can master you."

"That's bull!"

"Master you and mak you desire more'n just succeedin' in a career."

She stormed back to the settee and plopped onto it. "You'll never make it as a fortune teller."

He turned and stared down at her, his expression bland, his emotions at bay. "You envy Laura and Beth."

"Get a grip," she grumbled.

"You dinna understand wha' they have."

"Oh, are we talking about love, now?" She jumped to her feet and jabbed an isolated finger in his middle. "Love is crap, Lachlan. For men it's lust, and for women . . . oh, hell, who knows. I don't envy anyone! I'm a damn good photographer, a better than damn good writer, and *damn* good at getting my stories!"

"Wha' abou' the womon, Taryn?" he asked softly.

"What about her?" She put her hands on her hips. "Did you see anything in my room that wasn't appealing?"

"There's more to a person than the packagin'."

She laughed. "But isn't that what first attracts notice?"

Lachlan jerked back as an impression slammed his awareness.

"What? Did I offend your sensibilities?" she asked sarcastically.

"Where are you plannin' to go when you leave here?" he asked, his face darkening with a scowl.

"Home," she lied smoothly.

Lachlan's dark, riveting eyes bored into hers. "Dinna go."

"Home?"

" 'Tis no' home you're headed."

"Oh? Then where?"

"Heed this warnin', Taryn," he said huskily. "There's a mon waitin' for you at the end o' your destination. Dinna provoke him."

Taryn shivered as an inexplicable chill pierced her spine. "It's what I do best."

Lachlan backed away two paces and shook his head. "He'll no' understand your ways."

"You're cute, but crazy," she muttered.

"Go back to the States, lass. Whatever you're efter, 'tis no' worth the price you'll pay."

"My heart?" she laughed. "Is that the price you're talking about? Well, my big-shouldered friend, I don't have one. At least, that seems to be the consensus around here."

He stared at her a moment longer as he tried to lock onto what the *knowing* was attempting to formulate in his mind. When no more information came to him, he gave a departing gesture with a hand and headed for the dining room.

Taryn watched him disappear into the next room. Anger simmered in her heart of hearts. Anger and a measure of sorrow.

To say she had somehow developed a crush on the laird was a gross understatement. She couldn't remember ever being so attracted to anyone. From the instant they had made eye contact across the crowd two nights prior, every time she saw him she had felt a sickening jab to the pit of her stomach. It was both mind-reeling and frustrating. And frightening. With a glance he made her feel vulnerable. With a glance he stirred her blood. She'd lain awake half the night fantasizing about him, which had only worsened her frustration to maddening ambivalence. She wanted his approval, but she couldn't give up the story she was after. It was so much easier to invade people's privacy when they were but a name, and not someone she personally knew or wanted to know. Before the ghost had scared the wits out of her, she'd already decided she had to get away from Baird House. Away from Lachlan. It was one thing to be criticized for her bitchiness and her actions, another to be ridiculed for matters of the heart. She wasn't as arrogant or as confident as they all believed.

Lachlan belonged to Beth.

The pathetic irony of it all was, for the first time in her life, Taryn Ingliss had fallen in love. Damnably in love and it hurt like hell to know there was nothing she could do about it. Her sarcasm and flippancy were ways to shield her true feelings for him. Miss Goody Two Shoes Beth would have a coronary if she suspected.

Taryn was given a jolt of surprise when she realized Roan was standing a few feet away, watching her. Again, her instinctive verbal defense rose to the fore before she could suppress it. "Missed me, huh?"

"Where's Lannie?" he asked curtly.

Beth's words came back to haunt her. If she thought for one moment the rift between herself and Roan could be closed with a heartfelt apology for her behavior, she would give it. But of course it wasn't that simple. Nothing in life was ever that simple, and she wasn't in the mood to endure another lecture about her character failings. It was easier to let Roan believe she cared for no one but herself. He would only mock her if she told him how much she'd missed him over the years, and that her bitter letters had been her way of trying to provoke him into visiting the States. Of course, he hadn't responded to those childish tactics. Neither would she, if she were in his shoes. And despite his dislike of her, they were very much alike, only Roan had found people to care for, and people to care for him. People he trusted. People he considered his family. So, instead of asking him if they could have a serious talk, a brother and sister bonding—or at least come to some kind of understanding—she pointed in the direction of the dining room. He left with barely a nod to her and, when he, too, was gone from sight, she felt as if her insides had shriveled.

"See you in the morning," she murmured, then went into the hall.

At the second floor landing, she realized she was developing a headache. She entered her room and closed the door, then massaged her temples with growing impatience as she walked toward the bed.

"Tomorrow morning can't come soon enough."

Something struck the back of her head with such force

that lights burst in front of her eyes as she pitched forward. She struck the edge of the mattress, bounced off and hit the floor, oblivious to the man whose fist remained in the air where her head had been a moment ago.

CHAPTER TEN

A brief vibrating movement lifted Deliah through layers of sleep. Her eyelids fluttered open. Her mind disoriented from exhaustion, she peered into semi-darkness and wondered where she was and why the mattress beneath her felt so strange. As seconds ticked by, her recall gradually came into focus, mostly due to the odors lingering in the room. They had been unfamiliar scents—man-made florals—prior to her entering their hotel room. The bathroom reeked of disinfectants and she'd had trouble keeping her stomach calmed until she'd gotten used to the nasal invasion. She did like the fragrance of the soap and shampoo the hotel provided.

She lay on her side with her head pillowed by the hollow in Winston's left shoulder. The mattress beneath them was harder than the one they had at the estate, and it had taken her some time to settle into a comfortable position and fall asleep.

What a day it had been.

The sometimes blur of scenery and the jarring motion of the car on rougher areas of the road had made her a little anxious during the half hour drive to Ayr, where they stopped to refuel and eat in a small diner. Winston ordered hamburgers with lettuce, tomatoes, and cucumbers, and a large side platter of deep fried chips. Not only had she eaten her food to the last crumb, but she had helped him to polish off his.

The less than two hour drive to Edinburgh proved less stressful for her. Rolling hills of green and meandering roads held her interest and made the time pass quickly. When they reached the outskirts of the city, though, she was ravenous again. They ate in the hotel where Winston had booked their room from a pay phone in Crossmichael. Then they toured the city, took care of Winston's business with the gemologist, and shopped until Deliah laughingly pleaded to go to their room. Amidst the packages containing her new wardrobe, they ordered room service and ate their fill. They made love on the bed and, later, in the shower. No sooner had his damp head hit the pillow, Winston fell asleep, while she sat staring at his face, falling deeper in love with him with every minute that passed.

Deliah snuggled closer to his warmth. Hunger pains nipped at her stomach, but she was too tired to do anything about it. She closed her eyes and laid her hand atop his bare abdomen. It was then she realized his skin was feverish, clammy, and that what she'd thought a vibration was in fact his shuddering and twisting.

He moaned, a piteous sound. Reaching for the light switch on the nightstand lamp, she engaged it and sat up. It took a moment for her eyes to adjust to the brightness.

Winston lay on his back, his arms and legs rigidly angled out from his sides. The sheet, which was the only cover they were using, covered his legs and lower hips. His exposed skin was shiny with perspiration. He twitched again and again, and his eyes moved spastically behind the closed lids. His features were taut, as if he were caught up in a nightmare from which he couldn't escape.

She didn't need to touch him to feel the hammering of his heart.

"Winston," she said, shaking him.

He remained locked in his realm of sleep.

"Winston, ye be frightenin' me!"

Still, he didn't respond.

Deliah pushed out with her mind until she was able to enter his thoughts. Images flashed across his mindscreen. Two consecutively blinked in and out so rapidly that she couldn't formulate a clear picture of what he was seeing. What was readily available was the terror he was experiencing. Its cold, shadowy tentacles reached out from his body and sinuously wrapped around her tighter and tighter. When she could no longer bear her own magnifying terror, she broke the link and climbed off the bed.

She padded into the bathroom, to the sink. Her hand trembled as she filled a glass with cold water. She was lightheaded and queasy, but more worried about Winston than fainting again. Returning to the bed, she threw the water into his face. It should have rescued him from the nightmare's clutches, but he only shuddered and twitched. Shuddered and twitched.

His breathing became louder, faster, and hoarse. Deliah made a graceful swirl of her right hand, then blew from the palm the golden dust her skin had produced. It should have gently awakened him, but instead the glittering particle turned black before touching his skin. Breathless with dread, she willed herself to view his aura. It was black, lifeless, and reeked of death and decay.

Kneeling on the bed and gripping him by the shoulders, she shook him until her arms ached and her heart had risen into her throat. Then, not knowing what else to do, she struck him hard in the face. The sound of flesh hitting flesh sickened her. She dashed into the bathroom and knelt in front of the toilet.

Winston awakened to the sounds of her retching. Groggily, he swung his legs off the mattress and got to his feet. Dizziness gave him a moment's pause. He blew air out the side of his mouth and stretched the kinks in his legs and the small of his back. By the time he reached her side the spasms had waned and she sat dazedly on the floor, looking up at him as if he was solely responsible for her condition.

He crouched and tenderly cupped her chin. "Can I get you anythin'?"

"An explanation, if ye please."

A wry grin masked his face. "O' wha'?"

"When did ye start influxin' again, Winston?" She wiped the back of a hand across her mouth, then released a shuddering sigh. "I thought ye had learned to shut off your mind from extraneous brainwaves."

Winston touched her brow. "You don't have a fever," he said humorously.

"Neither do ye . . . *now.*"

"Meanin' wha'?"

She heaved a sigh of impatience and cocked her head to one side. "Meanin' you were twitchin' like a fly caught on a spider's web. Winston, wha' be the nightmare wha' had ye so fiercely in its hold?"

A denial that he'd had one at all was about to spring past his lips when the two images Deliah had seen returned. He shot to his feet, oblivious that she also rose to hers. At first the images came and went too swiftly for him to grasp, but then they slowed, little by little, and he strained to understand their meaning and more closely focus on the features.

It was the burglar's face behind the ski mask he kept seeing over and over again. Alternately, the black knitted piece changed. Sometimes the man's mouth was visible, other times it wasn't. Sometimes the man's pale eyes were fearful, and other times so evil in their deadness that his gut muscles clenched.

"Winston?"

He lifted a hand to silence her. Flick in, flick out. Mouth visible, mouth not. In and out, slower and slower and slower until finally the two faces were side by side on his mindscreen, and the reality of what had been trying to fully escape his subconscious slammed to the fore of his brain.

His legs buckled beneath him and he sat hard on the white tiled floor. The small bathroom went into a tailspin. From far away he heard Deliah calling to him, and he forced himself to concentrate on her in order to find his way back to reality.

Coldness pressed to his face and helped to revive him. Once Deliah lowered the dripping wet face cloth, he braced his back against the tub base and nodded that he was all right.

"Can I fetch ye anythin'?" she asked.

"We have to get back to Baird House."

"Now?

He nodded, then heaved in ragged breath. "He's there. The Phantom. God Almighty, he's been there all along."

" 'Tis no' possible."

"Deliah," he said weakly, "he is. The mon who attacked Alby, and then me wi' the knife, his ski mask didn't cover his eyes or mouth, and his eyes were almost colorless.

"The mon who broke into the house the same night wore similar dark clothes, but his mask covered his mouth, and his eyes were light blue, but definitely blue. And he was right handed, no' left like the Phantom."

"But I would *know* if this mon be in the house!"

A choked sound rattled in Winston's throat. "I've finally figured ou' how he's managed to elude us all these years. He's psychic, Deliah, and a telepath. That's why."

Deliah's expression turned to one of stark bleakness. "So he be blockin' our reception o' him?"

"And manipulatin' us. Deliah, he's after Laura and Beth, and there's no telephone at Baird House to warn them."

Lachlan looked up and smiled from the island counter in the kitchen. "Dinna tell me you're hungry again?" he asked teasingly, and placed the tenderized steak into the frying pan he had heating on the stove.

"No," said Roan. "I remembered I hadn't fixed anythin' for Reith."

"It willna tak me long."

Roan nodded, then grinned pensively. "I was checkin' on the laddies, and Kahl asked me why I talk more like you now."

Looking up from the stove, Lachlan asked, "Do you?"

"It seems so."

Lachlan placed two large potatoes in the oven to reheat, then faced Roan. "You sound normal to me."

"Accordin' to young Master Kahl, I've 'fallen into the Scottish lingo.' Then I remembered you tellin' me some months ago tha' I talked more like an Englishman. Remember?"

After a moment, Lachlan nodded. "Aye, I do, now. 'Tis true. You barely use 'can't' and 'don't' no more."

"You were raised speakin' Gaelic, though. Right?"

"Aye, but many a lowland Scot worked for my faither. When I moved here, I adapted to their language." Lachlan flipped the steak over and deeply inhaled the aroma before adding, "No' many Lowlanders speak Gaelic. 'Tis a pity, for sure, for Gaelic comes from the heart."

"Maybe I'll get around to learnin' it one o' these days."

Lachlan's eyes held an internal light of amusement as he regarded his friend. "You should. Efter all, mon, you have a Highlander's blood in your veins."

Several seconds passed in silence. Lachlan was aware that Roan was a little unsettled by his remark. He hadn't said it to belittle Robert. Robert Ingliss Baird was no more responsible for his parentage than was Lachlan.

Roan sighed, then asked, "Now tha' Robbie's fragmented soul has passed over, does it mean you and me . . . weel, tha' half brither business no longer exists, does it?"

"Did you fancy the idea?"

Roan glanced downward for a moment. "Actually, I think I did. Itherwise, I'll have to think o' you as a verra distant uncle."

Lachlan laughed, then faked a shudder. "How many greats would tha' mak me?"

"Too bloody many to count."

Lachlan nodded. He turned off the gas burner beneath the steak, then reached for the paring knife in the oak rack on the island counter. Walking up to Roan, he jabbed the point into his right palm, just enough to draw a bead of blood. Roan was hesitant at first. He stared at Lachlan's palm for a time, frowning, then finally held out his own. He winced when the knife point pricked his skin, then Lachlan clasped his palm against the inside of Roan's right wrist. Roan did likewise, and experienced an inexplicable warmth building up inside his chest. The men stood with their hands and gazes locked.

"We're brithers," said Lachlan, his voice husky with emotion. "There is no' anither mon in all the world I trust more'n you. So from this day forward, our blood to one anither's wrists, I claim you as my brither and my only livin' clansmon."

Roan lowered his head in a bid to hold back the tears pressing behind his eyes. He felt as though he had just been bestowed the greatest honor of his life, and he was too choked up to speak right away. When he did, his tone was soft with reverence. "And I claim you as mine." He looked into Lachlan's eyes and smiled a bit tremulously. "You're too generous wi' your heart . . . *old mon.*"

With a laugh, Lachlan embraced Roan, clapping him soundly on the back. "Are we a pair o' sentimental fools, or wha'?"

"Brithers."

They separated and stared at each other, both lost to the emotional moment, both straight-backed with pride.

"I had best feed Reith afore he thinks I've forgotten him."

"I'm sure Laura is wonderin' where I am." Roan turned to the door, but paused to regard Lachlan. "Lannie, are you really thinkin' o' movin' to the States?"

Lachlan nodded. Although he thought he was careful to guard his apprehension, Roan seemed to sense it.

"This will always be your home," said Roan softly.

"I know. But you see, I *can* leave, because my brither will be here, raisin' his family and carin' for these old walls wi' the same devotion I have all these years."

Swallowing hard, Roan nodded. "Aye, tha' goes withou' sayin'."

"Dinna dwell on what's to come. Fegs, Roan, you'll have your hands full, wha' wi' Laura and the boys, and openin' this place to the public. You willna have time to miss me."

A strangled laugh escaped Roan, and the tears in his eyes made them glimmer. "Wha' will I do withou'' your sage advice?"

"Probably stay ou' o' trouble."

Roan smiled, nodded, then opened the door to the dining room. "Good night *old* mon."

"Good night, you Ingliss swine."

It amazed Roan that what once had been grievous insults between them had somehow become endearments. As he crossed the dining room toward the hall he flashed back to the verbal battle he and Lachlan had shared during those first stormy days of their acquaintance. Back then, if anyone had predicted that he and the ghost would eventually become friends, he would have had them measured for a straitjacket and a padded room. And now they were more than friends. Blood brothers. Brothers by *choice,* which to him was more meaningful than if genetics had thrown them together.

"In a way, genetics did," he murmured humorously as he started up the staircase.

He was on the fourth step when a sound gave him pause. Frowning, he listened intently, and when he heard the rap again he descended and went to the cellar door at the side of the stairs. More than a minute passed while he kept an ear to the wood. The sound didn't come again, but his curiosity wouldn't let him walk away. He thought about Laura and Taryn's ghost. Was the unwelcome visitor in the cellar, or was he so tired he was hearing things now?

Opening the door, he peered into the bottomless darkness. A twinge of apprehension pricked at his awareness. "Hello?"

No response. Still, he couldn't shake the notion something wasn't quite right. Gooseflesh rose on his arms, and the hairs at the back of his neck squirmed against his sensitized skin. He considered fetching Lachlan, but then told himself he was overreacting. So what if he encountered a ghost? It wouldn't be the first, but he preferred to believe only the living now remained within the walls of Baird House.

His spine stiffened when he detected what sounded like something dragging across cement. The sound was so soft that he nearly convinced himself it was his imagination playing tricks on him, but he had to know for sure. Taking a candle from the bar and lighting it as he returned to the door, he held it out and squinted into the shadows below. A grimace twitched on his face. What if this ghost were endowed with Lachlan's previous abilities? Could he be faced with a physical confrontation?

"Damn me," he grumbled, and took the first step before his courage deserted him. By the time he reached the cellar floor he was mentally berating his imagination. He stepped away from the stairs and held out the candle. Although the meager light left little for him to view from his standpoint, he convinced himself he would find nothing to warrant a further search. Laura would be anxious by now. He'd only told her he was going to make sure the boys were still in bed.

He chuffed a scoffing laugh and turned toward the staircase, then froze in shock when a grotesque visage materialized within the golden glow of the flickering candle flame. Pale eyes devoid of life stared at him. Blistered cheeks puffed up and then the pursed lips expelled air. The flame extinguished. Plunged into darkness, Roan snapped from his stupor, but too late. Two swift successions of impacts staggered him, one just below the right collarbone, another in his right shoulder. Excruciating pain turned out the light in his mind. Internal darkness yanked him into its clutches, and he collapsed to the floor.

Unaware that Roan lay bleeding in the cellar, Lachlan ambled in the direction of the carriage house with Reith's meal on a tray. He'd left by the kitchen door, deciding to take advantage of the fresh air instead of taking the shorter route via the front doors. The night was cool, but the indigo awning above him was speckled with countless resplendent stars, some seeming so close that he was tempted to reach up to see if he could touch one.

He looked above him again as he stopped by the new oak, and saw a shooting star in the southern sky. Wonder gladdened his heart, and he thought about Winston and Deliah, and hoped they were enjoying their stay in Edinburgh. He wouldn't mind seeing the city again before he left Scotland. Especially visit Edinburgh Castle, which majestically crowned the core of an extinct volcano. He'd stopped to ogle it on his move to Crossmichael, and had planned to one day tour its interior. That hadn't happened prior to his death, and now the possibility of seeing it with Beth made it all the more exciting.

Reith wasn't in the lower part of the carriage house when he arrived. Thinking he might be asleep in the loft, he called out his name, but got no response. He placed the tray on the cot and the coffeepot on the floor. The wood stove was cold. No lanterns were lit. The latter he found on the floor by one of the crates, but he had no idea where Reith kept the matches.

"Where are you, lad?"

Silence.

Lachlan quirked an eyebrow when he remembered Reith had talked about trenching the field. Surely the young man wouldn't be working in the dark?

Lachlan spied a lit lantern across the field before he'd fully exited the woods. With a rueful shake of his head, he walked toward it, and was nearly upon Reith before he saw him.

"Laddie, have you no concept o' callin' it quits for a day?"

Bent over the trench he was expanding, Reith straightened into a kneeling position and peered up at his employer. "I be nearly done wi' this section."

"Wi' a trowel?" Lachlan asked disapprovingly. "There *are* shovels on the property."

"I was usin' one, earlier. I'm only usin' the trowel now to loosen up these rocks, sir."

" 'Tis night!"

"Sir, I can see by the lantern's light weel enough."

Lachlan crouched at the young man's side and humorously looked him in the eye. "You lookin' for a raise in wage, are you?"

A rueful grin appeared on Reith's mouth. "If aught, I be tryin' to earn the clothes on my back."

Lowering his head below the line of his shoulders, Lachlan gave it a shake, then looked up with a paternal frown. "Have I been harsh wi' you?"

Startled, Reith said, "No, sir!"

"Then pray tell, Reith, why do you feel so bloody compelled to break your young back as you are?"

Reith rested his buttocks on his heels. "My back be fine, sir. I told ye I like to work. Besides, if I'm no' bone weary when I lie down, I canna sleep for thinkin' o' my wife."

Lachlan stood. Reith followed suit and said, "I didna mean to complain, sir. It was but an explanation why I dinna mind workin' so late."

"Your dinner's in the carriage house."

On cue, Reith's stomach grumbled. "I havena much to go," he said, looking down at the trench. "Maybe anither hour's work."

"At least eat first." Lachlan's tone took on a teasing lilt. "Steak, and potatoes in their jackets, bread, and a pot o' coffee. Nocht tha' will taste good once cold."

"I am a wee hungry."

"By the sounds o' your stomach, your more'n a wee in

need o' nourishment. If you must, the work will be waitin' for you when you're done."

Reith offered a grateful smile. "How does a mon become so wise, sir?"

Lachlan laughed. "You silver-tongued deil, you. Wise, you say? Weel, my lad, 'tis a sorry fact I've no' a wise thought in my head itherwise, I wouldna be so prone to trouble. Now, come along." He lifted the lantern by its handle and passed it to Reith. "I've a date wi' my Beth."

They walked silently until reaching the woods, where Reith stated, " 'Tis good to see ye so happy, sir. Ye deserve no less."

Lachlan looked wistfully up at the stars and sighed. "You'll see your wife soon," he said, the conviction in his tone taking Reith aback.

"I no' be sure that's good news."

Lachlan looked at him, perplexed. "Why?"

Reith shrugged. " 'Tis too soon to expect her forgiveness."

"Was your wrong so great?"

Lowering his head, Reith murmured, "Aye."

"I canna imagine you ever hurtin' anyone."

Reith looked up. "Sufferin' can either break a mon or build his character. I refused to be broked."

"Who made you suffer?"

"I pray ye, sir, dinna ask me. I shouldna spoken o' it. I am aware ye have the *knowin'*, but learnin' o' my past will only confuse ye."

Lachlan chuckled. "Confuse me more'n dyin' and returnin' to the land o' the livin'?"

He sobered when Reith gave a solemn nod.

"I willna pry," Lachlan said on a sigh of resignation. "But I want you to know you can tell me anythin'. Whatever is in your past, it canna alter my opinion o' you."

"Thank you, sir."

Patting Reith on the shoulder, Lachlan said, "Eat your supper. I'll see you in the morn wi' your breakfast."

"*Taitneach aislings*. sir."

Pleasant dreams.

"You speak Gaelic?"

"Aye. 'Tis my first language."

Lachlan grinned appreciatively. In Gaelic, he said, " 'Twould be grand to speak in my native tongue now and then."

Reith nodded, then lifted a hand in a parting gesture and headed for the carriage house.

Lachlan watched him for a moment before taking the path through the woods which led him to the south side of the house. Instead of going on to the front doors, he leaned against the cold brick of the wall a few feet away, and stared up at the stars. He was convinced he was the luckiest man alive. *The Lucky Baird* of old had been carried over to the new Lachlan.

His steps buoyant, he entered the house with thoughts of snuggling next to Beth. It had been a long, exhausting day, and he was glad it would soon be over. Beth had not mentioned her murder since that morning, but it remained at the periphery of Lachlan's mind, gnawing at his resolve to leave the past behind him.

He looked down at his left hand. It was suddenly numb, somehow leaden, and when he tried to move the fingers he couldn't.

"Old age," he muttered.

Entering the house, he headed for the staircase. A maddening, tingling sensation pulsed through the hand, and he paused on the bottom step and forcefully worked the fingers. They moved sluggishly like disembodied digits attempting to function through the willpower of someone gifted with telekinesis. The concentration necessary for him to accomplish this small feat soon tired him.

He was on the third step when a piercing pain lanced his right shoulder. Staggering to the first floor landing, he leaned against the balustrade and breathlessly massaged the area.

"I'm falling apart," he muttered.

He sucked in deep breaths to clear away the nauseating

roaring in his ears. Now his entire system tingled. He glanced down at his legs, asking himself if he trusted them to carry him to the third floor. It would be bitter irony if he plunged to his death on the stairs—an insult to the powers that had brought him back, only to have his corporeal existence diabolically work against him.

It crossed his mind to call out to Beth, but he was reluctant to worry her needlessly. Besides, if he did take a fall, he doubted she would have the strength to stop it, possibly breaking her own neck for her troubles.

Grimacing at the image of a double catastrophe, he peered up the staircase. It seemed an inordinately long climb, now, the stairs looming and intimidating.

"Fegs, mon! Get a grip!"

His hearing cleared of the internal noise. The numbness waned. The left hand still felt odd and somehow disconnected from his wrist, but he was grateful for whatever blessing came his way at this point.

Again he stepped on the first stair. This time, he detected an external sound. Distant. Muffled. His gaze crept to the midway landing. He told himself the sound could be coming from the second or third floor, but a niggling suspicion suggested otherwise.

To satisfy the sense of dread yawning through him, he opened the parlor door and peered in. Nothing. Next he checked the bar. Nothing. He was standing in the hall near the balustrade when he looked at the cellar door. A chill gripped him. The dread transformed into something so dark and vile that his vision blurred. However, his hearing sharpened at the same time. Now he heard the distinct sounds of someone moaning and someone weeping.

The instant he opened the door, a gust of psychic waves rolled over him. He descended the stairs in the dark. When he reached the bottom the door slammed, and he heard the exterior bolt grind into place. He didn't have time to panic, for Kahl wailed, "Lannie! The boogeyman got us!"

A groan followed, then a grunted, "Damn me, it hurts."

Lachlan's feet soon found Roan's legs. Going down on

his knees and groping in the darkness, he discovered Roan was slumped against the stair rail. Close by, Alby was sobbing. Kahl and Kevin inched closer to Lachlan.

"Roan, wha' the hell happened?"

"A mon came at me wi' a knife. Got me twice. Shoulder and my chest, I think."

"Have you lost a lot o' blood?"

"Dinna think so," Roan murmured. "Lightheaded, though."

"There's a lantern and matches by the Scotch cellar," said Lachlan, easing onto his feet. "I'll be right back."

"Watch your step. I canna even see my hand in front o' my face down here."

"Roan, my lad, I could find my way around this place in my slee—*Ouch!* Fegs! Bloody hell, wha' do I need wi' two shins, anyway?"

Roan's attempt to laugh resulted in a coughing fit, which only aggravated his wounds.

Shortly, Lachlan had the lantern lit and returned to Roan's side, where he placed it on the floor. He spied Alby cowering beneath the stairs, wretched sobs quaking through him. Going down on one knee, Lachlan held out his arms. "Come here, son. Come to Lannie."

Alby closed his eyes and sobbed harder. Finagling as best he could beneath the cramped space, Lachlan managed to pull the boy toward him until he was able to cradle him in his arms. Alby hid his face against Lachlan's chest and held on for dear life.

"I need to check your uncle's wounds, Alby," said Lachlan softly. " 'Tis a lot to ask, I know, but can you help me?"

The boy's head lifted fractionally. "How can I help?"

"Weel, do you think you can hold his shirt open for me? Dinna look at the wounds, though. No' a pretty sight if two o' us are left to toss up our innards."

A hoarse chuckle escaped Alby, then he fully lifted his head and peered into Lachlan's eyes. The boy's face was swollen and blotchy.

"God," Lachlan breathed, then swallowed past the tightness in his throat. "Alby, you have my word, whoever did this to you will pay dearly."

"He put his smelly hand on my face and dragged me down here," Alby whimpered.

"He did the same to Kahl and me," said Kevin.

Lachlan regarded the oldest boy. Although he knew Kevin was as frightened as his brother, his eight-year-old face held the anger of an adult.

"He said he was gonna kill us if we went up the stairs," Kevin continued, his voice surprisingly level considering the circumstances. "He locked us down here, but he undid it a little while ago until you came down."

"He has us trapped down here," Roan said sickly. He attempted to sit up, then slumped back against the railing. "He's efter the women, Lannie. We have to get ou' o' here."

"Hold on a minute."

Lachlan ran to the Scotch cellar. He returned moments later with a bottle and a cork.

"Tak a swig o' this," said Lachlan, passing the opened bottle of whisky to Roan.

Without hesitation, Roan took three hefty gulps, shuddered, then downed two more and grimaced as they hit bottom. Lachlan took the bottle and sent Alby a visual gesture to do his part. The older boys stood aside and allowed Alby to unbutton Roan's shirt. Following Lachlan's instructions, he was careful not to look at the wounds as he parted the material. He turned his back to Roan and calmly waited for Lachlan to proceed.

"You've lost a fair measure o' blood," Lachlan said. "Close your eyes."

"Why?"

"Just do as I say. I need to check the wounds more closely, but I canna concentrate if I have to see the sufferin' in your eyes."

Believing Lachlan, Roan complied, but released a howl of pain and surprise when Lachlan poured some of the

Scotch on the wounds. "Are you daft!" Roan shrieked, blinking rapidly, his face as pale as a sun-bleached skull. "You lied to me!"

"Aye. Now listen to me, Roan. There's anither way ou' o' here through the north cellar. If I get you on your feet, do you think you can walk?"

Roan held out his hand for the whisky. Lachlan reluctantly passed it to him. Roan downed several gulps, gasped, burped, then placed the bottle on the ground next to him.

"Damn me, I'll walk or crawl. Whatever it taks."

"Concentrate on the women," said Lachlan, positioning himself behind Roan as he leaned forward. He hooked his hands beneath Roan's armpits. "Ready?"

"Aye."

One try brought Roan to his feet, but he swayed, and would have keeled over if not for Lachlan holding him up.

"Kevin, you're in charge o' the lantern," said Lachlan.

"I want to carry it," insisted Kahl.

"I need you and Alby to walk behind me."

"Why?"

"To guard the rear in case your boogeymon tries to sneak up on us," said Lachlan.

To his relief, the boys obeyed without further question.

Midway to the farthest end of the basement, Roan managed to hold his own walking. His steps were slow but steady. He kept himself focused on the women, not the pain radiating through his upper torso.

"Who is he?" he asked Lachlan.

"I suspect he's Winston's Phantom."

"He's the boogeyman," Kevin insisted.

"No, he's just an evil mon," Lachlan said. "Roan, I'm going ahead a bit. The door's flush wi' the wall to conceal it."

"Wha' if that's locked, too?"

"Hopefully he doesna know it exists. I designed the sections of the cellars to look as though they're sealed off from one anither."

"I'm all right. Go ahead."

"Kevin, remain in front o' Roan. I dinna need the light to find my way."

"Tell tha' to your shin," Roan quipped.

Lachlan spared him a wry grin, then disappeared into the darkness beyond the glow of the lantern.

"Uncle Roan?"

"Wha', Alby?"

"You ain't gonna die, are you?"

A choked laugh burst from Roan's dry throat. "No' intentionally. Besides, I'm too mean to die young."

"You're not mean," Alby murmured with a whimper.

"Uncle Roan?"

"Aye, Kahl?"

"We love you."

A moment of profound silence followed, then Kahl added, "I know we give you a hard time, but it's 'cause we know we can and you won't hate us."

His eyes misting, Roan nodded. "Weel, laddies, I've got plans to see you tortured by your own children one day. Do you think I would miss ou' on tha'?"

Alby and Kahl exchanged a quick grin.

"Retrabition," said Kevin.

"Retribution," corrected Roan with a chuckle.

"That, too," said Kevin, then asked over his shoulder, "The boogeyman won't really hurt Aunt Laura, Beth, and Taryn, will he?"

"They'll hold their own. They have to. The plan, laddies, is to time the rescue so we come ou' the heroes."

"I like that plan," said Kevin. "When we catch the Phantom, can I bite him good for scarin' us?"

Roan smiled through a grimace. "Weel, I dinna think so, Kevin."

"Why not? I can bite real hard."

"Aye, I know. Remember when I tried to pull you ou' o' your aunt's car when it hit the oak?"

"That was a long time ago."

"Seems so, it does. But, Kevin, if you bite this Phantom, you could get sick."

"How?"

"Och, 'tis a lie. You willna get sick, but I'm worried he'll bite you back, okay?"

Kevin thought this over, then nodded. "Okay. I'll just kick him in the nuts, instead."

"Me, too!" said Kahl.

Alby remained silent as he repeatedly looked over his shoulder to make sure the boogeyman wasn't following them.

"Okay, Uncle Roan?" asked Kevin.

Roan grimaced in pain and exasperation. "Stay away from him."

"He can't scare us!" said Kevin.

"Yeah," said Kahl.

From up ahead, they heard hinges screaking. Then Lachlan called, " 'Tis opened!"

The lantern's radiance crept up Lachlan's tall frame as they closed the distance and Kevin held up the lantern as far as his small arm would permit. As they approached the doorway Roan couldn't help but admire the boys' courage. They were terrified of what awaited them, and he couldn't have faulted them if they resorted to hysterics, but they wouldn't. They were little men who were determined to see the boogeyman stopped from hurting anyone else.

"God, the smell!" Roan choked.

"Aye. Somethin's afoul down here."

Lachlan gestured them over the threshhold, then followed and closed the door behind him. He took the lantern from Kevin and led the way toward the steps of the bulkhead. They hadn't gone but ten yards when Kahl released a squeal and pointed to another door. It was closed, but a black pool was visible beneath the door spacing.

"Stay back, laddies," Lachlan warned.

Roan remained with them. He was lightheaded again, and the stench was so overpowering, he found it impossible to breathe.

Lachlan knelt by the pool. "Looks and feels like blood." He stood, opened the door, and held out the lantern to see into the room, then jerked back and shut the door, a hand clamped over his mouth for several seconds longer.

"Wha' is it?" asked Roan.

"From Laura and Taryn's descriptions, 'tis Stephan Miles. He's dead."

Roan teetered on his feet.

"And by the looks o' it in there," Lachlan said grimly, "our boogeymon has been makin' himself at home for some time."

"I don't feel so go—" Kevin bent over as his stomach ejected its contents.

"Lannie, we've got to get ou' o' here."

Lachlan ran to and up the steps to the bulkhead and pushed open one side of the doors. He'd never put locks on them. With this part of the cellar used for storing junk, it hadn't been necessary.

"Come along," he urged from the bottom of the steps, where he remained until everyone else had gone into the night. By the time he joined them his own stomach was churning, and his eyes were watering from the fumes of decay.

He knelt in front of the boys. "Go to the carriage house and wait till you hear from us."

"We wanna help," Kevin insisted.

"Listen . . ." Lachlan paused to draw in a deep breath of fresh, cool air. "You're brave lads, but I canna be worryin' if tha' sick bastard can get his hands on you again."

"But—"

Lachlan framed Kahl's face and planted a kiss on his brow. "Now listen to me, Kahl. Go to the carriage house. Tell Reith we need his help, but *dinna* leave tha' buildin'. Understand?"

"What about the boogeyman's nuts?"

"Kahl, we'll discuss tha' later. Right now I need your promise you'll no' leave the carriage house, no matter wha' happens."

"Okay," said Kevin, his chin quivering. "I'll make sure we stay out of the way."

"In the carriage house!"

"Okay! Geez!"

"Tak the lantern, and be careful no' to place it near anythin' inflammable. Now scat."

While the boys ran in the direction of the carriage house, Lachlan led Roan to the kitchen door. It was locked.

Roan sat on the stoop and lowered his head.

"How are you farin'?" Lachlan asked him, peeling out of his shirt.

"Gettin' weaker."

"You need to drive to town for a doctor."

Roan shook his head. "I'll be all right."

"Roan—"

"I'm too lightheaded to drive. Stop worryin' abou' me and get to the women!"

Lachlan swiftly wound his shirt around his fist, creating bracing layers. "Then stay here." He popped the covered fist through one of the glass panes, reached in with the other hand and unlocked the door. "Dinna move. I'll be back for you."

Roan attempted to stand, and fell back on his buttocks. Lachlan crouched alongside him, a hand on Roan's trembling shoulder.

"Dammit, Roan, stay here! I can best sneak up on the bastard."

Breathing erratically, Roan nodded. "Be careful."

"Do you pray?"

Roan stiltedly shook his head.

" 'Tis a good time to start," Lachlan quipped. He ran into the house, his footfalls on the glass tinkling in the otherwise stillness of the night.

CHAPTER ELEVEN

After searching the second floor bedrooms, the tower, kitchen, dining room, parlor, bar and library, Laura was mentally threatening to hang her nephews and Roan when she found them. She plodded up the stairs to the third floor, muttering under her breath and trying not to think about the headache blossoming in her temples. She opened every door on each side of the hall and called out for Roan and the boys. No response. With each door she closed, her face grew redder with vexation.

She stopped at the closed nursery door. It was always left open. Beth and Lachlan were relatively paranoid about not hearing the babies if they awakened.

Opening the door just wide enough to peer in, her gaze searched the room. She couldn't see anyone. The bumper blankets blocked her view of the babies and, for this reason, she quietly walked to the crib. Broc and Ciarda were asleep, both propped on their sides, facing one another. Laura murmured cooingly to them, then retraced her steps and eased the door shut.

The door to Beth and Lachlan's room was open about an

inch. Laura lightly rapped and ventured, "Beth? Lachlan? Have you seen Roan or the boys?"

Silence.

"Beth?"

She pushed the door open a little further.

"Beth?"

Silence.

They could be in the bathroom, she reasoned, indulging in a bubble bath or . . . whatever. It was unlikely she would find Roan and her nephews in there, or anywhere else in the master suite. The only other place they could be was outside. No. It was more likely the boys had slipped from the house, and Roan was looking for them.

The pain pulsing at her temples expanded to her nape. A tension headache. All she needed now was another visit from that Peeping Tom, "Tales From the Crypt" reject.

Laura froze as she turned. About six feet away, he hovered just above the floor, his eyes wide behind his round-rimmed spectacles, and his hands held out in a beseeching manner. His translucent mouth moved rapidly in a succession of words, only one of which she could make out: Help.

Forgotten were Roan, the boys, and her headache. Beth needed to see him! Abstractly, she wondered why he didn't come closer. Not that she wanted him to. If he touched her, she was sure she would be reduced to hysterics. Now she was still angry enough to keep her adrenaline pumping and her mind focused.

Help.

For help.

His lips slowed enough for her to grasp, Go for help.

Backing into the door and bumping it wide open, she crossed the threshhold.

The spirit flagged his arms. The cut of his hair made it look as though it was standing on end. That, combined with his wild expression and gesticulating arms, made him almost laughable.

"Come with me," Laura said softly, through a strained grin. "There is someone I want you to meet."

His motions became humorously frantic.

Laura backed up, one slow step at a time. "Come up, you handsome dead person you." *Perverted jerk!* "It's time you met the lady of the manor. Her name's Beth. You'll *like* Beth. Beth goes for the silent, dead type."

The ghost lowered his arms and slumped as if too weary to go on. He stared at her dejectedly, and for a moment—a blink of time, actually—she almost felt sorry for him.

"Beth? There's someone here to see you. Beth!"

What the hell is going on? she thought, fear twisting through her stomach. Had everyone gone deaf, or stepped into the "Twilight Zone"?

Her nose wrinkled when it detected a faint putrid scent. A chill licked up the nerve endings of her spine. An immediate sense of danger detonated her awareness, locking her joints and causing her heart to thunder behind her breast. At the same instant that she turned her head and saw two unconscious figures bound in duct tape on the bed, the stench was upon her like a cloud of death. A beefy arm shot out from behind her and wound about her neck. The muscles at the crook of the arm tightened at her throat, cutting off her oxygen and her outcry. A curtain of darkening grayness descended in front of her eyes as she clawed and pounded at the human vise.

Wheezing, hot breaths filled her right ear, then the gutturally spoken words, "I'm the chosen one."

Although her world was darkening by the second, she was more terrified for the children than herself. She closed her eyes and went limp. For a moment she thought her ruse had failed, for his hold didn't lessen. But then he gushed a sigh and pressed his lips to her neck, just below the right earlobe. It was nearly her undoing. Repulsion rose up into her throat. She forced it back, back for the sake of the children, the man she loved, her friends, and for herself.

His arm slackened. It took all of her willpower not to suck air into her lungs, only a little through her nostrils so as not to warn him she was conscious. He clumsily repositioned the arm beneath her breasts, grunting in the process, and began to drag her. Toward the bed, she knew.

Her mind scrambled to assess the possibilities of escape. She was barefoot. If she attempted to ram one of his shins with a heel, she could miss or not do the damage she hoped for, and knew she wouldn't get another chance at catching him off guard. The same applied if she tried to drive a fist into his face. She had to do something, but the wrong move could end her life in a heartbeat.

One of the babies began to cry. The other joined in.

The assailant trembled. For a fleeting moment she hoped it was out of compassion for the infants. But no. With sickening clarity, she knew the sound was enraging him. She had no way of knowing the Phantom had lost his hearing, and that the rage she sensed in him was for the awakening Taryn. The louder the cries grew, the more he quaked, until she was sure her insides would vibrate up and out of her mouth. She couldn't see Taryn stirring on the bed.

How many times during the past years had she thought about taking self-defense classes? *Thought* about, but never followed through!

She was at a gross disadvantage. Unless she could see her target, she couldn't risk blundering a shot at him.

At the same time that Lachlan ran into the main hall, Winston and Deliah charged into the house through the front doors. They met at the staircase.

"He's here," said Winston.

Breathing heavily, Lachlan nodded and glared up the stairs. "The women are up there. Roan's been stabbed. He's ou' on the north stoop. The lads—"

"We talked to them," said Winston.

"I'll see to Roan." Deliah fearfully searched Winston's face. "Be careful. Both o' ye," she added, glancing at Lachlan.

"Don't come upstairs," Winston ordered.

"But—"

"Deliah, stay wi' Roan!" he demanded in a stage whisper.

Without hesitation, she ran down the secondary hall toward the kitchen.

Lachlan and Winston headed up the stairs, mindful of their footfalls until the infants' shrill demand to be fed reached their ears. They sped up, but stopped at the third floor landing when greeted by the spirit of Stephan Miles. The ghost frantically pointed toward the end of the hall, his eyes wide with terror, mouthing words neither man had time to understand.

Side by side they raced toward the master suite, bursting into the room and halting simultaneously at the sight of a massive man standing at the side of the bed, his right arm holding up a seemingly unconscious Laura and a knife clutched in his left hand.

"Let her go!" Winston shouted, his fists quaking at his sides.

The sound of his voice jerked Laura's eyes open.

The Phantom flung her onto the bed and raised the knife as if to plunge it into her. At the same time she drove one heel into his abdomen, Winston and Lachlan were on him, the latter attempting to wrest the dirk from the Phantom's hand, Winston attempting to subdue his other arm.

Three bodies staggered away from the bed and crashed to the floor in a heap of flailing arms, pounding fists, and a cacophony of growls and curses.

Laura scrambled to her knees atop the bed. Both Taryn and Beth were lying facedown. Taryn's head turned, and she blinked dazedly at Laura. Beth began to come around. Laura yanked the duct tape from Taryn's mouth. Ignoring the woman's gasp, she worked feverishly to unwind the tape about Taryn's wrists, and then her ankles before focusing on Beth's. Within a short span of time, she was helping both women off the bed and urging them out of the room. With the men still struggling on the floor, the women took the babies and escaped down the stairs, the new specter resident in their wake.

To Lachlan and Winston's surprise, the Phantom managed to overpower them. The knife first slashed across Lachlan's upper chest, then drove into Winston's upper left arm. Both men were shucked off the enraged bulk of muscle and fat, and the Phantom jumped to his feet, spewing foaming spittle past his curled back lips. He drove the point of the dirk into Winston's right thigh, and would have targeted Lachlan's middle if the laird hadn't driven the heel of one boot into the Phantom's left kneecap.

With a feral howl, the Phantom staggered back. Lachlan, despite the pain radiating through his chest, climbed to his feet and helped Winston to his. It was then, as they faced the giant of a man who stood not six feet away, they noticed his ravaged face.

Wade Cuttstone resembled something out of a child's worst nightmare. His shocking white hair stood on end, as if combed with static electricity. His protruding eyes were bloodshot with dark pockets of flesh hanging beneath them. The irises were colorless, as lifeless as marbles. The face and what could be seen of his neck were mottled with shades of gray, bluish tones, and raw red where there were open sores and rings of inflammation surrounding blisters.

"Good of you to join me," said the Phantom in a surprisingly cultured English accent. His voice was overly loud, prompting Winston to scan him.

"He's deaf," he whispered to Lachlan, moving his lips as little as possible.

"Ask me anything you like before you die," said Cuttstone to Winston, a skeletal grin mocking his adversary of four years. "You can't save yourselves or the begetters. I have the power of the Guardian on my side."

"You're insane," Lachlan growled, a hand pressed to his bloodied chest. He looked askance at the swords mounted on the wall. So close, yet so far. If he dashed for one of the weapons, he was sure it would further provoke the Phantom. He dreaded the idea of feeling the dirk's steel enter him again, but he was terrified one of the others would be the next target.

The Phantom's gaze never wavered from Winston's mouth. "No need to ask, my good man. Your mind questions the car chase and the resulting tragedy which followed." Cuttstone sighed with theatrical patience. "It was indeed my car, but not more than an hour prior to the chase a carjacker had the misfortune to choose me as his next victim." He grinned mirthlessly. "Imagine his surprise when he found himself surrounded by police, and he being such an unworthy criminal to warrant such attention."

Cuttstone lunged forward with the dirk extended. Winston shoved Lachlan to the floor, out of immediate danger, but was only able to twist himself out of the way enough to avoid a stab to the chest. The edge of the blade grazed his side, along his rib cage. The wound wasn't deep, but—combined with his injured leg going out from under him—painful enough to make him collapse to the floor. Cuttstone slashed to his right, the blade opening Lachlan's right palm. He swung to his left with the intention of driving the dirk to its hilt into Winston's chest, but another figure ran into the room, followed by yet another.

"Deliah, get ou'!" Roan thundered. His wounds were covered with the same root pulp she'd used on Winston two weeks ago. He reached out to grab her arm and stop her advance on the giant, but she eluded him and sprang to Cuttstone's right, behind Lachlan, a hand held out in warning to the intruder.

Her face was livid, her eyes inhumanly bright. The long strands of her hair flapped behind her as if she faced a gusting wind. Roan stood frozen, afraid that if he made a move, the Phantom would throw the dirk into her chest before he could stop him.

"I be Deliah o' the Kingdom Faerie. Ye have no power here!"

"He can't hear you!" Winston exclaimed, inching away

on his buttocks. "Get ou' o' the house, Deliah! You can't stop him!"

"Ye o' little faith, my love," she said in a strained tone, her fiery gaze riveted on Cuttstone's glassy eyes.

Lachlan struggled to his knees, then his feet, while Deliah hastily pulled her pale blue Cashmere sweater over her head and tossed it aside. At the same moment the Phantom thought to spring at her, she unfurled her wings, their rapid appearance causing him to jerk back in astonishment.

Put down the dirk! she projected into his mind. *Now, afore I call upon the oak beneath your feet to rise up and encage ye!*

Wade Cuttstone staggered backward across the room, his maniacal eyes daring her to carry through her threat.

Her wings fluttering at her back, Deliah rose into the air and settled on her feet atop the mattress. Cuttstone advanced backward toward the windows, the dirk held out, the hand holding it trembling. With a wave of her right hand, millions of glittering specks of golden dust swirled through the air between herself and the Phantom. No sooner did they settle on the oak planks, roots sprang up, spiraling upward.

Cuttstone snarled and kicked at the manifestations with one of his steel-toed boots. Snapping sounds rent the air. He stomped and kicked with a frenzy, breaking off the roots in his immediate vicinity, unaware that the three men were closing in on him until it was almost too late. His mind forewarned him, and he swept out his left hand. The razor-sharp edge of the dirk's blade came within a hair's breadth of Roan's throat. Roan fell back out of surprise, unwittingly sending himself and knocking Winston to the floor. The roots vanished beneath them a second before they hit the surface.

The Phantom whirled to look out the window in a futile search for an escape route.

Lachlan was too enraged to feel his wounds. No sooner did the Phantom turn his head toward the window than Lachlan hunched low, then cast off in a dynamic launch.

He plowed into the killer like a linebacker, one shoulder positioned to take the brunt of the impact.

"Alby, wait up!" Kahl panted, amazed that his younger brother could outrun him. "Alby!"

Deaf to his brothers' entreaties first for him to remain in the carriage house and now for him to wait for them to catch up, he pumped his legs in the direction of the field, then toward the golden beacon in the distance. When he reached his goal he stumbled to a stop and fell into waiting arms, the roar in his ears blocking out Reith's, "*Och*, lad!"

Kevin dropped to his knees when he reached Reith. His lungs ached from both the run and fear. Kahl stopped next to him and bent over, trying to catch his breath.

"Wha' be wrong?" asked Reith sharply, checking each boy for injury. When he found none, he frowned with paternal concern. "Does anyone know you be ou' in the night?"

"In the house," Kahl panted.

"Aye, tis where ye should be."

"*Him!*" Alby wailed, then pressed his face to Reith's chest.

Smoothing the hair at the back of Alby's head, Reith studied the two older boys. "Tak your time and tell me why ye be here and no' in your beds."

"Lannie told us to . . . wait in the carriage house for you," Kevin explained. "Alby got too scared to wait for you to come back, so he took off to find you."

"Why would Mr. Baird tell ye to wait for me?"

"The boogeyman!" Alby cried.

Reith laughed, but with compassion, and wound his arms around Alby's quaking form. "Bogeymen be but creations o' our minds. Ye have yourselves worked up for nocht."

"He put us in the cellar!" Kevin said indignantly. "And he stabbed Uncle Roan!"

Reith's spine stiffened as he released Alby. "Ye be tellin' me the truth?"

Kevin stomped a foot and angrily exclaimed, "He's gonna kill everybody if you don't get up off your ass!"

A horrendous boom of glass and wood shattering blasted into the night. Shrill cries of anguish soon followed.

"Return to the carriage house!" Reith ordered the boys, then lit into a run. Blinded by fear, he only knew he was headed for the woods. By the time he reached the perimeter, discordant voices rang in his ears. He was careless in his haste. One of the branches of the ground shrubbery pierced one of his pant legs and he pitched forward into evergreen nettles and dried twigs.

Immediately following Lachlan and the Phantom sailing through the window, Deliah flew after them. Roan and Winston ran for the stairs, the adrenaline pumping through their veins making it possible for them to overcome shock and injury. They went out the back door through the library and ran to where Beth, Laura, and Taryn stood, which was several feet from Deliah's kneeling position amid shards of glass and wood splinters. Between herself and the wall was a mound—Lachlan atop the Phantom, motionless.

"Lachlan," Beth sobbed, holding Broc against her. "Is he . . . ?"

"He be alive." Deliah glanced at the others. "The ither mon be dead. His neck be broked."

"Why isn't Lachlan moving?" Beth asked tremulously. Like Laura, she couldn't bring herself to move closer. Not only didn't she trust her legs, but it was all she could do to hold in the fear gripping her.

Her wings fluttering, Deliah placed a hand on Lachlan's back and gently shook him. "Lachlan. Lachlan, come round! Lachlan!"

He moaned.

"Ye are no' broked," she told him, excitement in her tone.

He moaned again, longer.

"I wouldna say ye flyin' skills be as grand as mine," she said as cheerily as she could muster, hoping to ease him back into full consciousness, "but ye did yourself proud, ye did."

"Dinna mak a funny." Lachlan grunted. "Hurts."

Deliah stood back when Lachlan started to roll off Cuttstone. Roan and Winston stepped forward to help, but stopped cold when Lachlan flopped onto his back.

Protruding from Lachlan's naked, blood-soaked chest was the dirk, embedded to the hilt.

"Oh my God!" Beth wailed.

Coughing up blood, Lachlan looked at Deliah and pleaded, "Dinna let Beth . . . see me . . . die."

"Do something," Taryn rasped, her tear-filled eyes riveted on her brother.

Deliah went down on her knees alongside Lachlan, her hands held out in helplessness and her features contorted with anguish. "Remove the cursed dirk!" she cried, to no one in particular.

Roan was the first to step forward. He dropped to one knee and flinched with pain as glass cut through his slacks and the taut skin covering the area. Reaching for the dirk's handle, he hesitated inches away from touching it. His hand trembled so that he had to flex it several times before he felt steady enough to proceed. Lachlan was unconscious. Roan pulled a clean handkerchief from his back pocket then, staring into Lachlan's slack face, he gripped the handle and jerked it free. He vehemently tossed the weapon aside and applied pressure to the wound, using the folded cotton beneath his hands.

Winston positioned himself behind Deliah, and Beth forced herself to stand next to him. She couldn't breathe. She couldn't look away. And she couldn't bring herself to pray for his life. The only thought echoing through her mind was that she was willing to return to the grayness to be with him. She didn't think of the twins or anyone else. Without Lachlan, she did not possess the strength to stay even one day in the world of the living.

"The damage be too great," Deliah whimpered, her palms pressed to Lachlan's chest, below where Roan's were placed. A golden glow passed from beneath her palms, upward over his chest, then seeped into his skin. "I dinna have the power to undo this!"

She balled her hands atop Lachlan and threw back her head. Her eyes closed, she wailed, "MoNae! MoNae, I *need* ye!"

The tormented depths of her voice broke the dams of Laura and Taryn's tenuous control. Both wept hard. Although Laura could only clutch Ciarda against her, Taryn's mind was burning with the knowledge that the dirk lay a few feet away. Without anyone noticing she inched toward it, crouched low as if unable to stand a moment longer, and slipped the bloodied dirk into the sleeve of her blouse. As yet, her mind hadn't processed the fact that Deliah had wings. The assault of the Phantom, grief over Lachlan, and not missing her chance to get the dirk, were all she could handle at the moment.

"MoNae!" Deliah repeated, quaking with sobs and vexation. "I beg o' ye to come!"

"Deliah?"

Reith's voice crashed upon the scene. Deliah shot to her feet and swayed with a wave of dizziness. Winston dumbfoundedly stepped aside as Reith elbowed his way to Deliah, who flung herself into the young man's arms.

"Deliah, Deliah," he said in a chanting manner, his tone laden with joy and bewilderment. "I thought I'd lost ye forever!"

"Reith!" Deliah choked, part in laughter, part in anguish, as she leaned back and searched his face. "I need your help. This mon be dyin', and I canna—"

Reith jerked as he looked down at Lachlan with horror-filled wide eyes. "No, *no!*" he cried angrily, and knelt beside

Roan, whose tearful gaze looked at him with a plea for help.

"Maybe our combined powers can save him," Deliah said. "His spirit is holdin' on as best it can."

Bleakly, Reith glanced up at her. "Blue stripped me o' my powers and cast me ou'. But ye go to them! The new oak."

"The kingdom be back?" she asked dazedly.

"They all be there. *Hurry!*"

"I have no' my Ring O' Passage!" she wailed. "Will they hear me, ye think?"

Reith stood and swiftly yanked a cord from around his neck, over his head. "No. She cast a spell to shut ou' the sounds o' this world. Hurry, Deliah. His pulse be verra weak. I'll carry him to the oak, and meet ye there." As he spoke, he untied the cord and removed a band made from an oak root. He placed it on the third finger of Deliah's right hand, kissed her on the cheek, and breathed, *"Hurry!"*

Deliah flew into the air and out of sight.

Reith whirled about and dropped to his knees in one fluid motion. "I'll carry him," he said to Roan, determination accentuating the lines of his face. "It mayhaps be wise if ye all remain here. No tellin' if my kin will come if they sense more humans abou'."

Roan rose to his feet while Reith effortlessly lifted Lachlan, stood, then faced the stunned onlookers. A retched sob came from Beth, and Reith compassionately met her gaze. " 'Tis hard, I know, to wait here, but this I must ask ye. The Circle O' Magic can save this mon, but my kin isna fond o' practicin' it on humans."

Releasing a shuddering breath, Beth stated, "Then more's the reason for all of us to be there. They need to know how much Lachlan is loved. Reith, you must help us convince them. You're Deliah's brother, aren't you?"

"Aye, but I no longer hold status among my own." He glanced at Lachlan's colorless face, then again looked into Beth's eyes. "But ye are right, m'lady. 'Twould be best if we all beseeched the Keepers O' The Circle. Follow me."

Leading them around the house to the new oak, he instructed them how far back to stand, then placed Lachlan, who came to with a moan, on the ground. Roan knelt to Lachlan's other side and again applied pressure to the wound.

"Lie still, sir," cautioned Reith, "but dinna give in to death. My sister has gone to fetch the Keepers O' The Circle."

Lachlan's eyes rolled, then he focused on Reith with difficulty. "Too weak."

"No, sir," Reith said firmly. "For the sake o' your womon and younglings, ye *must* fight for your life!"

"Tell Beth . . . ."

"I'm here, Lachlan," she sobbed, stepping closer until he could see her. She tried to smile, but her face crumbled as she broke down into a torrent of tears.

"Beth," Lachlan murmured, his eyes growing more glazed by the second.

"Listen to me, Master Lachlan Iain MacLachlan Baird!" Reith shouted. Lachlan blinked in bewilderment, then scowled up at the face swimming above him as Reith went on, "Ye will *no'* die!"

"For the love of God," Taryn sobbed, "leave him alone!"

"He's trying to keep him alert," explained Winston.

Guttural sounds of misery escaped Roan's control, and he lowered his head in shame. His tears dripped onto Lachlan's chest, despite how tightly he closed his eyes to hold them back.

With life-ebbing languidness, Lachlan's gaze shifted to him. It took two attempts before he could summon the strength to speak. " 'Tis all right . . . to let go. My Beth. My bairns. My . . . brither."

The words only magnified Roan's sorrow. He repeatedly shook his head, gulping in air and tasting the saltiness of his own tears.

"W-we could have gotten him to the hospital by now!" Laura said angrily.

Before anyone could respond Deliah appeared, seeming to have emerged from the twisted trunk of the oak. Her features were gaunt and ravaged by confusion, sorrow, and anger, each distinctly visible. She staggered toward her brother, her wings drooping at her back as though she didn't possess the energy to lift them.

"Blue will no' listen to me," she sobbed, and sat on the ground next to her brother, draping an arm about his shoulders. "I mistakenly told her ye had sent me."

"Ye did your best. But, Deliah, ye dinna look weel."

"I be fine," she murmured, although she was not.

Winston brightened. "Deliah, can you guide me into their minds?"

She looked at him a bit puzzled, then slowly rose to her feet. " 'Twould no' be proper," she said dazedly.

"Screw what's proper."

"Aye." She walked to him and laid her hands on his chest. "Aye, screw wha' be proper. But they'll no' tak this invasion lightly."

"Good. Anger is better than detachment. So wha' do we do?"

Deliah took him by the hand and led him to the oak. Retaining her hold on him, she placed her free hand to the trunk. "I be ready. Channel your message through me."

"Okay." Winston was having second thoughts. It was one thing to get inside the minds of criminals, another to trespass into the sanctuary of beings he'd only learned existed a short time ago. But knowing he had no other choice, he heaved a fortifying breath, then closed his eyes and pushed out with his mind.

Beth sat on the ground near Lachlan's head and brushed her fingers across his cold, perspiring brow. His eyes rolled up, but he couldn't make out her features through the haze of his vision. He knew it was she, though, and despite his pain and increasing lassitude her touch warmed his heart of hearts.

"I love you," she whispered, the bleakness in her tone

spearing him with regret. "Don't leave me here. I can't live without a soul, and you know if you die, you'll take it with you. So hang on for *us*, Lachlan."

He couldn't reply. The strength required to move his tongue was more than he could manage. His world was narrowing to a space no larger than a penny, with infinite darkness surrounding it. And it was also the measure of what remained of his life. Too soon it would blink out, as it had in eighteen forty-three. Only this time he wasn't alone, hidden behind a brick wall. He was beginning to believe that was preferable to having his loved ones watch him die.

Hold on, his Beth had said.

Wi' what? he wondered. *Wha' is left when the body canna resist the need to let go o' the soul?*

New sounds invaded the layers of his thickening daze. The boys. Somewhere in the distance. Crying as only children can cry, hard and from the depths of their emotional wells.

He tried to say, "Dinna let them see this," but no words passed his lips.

His pain grew more distant, his mind more uncaring about his fate. He didn't fear death. Second time around. He knew what was coming. . . .

Energy sparked from the trunk. Deliah and Winston shrank back, then she shook the hand that had been on the wood.

"Are you hurt?" he asked, taking the hand into his own and massaging it.

"No. Surprised me more'n anythin'."

"Wha' happened?"

Deliah made a sickly, rueful expression. "They reacted to ye callin' them heartless cowards."

"They are—"

A figure emerged from the trunk, swept past them, and turned to indignantly confront the couple. Ignoring the gasps and murmurs of the others she knew to be present, she lifted her chin and stated, "How dare you side with these mortals!" Her voice held but a hint of a Scottish accent. "Have you forgotten our ways, Deliah?"

"She has forgotten nocht," Reith said, the anger in his tone mocking his display of deference by going down on one knee to the newcomer's right. With his head bent low, he went on, "It be beneath ye, Blue, to tak ou' your anger for me on my sister, or anyone else o' my family."

"Get off your knees!"

"As ye wish, Your Majesty." He stood and faced her, his stance as hostile as her own. "Behind me lies a mon o' immeasurable worth," he clipped, staring into her eyes with an arrogance he believed he'd long ago abandoned. "Withou' the help o' the Circle O' Magic he will die, and be the shame o' tha' loss on *your* conscience."

"Deliah!" Winston cried, and reached out to stop her fall. Her dead weight dragged him down into a sitting position, where he cradled her head and shoulders in his arms. "Deliah, tell me you're just faint again. Deliah!"

Her eyelids fluttered open.

"Why would she be faint?" asked Blue coldly. "She is not mortal."

"She's pregnant!" Laura bit out.

The luminescent blue of Blue's eyes riveted on Winston. "That's not possible."

"Wha' isn't possible?" Winston asked bitterly. "Tha' we could love each other enough to create a *uirisg*?"

Perched atop the multiple rooftops, more than a dozen peafowl squawked, as if lending their voices in support. The fluttering of their wings was inordinately loud, preternatural, and Blue tore her gaze from them and stared at Winston.

"We be dyin' soon," Deliah said weakly. "Forgive me, but I gave Lachlan a piece o' my life, so he could hold on."

"No, Deliah." Winston's throat constricted. "No' you, too!" He glared at Blue, tears from fear and outrage brimming his eyes. "Do you have the power to save them, or no'!"

"Blue, I beg o' ye to help my sister and Master Baird," Reith said. "I know ye still have a heart."

With a cry of vexation, Blue held out her hands, palms upward. Thunder rolled across the heavens. Lightning mauled the sky like massive claws seeking to claim the occupants by the new oak. Winds rose and swirled with deafening speed around the area, closing them all within its wall.

"Blue!" Reith shouted in fury, misunderstanding her intentions.

A ring of what at first glance seemed to be fireflies appeared around Lachlan. The blue-black, ground-length hair belonging to Faerie's queen rose and snaked through the air, outlining her stance. A song crooned from her throat, a hauntingly sweet melody that evoked a warbling sensation in the hearts of the listeners.

Beth and Roan had scooted back at the appearance of the mysterious ring. Now, they stared at Lachlan in wonder and trepidation. He was levitating three feet above the ground, fully cocooned in a mist of vibrant, rainbow colors.

Tearing his gaze from the phenomenon, Reith gratefully bowed his head to his wife.

CHAPTER TWELVE

Beth tore her gaze from Lachlan and stared at Blue with burgeoning horror. She wanted to cry out to the Faerie queen to stop the theatrics, but she couldn't force out a breath or take one into her aching lungs. The sound of the winds circling them in the elemental prison, had dimmed to a tolerable volume, but she was no less aware that she and the others were cut off from the rest of the world. Beth had no way of knowing what the queen had planned for them. That she was outraged to have been forced to leave her realm, was obvious. That she was angry at Reith, was unmistakable. That she held the human race in contempt, was frightening.

Everything Beth held most dear depended on this magnificent being's ability to show compassion. Without Lachlan, her heart of hearts would shrivel into a hard pit. What kind of mother could she possibly be? How could she hope to offer her children love when she knew if she lost Lachlan, the wellspring of who she was would be as dried out and as barren as a desert.

Without thought to her actions, she somehow broke through her fear and approached the queen, stopping within arm's reach. Reith, standing to her right several feet away, cast her a look of alarm, but she paid it no heed. There was nothing the black-haired entity could do to her that wouldn't pale compared to the desperation clawing at her insides.

Vibrant aqua eyes shifted to regard Beth with wariness and a measure of indignation. That she considered Beth's boldness in coming so close a challenge was painfully clear, and Beth nearly buckled under the being's intimidating presence. Perhaps she would have if Reith hadn't stepped to her side and entwined the fingers of one hand with hers, in offering of support. He glared at his wife as though daring her to ignore Beth's existence, then lifted Beth's clasped hand and pressed its back to his heart.

The gesture infused Beth with a powerful sense of rightness. Her voice calm yet firm, she said, "If you do have the ability to save Lachlan, it would be a grave injustice to let him die."

"And what shall you offer me in return?" Blue asked, her tone edged with sarcasm. "Your firstborn?"

Beth stiffened and looked defiantly into the mesmerizing eyes. "No. I can't sacrifice one life for another. Not even my own, because Lachlan and I are one, and the children are the product of our love." She hesitated, unsure what to call the queen of the faeries, then continued, "Your Majesty—" She gulped and mentally cursed the tears spilling from her eyes. "Do you know what it's like to love someone so much it hurts to even think of a day when you won't be together?"

The aqua eyes flicked but an instant to Reith, then were again staring deeply into Beth's with such detachment, a sob caught in Beth's throat.

"She knows," said Reith, his gaze on Blue both accusatory and challenging. "It be the shame I brought upon my wife, my clan, and myself wha' has embittered her."

Blue's shoulders drew rigidly back as she met his gaze. Beth could almost feel the animosity emanate from the queen, and it frightened her. "My *husband* is dead," said Blue, her voice devoid of emotion.

"Annsachd," said Reith, calling her "darling" in Gaelic, "he stands afore ye, as weel ye know." He frowned scoldingly, one eyebrow arched and his head tilted to one side. "But this isna abou' us, Blue. Aye, it pains me deeply to see these good people made to suffer, and there be the reason o' your hesitation to follow the dictates o' your conscience."

"You're incapable of caring for anyone but yourself!"

Releasing Beth's hand, he stepped up to Blue, too close, for her right hand shot up and smacked against his chest, stopping further advance on his part. With a sigh of impatience, he glanced down at the long-fingered barricade, then placed one of his own atop it. She attempted to withdraw her hand, and looked startled when he held it firmly in place, his unwavering gaze locked with hers.

"I care, especially for this mon, Lachlan," he said, his voice inordinately deep. "Aye, as laird o' this outer world, his hirin' me thwarted your banishment o' me from the land, too, and how tha' must gall ye. But I know ye will no' permit an innocent to die."

She wrenched her hand free and reared back, her wings fluttering in cadence with her anger-induced pulse rate.

"To spite me," he challenged, "would ye truly disgrace yourself, my queen, my wife, my love? For disgrace ye would bear were ye to let Lachlan die. He be no' like ither men. No ither mortals. Why else would Deliah risk her life to give him more time?"

When she remained belligerently silent, his temper flared. *"Och,* your stubbornness be unfounded in this matter!"

"It's not a faerie's place to interfere with a mortal's fate," she declared.

With a guttural sound of frustration, Reith threw his hands up, then slapped his thighs. "I demand an audience wi' MoNae!"

"She is far away, on a dire mission concerning one of

our cousin kingdoms," said Blue coldly. "I did try to summon her. To no avail."

Reith's face darkened. "Then hear me weel, Your Majesty. Afore ye mak an error o' which I vow will haunt ye the whole o' your existence, think wi' your mind, and no' your heart!"

"Are you threatening me?"

A sour laugh escaped him. "Wi' wha'? I be stripped o' my powers and my status. But mak no mistake, Blue, I *allowed* all that to be."

"You arrogant—"

" 'Twas penance proper for my crimes, but it be *ye* who be arrogant if ye fancy the notion I couldna have countered the spell!

"Ye talk o' no' interferin' wi' wha' fate decrees on mortals?" he asked snidely, his hands on his hips as he leaned his face closer to hers. "Wha' o' The Sutherland, and the mortals we rescued? I dinna recall us questionin' fate then!"

Blue's nostrils flared. "It was to free our own."

Reith flagged a hand in exasperation. "The mortals worked wi' us, mayhaps ou' o fear for their own lives, but fought alongside us, nonetheless. MoNae didna frown upon *tha'*, did she? No." He pointed to his sister. "And wha' o' Deliah? She be wi' a mortal's child, and carryin' it in the mortal way. A *uirisg* has been but a myth in the past. Do ye think yourself so grandly empowered now tha' MoNae's wishes be beneath ye? *Och!* Surely Deliah couldna be wi' child withou' the blessin' o' our goddess!"

Suddenly, as if too drained to defy her any longer, he sank to his knees. His arms hung limply at his sides as he lowered his head in deference. His tone low and pleading, he said, "Do wha' ye feel ye must to punish me, but dinna mak these people pay for my mistake. Long ago, this land was cursed wi' The Sutherland. 'Tis Baird land now, and this mon has given the earth his heart and soul, and a respect and love only equaled by tha' o' a faerie kingdom."

"Don't make him beg for us," said Beth softly, her face

wet with tears. "I don't know what happened between you two, but the Reith I know and the Reith Lachlan cares deeply for doesn't deserve your anger."

Blue stared at Beth for a long moment, her expression unreadable, her posture regal, but no longer hostile. "If I grant your man his life through the magic of the circle, it will open the two worlds to one another. I must first consider the welfare of the kingdom."

"We're no threat to you or your people," said Winston, coming to stand to Beth's left. He gave a curt, awkward bow of his head to Blue, then released a shuddering breath. "Deliah told me about the warlock, and how the kingdom vanished."

Blue nodded grimly. "My people were held captive for over three hundred years, Mr. Connery. We've barely settled back into our home."

"I know." Winston cleared his throat. "I-um, picked up tha' piece o' information when I invaded your mindspace."

One of her eyebrows quirked up in disapproval.

Winston shifted with unease. He couldn't help but wonder why the queen's feet never touched the ground, but forced himself not to scan her for the answer. Instead, he stated, "Your Majesty, Lachlan has brought his own element o' magic to this place. He has this ability to bring light to darkness, and hope to despair. All the mortals you see before you are better people because o' Baird House."

Her gaze shifting, Blue pointed to Taryn, who jerked in alarm and indignation. "That one cannot be trusted."

Beth almost felt sorry for Taryn, for suddenly all eyes were on her, suspiciously questioning the queen's declaration. But Beth's sympathy went only so far, for if Taryn in any way ruined Lachlan's one chance to live she vowed she would choke the life out of the woman.

"My sister has no' been here long enough to—" began Roan, but Taryn heatedly cut him off.

Her face pale and gaunt, she kept her arms folded against her midriff. "Who the hell do you think you are!" she cried at Blue. "You don't know anything about me!"

"I know enough."

"Be silent," Roan demanded of his sister, but she was too incensed to listen.

"You think I'm going to write about this?" Taryn laughed at Blue. "Lady, I could publish a piece declaring the president was from Mars, and it would read more believable than anything I could expose about what I've seen *here!*"

"Taryn, let it go," warned Beth.

"Why is she picking on *me?* I've taken all the guff I'm going to! It's one thing to get ragged on by someone of my own species, but this winged wonder declaring I'm untrustworthy goes beyond my tolerance!"

"You're an outsider," Blue said, not unkindly.

"Only because o' circumstance no' o' her doin'," said Roan, surprising Taryn in his defense of her. "Your Majesty, Taryn may be a wee rough around the edges, but she isna heartless." He passed his sister a fond although sheepish look. "She willna expose the existence o' your kingdom. No' because she's worried no one will believe her, but because she understands tha' there are some realities the world doesna need to know."

Blue sighed as if bored. She looked down at Reith's bent head and said curtly, "Get off your knees."

A moment passed before Reith stood and stared into her fiery eyes. Beth's gaze darted between the couple. She couldn't begin to imagine what Reith could have done to warrant his wife's mistrust and contempt, but they were a stunningly beautiful couple, and she was struck by a strong notion that Blue did in fact still love her husband, and that her austere demeanor was but a front to conceal her raw emotions.

Winston returned to Deliah, who was barely conscious, lifted her into his arms and returned to Beth's side. Blue's gaze lowered to Deliah's wan features, and her expression melted to one of poignant sorrow. She grazed the fingertips of one hand along Deliah's clammy cheek, then sadly looked into Beth's eyes.

"In all good conscience, before I can bring your world

and mine onto one plane of understanding, you, Beth, must choose one amongst you to represent a Pledger. It shall then fall upon this mortal the responsibility to protect our realm from outsiders, and to arbitrate matters which will come to concern faeries and mortals alike."

Beth's head shot around in Roan's direction. After a moment of hesitation, he came forward. He stood behind Beth, his hands on her shoulders, an uneasy looked at Blue, who stared at him through a guarded expression.

"I choose Roan," said Beth, "because he is the new laird of the Baird estate. He is also a man of compassion and honesty."

"Wait, Beth," Roan murmured. He stepped to Reith's right and, keeping his gaze on Blue, said, "It would be an honor to accept this position o' Pledger, but I canna help but feel Lachlan would choose someone else, and it is *his* life we are bargainin' for."

Blue nodded slowly.

"There is someone Lachlan is verra fond o'," Roan continued, sparing Beth a quick glance. "Someone he trusts, and someone I believe Lachlan would say was best to negotiate matters atween our worlds."

Blue's wings batted the air in a flurry of irritation. "I will not accept him."

Beth's face brightened, and she smiled as she locked gazes with Roan. Then they both looked at Reith, who glanced at each of them as if unaware of what was coming.

"Reith has lived in both worlds," said Roan, resting a hand on one of Reith's shoulders.

"He was banished with just reason," Blue said defensively.

Reith's breath hitched as he gratefully nodded to Beth, then Roan. He met his wife's heated gaze and said calmly, "Ye canna accuse me o' no' offerin' my life to protect my people, nor can ye say I dinna have respect for mortal ways. Aye, Blue, I be the best Pledger, for I can and will guard both worlds to the best o' my ability."

He grinned ruefully. "I understand your loathin' o' such

an appointment. 'Tis far easier for ye to keep your heart hardened against one you dinna have to face."

"You will abuse the position," Blue accused.

"No. I be no' tha' younglin' who nearly destroyed Faerie and betrayed ye. I earned my measure o' trust wi' these people. Mock me if ye so deem it necessary, but MoNae, my parents, my kingdom—and aye, *ye*—will one day welcome me home. Till then, I will serve as groundskeeper *and* Pledger, and no' regret anither day o' my life."

"Your intentions are as flighty as the winds, and about as reliable as chance."

"In the past, aye. But I know ye now see me as tha' prince you once held so dearly in your heart. Blue, I do no' accept the position o' Pledger to get closer to ye, but because it be right for both faeries and mortals."

Blue's head jerked to the left, and she frowned. She pointed in the direction of the carriage house, which couldn't be seen through the swirling winds, and she opened a small gateway with an impatient wave of a hand. Kahl, Kevin, and Alby dashed into the circle, their faces red and swollen from crying. The older boys ran to Laura, while Alby headed toward Roan. Reith intercepted the boy and lifted him into his arms. Roan went to Laura, knelt, and enclosed the boys in his embrace, for Laura still held Ciarda and could do no more than sit on the ground next to her nephews.

Beth nestled Broc closer to her body and watched Blue's wistful expression when Alby's small arms wrapped around Reith's neck. Somehow she knew the Faerie queen longed for a family of her own, and sensed such a vastness of loneliness in the being that she wanted to weep for her. Over Reith's shoulder, Alby stared miserably at Lachlan's body as it hovered. Sobs racked his small frame, and he whimpered, "Uncle Lannie."

"Dinna worry, lad," Reith soothed, and kissed Alby on the cheek. When Alby's blue eyes searched Reith's face with an unspoken question, Reith smiled. "Do ye believe in magic, young Master Alby?"

He nodded vigorously.

"Weel, lad, let me introduce ye to the queen o' all Faerie's wee folk. Her name be Blue, and she holds in her heart the makin' o' the magic o' this land."

Alby twisted around to stare at Blue. Beth noticed the queen was ill at ease now, unnerved by the attention of the boy. Blue shrank back when Alby held out his arms to her and, hurt by her rejection, he wept hard against Reith's neck. Blue glanced at Beth, conveying her regret for her reaction. Then she hesitantly glided closer to Reith and held out her arms. At first Alby refused to release his hold on Reith, but the Pledger laughed softly and murmured in the boy's ear, "Ye startled her. Can ye no' find it in your heart to give her a wee hug?"

"She hates me!"

"No," Blue said, gently placing a hand on Alby's back. "A hug would surely brace me for the magic to be conjured up to save your Lachlan."

Alby turned and permitted Blue to take him into her arms. He stared in wonder at the wings at her back, then briefly looked her in the eye before linking his arms around her neck. A mask of serenity fell across Blue's face. She looked at Reith with uncertainty, her heart warring with her mind, her hand stroking the back of Alby's head with the tenderness of a mother. Finally, she sighed and held the boy out to look into his expressive eyes.

"Your Lachlan must be a very special man," she said softly.

Alby nodded, then touched her cheeks with his fingertips. "We were sad when Beth and Lannie went to Heaven, 'cause we thought we wouldn't see them no more," he said, his voice hitching now and then from crying so hard. "The boogeyman tried to kill Lannie. That's not fair. The boogeyman wanted to hurt everybody. He was bad. I'm glad he's dead."

"I don't mean to be disrespectful," said Winston anxiously, "but while we stand around chattin', Deliah and Lachlan are dyin'."

"They're in stasis," Blue assured.

"Do you have lots of magic?" Alby asked hopefully.

"The kingdom has lots. I'm only the channeler."

"If you help my Uncle Lannie, I promise not to cry no more," he said, his chin quivering.

"It's good to cry when you hurt," Blue said, her eyes misting. "We will all save your Lachlan."

"I don't have no magic."

Blue smiled. "But you do, in here," she said, tapping a fingertip to his heart.

His eyes wide with awe, Alby said, "You can have it all, if you want."

"We'll share, okay?"

He nodded.

"All you have to do is wish as hard as you can for Lachlan to accept the magic."

"Wish hard?"

"Very hard. Can you do that, Alby?"

"Yep. I can wish so hard my eyeballs will pop out."

A short time ago, the Faerie queen had emerged from the oak belligerent, hostile, and angry. Now she laughed, and the dulcet sound rippled through the air as sweet as a bird's song, allaying any remaining fears that she would not choose to intervene on Lachlan's pending death. She lowered Alby to his feet and told him to stand with his brothers. Then she looked at Beth, her beautiful features radiant, as if a great burden had been lifted from her shoulders.

"I am ashamed to admit that I had forgotten what mortal children and faeries share alike," she said to Beth.

"What is that?" Beth asked.

"Hope everlasting." Her gaze swept the others, then returned to Beth. "Without it our kingdoms would vanish, and your children would become apathetic adults who would eventually destroy each other and what they could of the world."

She glided to Beth and lightly touched the sleeping

Broc's brow. "Children are the hope of all kingdoms, are they not?"

"Yes," Beth said, "but so are all the people we love."

Blue stared deeply into Beth's eyes for a long moment, her expression unreadable. "Is this Lachlan truly worthy of you?"

"No," Beth said with a strangled, low laugh.

"In saying 'no,' you mean yes?"

Beth sighed raggedly and briefly rolled her eyes to the heavens. "Yes. If anything, I'm the one who isn't worthy of him, sometimes. To know him is to love him. He's . . . Lachlan."

"Then I guess the time has come to call upon the Circle Of Magic."

Blue unwittingly locked her gaze with Reith's. A blush rose to her cheeks and she rapidly looked away as if she had displayed weakness instead of compassion. Then her wings twitched in an unmistakable show of annoyance, and she glared at Reith in a mute demand he step aside to let her pass. When instead of complying he casually folded his arms against his chest, she soared above his head, deliberately letting her toes bump his brow. Beth, too, had wondered about the queen's reluctance to set foot on the ground. Now she knew why. Blue's legs remained motionless during her short flight to Lachlan—not extended, but hanging as though leaden. She positioned herself at his head. Again her feet remained a few inches off the ground as she extended her arms over Lachlan's stiff, hovering form. The swirling specks of light around his body slowed, then abruptly stopped. Each transformed into a mortal-sized faerie, wings unfurled, their arms held out over the center figure of their gathering. Lachlan. Glittering dust of every imaginable color formed a ring above their heads, then another behind their calves. The queen began a chant in Gaelic and the others joined in, the voices an orchestration of harmony.

"The females be the channelers," Reith explained to

Beth, his voice kept low so as not to disturb the concentration of the ring. "Till Blue, males always ruled."

"Thank you for defending us," Beth whispered.

His forlorn gaze drifted to his estranged wife. "I could do no less. Think no' unkindly o' her, Beth. In truth, she be kind and compassionate."

Beth didn't comment on his commendable loyalty to Blue. She glanced at Roan, Laura, and the boys. Their attention was riveted on the ring of faeries, whose melodious chant was becoming increasingly hypnotic. Only Beth was aware of more faeries emerging from the oak. They stood in the distance, their heads bent and eyes closed in exclusive concentration of the ritual in progress.

She looked over at one winged couple, who lifted their heads in unison and opened their eyes to return her stare. Somehow, Beth knew they were Reith's parents. He bore no resemblance whatsoever to either of them. Their gazes flicked to him, then back to her, and she offered them a small smile. His mother returned the greeting, but his father remained poker-faced, and she reasoned that he missed his son and was too distraught to approach him. Distraught or proud. She wasn't sure which.

Beth forced herself to observe the ritual. She was dimly aware that the circle of winds had expanded to allow for the hundreds of faeries now attending the gathering. Serenity mantled the site. Lost to the tune of the chant, she dazedly stared off into space. Lachlan's body was blocked by those of the channelers. Her blood felt as if it throbbed with the chant's cadence. She was no longer worried if Lachlan would make it. He would. She had sensed in Blue a determination to succeed.

An image of the Phantom's broken body formed on her mindscreen. It didn't upset her to see him. He would never hurt anyone again, and that was all that mattered. Someone would have to go for the police. Not all of the details could be given, but there was time enough to work out a viable story.

She thought of Stephan Miles. Now she understood that

he'd come to warn her, but when he'd materialized in the master suite at the foot of the bed, the shock of seeing him hadn't put her in a frame of mind conducive to rational thought. Assuming his flailing tactics were but a childish attempt to frighten her, she'd vented her outrage through a diatribe, during which the Phantom had come up from behind and overpowered her.

How easily they all could have fallen victim.

Again, Baird House would become besieged by reporters. Another tragic death would hit the newswires. If there had been even a slim chance she and Lachlan could raise their children on the estate, it was lost.

A soft hum drew her from her musings. The air was alive with energy. It vibrated pleasantly against her skin, tickling. To her right, Winston was lowering an alert and wide-eyed Deliah to her feet. Four female faeries approached and, although outwardly wary of Winston, eagerly pulled Deliah aside. Again, Beth somehow knew these were some of Deliah's sisters.

With a dreamy smile, Winston observed the exchange of hugs, and it struck Beth that he had come a long way from being that tortured soul who'd first returned to the estate. Then she wondered how she knew about that, too. No one had mentioned why or when he'd come to stay, and yet she clearly remembered seeing him in his car, unshaven and half frozen, hoping death would free him from the misery that had been his life. That Winston Ian Connery no longer existed. This Winston was happy and unafraid of the future, hopeful and passionate in his love for Deliah.

Beth unwittingly focused on a male faerie standing behind Laura and Roan's position. He wore an oddly rapt expression, his attention on Laura's nephews as if this were the first time he had been this close to mortal children. Leaning over, he peered down at Ciarda in Laura's arms. His smile was pixyish, and Beth felt a flutter of warmth behind her breast. Then he looked up directly at her and straightened, his worried expression conveying his concern that she didn't approve of his proximity to the children. Beth smiled and nodded her head. After a moment's hesitation, he walked toward her, paused midway, then proceeded when she continued to smile. Winston spared him a measuring glance before turning back to watch Deliah and her sisters, and the parents, who had now joined the small group.

The male faerie was younger than she had first thought, although it was impossible to actually determine his age. Lookwise, she would say he was in his mid-teens, but he could be over one hundred years old for all she knew. He stood three feet from her, his arms relaxed at his sides, his wings twitching nervously. He cast the Circle of Magic a cursory look, then grinned shyly at Beth.

"I'm Beth Staples," she said, her voice low, her right hand outstretched.

Again he hesitated, then cautiously clasped her fingers with his left hand. His skin was warm and soft. Dark blue eyes watched her with the curiosity of a child. He was slightly shorter than she, lean and muscular, his shoulders broad for his size. Shaggy brown hair fell to his shoulders, and even in the overly bright starlight which shone on the wind-enclosed area, she saw that his eyelashes were long and thick. His lips were full. When he smiled deep dimples were visible in his cheeks. He wore a dark green tunic and black leggings. The other faeries wore tunics, too, of various lengths and colors, and leggings. Some, she'd noticed wore delicate slippers, while many, like this one, were shoeless.

"Jondee," he said, his voice barely above a whisper.

He released her hand and tilted his head to one side. His scrutiny was like that of a child encountering something new and wondrous, and Beth felt the heat of a blush bloom on her cheeks. He was far younger than Deliah, of that Beth was sure.

He passed another glance to the circle, then said, "Your male be nearly healed."

"I'm forever in your people's debt."

This surprised him. "No, mistress."

"I am," said Beth happily, "and gratefully so."

His eyebrows rose and fell, then he glanced in Laura's direction. When he looked into Beth's eyes, he frowned. "When I was a chair, several mortal younglin' sat on me, but I have no' had the experience o' touchin' one wi' my hands."

When you were a chair? Beth thought, bemused.

"Would be it improper to ask ye if I may hold one o' your younglin's?" He rushed on, "I vow to be verra careful."

Beth's gaze swerved to where her babies were. Without further hesitation, she led Jondee to Roan and Laura. The couple smiled a bit dazedly in greeting. Laura's nephews were uncharacteristically quiet, sitting on the ground side by side and staring transfixedly at the Circle of Magic. They didn't even look up at Beth's approach.

"How are you holdin' up?" asked Roan. Ciarda, now in his arms, squirmed, and he absently lowered his head to kiss her brow.

"Kind of numb," Beth replied. "Is it me, or are we all dreaming?"

"I don't think I've ever seen anything more beautiful," said Laura, her gaze on the faerie ring. "I'm ready to believe in Santa Claus and the Easter Bunny."

With a soft chuff of laughter, Beth took Jondee by the hand and coaxed him to stand alongside her. "This is Jondee." Roan and Laura offered another smile. "Jondee, this is Roan Ingliss, the new laird, and his fiancee, Laura Bennett."

Jondee bowed his head graciously. " 'Tis an honor."

"Jondee would like to hold one of the babies," said Beth to Laura and Roan, then she asked Jondee, "Broc or Ciarda?"

His face beamed with joy. "Be one a girl child?" he asked breathlessly.

"Ciarda."

Roan gingerly placed the infant into Jondee's waiting arms.

At first he stood as still as a statue, staring into Ciarda's face as if awestruck, as if to move would somehow break the baby. Then he gracefully lowered himself to the ground, folding his legs beneath him. He shifted Ciarda into the crook of one arm, and shifted her again to test her willingness to be handled by a stranger. Then he gently unfolded the blanket and lifted her with his hands positioned beneath her arms. He held her face level with his own. She no longer squirmed, but seemed to stare at him as if content and secure in his hold.

"Ciarda," he said on a wistful sigh. "Ye be as lovely as your name." He looked up at Beth, grinning broadly, his youthful features illuminated by the starlight. Looking again at Ciarda, he cradled her against one shoulder and rocked to and fro, humming sweetly.

Roan's deep sigh drew Beth's attention.

"When I think I've seen all there is to see in the world," he said, "anither miracle unfolds. Canna imagine anythin' grander than this, though," he added, his gaze darting in the direction of Lachlan's benefactors.

Beth nodded. She was about to voice her agreement when she felt compelled to look at Taryn. She stood away from everyone else, her arms pressed against her middle, looking lost, vulnerable.

Glancing at his sister, Roan said grimly, "She willna join us. I'm worried abou' her, Beth."

"I'll talk to her," said Beth, and passed Broc into Roan's proffered arms.

She went to Taryn and placed a hand on one of her slumped shoulders. The pale amber eyes flicked her an acknowledging glance, but then returned to staring off into space.

"Are you all right?"

Taryn's shoulders twitched in response.

"I'm sorry your visit has been so harrowing."

Taryn dully regarded Beth. "Don't worry. I'll be out of your hair, first thing in the morning."

The dispassionately delivered statement caused Beth to frown. "No one is forcing you to leave, Taryn. So we didn't hit it off. We really haven't had the chance to get to know one another."

"Don't get mushy," Taryn sneered.

"I'm trying to apologize for my behavior."

The arrogance vanished from Taryn. "Fine, but you don't owe me anything, including an apology."

Sighing, Beth said, "You really make it tough to like you."

"One of my better qualities."

"I like your spunk, Taryn. It's not always easy to cope with, but I imagine you need it in your career."

"It helps."

"Did he hurt you?"

Taryn looked Beth in the eye. "Not really. I'm more pissed than anything that he got the jump on me. Do you know who he was?"

While Beth explained what she knew, Taryn stared at Winston and gave a single nod when Beth finished.

"Makes you wonder what makes a man like that tick, huh? They're coming out of the woodwork these days."

Beth agreed. "Have you ever thought of going into serious journalism?"

A wry grin appeared on Taryn's mouth, and she shrugged. "I think about a lot of things."

"Have you ever considered settling down and having a family?"

Taryn's astonishment swiftly vanished. "I didn't figure you for someone who believes a woman's greatest expectations should revolve around a man and kids."

"You make it sound like a nasty proposition." Beth glanced at Jondee. "Of course, it isn't the answer for every woman. There was a time when all I wanted was to finish college and decide what I wanted as a career."

"What happened?"

With a grin, Beth looked at Taryn. "Scotland. Lachlan."

Somberly, Taryn nodded. "I guess I would opt for the domestic life if I found someone like him. You're lucky, you know. Too bad he doesn't have an identical twin."

Several moments passed while they watched the Circle Of Magic. Then Taryn asked in low, husky voice, "Do you think there's a chance they can pull this off?"

A pang of realization took Beth by surprise, but instead of addressing the issue of Taryn being in love with Lachlan, she said, "One of the male faeries assured me it's almost over."

"It's funny, but none of this is real. I mean, I know I'm seeing it, I'm not dreaming, but it's . . .not real."

"Life at Baird House," Beth said wistfully.

"The police are gonna raise hell about the stiff."

Beth grimaced. "I know, but I'm more worried about the press—sorry."

"Forget it. You know, we need to compose a believable story that will satisfy the police and the press. I don't think you and Lachlan should be involved. Let Roan or Winston say they pushed the bastard out the window."

"You're willing to omit part of the truth?"

"Yeah. Why are you so surprised? We can't say anyone was stabbed, because Deliah-The-Wonder made all the boo-boos go away. Can't even claim the sick prick had a weapon at all. Whatever is decided, we *all* have to stick to it."

"I agree."

Beth's deep voice lifted Taryn's eyebrows. "You thought I'd rush to my laptop and spill the whole story, huh?" She shook her head disparagingly. "No, thank you. Some truths are better left unsaid."

"Thanks, Taryn."

"For what?"

"Being a compassionate woman first, a reporter and paparazzi second."

Taryn groaned. "Gads, I'm gonna puke. Beth, I'm going along with this because no one would believe it if I wrote up the entire story. Sure, there's acceptable weird, but this soars far out of that range. I'm just protecting my ass, so don't get misty-eyed thinking I have a magnanimous bone in my body."

"You're really opposed to anyone knowing you have a heart, aren't you?"

"Me? No one really cares if I do or I don't." She nodded in the direction of Roan and Laura. "Go bug them. I'd like to return to the comfort of a stupor."

Beth smiled. "Roan's worried about you."

"Yeah, well, tell him to keep his big brother sentiments to himself."

"I'll just say you're all right."

"Whatever."

Beth was reluctant to leave Taryn alone, but nonetheless returned to the group. Jondee rose to his feet and faced her, his eyes sparkling with delight. Ciarda lay in the crook of his arm, blinking at the world and cooing softly.

"I have pledged myself to young Ciarda," he said proudly, his head held high and his shoulders squared. "When she comes o' age, I will come to claim her."

Beth's mind went blank, her expression deadpan, while a startled Roan and Laura exchanged a harried glance. Perplexed, Jondee looked at them, then seriously regarded Beth. "I have long had dreams o' pledgin' to a mortal girl child."

"Really?" Beth tried to smile and failed. "But, Jondee, mortals don't pledge to children."

Jondee's perplexity deepened. "She has accepted me."

"She can't even talk yet."

"Aye, she canna speak, but her mind acknowledges me. Do ye deny me the right to win her when she comes o' age?"

Beth cast Roan a look of helplessness.

"Now, Jondee," said Roan kindly, "mortal females are fickle. Wha' say we wait till she's grown?"

Jondee searched Beth's wary expression. "I be untried." When Beth frowned, he explained, "Chaste, mistress."

He went on, "In my dreams, MoNae tells me—although

it has been forbidden to claim a mortal as a lifemate—mine be, in truth, one o' your world."

Beth laughed a bit unsteadily. "Dreams aren't usually premonitions."

"To a mortal, no?" he asked with genuine surprise.

"Well . . . no. I mean, it could be true, but not necessarily that my daughter is the one."

"Aye, it be her. Patient and chaste I will remain for Ciarda."

"Beth."

Roan's curt tone stabbed her with alarm, and her gaze followed to where he was pointing. The rings that had been around the Circle Of Magic were gone. Stillness and absolute quiet pervaded the enclosure. Apprehension crept up Beth's spine until the channelers began to separate and she spied Lachlan sitting up, his hands cupping his head. Running to his side, she dropped to her knees and threw her arms around him.

"My head," he groaned. "Fegs, Beth, tell me I didna raid the bloody scotch again."

Laughing, Beth replied, "You fell out the window with the Phantom. The dirk was in your chest when you hit the ground."

"Tha' explains my heart burn."

"Lachlan, you almost died."

"How did I—" His head shot up and his eyes widened at the sight of the other onlookers. He couldn't absorb anything more at the moment than the fact they had wings. "Beth, what's goin' on?"

"Deliah's people have returned, Lachlan, and the queen, Reith's wife, called the Circle Of Magic to heal you."

"Reith's *wife?*"

"He's Deliah's brother."

A longer moan rattled in his throat. "My head's reelin'. Tell me one thing, love."

"What?"

Deadpan, he stared into her eyes. "Am I goin' to sprout wings now?"

"God, I love you!" she laughed and, framing his face with her hands, kissed him.

But of course it wasn't the time to rejoice. Winston's grave statement reminded them there were serious matters to attend to, and as soon as possible.

"I have to go into town for the police." All eyes, human and faerie alike, trained on him. "Beth, you and the twins can't be here when they arrive."

CHAPTER THIRTEEN

Beth tried not to think of what was going on in the main house, or of how extraordinary was her temporary refuge. The babies had been nursed and their diapers changed, and were now with their self-appointed guardians in another part of the dwelling.

She absently sipped her herbal tea. Its flavor was strong yet soothing, bitter yet sweet. When she placed the cup down, her hostess immediately topped it off with hotter brew, and she murmured, "Thank you." She'd had her fill of the round herbal cakes and sweetened root mash. There was so much for her mind to absorb. New sights and smells and flavors and impressions.

Lifting the cup, she took a moment to study the intricate floral design hand painted on its surface. Some of the flowers she recognized, others, she didn't, but they were all so perfectly detailed, she almost believed she could smell their fragrance.

She was in the main dining room, seated at one of the elongated oak tables, atop one of countless high-back chairs. All the furniture she'd seen thus far had engravings depicting nature scenes, and the walls were painted with murals of exquisite gardens. Torches were used to light the mazework of the dwellings, yet none of the rooms were smoky, nor the air stuffy.

It was a world unto itself, and no less miraculous or beautiful than that of Beth's.

"You surprise me, Beth."

She looked up into Blue's smiling countenance, a bit puzzled by her remark.

This morning, a full-length, backless gown of blue and white enhanced the queen's graceful figure. The sides of her hair were braided and woven with ribbons, the rest left to hang in strands of satin ebony. Beth had yet to meet a faerie who didn't possess beauty of face and figure, who wasn't as graceful as a butterfly. She felt awkward among them. Gangly and plain. For the second day since entering Faerie, Beth had chosen to wear a tunic. Although the tweedlike fabric was soft, its texture was unfamiliar and had an earthy scent.

"Plant fibers," Blue said, and added when Beth gave a start, "Our fabric is woven from plant fibers."

"You can read my mind?"

Blue laughed, a musical sound. "I could, but haven't." She pointed to Beth's chest, her eyes lit with amusement. Beth glanced down to see she had a section of her tunic between a thumb and forefinger. "You were rubbing it, and had a most thoughtful look in your eyes."

Placing the cup back on the table and folding her arms atop the oak surface, Beth grinned sheepishly. "I'm sorry. My mind keeps drifting."

"I wonder why," said Blue impishly. "I must say, I was reluctant to allow you passage. Even the older faeries can't remember when last a mortal was brought into our nest. I'm glad Deliah persuaded me to reconsider. I've enjoyed watching your reactions to our ways. You've been very gracious—surprisingly so, considering I know you long to return to your Lachlan."

"Without you, I wouldn't have him, would I?"

Blue stirred the remains of her tea with a whittled implement shaped like a miniature oar. "I'm afraid I allowed my resentment for The Sutherland to prejudice me against all mortals." She solemnly met Beth's gaze, then smiled apologetically. "Foolish, I know, but I'm afraid I haven't had the time to polish my attitude." She became mockingly serious and deepened her voice. "There is a proper mind-set for royalty, after all."

Beth laughed. "May I say something?"

"Of course."

After a short hesitation, Beth ventured, "Why do I have the distinct impression you're not happy being a queen?"

Blue's eyebrows quirked upward, then settled in place. "I don't believe I'm the best qualified, especially in light of the fact we have only recently regained Faerie's populace and returned to our land."

Beth frowned thoughtfully. "What happened to the kingdom? During the gathering, I remember Winston saying something about a warlock."

Strain made taut the lovely features across from her. Blue sighed in contemplation, then said, "The Sutherland. I don't mean to sound so cryptic, Beth, but it's something I'm not comfortable talking about, right now."

"How did you manage to put this place together so quickly?"

A hint of a grin appeared on Blue's mouth. "Faeries are extremely resilient. We've been back less than a month, and already they have rebuilt the kingdom of old. Whatever the tragedy, they persevere. Whatever task is demanded of them, they accept without question. Only one among them ever rebelled, ever brought grief and sorrow into the fold."

"Reith?"

Her mouth twisted into a parody of a grin. "Another subject I choose to avoid, although I do understand your curiosity." She sighed almost woefully. "But some things are better left the way they are."

Beth nodded, then frowned "Even if it pains you?"

"Then, too. Please, Beth, don't push me where he's concerned."

"All right. But there is something else I want to ask you."

Wariness clouded the queen's eyes.

"Why do you believe you're not qualified to rule this kingdom?" Beth asked passionately. "I may be out of line, here, but your self-esteem sucks."

Faerie's queen was taken aback. "You are blunt."

Beth's head reeled. It wasn't her intention to sully her welcome, but it disturbed her to know Blue dwelled in an emotional bog of sorrow. "Forgive me," she murmured, staring down at her cup. "Yes, I have a tendency to speak before I think." Her gaze lifted timorously. "Your admiration for your people is undeniable, but you didn't include yourself when you spoke of their character."

Silence permeated the large dining hall for a time. Beth was uneasy. It was all she could do not to squirm on her chair, while Blue maintained a cool facade. At a point when Beth felt as if she would burst from the tension building up inside her, Blue made a dismissive gesture and relaxed with resignation.

"I will tell you this much, Beth Staples." She kept her gaze lowered, on nothing in particular. "I was born at a time when others in my kingdom hibernate, and I came into this world with a stigma that further set me aside."

"Your legs?" Beth asked softly.

Blue smiled ruefully. "No. Reith crippled me."

The statement drained the color from Beth's face.

"It was an accident," Blue went on, "and is not the cause of my estrangement from him. No, the stigma was the fact I was born with light blue skin, which lasted until the night of the accident. Anyway, my appointment as queen came from a marriage that Reith shunned. That, and the three centuries I've lived in your world, soured my outlook."

"Crippled isn't an acceptable word anymore. You're physically challenged. You just have wings instead of a wheelchair."

"I sit corrected," Blue said wryly.

"Why did you have to live in my world?"

"I was searching for my people. My kingdom. The Sutherland held them captive. It was a fluke that I found Reith, and later, the rest of Faerie. They were all accounted for, with the exception of Deliah. Until two days ago, we thought her forever lost to us."

The anger in Blue's tone saddened Beth. "How do you expect to put all that in the past, Blue, if you can't forgive your husband? I know you love him, and you're miserable with loneliness."

Beth nervously wound a light brown curl around one of her fingers. "Personality-wise, you and I are a lot alike. We think and react from our hearts, and we tend to withdraw into ourselves rather than face what hurts us. But I don't have powers I can use to force Lachlan away when I'm upset with him. I can't hide in another world. I'm not about to try to minimize whatever Reith did to you, but I don't believe you would still love him if he were a hopeless cause."

Blue's rigid posture warned Beth she was going too far, but when the queen spoke, her tone was deceptively calm. "I have never been able to deny loving him. How can I? I was created for no other reason than to be his wife."

"Literally?"

Blue nodded, then heaved a weary sigh. The blue and purple of her wings glittered in the torchlight, the silver veins shimmering like mercury beneath sunrays. Her thick black eyelashes lowered just enough to shield her eyes from Beth. "In that, too, I am unlike the others."

"Well, I don't know too many mortals who have died and returned—with the exception of Lachlan. Different isn't wrong, Blue. We're just in an elite class, that's all."

A smile strained to appear on Blue's mouth. Her lashes lifted and she humorously regarded Beth for a time. "You're determined to change my mind about Reith"

"I'm *determined* to see you happy."

"That isn't in the stars."

"Bullshit—" Beth choked as her face inflamed with

embarrassment. To her further chagrin, Blue laughed until tears misted her eyes.

"Don't apologize," Blue said merrily. "I've been known to color my speech. A habit from my life among mortals."

"Lachlan doesn't appreciate my vocabulary."

"In truth, you could sprout warts and I doubt he would love you any less."

" 'Tis Lachlan the subject, I be sure," someone said in a singsong voice.

Beth and Blue looked up to find Deliah standing in the archway, a smile enhancing her features. She entered the hall and stopped to bow her head in reverence to Blue, then turned to Beth as she left her chair.

"And speakin' o' our Lachlan, he be anxious to see ye and his younglin's."

Beth's gladdened heart rose into her throat. "Is the investigation over?"

"Aye. Two constables stayed to ward off the reporters, but they, too, have now gone. 'Tis safe for ye to come home."

With a strangled laugh, Beth threw her arms around Deliah and hugged her. When Beth released her, she turned to Blue with tears in her eyes. "I can't thank you enough."

"Nor I, you," Blue replied graciously.

Beth went to the queen's right side and stared into the upturned face. "Are there any laws that decree mortals and faeries can't be friends?"

"If there were, I would abolish them," Blue said humorously, trying to make light of the tension building inside her. "I have enjoyed our time together."

Beth quickly crouched and grinned mischievously. "Then come to the house for tea, or supper, or breakfast—*hell,* whenever you like. I don't know how long Lachlan and I will be staying in Scotland, but I want us to stay in touch."

"That's kind of you," Blue murmured.

"Don't keep yourself hidden down here to avoid Reith."

Beth clasped one of Blue's hands and gave it a gentle squeeze. "Anytime you need to talk, I'll listen. I'll even promise to stop playing matchmaker, okay?"

Blue nodded, then hesitantly embraced Beth. It was brief, and she withdrew as if embarrassed to have displayed open affection in front of Deliah. When Beth stood and looked at Deliah, she noticed a hint of sadness in her eyes.

"Forgive me for not seeing you through the passage," Blue said, her tone shaky. "But I shall visit you at Baird House, Beth. In a day or two."

"I'll look forward to it."

Deliah again bowed her head to Blue, then gestured for Beth to follow her. Beth complied, but felt torn about leaving. She was eager to rejoin everyone at the house, but she'd only just begun to nudge the truth of Blue's withdrawal to the surface. After two days of nothing more than companionable conversation, Blue was finally beginning to trust her enough to confide in her. Now she was leaving, and she suspected they would be back to square one when the faerie queen did visit the mansion.

They were nearly through the archway when Blue called Deliah's name. Deliah turned in place and offered another bow.

"Your Majesty?"

Blue stared across the table, keeping her profile to them and hiding any emotion her eyes could betray. "Kareena tells me you and Winston are planning to wed soon."

"Aye, Your Majesty."

"I realize you are now part of both worlds, but I strongly request your vows be exchanged in the tradition of your people."

Deliah's head lowered. "I respectfully wish to be mairrit wi' my friends. We are hopin' to have a triple weddin'."

"I wouldn't exclude them from the ceremony," Blue said stiffly. "I'm not *that* unreasonable, Deliah."

"No' unreasonable at all," Deliah countered. "The fact ye now be my queen doesna change the fact we were once close friends."

Instantly contrite, Blue shifted her gaze to Deliah. "I value our friendship, Deliah, but as queen I must insist your vows be exchanged within the Circle Of Magic."

"Wha' o' my brither?" Deliah asked in a tremulous tone.

"The ceremony can be performed in the outer world," she said dully, as if it had taken all of her strength to grant this.

"And Reith?" Deliah asked anxiously.

"Why else hold it in the outer world? I can't allow him to enter the kingdom, but I also can't deny your right to have him attend your ceremony."

"Wha' o' ye, though? In exchange, will I lose the company o' my queen and friend?"

Blue shook her head and sighed. "No. I'm too selfish to deny myself the pleasure of seeing you wed. You, too, Beth. I'm a sentimental fool when it comes to vows of the heart."

"Because ye love so unequivocally."

Blue was about to respond to Deliah's statement, but instead she made a dismissive gesture with one hand. "Perhaps we can discuss the plans when I come for tea?" she asked with an impish grin directed at Beth.

Beth chuckled. "Then you'd better make it supper. Juggling plans for a triple wedding is bound to be harrowing—*even* for a queen of your worldliness."

The strain and tension evaporated from Blue as she laughed, the sound filling the dining hall. "I'll strive to use my *worldliness* for your ceremony. Now go, before Lachlan decides to dig his way here to fetch you."

Deliah led Beth into the main corridor. Even here, the compacted dirt walls bore murals and were lit with torches, the smoke of which rose into the painted ceiling. They passed entries to other corridors, and through a vast, open room where Deliah explained that the Circle of Magic used in bad weather to hold their rituals. When they came to the end of the corridor, a crisscross of roots stood before them. Here was the passageway to the outer world. The human world.

"Aren't we getting the twins?"

"They be sleepin'. Dinna worry. My sisters will return them as soon as they awaken."

"I know they're safe," Beth assured.

"Afore we cross over," said Deliah, her grave tone sending a chill up Beth's spine, "there be somethin' ye should know."

"Is it about Lachlan?"

"Taryn. She left yesterday morn."

"I was hopin' to talk to her"

"Aye. I wasna happy to see her leave afore she and Roan mended their relationship. But now we believe she left in haste for a reason."

"Oh, God, what?" Beth groaned.

"The dirk be missin'."

Beth jiggled her head in confusion. "Why would she take the dirk?"

"Efter we had ye securely down here and Winston had left for the police, Roan noticed there was blood on the sleeves o' her blouse. But she wasna injured, nor had she touched Lachlan efter his fall. She was defensive when Roan asked where the blood originated. Lachlan had been searchin' for the dirk. If ye remember, Roan had tossed it aside efter removin' it from Lachlan's chest."

"Yes. It fell near the stoop."

"Aye."

Beth frowned. "Taryn was crouching near there."

"Roan said the same. The dirk was never mentioned to the police, nor the injuries, for I had healed them. The police were told the Phantom had attacked Lachlan in the master suite, and while strugglin' he had fallen through the window to his death."

"Taryn backed up the story?"

"Aye, and convincin' she was. But the dirk wasna found. Efter she left, the boys were playin' in the attic and found a pendant which had belonged to Lachlan's mither."

"I don't understand the connection."

"Apparently, Taryn had been goin' through his mither's trunks."

"For what purpose?"

" 'Twas my question, too. Lachlan thought perhaps she'd been browsin' through them ou' o' curiosity, but Winston picked up some peculiar trace impressions when he handled the pendant. Apparently, our Taryn was searchin' for a lead to the origin o' the dirk."

"In Lachlan's mother's trunks?"

"Aye. And she found somethin', but neither o' us could determine wha' it was. The pendant has a strong aura o' energy protectin' it. Unfortunately, it maks scannin' the piece verra difficult."

Beth released a breath through pursed lips. "So Taryn's after another story. But why that damn dirk? She can't write about it nearly killing Lachlan for the second time. She wouldn't expose him like that. Even if she traces the origin of the dirk, who cares? Lachlan's murder has been grossly overwritten, already. What could she be hoping to gain?"

"Reith may have given us a clue," said Deliah solemnly. "Lachlan showed him the pendant last night. We were all in the parlor, tryin' to come up wi' a viable motive for her actions, when Lachlan commented tha' the demon faces carved on the pendant resembled those on the dirk."

Now Beth frowned in amused bewilderment. "Okay. Demon faces. Why aren't I surprised?"

"No' demon faces, Beth. Lachlan thought them tha', but in fact, they be gargoyles."

Beth chuffed a laugh. "Which means what?"

"Weel, there be few relics remainin' o' the time o' their reign."

"Their what? Weren't gargoyles first made as water spouts?"

"Aye, for their speech resembled tha' sound."

"Gargoyles. You're saying they were once alive?"

"Aye, but they have been extinct for thousands o' years. Beth, most myths were real at one time. To my knowledge, the Picts were the last to worship the gargoyles. Accordin' to Winston, their temples remain. One be called—"

"Stonehenge," Beth interjected breathlessly.

Deliah nodded. "Winston scanned the pendant, and believes it dates long afore the time o' the Picts. Because o' its aura, he couldna get an exact fix on when it was made."

"How would Lachlan's mother come to have it?"

"Tha' *and* the dirk both. I agree wi' my brither. No coincidence be this. Taryn only came to Baird House to find the dirk. In trackin' its history, Beth, she be delvin' into matters verra dangerous. The secrets o' the ancient gods be no' for mortals to know—*or* faeries."

"Even when she's not around, she's a pain in the ass," Beth grumbled.

"More'n ye know." Deliah took in a deep breath and massaged her brow. "I be tellin' ye this because the men-folk dinna want us to know they be talkin' abou' goin' efter her. Winston let it slip from his mind in his sleep. I have already told Laura."

"How did she take it?"

Deliah shrugged. "Verra weel, but said she would shackle Roan to the bed if he tried to leave afore the weddin'. Our men have no right to think us too fragile to know the truth."

"I agree."

"Whatever is decided to do abou' Taryn, we six should discuss it through. I have no' lived this long to be coddled and expected no' to have a mind o' my own."

"Deliah," Beth laughed, "you may look as delicate as a flower, but you're as tough as a weed."

A dubious frown appeared on the faerie's face. "Thank ye . . . I think. Shall we go?"

"No more revelations?"

"No' at the moment."

Although the sky of the outer world was overcast, Beth had to squint as she emerged from the new oak behind Deliah. The air was cool and held a promise of rain, and from the sounds of the peafowl's chatter as they were gathered on the rooftops.

"Lachlan be waitin' at the south gazebo," said Deliah. "Are your eyes now sensitive to the light?"

"A little. Go to Winston. I don't see a gray haze in front of your face anymore. I'm sure I can find Lachlan."

"When the twins are returned to the house, Laura and I will watch them."

"I can't ask you to do that."

"Ye no' be askin'," Deliah interrupted. "Laura and I discussed it this morn. Efter wha' ye and Lachlan have been through, a wee time alone be wha' ye both need. He's been a bit o' a grouch withou' ye."

"I'll do my best to de-grouch him, then. Thanks, Deliah."

"My pleasure."

Deliah headed toward the house. Beth watched until she entered the front doors, then headed for the gazebo. As she walked through the rose gardens she searched for him, but didn't see him until she'd stepped onto the planked floor of the gazebo. He sat on the lower step across from her, talking to himself—or so it seemed, at first. His light blue, full-sleeved shirt was stretched tautly across his broad back, and she released a thready breath in anticipation of caressing his warm, naked flesh.

Barefoot, her tread was silent as she closed the distance and positioned herself against the arch post, behind him. Braussaw stood on the ground in front of him, looking eerily alert for a stuffed bird.

". . . and when you put two females thegither, my friend, time has no meanin'. They'll chatter away the hours, they will, wi' no' a thought for their poor menfolk waitin' on the side for a wee lovin'." He sighed dramatically, and Beth had to compress her lips to keep from chuckling out loud.

"Ah, Braussaw, to be fair to my Beth, when she gives me her all 'tis far more'n most men can hope for."

The peacock released a guttural coo, which nearly made Beth jump out of her skin.

Braussaw was alive?

"Ahhh, you have it bloody good, you do," he said to the bird. "You eat and you sleep, and strut your stuff for all you're worth. Wha' do you worry abou', eh? You have nocht to lose, except mayhaps your tail to a feather bandit. I'm sure, though, most are no' willin' to brave the ire o' Baird House's ghost to pluck you clean."

He sighed again, a lonesome sound that tugged on Beth's heartstrings.

"Two days withou' Beth is an eternity. I never knew how large was my bed till she wasna in it. 'Tis a curse, you know. Aye, Braussaw, a curse a mon must bear when he loves a womon so much he canna think beyond the strain in his breeks for want o' her."

Kneeling behind him, Beth said, "A curse, is it?" and wound her arms about his chest. He gave an initial start of surprise, then laughed and clasped her forearms.

"You took your sweet time," he said happily. He turned his head and she kissed him by the side of his mouth. "I was afeared the faeries had decided no' to let you go."

"Blue was worried you would start shoveling to find me."

He shook with a laugh. "It crossed my mind."

Braussaw released a shrill caterwaul and flew to perch atop the peak of the gazebo. Beth winced when the sound stabbed at her eardrums, then released a mock cry as Lachlan finagled her atop his lap. Her eyes were bright with excitement as she linked her arms about his neck, and peered into the passionate depths of his eyes.

"Miss me a wee?" she asked teasingly.

Lachlan's eyebrows arched and a slow, devious grin formed on his mouth. "Your pillow is no compensation for you, lass."

"And what were you doing to my pillow?"

A dark flush suffused his face. "*Och,* Beth. Shame on you! I was snugglin' with the bloody thing, nocht more!"

Burying her face to one side of his neck, she laughed until his arms tenderly enfolded her and drew her closer against him. Her pulse racing, her lungs suddenly heavy, she looked up to see him lowering his head. She'd thought herself ready for his kiss, but as his mouth covered hers and began to move with languid sensuousness, her blood turned to liquid fire and her head went into a tailspin. She had never thought of kissing as an art until meeting him. He had a way of making every nerve in her body feel as though it was part of her lips, part of his exploration.

The muscles of his arms flexed against her, thrilling her with their masculinity and strength. Beth moaned when his right hand cupped the side of her outer thigh. His palm was hot, causing the skin beneath it to tingle. Then he trailed the fingers of the same hand up her thigh, stopping to caress and pamper and taunt her flesh. She squirmed and lost her fingers in the thickness of his hair, and pushed at the back of his head to urge him to kiss her deeper, deeper. Maddening sensations built inside her, not unlike those connected with the throes of a climax. She was sensitized to his musky scent and every curve and hard plane of his body. Sensitized to the wild thudding of his heart, and to his fingertips sliding over the roundness of her left buttock. He was somehow carrying her to the brink of gratification when he reared back and gasped, "Beth!"

Dazed, breathless, she blinked and rasped, "What?"

"Where are your wee bloomers?" he asked in stunned indignation.

"Panties, Lachlan. They're called panties, and faeries don't wear them."

"Weel," he sputtered righteously, "you are no' a faerie, are you! Fegs, lass, are you tryin' to mak my heart come to a cold stop?"

With a sigh of resignation, she straightened atop his legs and primly folded her hands on her lap. Too sweetly, she asked, "Do you realize there's only your breeks separating us?" and wiggled her eyebrows suggestively.

His eyes wide, his face beet reed, Lachlan could say nothing for a long moment. Then he expelled a breath and leveled a scolding look on her. "You're wicked.

Exposin' your privates in the light o' day—ou'side, no less!"

She playfully nuzzled the tip of his nose with hers. "If we were in our bedroom, you prudish hunk you, we would both be naked and—"

Her sentence died in her throat when he shot to his feet with her cradled in his arms. He headed for the house in a trot-run, the strain of carrying her carved into his face. His gaze remained fixed on his objective, and he didn't slow down until they reached the outer doors and he grunted for her to open them. Once they were in the hall Beth demanded, "Let me walk. Dammit, Lachlan, my ass is hanging out!"

She buried her face against his neck when a surprised Roan stepped aside on the first landing of stairs. She heard him chuckle as Lachlan took on the ascent with all the speed he could muster and marveled at his stamina when they reached the third floor. The hall passed in a blur, a door slammed shut, then suddenly she found herself on her back atop the bed, watching Lachlan hastily peel out of his shirt. He was breathing heavily, and his face and chest were coated with a fine sheen of perspiration. She scooted into a sitting position, pulled the tunic over her head, and tossed it over the far side of the mattress, noticing when she watched it fall that the broken window across the room had been boarded up.

"You mak me crazy, womon," he panted, and sat on the edge of the bed. He grunted and cursed in Gaelic as he struggled to remove his boots. One at a time, he tossed them across the room.

While he stripped out of his breeches, socks, and undergarment, Beth's gaze went to his portrait above the fireplace. She faced it, sitting on her folded legs, and dreamily likened the painted image to the man she knew. The artist had captured both Lachlan's pride and arrogant bearing, and also the mischievous glint that was often in his eyes.

Naked as the day he was born, Lachlan stood and turned to Beth, but his intended pose became lost to the wonder he experienced at seeing her sitting like a wingless cherub, adoringly staring at his portrait. The light brown ringlets of her hair fell past her shoulders, framing a face he believed grew more beautiful every time he looked at her. Tears welled up in his eyes and filled his throat. Of all his treasures she was his most precious, the one thing besides his children that he would fight to hold on to with everything he had in himself.

He placed a hand over his heart and sank to his knees, then folded his arms atop the mattress and rested his chin on them. The joy he felt eased his breathing. And when her head turned and her blue eyes met his, the devotion in their depths caused a tear to slip down his cheek.

"Beth," he said, the way he spoke her name a declaration of love in itself, "wha' you do to my mind, my heart, and my soul."

A ragged breath passed her lips. Stretching out on her front, she rested her chin atop her folded arms and brought her nose to within an inch of his. "If it's anything like what you do to mine, then I think we're in love, Lachlan."

He smiled timorously. "Love, you say? Probably so."

Nearly a minute passed while they contentedly stared into each other's eyes, then Lachlan lowered one side of his head atop an arm and said, "I do love you, lass. Bare arse and all."

"Even when I'm wicked?" she grinned.

"Shame on me," he said, sighing with exaggerated desolation, "but even then."

"It's chilly in here, Lachlan."

"Is it?"

"There are goosebumps the size of my ass, on my ass."

He winced, then closed one eye and gave her a thoroughly paternal look. "You love to shock me."

"Only when your nineteenth century prudery surfaces."

"Prude, am I?"

His movements slow and as graceful as a prowling panther, he climbed onto the bed. Beth luxuriously stretched out on her back and opened her arms to receive him, but this time Lachlan would not be rushed. Impish delight gleamed in his eyes as he knelt between her thighs and braced rigid arms to each side of her rib cage. Her legs and feet stroked his hips and outer thighs, and her hands caressed his face, throat, and chest. She was ready. No foreplay, this time. She wanted him now. He wanted to hear her moan, though, especially that hitching sound she made deep in her throat when she reached the end of her patience for him to enter her. Her eyes were glazed with passion, her pouty lips parted in invitation.

"Prude, am I?" he said huskily.

For the next hour, he made love to her skin with his hands and mouth, bringing her just to the brink of ecstasy so many times that she weakened with need. He tasted of her salty perspiration and of her passion, leaving no part of her untouched. When she tried to touch him, he held her wrists to the mattress until she acquiesced, then proceeded to take her again and again on various paths of pleasure.

Caressing and kissing every part of her body, he took her through heaven and hell and everything in between. When he was satisfied she could take no more, he entwined his fingers through hers and gently anchored her hands to the bed above her head. He lowered himself atop her, entering the heat of her without the use of a hand, and drawing her into a kiss that caused her to shudder with the depths of its passion. His muscles were taut with his determination to hold back when she climaxed, and her inner muscles demanded his joint release. Coated in perspiration, his lungs aching to breathe, he continued moving inside her until he felt renewed throes gripping her body.

With a cry of primordial rapture, she clutched him tightly within her legs and forced him deeply inside her. Shudders of exquisite ecstacy racked him. For a matter of seconds, he was one with her. Time and space didn't exist, nor reality in any form. When he was finally spent, he collapsed to one side and nuzzled her damp neck with his face.

Their panting breaths fell into synchrony. Lachlan laid a hand on her slick abdomen. He wanted to knead her soft skin, but he couldn't summon the strength.

"I think that . . . bordered on . . . torture," she wheezed.

"No' bad . . . for a . . . prude, eh? Fegs, I'm exhausted."

"You? Exhausted?" she chuckled.

"Lass, I did all the work."

"Torture, you mean."

"Whatever you say, love."

"Okay." She grinned up at the ceiling. "Again."

Lachlan frowned into the moist tendrils of her hair. "Wha'?"

"Again."

"Mak love?"

"Aye," she gurgled.

Weakly, he managed to prop himself up and look into her eyes. "Are you serious?"

In response, she arched one eyebrow.

Muttering Gaelic, he lowered his brow to the area between her breasts. "I canna . . . for a while, at least."

Stroking the back of his head, she whispered, "Wanna make a bet?"

CHAPTER FOURTEEN

Everyone at Baird House had practically forgotten about the attempted burglary of over a week ago, until two officers arrived to remind them. For the next three days, there had been no time to relax and begin the plans for the wedding. The younger of the two constables had been present the night of the break-in. The second was an older man, an inspector, with a burly attitude. Mornings, afternoons, and sometimes twice at night, they had come to question the original statements made by Laura, Roan, Lachlan, Deliah, and Winston.

No one in the household had ventured near the backyard to see the bulkhead, where the area had been cordoned off with yellow police tape. Beth and the infants remained hidden on the third floor, while Winston mostly handled the officers, for which Lachlan, Roan, and Laura were immensely grateful.

Inspector Douglas Grant was the problem. He was fond of telling them he didn't believe in coincidence, especially the convenience of Cuttstone and the burglar, Robbie Donnely, targeting the same house. It was this that made Grant a tenacious investigator. Winston again and again went over the details of the night the Phantom died, only omitting the MacLachlan dirk, Beth, and the twins. During each visit, Winston had remained calm—until the inspector had deviated from his questioning last night and asked about "Horatio" Lachlan's background, birthdate, place of birth, and occupation. Before Lachlan could think up a viable history, Winston informed the inspector they had been patient and cooperative till that point. Then he informed him that no more questions would be answered without a solicitor present. Inspector Grant had been wryly amused by this tactic, and assured Winston it wouldn't be necessary.

This morning Inspector Grant came to the house without another officer in tow, and on a different matter he said might possibly tie in with the recent deaths. To everyone's discomfort, he had encountered Reith at the carriage house and insisted the young man join the questioning.

Laura, Roan, Winston, Deliah, and Reith gathered in the parlor, while the boys remained in their rooms despite Grant's insistence they, too, be questioned. Roan adamantly warned the inspector he was stepping over the line, and Grant had acquiesced.

It was barely 8 A.M., and tempers were on the rise. This time, Laura refused to offer Grant coffee. His mood was overly cheerful as he sat in one of the high-back chairs and thumbed through a small pad. When he looked up he insisted everyone take a seat, then waited until they had followed his order.

Then his bombshell detonated, and the immediate tension in the room was so thick that it couldn't have been cut with a chain saw.

"Wha' can you tell me abou' Beth Staples's headstone?"

Silence and grim expressions met his inquiry.

"The one in the field?" he asked with a sardonic grin.

Again, silence was the only response, and Grant sighed with a theatrical flair. His gaze lingered for an excruciatingly long moment on Deliah, then Reith. During this time Winston scanned the man's mind, and his stomach clenched in to a sickening knot to discover that this time there wasn't a lie which could save them, or even bide them enough time to get Lachlan, Beth, and the twins out of the country.

The inspector's smug attitude permeated the room as he crossed one leg over the other and bobbed the raised foot. "We're no' verra cooperative this mornin', are we?" He grinned, his bushy dark eyebrows stretched upward as far at they could go. "Perhaps I'm confusin' you. Forgive me if I am. I'm sure you were prepared to go over your previous statements. Yet *again.*"

Lachlan rose to his feet, despite Roan's terse advice for him to sit and remain calm. But Lachlan wasn't in the least calm. A brewing storm of anger was visible in his dark eyes.

"Mr. Baird, I prefer you remain seated, if you will."

"I'll stand if I please, in my own home."

The inspector's mouth stretched a bit further in its condescending grin. "Your home? I thought Mr. Roan Ingliss—"

"Wha' do you want from us?" Lachlan asked heatedly.

"Don't say anythin' more," Winston warned.

"Bloody hell!" Lachlan sucked in a breath and glowered at the inspector. "Fegs, mon, the members o' this household have gone through quite enough!"

The inspector nodded in mock appreciation of Lachlan's statement, then eyed the information on his pad. "To be sure, Mr. Baird, and my heart does go ou' to each and every one o' you. However, there's more goin' on here than a couple o' dead bodies. So let's stop playin' games and get to the truth."

"You believe one or more o' us is capable o' murder?"

Grant chuckled a bit nastily. "Mr. Baird, I'm satisfied Cuttstone murdered Miles. And, though I shouldna admit to this, I really dinna care how tha' murderin' bastard—pardon me ladies—met his end. But I have been curious abou' the happenings at this house for a long time. You see, Mr. Baird, some years ago, I came here on one o' the tours, and I met your ghostly relative. Oh, no' in the context tha' I spoke to him. No. Unfortunately. But I saw him as clearly as I now see you."

"He had the ability to appear verra much alive," said Lachlan, his voice husky from the stress squeezing his insides.

Grant nodded. "I'll never forget tha' day. You could say it led me to tak up readin' abou' the paranormal as . . . oh, kind o' a hobby. I'm a curious mon by nature, and I'm curious abou' the anomalies surroundin' this house and its occupants."

He gestured expansively with his free hand, the grin intact and his gaze unwaveringly fixed on Lachlan's face. "So wha' does a mon in my position do abou' all the questions runnin' round in his mind?"

"I repeat," said Lachlan bitterly, "wha' do you want from us?"

Grant released a breath through pursed lips. "Mr. Baird, park yourself back on tha' couch, I'll tell you exactly wha' it is I want to know."

Lachlan hesitated, then lowered himself next to Winston.

"Thank you," said Grant cheerfully. He thoughtfully rubbed the spiraled top of the pad beneath his chin. "Okay, here's wha' I have. Feel free to jump in at any time wi' an explanation."

He looked upward, as if taking a moment to gather his thoughts. Lachlan's hands were fisted atop his lap, but he loosened them when Winston nudged him.

"There are four headstones ou' by the oak in the field," the inspector began, his gaze riveted on Lachlan. "Now, o' course Lachlan Baird's grave is duly registered, and I found the paperwork grantin' the Cambridges' burial on the property. However, Miss Staples is anither matter. It has come to my attention tha' the news media misspelled her last name, but there are no records regardin' her death wi' the county, under either name."

"It happens," said Roan.

The inspector's gaze shifted to him for but a second,

then returned to Lachlan with disquieting intensity. "On the night o' the attempted burglary, my dear friend and co-worker, Constable Clare Bruce, handed me a most curious report. Accordin' to him, no' only did a mon in this house claim to be *the* Lachlan Baird, but a womon said she was Beth Staples. Then o' course, we have the newspaper articles statin' Mr. Baird is in fact a descendant, but I found it a wee strange tha' there was no mention o' Miss Staples. And more curious still, I havena encountered her durin' my investigation, which maks me wonder why this womon is hidin'. So, either there's a verra cunnin' scheme afoul here to defraud the public, *or* . . . a no' so cunnin' scheme to confuse the police. Whichever the case, I intend to have those bodies in the field exhumed and examined."

"The *hell* you will!" Lachlan bit out, jumping to his feet.

"Sit down!" Grant ordered.

Lachlan defiantly glared at the man. When at last he sat, Grant gave an irritable shake of his head. "I *know* Beth Staples arrived at Prestwick Airport in July o' last year. I also *know* she arrived at this house by taxi. I have in my possession a copy o' the list o' passengers—bearin' her name, thank you—*and* Callum MacGregor's log o' his fares tha' same week. Imagine my surprise when his log revealed he had picked up a fare at Prestwick, and delivered this same fare to our verra own Baird House."

"Wha's the point!" Lachlan snarled. "I dinna deny she was here!"

Grant's eyebrows, as dark as his curly hair was white, quirked upward. "So you *were* here, then?"

"Aye!"

Winston shot to his feet, his face livid. "Are any o' us bein' charged wi' somethin', or are you here based on your curiosity, Inspector? Whatever your answer, I can't allow this questionin' to continue withou' a solicitor present."

Grant pinched the bridge of his nose for a short time. "And will you tell this solicitor why you have a Yank buried in the field, o' whom there isna a single report to verify her death? And will you explain to this solicitor where this—'' He gestured impatiently to Lachlan. "—*Horatio* character actually hails from, and how is it Miss Deliah and Mr. Reith's fingerprints canna be found on anythin' in this house or in the carriage house?''

His knees suddenly unable to support his weight, Winston sat. He was dimly aware of Deliah entwining the fingers of a hand through his, but he found no comfort in this gesture. His mind raced to no foreseeable end, and his heart seemed to be lodged in his throat.

''Aye, we did a thorough dustin' for fingerprints,'' Grant went on, no trace of his usual sarcasm present in his voice. ''And you know, Mr. Connery, anither matter which has me a wee confused is, you bein' a renowned psychic and all, how is it you didna know the Phantom was hidin' in the cellar?''

''Do ye know wha' be a telepath?'' Deliah quietly asked the inspector.

He nodded.

''The Phantom was verra strong in this ability.''

''Don't say any more,'' Winston told her.

''Ahhh. So, Miss Deliah, you're tellin' me he was able to block his presence from Mr. Connery?''

''And myself.''

Grant bobbed his head. ''Another psychic. Fancy tha', miss. And wha' o' Mr. Reith? Is he also psychic?''

''My brither only just arrived here a few days ago,'' said Deliah, a maternal frown leveled at the inspector.

''Your brither?'' Grant chuckled, and again it was an unpleasant sound. ''I dinna see a family resemblance. Tell me, does he also sprout wings?''

This time, Lachlan, Roan, and Winston shot to their feet, their expressions protective, almost murderous. The inspector studied them for a time. He curtly gestured for them to sit, then gestured again more forcefully when they remained standing. One by one they sat and exchanged conspiratory glances, all of which Grant filed away in his mind for later reference.

"Donnely insists Miss Deliah had wings afore Constable Bruce arrived the night o' the break-in."

Winston snorted derisively. "And you believe him?"

"Normally, I'd think the mon daft. But as I said, I dinna believe in coincidence. So how is it the siblin's here dinna have fingerprints?"

"That's ludicrous," Winston charged, trying to make light of the question. "Obviously, your team missed them."

"No. Even if someone believes themselves diligent in erasin' their prints, there's always at least one we find." Grant leaned forward and braced his forearms on the top of his thighs. His expression was deadly serious as his blue eyes glanced at each person with practiced scrutiny. "You might say I'm like a dog wi' a favored bone. I willna give up searchin' till my teeth are firmly locked onto wha' I consider my prize."

"Some dogs choke on bone slivers," said Beth, entering the room. Ignoring Lachlan rushing to her side and the others' horrified expressions, she stopped in front of the cold hearth, folded her arms against her chest, and met the inspector's startled gaze with one of cool disdain. "Kindly permit me to introduce myself."

"Be quiet!" Lachlan warned, at which she dealt him a scolding look.

Grant stood and faced Beth. Although his expression was one of deepening interest, his demeanor betrayed his wariness.

"Inspector Grant was abou' to leave," said Winston to Beth. His piercing gaze shifted to the inspector. "Don't return withou' a search warrant."

The inspector spared Winston an impatient glance, then looked at Beth and Lachlan for a long moment before his gaze lifted to study the portrait above the mantel. He blinked in mild confusion and scratched the nape of his neck. "Anither relative, are you?" he asked her.

"I was listening in on the conversation," she said stiffly. "I'm the *dead* Yank. Or rather—"

"Beth," Lachlan moaned.

"—I *was* the dead Yank," she completed, undaunted by Lachlan stepping behind her and winding his arms around her middle. He kissed the back of her head, then sighed heavily into her hair.

"Beth Staples," said Grant in a monotone. "And you claim you *were* dead?"

Beth glanced at the others with a mute apology. Her cheeks were flushed and her heart racing, but she couldn't allow the inspector to keep verbally hammering at the people she loved. Winston offered her a slight nod, telling her he understood her motive. It helped her to again focus on the officer.

"Answer me one question, Inspector."

His right eyebrow shot upward, then relaxed as he nodded.

"Are you seeking answers to assuage your curiosity, or looking for information to open another investigation?"

He blinked in bewilderment, then smiled in an offhanded manner. "In truth, my curiosity."

"Beth," Lachlan murmured, and she leaned the back of her head against his shoulder for a second.

"All right," she said to the inspector, "I'll tell you everything you need to know. But if you use what I say against anyone in this house, I swear I'll rip your heart out with my bare hands."

Grant's right hand went to the breast of his impeccable dark blue suit. "Does wha' you have to say involve criminal activities?"

"No."

Beth gestured for him to sit. She escorted Lachlan back to the sofa he'd been on previously, then briefly stopped in front of Deliah and Reith and passed them a look that told them she wouldn't reveal their backgrounds. She took one of the other chairs and positioned it in front of the inspector. She sat, her knees approximately eight inches from his, and primly folded her hands atop her lap. For the next half hour, she calmly told him of everything she now knew had led to her death, what had occurred during her existence in the afterlife, and how she and Lachlan had been given a second chance. Lastly, she told him about the twins, ending her revelation with, "So you see, Inspector Grant, we haven't been secretive without just cause. All Lachlan and I want is to live a relatively normal life with our children."

Silence stretched on for an inordinately long time. The inspector's gaze flitted repeatedly to each of the guarded expressions, then he released a burst of laughter. "You almost had me, miss," he said, wagging a finger at Beth. Hardness crept into the lines of his visage as he straightened his shoulders and crammed the pad into the breast pocket of his shirt. He stood and cast the group a scowl before cutting his gaze to Beth. "I'm retirin' in four months, but that's four months I'll be visitin' you people till I get to the truth. You've a fine imagination, Miss-Whoever-You-Are. Perhaps you should be pennin' stories for one o' the pulp publishers."

He brusquely headed for the hall door, but released a cry of alarm when something whizzed past him and blocked his path. He staggered backward, a hand to his brow, and stared in horrified fascination at the woman hovering in front of the doorway, her wings beating the air so swiftly, they were nearly invisible. Nearly, but not quite. He plopped back onto the chair he'd been using, his eyes transfixed on Deliah as she flew closer and then settled soundlessly on her bare feet. Her wings fluttered to a stop, and she folded her arms against her middle as she eyed him with an unmistakable challenge to deny what he was seeing.

"I be Deliah, princess o' the kingdom Faerie. 'Twas I who helped Lachlan and Beth return to the livin'."

A strangled laugh escaped Grant.

Lachlan rose and approached the inspector, positioning himself alongside Deliah. "In August o' nineteen eighty-eight, you came wi' a womon to this house."

The inspector's eyes narrowed, and he nodded. "My wife. She died soon efter o' cancer."

"You tried to tak my picture, but I wouldna allow your camera to work."

Grant unsteadily rose to his feet, his face blanched, his eyes misting with tears. "It *is* you," he murmured.

"Aye. Wha' my Beth told you is the truth. Horatio was invented to protect my return, and Beth was hidden to protect her and our children."

Grant loosened his tie, then the top two buttons of his shirt. "How . . . how the hell have you kept this secret? Rebirth and . . . faeries." His gaze shifted to Reith, who shrugged.

"Aye, I be a faerie prince."

"King," Deliah corrected, smiling at him adoringly.

"Wha'?" asked Lachlan, bewildered. "King?"

Reith stood and shifted on his feet, chagrined at the attention he was receiving. "Dethroned and de-winged, for the time." He smiled ruefully at the inspector. "My wife. She has a temper."

The inspector walked around to the back of the chair and gripped its top so fiercely that the ruddy color of his knuckles turned white. He made two attempts to speak, failed, then managed, "I knew there was something more no canny goin' on here, but this . . ." He tried to smile, and again failed. "My mither-in-law used to swear she'd seen faerie circles in her yard, and I thought her daft. And my wife, Kathy, God rest her soul, would say to me, 'Tis better to believe in faerie circles than believe in nothin' atall.' If only they were here to see you."

"Now that you know everythin'," said Winston, "wha' do you plan to do wi' the information?"

Grant shrugged. "Tak it to my grave."

Several sighs of relief were heard.

"But I canna guarantee anither officer willna get curious in the future. There's a lot o' unanswered questions involvin' this house." He looked at Lachlan dazedly. "If I were you, I'd tak my family and go somewhere you're no' known. But you'll need papers."

"I'm takin' care o' tha'," said Winston, surprised he'd offered the information.

"Good. Good." The inspector's head bobbed as he fell thoughtfully silent for a time. Then he looked at Beth. "You need to have tha' headstone removed and the . . . kist. Dinna leave any evidence you died, lass."

Lachlan nodded. "Aye, we should remove them. Fegs, so much to think abou'." He acknowledged Grant's shaken look and added, " 'Tis a lot to digest, I know."

"Aye. Aye, it is."

"Would you like a cup of coffee, Inspector Grant?" asked Laura, now feeling sorry for the man.

With a strained grin, he shook his head. "Thank you, but I dinna think my stomach would keep it down."

"How long will the cellar be cordoned off?" asked Roan.

"It can be taken down now. I've no doubt the Phantom murdered Mr. Miles, or tha' the killer's death was anythin' more than an accident."

"Thank God," Roan muttered, and raked the fingers of one hand through his hair. "The sooner tha' mess is cleaned up down there, the better I'll sleep."

"Me, too," said Laura. "At least Miles hasn't been seen since—" She clamped a hand over her mouth and winced at her own stupidity.

"Since when?" asked Grant.

"Miles' spirit was here for a while," said Lachlan wryly, "but he hasna been seen since the Phantom's death."

"Weel, I think I've heard all I can tak for one day." The inspector laughed. He sobered and added, "I'm sorry I've been a royal pain. Since my wife died, I havena had much to keep my mind busy. Crossmichael's a quiet place. No' much happenin'."

"But you do understand why we've had to do some creative juggling to protect ourselves?" asked Beth.

"I do. You're from Washington State, tha' right?"

"Yes. Kennewick, Washington."

The inspector sighed. "Might be best if you and yours head for the States."

"Lachlan and I have been discussing the possibility."

Grant nodded, then glanced at Roan and Winston. "I'll tak my leave now. If you need anythin', feel free to call on me. I'll do my best to discourage any further investigation into the occupants here. But as I said, get rid of Miss Staples' kist and headstone. If any questions are asked, play dumb. That's the best advice I can offer."

Beth stood and extended a hand to the inspector. He hesitantly clasped it. "Thank you."

"Thank *you.*" He laughed a bit shyly, and his eyes took on a sparkle as he regarded Beth. "Wha' do you think o' Scotland?"

"I hate to leave. If you ever come to the States, give us a call. I'm in the phone book."

"That's verra kind o' you." He walked around the chair and clapped his hands against his small paunch. "I best be leavin'. I came on my free time, but I should be checkin' in, soon." A genuine smile youthened his face as he took a long look at the others in the room, lingering lastly on Deliah's serene features. "I canna thank you enough for sharin' the truth wi' me. Miss Deliah, I feel as if I've been given a second chance, too. I believed in faeries as a verra young lad, but grew dour as I got older."

"Whenever ye feel a dour moment, Inspector, feel free to have a visit wi' me," she said with a smile.

Roan asked Grant, "Do you like to fish?"

"Verra fond o' the sport, aye."

"Then let's plan to mak a day o' it when the weather warms up a bit."

The inspector beamed. "Whenever you say, Mr. Ingliss. Good day, all. My thoughts will be wi' you."

Everyone in the parlor remained silent until they heard the front doors open and close. Deliah continued to stare down the hall, a wistful expression on her face. "He be a lonely mon." Her gaze shifted to Roan. " 'Twas kind o' ye to offer to tak him fishin'. Wha' be fishin'?"

Laughing, Winston closed the distance and drew her into his arms. "It's usin' a rod and a hook to catch fish."

"For wha' purpose?"

"To eat, and for sport."

She looked aghast. "Ye hook the poor wee things?"

"They don't feel it," Winston assured. He turned his attention to Beth and Lachlan. "I'm goin' into town to call Grayson. If he can meet us, Deliah and I should drive to Ayr and pick up the identification papers he's made for you. He's probably wonderin' wha' happened to us when we didn't meet him in Edinburgh. The sooner we get your paperwork, Lachlan, the sooner we can arrange the weddin' and get you both and the twins away from here."

"Wha' abou' Taryn?" asked Deliah.

"Wha' abou' her?" Winston volleyed hesitantly.

Deliah gave each of the men a measuring look before addressing Winston, "We know o' your talks to go efter her."

"How can you?"

"Your mindshield lowers when ye sleep."

Astonished, he gasped. "You invaded my mind? While I slept? Then told the women?"

"Aye," she said proudly. "I be a weed, no' a fragile flower."

"A weed?" Winston muttered, glancing at Beth and Laura for an explanation. None came.

"Fegs," said Lachlan, shifting uncomfortably when Beth's challenging gaze met his. "Aye, we talked abou' goin' efter her."

"That's my responsibility," said Roan, then looked at Laura apologetically. "I had planned to bring it up to you efter the weddin'."

It took a moment before she could ease her pique and say, "If she really is in danger, we shouldn't wait." She sighed in resignation. "Besides, she should be here for the wedding. I don't want your mind on anything but us during the ceremony."

With a loving smile, Roan walked up to her and gently took her into his arms. "I love you. I know how much the weddin' means to you. To postpone it for my sister is verra generous."

"Oh, darling," she purred, "I plan to get even when she returns."

"Oh?"

"Nothing drastic. I promise."

"I could track her," said Reith.

"No doubt, but you have business here, lad," said Lachlan.

"The gardenin' isna verra demandin' right now, sir."

Lachlan grinned. "Aye, but you need no' put more distance atween you and your wife. Wha' if she comes o' a mind to see you, and you're no' here, eh? No. 'Tis my mither's belongin's Taryn took, and somethin' in my mither's family she's investigatin'. Roan and I are the logical ones to go efter her."

"Wha' abou' me?" Winston asked indignantly.

"Deliah needs you close by," Lachlan said.

"I be a—"

"Weed, I know, lass," said Lachlan, "but we dinna know if you'll have problems wi' the pregnancy. 'Tis better Winston stay close."

"I agree," said Laura.

Beth nodded.

"Okay." Winston sighed. He cast Deliah a forlorn look. Realizing that she believed he was disappointed to be stuck at home with her, he released a laugh and kissed her on the tip of her nose. "I was jokin'."

"Were ye now?" she asked suspiciously.

"Why is it you don't read my mind when I want you to?"

She grinned mischievously. "No fun when I have permission."

Beth whispered in Lachlan's ear. When he nodded, she said, "Roan, Laura, would you mind if Lachlan and I take the boys out for a picnic? A *long* picnic . . . say, for three or four hours?"

Roan and Laura looked at each other as if unable to believe what they'd heard.

"When?" Roan asked.

"Now, if you like." Beth winked at them. "Send the boys down to help make the sandwiches, then disappear to your room. Take a little time for yourselves."

"Aye," Lachlan grinned. "You've both been lookin' a wee frazzled o' late. We'll mak sure you're undisturbed."

A delicate blush rose in Laura's cheeks, and excitement brightened the emerald green of her eyes. "Are you sure you're up to handling five kids at once?"

Roan gushed, "O' course they can!" He sent Lachlan and Beth an eager look. "Right?"

"No' to worry," assured Lachlan.

"It will rain shortly," said Reith, and smiled at the fallen expressions. "The carriage house loft would mak a grand picnic retreat. Do the lads play hide-'n'-seek?"

"It's their favorite game," said Laura.

Reith humorously bowed at the waist. "Then may I prevail to invite myself to this picnic. I would enjoy playin' wi' the lads."

"You're invited," said Beth.

"I'll go and rearrange the bales o' hay," said Reith. "Do ye need me to help bring anythin' to the carriage house?"

"We'll manage," said Lachlan.

Reith went to his sister and kissed her on the cheek. "Ye have a safe journey to Ayr with your Mr. Connery."

"Winston," Winston said. "We'll be in-laws before long."

"Aye, sir. Just remember ye have valuable cargo wi' ye in your car."

"As if I could ever forget," Winston said amicably "Deliah, do you want to come into town wi' me?"

"To mak the call to Mr. Grayson?"

He nodded.

"Aye, I would like to go. Might we stop for sweets? I've a cravin' I canna ignore."

"Then stop, we shall. But put shoes on."

She looked down at her bare feet and lifted a pathetic

expression for him to see. "Must I? They mak my toes feel broked."

Winston turned to the others and shrugged flamboyantly. "Wha' can a mon do? Barefoot and pregnant she wants to be, so who am I to argue?"

With a merry salute, Reith headed into the hall. Before he reached the front doors, the sound of the brass knocker being engaged echoed through the first floor. Other more forceful raps followed before Reith opened the outer doors to see who was on the other side.

A mantle of gloom fell over those remaining in the parlor. Lachlan, his expression one of annoyance, remarked, "If the police have returned, I'll throw myself from the tower!"

Winston stood at the threshold to the hall. Voices carried his way. After several moments he turned and delivered a dubious look to his friends. "We have company."

"Who?" asked Beth, peeved. "The police again?"

Winston shook his head as the voices grew louder in their approach. "No. But you might wish they were, though."

He stepped aside. Reith, his face flushed and eyes offering a mute apology, led four people into the room. Shocked silence prevailed for a time as two couples in their sixties stood haughtily appraising the occupants of the room.

"This is a fine hello," said one of the women. She was tall and slender, with crisp hazel eyes, short blond hair, and austere features. The man next to her was two inches taller, portly around the middle, blue-eyed and white-haired, and his cheeks rosy.

"Mother," Laura said weakly, "Dad . . . what are you doing here?"

Before Lauren or William Bennett could reply, Eilionoir Ingliss cut in. "Taryn called us, of course, and told us about the wedding."

Roan inwardly fumed at his sister's audacity. Utilizing all his willpower to appear outwardly calm, he nodded to his parents, then asked, "How do you come to know Laura's parents?"

"I called them," Eilionoir snipped, giving her salon-dyed, reddish-blond head a toss. "Taryn supplied their number. I guess *some* good comes of her chosen profession."

Laura went to her parents and put an arm around each of their necks, while Roan stood in a silent battle with his own. His mother looked a little older than he remembered, but she was still a beautiful woman and obviously still full of herself. His father, however, looked years older than his actual age. His hair was gunmetal gray, and dark circles underscored the bags beneath his amber eyes. His cheeks were sunken, his face sickly and pale. It occured to Roan that his mother had worked her husband nearly to his grave. Dugan had always been a large man to Roan, but now he seemed shrunken and barely Roan's own height.

"Son," Dugan said with a terse nod, "you're looking well."

Roan could barely detect any hint of Scottish in their voices. It left a chilling void in his heart, and he tensed despite his efforts to the contrary. They were strangers to him. Dim memories, most of which were not pleasant. In his father's eyes, he could do no right, and his mother had never had an ounce of patience with him. That they would assume he wanted them to attend his wedding irked him.

His mind drifted into a daze. One moment he was wondering how to convince them to leave, the next he realized everyone but Deliah and Winston was sitting at the dining room table. Pots of tea and coffee were being served by Lachlan and Beth, and the boys were uncharacteristically waiting for permission to dive into the sandwiches stacked on two platters on both ends of the table. He was surprised to find himself seated at the head of the table. Laura was to his right, her parents to her right. To his immediate left was his mother, and next to her, his father. She was staring at him with a familar look of disapproval. His father was avoiding looking at him at all. Laura's parents, on the other hand, were cheerful although exhausted from the trip. Beth, he noticed, was quietly observing the guests, and he suspected she was wishing she had family to attend the wedding.

"Must we suffer that mouse staring at us from the cage?" Eilionoir snipped. "And what *is* a cage doing on such a fine sideboard?"

Since she was staring at Roan, no one answered, and he was lost in his thoughts.

"You're as rude as ever," his mother commented, a cup held with both hands, poised inches from her enhanced lips. "Roan? Did you hear me?"

He nodded dispassionately.

"Taryn failed to tell us you were marrying a woman with three children."

The room fell silent as Roan shifted a dark, warning look at his mother. "They're Laura's nephews."

Eilionoir smiled thinly across the table at Laura. "Are they in your charge, dear?"

Laura passed Roan a worried glance before answering, "Yes. My brother died and their stepmother—"

"Abandoned us," interjected Kevin with a smile. "Good thing, too, cause she wasn't right for us. We belong with Aunt Laura and Uncle Roan."

"Charming boy," said Eilionoir, her tone implying quite the opposite. Her gaze met her son's. "Are you able to support a ready-made family?"

The question came as Lachlan seated himself at the opposite end of the table. "The mon is wealthy enough!" he boasted for Roan's sake. "This estate is his."

"You don't say?" Eilionoir murmured.

"Actually, it belongs to Lannie," said Roan with a deadpan look fixed on Lachlan. "He's been gracious enough to share it wi' us."

"Gracious, my eye," Lachlan blustered, grinning broadly, his eyes sparkling with mischief. " 'Tis yours."

Roan flagged a dismissing hand, and sighed with annoyance as he looked at his parents. "Dinna worry yourself abou' how I'll tak care o' *my* family."

"Roan, I couldn't be happier with my Laura's choice," said Lauren happily, and gave her daughter's hand a loving squeeze atop the table. "And I know Jack approves of you as a father for his sons."

"Grandma," piped up Kahl, "will you tell us about our daddy, later?"

"It would be my pleasure, Kevin."

"I'm Kahl."

Lauren blushed, and her husband chuckled "We're suffering jet lag," he told the boys collectively. "Be patient. We'll get the names straight, soon enough."

The boys passed skeptical glances amongst themselves.

"I'm sure you do approve of Roan marrying your daughter," said Eilionoir to Lauren, her cold tone raising Roan's hackles. "There aren't many men who would take on a woman with three boys."

"Mither, shut up."

She stiffened and shot him a horrified look. "Excuse me?"

"You heard me."

"Roan," Laura pleaded softly.

"Dinna mistak her rudeness for jet lag, Laura," he said, clenching his hands on the table top. "She doesna have a maternal bone in her body."

"That's enough!" his father warned.

"No, Dad, it isna, by far. This is my home, now, and these people my friends and family. I willna stand for your wife puttin' down Laura, the lads, or anyone else I love." He glared into his mother's cold stare. "For as long as you're under this roof, you will conduct yourself like a lady. 'Tis bad enough you didn't wait for an invitation."

"Has one been mailed?" she asked curtly.

Roan shook his head. "I didna want you here. But now tha' you are, you're welcome to stay for the weddin'."

"You make it sound like a privilege," she retorted.

"Hardly, mither," he wryly cut her off. He gulped down

some of the chilled water in his glass, then heaved a breath to quiet the anger stirring inside him. "If I recall, I sent you an invite for my first weddin'."

"We were away on a business trip," his father said defensively.

Roan nodded. "And where were you both when Adaina and our son were buried? *Anither* business trip? I know Aunt Aggie called you. But I guess it wasna important enough for you to return to Scotland."

"We're here now," his mother clipped.

"Why?" he asked softly.

Eilionoir glanced at her husband, then lifted her chin and met her son's probing gaze. "Taryn begged us to be here for you. That's why."

Lachlan was about to get to his feet when he felt something move at the nape of his neck. He reached to scratch the annoyance, but stopped when he realized what was causing the sensation.

"Tell me, Mr. and Mrs. Ingliss," Lachlan said, "have you no idea wha' a grand son you have in Roan?" He scowled when they silently looked down the table at him. "Weel, *I'll* tell you!"

"Lannie—"

"Roan, be quiet," Lachlan said wearily, still scowling. "Do you know who I am?" he asked Roan's parents, and went on before they could reply. "I'm *the* Lachlan Baird, the same Lachlan Baird who Robbie and Tessa Ingliss murdered and walled up in the tower."

Eilionoir stiffly rose to her feet and gestured for her husband to follow her example. "I'm too tired to listen to this nonsense. Roan, you know where our room is. Let us know when you're up to acting civil."

"Sit down, ma'am," Lachlan said in a deadly quiet tone as he stood. The elder Bennetts' eyes were wide with amusement and wariness combined. "Nonsense, am I?" he went on and slowly walked to Roan's back. "Sit down . . . please."

Eilionoir glared through him. She had no intention of folding to his intimidation until her husband sat and tugged on her sleeve. She sank onto her chair, her unwavering gaze locked with Lachlan's in a war of wills.

"Mrs. Ingliss," Lachlan continued, the anger in his eyes belying his smile, and his hands resting on Roan's shoulders, " 'twas Roan who ended the Baird Ingliss feud, and no small accomplishment it was. You havena a clue wha' he's suffered all these years."

"Lannie, please," Roan said testily, but quieted when Lachlan playfully whacked him on the head.

"But your son's sufferin' didna prevent him from bein' a mon o' compassion. I canna stand by and hear you talk to him like he's beneath you, no' deservin' o' your love and respect. In truth, despite his lineage, he's more o' a mon than any I've had the pleasure or displeasure to meet. So, my good people, unless you wish to incur the wrath o' all here who love this mon, I suggest *you* change *your* attitudes, and be grateful he's allowin' you to attend a weddin' tha' will be like no ither your sorry eyes have seen, or ever will see again."

"You're a long-winded so-and-so, aren't you, Mr. Baird?"

" 'Tis one o' my charms," he said smoothly. "This weddin' is verra important to the couples involved, and I willna stand for disharmony spoilin' a moment o' its plannin' or the ceremony itself."

"Nor I," whispered a voice in his left ear. "Are they to know about us?"

"Canna be helped," said Lachlan.

"What can't be helped?" Eilionoir asked impatiently.

"My conscience," Lachlan lied with a disarming grin. "Eat up," he said merrily, gesturing expansively with his hands. "And tomorrow when you're fully rested and Deliah and Winston have returned from Ayr, we'll start on the particulars."

"Particulars of what?" asked Lauren Bennett.

Lachlan bowed his head to her. "Sweet lady, there's a few wee matters you need to know afore we can get down to the business o' the weddin'."

"Just a few," Laura said, and started to laugh. Before

long, everyone but the mystified parents were releasing their tension with laughter.

Snuggled within the thick strands of hair at Lachlan's nape, Blue smiled in response to the musical sounds.

CHAPTER FIFTEEN

With the arrival of "The Parents", Roan and Laura didn't get to spend time alone, and the picnic was canceled. For the residents of Baird House, the day seemed to drag on without end. Their guests were shown their rooms and helped to settle in. Then came a tour of the mansion, and later, grueling hours spent in the parlor trying to get reacquainted and relatively comfortable with one another.

For the most part, the Bennetts were a cheery couple. They were quite different from the parents Laura remembered, and were eager to please their hosts and hostesses, despite their exhaustion. Lauren Bennett asked to help in the kitchen, and was delighted to discover Roan did most of the cooking, and was willing to share some of his favorite Scottish recipes with her. While she was at ease conversing with Roan, William Bennett preferred to stay in the background, observing his future son-in-law. This suited Roan just fine. He'd already lost points with the man. William didn't approve of a man cooking unless he was a bona fide chef. Nonetheless, the Bennetts were not a problem in Roan's opinion.

However, such was not the case with his own parents.

Also given a room on the second floor, Eilionoir complained it was too small, the bed too soft, and Dugan claimed he nearly suffered a heart attack when a "hideous" creature perched on the window sill and gawked in at them. They made no effort to talk to Laura, and complained that the boys were too noisy. The house was *too* large, *too* drafty, *too* isolated. The topper for Roan came when his mother disapproved of what he'd planned to make for dinner, and the fact that he cooked, and not the woman he was soon to wed. Eilionoir was "hurt" that her son wasn't willing to fix one of the few Scottish meals she liked. He decided it best not to tell her he had no idea what she liked or disliked, and certainly wasn't inclined to care, either. He cooked one of his own favorites, Mince and Tatties, a meal of minced steak and potatoes with a spicy brown sauce. The dessert was Dundee cake, a rich fruit cake with almonds on top.

Dinner was a hit with everyone but his parents.

Reith diplomatically excused himself after the meal, and retired to the carriage house.

Deliah and Winston returned from Ayr sometime after ten that evening. Roan's parents had retired an hour earlier, around the same time William had said his good nights. Exhausted, Winston inquired about the new guests over the sandwiches and tea Beth had made for him and Deliah, and they listened to Roan's account of the day before discussing the paperwork Winston had brought back with him from Ayr. They went over Lachlan's new identity. It was all in a manila envelope, and Winston assured Lachlan all the information was in the computers—a statement that meant nothing to Lachlan—including a credit and travel history. The fake passport showed Lachlan had traveled to Greece, Italy, France, and Germany, which he had, but not in this century. The birth certificate was chemically aged, folded, and crinkled in places. Every document looked used and authentic The only complaint Lachlan had was his name. *Horatio* Lachlan

Baird. *Horatio!* It left a bitter taste in his mouth just to say it in his mind.

The boys were too wired up to go to bed before eleven. They were very young when they'd last seen their grandparents, and Lauren promised not to wait so long again to visit with her only grandchildren. All in all, Laura had a tiring but exhilarating day. She'd always thought her parents stuffy and distant, but after meeting Roan's she now looked at them in an entirely different light. She fell asleep on the foot of Alby's bed after reading him a story.

Sometime after 1:00 A.M. everyone slept in the main house, except Roan.

Melancholy kept him imprisoned in a daze as he stared into the fire he'd built in the library. He sat cross-legged on the stone extension of the hearth, dimly hearing the crackling and spitting of wood as flames reduced the paper and kindling to ash and lapped and rose into dancing peaks around two hefty logs. The firescreen was in place. Waves of warmth spilled over him and, although he should have felt secure and at peace, he didn't.

His mind kept replaying one evening when his parents had gone into his room and told him of their decision to move to the States. An argument had ensued, in which he'd told them he refused to leave his Aunt Aggie and Scotland. Not once had the subject come up again after that night. Two months later, as he watched his parents pack everything that was familiar to him, he waited for them to tell him he had no choice but to go. They never did. His toys and book collection had been given to the local Catholic church, his clothing and toothbrush taken to Aggie's, and he was left without another word from them. His last image of Taryn that last cold morning as his parent's car pulled away from the curb in front of his aunt's house was her face pressed against the rear window and her tongue stuck out to taunt him.

He hadn't wanted to move to the States, but neither had he wanted to be left behind.

To the best of his ability he couldn't remember ever

being a difficult child. He had never liked school and, his grades had attested to that. His teachers had liked him. He'd graduated by the seat of his pants, but he had graduated. For Aggie, he had. She'd tried to make up for his loss. Loved and cared for him as she'd done for her son, Borgie, never showing favor. That she wouldn't be here for his wedding hurt like hell. That his parents would be, hurt worse.

Taryn.

He wanted another chance to bond with her. She couldn't help her attitude. Their parents had always doted on her, but he really hadn't been envious when they were children. Taryn was beautiful, and had always possessed an impish quality that instantly swayed their parents' frustration with her. When their mother was upset with her, Taryn helped in the kitchen, and soon had their mother laughing at her ability to wear more of the ingredients than went into their meals. Were their father peeved with something she'd done, she curled up on his lap and told him how much she loved him. Roan had admired her ability to manipulate with cuteness. She'd even done it to him countless times. If she broke one of his toys or ripped one of his books, she offered up her favorite baby doll, which of course he wouldn't take. He wished that little girl still existed. He wished he'd been around to coach her for her first date, her first serious relationship.

He choked up with tears and lowered his face into his hands for a time, miserably regretting the years he'd lost with his family.

When he looked up, he thought he saw Adaina and Jamey's faces staring at him from within the flames of the hearth. In a way, they, too, had left him behind. And Borgie and Aggie.

Taryn had left, but at least she could be found—he hoped. He wanted her at the wedding. He didn't understand why it was so important to him, but it was. If she were still in Scotland, how difficult would it be to find her? All he needed was a possible location and a few days. He couldn't remember if it had been decided to search first for her, or wait until after the wedding. He couldn't disappoint Laura. She'd already waited long enough to exchange vows. He really did want Taryn there, and he desperately wanted another chance to repair their relationship. If only he had given her a portion of the patience he gave the boys.

God, what if he became the kind of father to them his father had been to him? Was this a genetic flaw, and could it be ticking away inside him, waiting to surface? Was to look at his father to see himself in a few years?

"Roan?"

He jerked in surprise and swung his head around. Laura's features swam in front of him, and he blinked hard to remove the tears blurring his vision.

"What's wrong?" she asked with concern. She brushed back the hair at the sides of his face, then tenderly cupped his jawline in her soft hands. "Honey, you're scaring me."

With a shuddering breath, he turned on his bottom and pulled her onto his lap, then buried his moist face into one side of her hair and silently wept.

"They really got to you, didn't they?" she asked tremulously, stroking the back of his head. A short time of silence passed, then, "Do you know what I love most about you?"

His arms snugged her closer.

"You feel so much," she whispered. "Most men refuse to show pain or sorrow, or even how much they love. Not you, Roan. You wear your emotions on the surface, for all to see."

He made a grunting sound in response, and she smiled.

"Do you know what I thought the first time I looked into your eyes?"

A second passed before he lifted his head and despondently stared into the green depths of her eyes. "I'm afraid to ask."

She laughed low and kissed him briefly on the lips. "I knew I was in trouble."

He frowned. "Why?"

"Because I thought you were the most drop-dead gorgeous man I'd ever seen. And burly. Let's not forget that."

"Me? Burly?"

"Remember, I woke up to hear you shouting at the boys. Alby had gotten into the matches."

"Aye." A hint of a smile appeared on his face. "I also remember you vomiting on me."

She grimaced playfully. "How about if we forget that part?"

Now he grinned in earnest. "How could I? 'Tis when I fell in love wi' you."

"That's so gross."

He laughed, its deep, rich sound vibrating in his chest. "True, though. You were achingly embarrassed, and your irises looked as if they possessed emerald fires.

"Oh, Laura." He sighed deeply. "I shudder to think wha' my life would be like withou' you and the lads."

"Probably a lot more quiet and uncomplicated," she said whimsically.

He somberly shook his head. "Damn miserable. I used to have this terrible emptiness inside me, Laura, and thought it had begun efter Jamey died. But I was sittin' here, thinkin' back, and realized it began when my parents left for the States."

"You can't let them upset you like this."

Again he sighed, and again he shook his head. "I don't understand this love hate stuff, Laura. It maks me crazy, and scares me to think I could be like them."

"With the boys?"

He nodded, swallowed hard, then cleared his throat. "I love them, Laura." He laughed unsteadily and lowered his head. "I love the feel of them in my arms, their scent and their mannerisms, and even their pranks. I don't just want to be their Uncle Roan, but their dad, wi' every responsibility tha' comes wi' it. I want to adopt them, and give them my name as weel as my love. I know tha's selfish, Laura. They have a faither and a mither."

"I've thought about it, too," she said softly.

"You have?"

She nodded. "I planned to talk to you about it after the wedding."

His tears glimmered to the glow of his smile. "Abou' adoptin' them?"

"Yes. I don't know how my parents will take it, though."

"I like them."

"You do?"

He grinned crookedly. "Your faither tells the corniest jokes, but I canna help but laugh at them. Somethin' in his facial expressions durin' the tellin', I guess."

"They like you. A lot."

"Do they?" he chuckled.

"Daddy told me after supper that you're a man's man, even though you cook like a woman."

"Meanin' wha'?"

She laughed and shrugged. "Beats the hell out of me, but he said it with pride, so it must be good. And Mom said I sure have an eye for a hunk."

"A hunk, eh?"

Laura nuzzled her brow against his left cheek. "You're my hunk, Roan Ingliss, and I love you more than I ever thought possible."

"Even when I'm in a foul mood?"

"Yep."

"On my lips?"

"Depends where you have them."

"On the rim o' a glass o' Scotch?"

She paused, then said, "Yep."

"Hmm. Remember you said tha' when next I transgress."

She gave a low murmur of contentment. "I'm sure you'll remind me. Roan?"

"Wha', love?"

"I'm worried about how our parents are going to take meeting the faeries."

He thought about this for a time, then twisted his mouth

in wry amusement. "It'll rock my parents' comfortable little world o' reality."

"Now, Roan, be nice."

"I am nice—nice and disappointed that efter all these years they still mak me feel like the boy who stood in front o' Aggie's watchin' them drive away. Damn me, Laura, I don't like this side o' me. They're my parents. Maybe I just think I'm mon enough to get past the hurt and go on wi' my life. Obviously, I'm no'."

"*Think* you're man enough?" she challenged, sitting up and looking him in the eye. "Roan, stop beating yourself up over this! You have every right to be angry. Parents have to earn respect like anyone else. Considering what you've been through, I'm amazed at your ability to love so openly."

"But I don't," he murmured. "I've held back on you and the boys from the verra beginnin'."

"Oh, bull. Short of ripping out your heart and handing it to me on a platter, what more could you possibly give?"

"A snip o' parsley on the side," he quipped, laughter in his eyes.

With a groan, she pressed her brow to his. "You know what?"

"What?"

"You're talking like yourself again."

Frowning, he leaned his head back to look at her. "Talkin' like myself, how?"

"For a while, you've been using Lannie's lingo."

"Lingo?"

"His 'dinna' and 'canna.' "

"Kevin mentioned tha' a few days ago."

"There's nothing wrong with it," she laughed. "You admire Lachlan, and I think you wish you were more like him."

"Aye, I do."

"Why?"

"He has a knack for acceptin' the good and the bad wi' equal measure, and he finds humor in almost everythin'.

You know, Laura, considerin' his history, he should have a big chip on his shoulder, but no' him. And I guess I admire the way he brings ou' the best in people. Like Reith. Here was this scruffy kid we caught, who we thought at first was diggin' up the graves, and within a few minutes, Lannie hires him. He hires him, gives him a home, and puts warmer clothes on his back."

"You wouldn't have done the same?"

Roan shrugged and stared into the fire. "I don't know. I'm too suspicious by nature."

"Bull twinkie."

Her words brought his gaze to her face, and he chuffed a laugh. "Bull *twinkie?*"

"Yeah, bull twinkie. Now you listen to me, Roan Ingliss. You and Lachlan are very much alike, so there's no reason for you to want to be him."

"I don't exactly—"

She pressed a forefinger to his lips, silencing him. "Yes, you do." She lowered the hand and eyed him adoringly. "But I'm in love with *you,* Roan, not Lachlan."

"If we're so much alike . . ."

"There are differences, obviously. Looks. You're quieter. You were born in this century."

He laughed. "Okay, I get the point."

"Do you?"

Her soft tone was like a caress to his ears. "Aye, I do. I was just havin' a wee fun wi' you."

"Hey, I have an idea!"

Humorous wariness shadowed his features. "And wha' is this idea?"

"Maybe the faeries have a spell that will make our parents *think* they're attending a normal wedding."

Roan threw back his head and laughed. "Lass, I think you're thinkin' too much. Besides, Reith doesn't seem concerned, and he is the Pledger."

After a moment, Laura nodded. "You're right. Besides —and please don't take this to heart—I think your mother could do with a dose of Blue."

A wicked gleam appeared in his eyes as he contemplated this. "I can't imagine her takin' guff from my mither."

Laura made a rueful face and grinned. "Lachlan told me Blue was hiding in his hair most of the day."

"Wha'ever for?"

Laura laughed. "To keep him calm."

Roan's face crinkled with a smile. "I'm growin' more and more fond o' our faerie queen. Shame abou' her and Reith, though."

"I know. They're so cute together."

"Laura, we have a faerie king workin' as a groundskeeper."

She shrugged flamboyantly, a mischievous glint in her eyes. "Doesn't everyone? Oh, and by the way, guess what?"

He arched an eyebrow.

"We're alone. Sitting in front of a glorious fire. Just you and me."

He looked about the room. "So we are."

"So?"

Both of his eyebrows jerked upward. "Are you suggestin' wha' I think you're suggestin'?"

She gently nipped his lower lip. "I don't know. Am I?"

Roan's chest expanded with an intake of air into his lungs. "The ceilin' might fall on our heads. Or the boys burst in."

"We're wastin' time," she purred, running her palms along the muscular contours of his pectorals.

"Do you want to go back to our room?"

"Not a chance. I want you here and now, Roan."

"This verra minute?" he asked breathlessly.

She kissed him. "Right—" She kissed him again. "—now."

Her eyes riveted on her task, she unbuttoned his shirt and swept aside the material to expose the breadth of his chest. She swallowed as desire quivered through her, and her hands trembled slightly as she touched the fingertips to his warm flesh and ran them over the enticing curvatures. She saw his eyes close. He shivered, and she knew she had awakened his nerve endings. With her own eyes closed, she leaned forward, pushed his hair aside, and directed her mouth to one side of his neck. She nibbled at his skin with her teeth, relishing his spasms of delight, then languidly caressed him with the tip of her tongue. He tasted of salt and mild soap, of heaven and earth and the sweetness of love.

Roan's hands eased around to her back and kneaded the solidity beneath her cream-colored pullover sweater. It amazed him that no matter how insecure or lost he felt, a touch or a kiss from her could banish it all and make him feel as if the world were his for the asking. How could a man hurt because of something from out of his past, when his present and future were so filled with love and promise and hope? Nothing should matter but what life had offered him in this woman and her nephews. And he vowed to himself, nothing would again.

With a rumbling moan, he dipped his hands beneath her sweater and explored the satin of her camisole, then the softness of her skin. Her lips and tongue and teeth had erupted tiny flames behind his breast and a haze of desire in his mind. Hooking his hands on her shoulders, he urged her back and hungrily sought her mouth. He kissed her deeply, passionately, his tongue sweeping along the lining of her lips and then venturing into her mouth. They kissed for an indefinite time, wrapped in each other's arms, sharing body warmth and the intricate matrix of their sexual nature which had initiated their bond during their first union as Roan and Laura.

"I love you," she rasped when the kisses ended.

He loved the way her eyes looked when she was passionate. Green and fiery. An entity in their own right. Eyes that could say more with a glance, than most people could vocalize.

Framing her face with his large hands, he took awhile to gaze over her features. He had always thought her beautiful, but of late there'd been a glow about her, softening and yet enhancing the qualities her genes had bestowed on her. It struck him again how much he wanted to have a child with her. A daughter with her eyes and blond hair, pouty lips, and pert nose.

Impatient with his delay, Laura pulled her sweater and camisole over her head in one motion and tossed them on the sofa. Roan's gaze dropped to her heaving breasts, and his mouth went dry at the sight of her rigid nipples. Static roared in his ears. The haze in his mind slipped down to blur his vision.

"What's wrong?" she asked in a small voice.

"You're so . . . exquisite."

"Then why aren't you making love to me?"

He couldn't answer right away. Jiggling his head, he cleared his throat and blurted, "I was thinkin' o' our daughter."

Laura leaned back, eyes wide in a shocky face. "You're psychic?"

"Wha'? No." He chuckled. "I was thinkin' wha' it would be like to have a daughter who looks like you. I suppose I shouldna been thinkin' abou' anythin' but you. I'm sorry, Laura."

"It's okay. Umm, why would you be thinking of a daughter at all? We-ah, haven't discussed having a child of our own."

"True, we haven't."

"I figured you would think the boys were all you could handle for now."

"I thought the same abou' you." He smiled a bit sadly. "Truth is, Laura, I think a lot abou' us havin' a baby, but then I tell myself it wouldn't be fair to you or the lads."

"Do you really think they would mind?"

"I don't know. Probably no'. Look how attached they are to the twins."

Laura's eyes brimmed with tears. She attempted to look away, but Roan gripped her chin between a thumb and forefinger and forced her to face him. "Laura, have I spoiled the mood for you?"

A single tear escaped down her cheek. "No. I've just been frantic about how to tell you."

"Tell me wha'?" Concern masked his features as he cupped a hand at the back of her head. "Laura, you can tell me anythin'. If you don't want or can't have a child, I'll understand."

"My last period was two months ago."

Her strained statement hung in the air for a time, then Roan blinked in bewilderment and opened his mouth to speak.

Laura rushed on to say, "I didn't know how to tell you. I didn't want you to feel trapped. So much has been going—"

He silenced her with a kiss, then again framed her face and gazed wondrously into her eyes. "You're pregnant?"

She nodded.

"Are you sure?"

"Yes. Winston and Deliah told me I was, for sure. I made them promise not to say anything to anyone until I worked up the courage to tell you."

She began to weep and Roan put his arms around her and rocked her trembling form. "Hush, Laura. Hush. Do I look afraid? Disappointed? Not as thrilled as a bleedin' sparrow when spring chases off the bite o' winter?"

A strangled laugh escaped her, and she peered with uncertainty into the amber depths of his eyes. "It's okay with you?"

"Okay?" A boom of a laugh burst from his throat. "I'm ecstatic! And so will be the lads when we tell them!"

"What about your parents?"

"What abou' them?"

"They're going to think you're marrying me because of the baby."

"Damn me, do I care wha' they think?" His face beaming, his head reeling, he laughed again. "My poor darlin'. All this time you've been keepin' this to yourself. But shame on you, Laura, for no' knowin' me better."

"You've been under a lot of stress."

"This isna *stress!* A baby. *We* created a baby!"

A dubious expression shadowed Laura's features. "You're going to be one of those zany fathers who spoil their kids, aren't you?"

"Aye. And I plan to be a protective and conscientious husband, as weel. No more liftin', and tha' includes liftin' the boys. You shouldn't stay on your feet for long at a time."

"If you don't make love to me, Roan Ingliss, I swear I'll—"

"Oh, dear," mewled a voice.

Laura released a squeal of shock and pushed her bare chest against Roan's as she looked in horror at the opened pocket doors. Her mother stood at the threshhold, her profile to them, a hand fanning her crimson face.

"Oh, dear," Lauren repeated. "Do forgive me. I'm so embarrassed."

Laura scrambled off Roan's lap and hastily retrieved her sweater and camisole from the sofa. The latter she balled and crammed into the left pocket of her slacks, then donned the sweater as quickly as she could. Roan stood and looked a bit dazed at the woman. Neither he nor Laura had thought to shut the doors, let alone lock them.

"Mom, I'm so sorry."

"No apology, dear." She laughed shakily. "Alby woke me and said he couldn't find you. I would have *never*—"

"It's okay, Mom."

Laura stepped into the hall and faced her mother, humiliation scorching her skin. "We should have closed the doors. Sorry. We weren't thinking."

Lauren's eyes were bright as she regarded her daughter. "One isn't supposed to think when in the mood," she said sagely, then fanned her face again. "Roan, I'm so sorry I intruded," she said without looking at him. "What you must think of me!"

With a sheepish grin, Roan walked around his soon-to-be mother-in-law and planted a kiss on her temple. This done, he draped an arm about Laura's shoulders and grinned like a fool at the older woman. "In a few minutes or so it would have been *verra* embarrassin'," he joked.

"My goodness, yes."

Laura buried her face into Roan's shoulder.

"Laura-lass, can we tell your mither?"

She looked up in panic, cast her mother a sickly look, then murmured, "If you must."

"Tell me what?" Lauren asked.

Roan couldn't wait. "You're goin' to be a grandmither again. Laura just told me she's carryin' our child." He loudly kissed the top of Laura's head. "And I couldn't be happier."

"Laura?"

"Yes, Mom, it's true."

"Are you happy about this?"

Laura frowned. "Are you?"

Lauren released a trilling laugh and clapped her hands. "I didn't think you could make me any happier, but you have! I was just tellin' your father tonight how I regretted missing so much of my grandsons' growing. Oh, Laura, it won't be the same as it was with Jack. I promise. We'll be here for you as long as you need us."

"Really, Mom?"

Lauren held out her arms, and Laura readily stepped into the embrace. Above her daughter's shoulder, Lauren mouthed a tearful thank you to Roan. It was a glorious moment for the three of them, although it did occur to him that once again he and Laura had been stopped from making love.

"I promise not to say a word to your father," said Lauren, holding her daughter out at arm's length. "It'll mean more to him, coming from you." She tweaked Laura's chin. "I'm so proud of you."

"Thank you, Mom. It means a lot to me to hear you say that."

"Me, too," said Roan.

Lauren looked at him with admiration. "Young man, I

liked you the moment I laid my old eyes on you. Welcome to the Bennett family."

She kissed him on the cheek, then withdrew, her cheeks again bright pink. "Goodness, I hope I don't begin to cry. The older I get, the more sentimental I am."

"Sentimental's good in my book," said Roan.

Without thought, Lauren blurted, "How on God's green earth did *your parents* manage to create such a handsome, sensible man?"

She placed the fingers of one hand to her mouth and then froze with disbelief. Laura and Roan laughed when she sputtered, "I can't believe I said that! Forgive me, Roan."

"Perhaps some o' your good taste will rub off on them."

"I do apologize."

"Please, don't," Roan grinned.

A shrill, bloodcurdling scream erupted from somewhere above.

Roan ran for the staircase. In his haste he stumbled and struck his right shin against the edge of one of the steps. Although it was covered with a Persian runner, it was not thick enough to dull the blow. He went down on a hip, howling with surprise, pain and raw vexation. Laura and her mother rushed to him, but another scream rent the air and he forced himself onto his feet. He ascended, the women behind him. Two more screams followed, then a cacophony of shouts. By the time he hobble-climbed to the second floor, he heard Lachlan demand, *"Haud yer wheesht!"*

"What did you say to me?" his mother shrilled.

Roan limped down the hall toward his parents' room, where others were gathered across from the open door.

"I said hold your noise!" Lachlan bellowed. "Your foolishness woke the bloody household!"

Roan stepped around the boys and stood at his mother and Lachlan's side. She was standing on tiptoe, pressing her face close to Lachlan's, her hands on her hips, and her chin thrust out in a manner Roan knew only too well.

She was furious, but also comical-looking in her night garb. The thin straps and lace cups of her negligee could barely support her large, sagging breasts. Her hair was wrapped in a satin turban, and a thick layer of pale green night cream covered everything but her mouth and eyes.

"How dare you talk to me like that!" she shrieked.

She whacked Roan in the chest with the back of a hand, then used the same hand to jab an isolated fingertip into Lachlan's chest, punctuating each shrill word, "I will not stand here and take this from an upstart like you!"

Livid, Lachlan glared down at the assaulting digit, then lifted his furious gaze to hers. "Are you sure you didna happen a glance in the mirror, Mrs. Ingliss?" he asked, delivering the verbal jab with a devilish grin. "You're a frightenin' sight, even for a mon o' *my* years!"

"You arrogant—"

"Mother!"

Her gaze cut to Roan and she jerked back as if stunned to see him standing so closely. "Where were you while I was being molested in my bed!" she cried, a fist emphasizing her words.

Intuition drew Roan's gaze to Laura's pale face. "Hon, tak the lads to their rooms. I'll handle this."

"For pity sake," Lauren huffed, glaring at Eilionoir, "get a grip!"

"Oh, shut up! Roan, what are you going to do about it?"

"Do abou' wha'?" he asked with his scowl, seeing from one corner of an eye his father standing back in the bedroom.

"The ghost! I woke up and he was standing over me with his hands clawed! He wanted to choke the life out of me! When I screamed, he melted into the wall near the bathroom. So what are you going to do about it?"

"A ghost?" Roan muttered, then looked at Lachlan and Winston, who both shrugged.

"He was hideous!"

"I'm sure he—"

She screamed again, pointing past Roan, and he fell back against the wall, a hand clamped over the ear her voice had pierced.

"Oh, my," from Lauren drew his attention to where his mother was pointing. There, between Laura, Lauren, the boys, and himself, was Stephan Miles. Transparent and luminescent green, he was pointing to himself and adamantly shaking his head.

"There's *two* of them?" Eilionoir wailed. "*Two* of them?"

Roan locked eyes with Winston, who stepped forward and leveled an intense look on Eilionoir. A moment later, he turned to Roan. "The memory image in her mind is of Cuttstone," he said disparagingly.

"Cuttstone," Roan muttered. Now his head throbbed with pain as well as his shin.

"Who is Cuttstone?" asked William Ingliss from inside the room.

Roan jabbed a thumb in Stephan's direction. "Cuttstone murdered this man in the cellar a while back. He died, himself, when he went through Lachlan's bedroom window five days ago."

Eilionoir's face sagged. "What kind of madhouse is this?"

Stephan, satisfied that he had been cleared of being the perpetrator, vanished.

"Neither have the power o' the grayness," said Deliah, then yawned. "They be harmless."

"Harmless?" Eilionoir snapped.

"Aye," Deliah said patiently, "harmless. They dinna have the abilities Lachlan had."

"That black devil tried to ruin my husband's family's good name!"

Roan gave a roll of his eyes as Lachlan positioned himself in front of Eilionoir. "Mrs. Ingliss, I didna do anythin' Robbie and Tessa didna deserve."

"Are you drunk?"

"I wish to hell I was," Lachlan grumbled. "Go to sleep, Mrs. Ingliss. We've enough o' your hysterics for the night.

If Cuttstone should return, give the bastard a boo and I'm sure he'll no' bother you again."

"Roan, are you going to stand there and allow this pirate wannabe to talk to me like this?"

"Pirate wannabe, am I?" Lachlan asked with comical affront.

"Dammit, Mother." Roan wearily massaged the back of his neck. "Go to bed. If I hear one more peep ou' o' you, I swear I'll toss you off the bloody tower."

For a second he thought she would defy him. Then she whirled into the bedroom and slammed shut the door, cutting her and his father off from the exhausted observers.

"Charmin'," quipped Lachlan. He clapped Roan on the shoulder. "You canna be from her womb. No way."

Deliah grinned at Roan. "I've a cure for wha' ails her," she said merrily.

"Oh?"

"Aye. On the morrow, though. Good night."

"Good night," Roan said to everyone.

He wasn't looking forward to another day with his parents, but he was intrigued by Deliah's statement. With that in mind, he followed Laura to help put the boys to bed.

CHAPTER SIXTEEN

Through a veil of fog and drizzle, Roan numbly watched the sun wink in and out above the horizon. It was cold and damp atop the tower, and the air held an unpleasant, dank odor. He knew he should park himself in front of a warm hearth. Instead, he secured about his shoulders the red plaid, wool blanket he'd earlier removed from the trunk at the foot of his bed.

He'd only managed three hours sleep the previous night. Afraid his restlessness would awaken Laura, he had gone to the library to sleep on the sofa, only to discover he was wide awake. Little wonder. His sister was off doing who knew what. A faerie kingdom had materialized on the property. Uninvited parents. Two ghosts. Laura pregnant. His mind couldn't juggle it all.

The peafowl were nowhere in sight. Smart birds. They knew enough to take shelter from the cold moisture. Not him. He'd come up to the tower in hopes of clearing his head, but for the past hour and a half the only thought he'd had that wasn't disjointed was he couldn't think worth a damn.

Life at Baird House was a guarantee against boredom.

"The household is awake."

The humor-laced feminine voice brought Roan's head around, then his body. Blue sat atop the crenelated wall on the opposite side of the tower. Her wings were retracted into her back. She wore a pale green, Grecian-style gown and sandals. Her heel-length, blue-black hair was loose, and glossy despite the lack of sunshine. Her skin was the color of fine porcelain, and her aqua blue eyes round and bright, smiling at him with a combination of sympathy and understanding. Like Deliah and all the faeries he'd seen during the ritual of magic, she possessed enchanting beauty and an aura of timeless serenity.

"Did I startle you?" she asked.

"A wee." He removed the blanket from his shoulders and was about to take it to her when she gracefully held up a hand to stop him.

"I'm not cold. Thank you." His dubious frown prompted her explanation, "I was born in late fall, but consider myself a winter faerie. I'm the first. Hopefully, not the last."

"I'm afraid I don't understand."

"Faeries have always been born in the spring." She laughed low. "MoNae decided to experiment." She held up her hands and shrugged. "And here I am."

"MoNae?" Roan asked hesitantly.

"Mother Nature."

"Oh." Roan frowned. Although the queen was friendly enough, he didn't know what to say to her.

"I spoke to Deliah a short while ago. She told me about the excitement you had here last night."

Roan nodded. "Apparently, a killer and his victim's spirit have decided to hang around for a while."

His dry tone brought added life to her eyes. "Poor Roan. You try so hard to keep a sense of balance, and so much works against you. I admire anyone who can look into the face of change and not cringe."

"On the inside, I cringe a great deal."

Her smile broadened. "You and I both know how strong

you are in mind, body, and constitution. Deliah has caught me up on everything that has happened here since her awakening in the root. Would you believe that she was once the most timid of Reith's sisters?"

Roan shook his head, and she sighed and looked heavenward, a wistful expression gracing her features. "I'm so looking forward to the birth of her child." Her gaze lowered to regard him. "I'm rambling. Forgive me."

Grinning a bit nervously, Roan said, "You're entitled."

"Am I?"

"Aye, Your Majesty."

She sighed. "Call me Blue, please. Royal titles are so syrupy, don't you think?"

An abrupt laugh burst from Roan.

"Besides," she went on merrily, "I'm not your queen, am I? So just think of me as one of the guys."

"Right," he chuckled, then sobered. "I'll never forget wha' you did for Lannie."

She nodded, her eyes downcast. When she looked up, she peered at him through the thickness of her lowered black eyelashes. "Gratitude isn't necessary."

After a moment, Roan closed the distance and positioned himself next to her, his lower spine braced against the top edge of the wall. "All right, Blue. I won't bring it up again."

She smiled appreciatively, then widened her eyes and sniffed the air. "Someone's cooking breakfast. Bacon."

"You can smell it from up here?"

She nodded. "And it's my worst weakness. Bacon, that is. Developed a hankering for it while I was living in your world. Can't eat enough of the stuff, and faeries don't eat meat or fish of any kind."

"Wha' do you eat?"

"Me? I eat anything," she said wryly. "Now, your ordinary faerie subsists on vegetation. Why, I don't know. It has just always been that way. My cooks can do up a mean root, let me tell you." She inhaled longingly through her nostrils, then flashed him a grin. "But *nothing* compares to bacon."

"Is this a wee hint for an invite to breakfast?" he asked, his eyes dancing with laughter.

"Unqueenly of me, I know," she said with a mock grimace. "Besides craving bacon, I'm anxious to begin work on the plans for the wedding. Because the ceremony will be held outside of our realm, the magic required to do it up proper will take several days to accumulate."

"Proper?"

She grinned mischievously. "You don't think we're going to just dance around in a bloody circle, do you?"

A wary expression slipped over Roan's face.

"Oh, my dear man," she gushed, her playful mood tickling his curiosity, "are you in for a treat! *Briar Roses'* wedding bash will look like a tea party with the *Mad Hatter* when I'm through. You did see Walt Disney's *Sleeping Beauty,* didn't you? She only had three faeries in her corner. Cute little characters, but I guess the artists didn't know that faeries *never* get chubby. How can they with what they eat? I'm excluding myself because I don't follow their diet. Anyway, I really need a bacon fix."

A burst of silence followed, and Roan blinked in confusion. He wanted to press the back of a hand to her brow, but instead asked, "Are you feelin' a wee jaggy? Feverish, perhaps?"

She looked at him almost shyly. "I love the roll of an R on a Scot or Irish tongue." She gestured excitedly as she went on, "It makes my blood sing and my heart go pitter-patter like the wings of a—oops, I almost said butterfly. Everyone knows there's no grander set of wings than those of a faerie."

Amusement sparkled in Roan's eyes as he nodded in agreement. "I think I should carry you down for breakfast afore you burst wi' good cheer."

"Carry me down from here? Hell, no. I'll fly ahead and meet you at the drapes to the hall, where, if you really don't mind, I'll borrow your arms to make my entrance into the dining room."

"They'll remain attached to me, won't they?"

"Your arms?" She chuckled. "Of course. I just don't want to shake up the parents before the right time makes itself known." A devilish gleam flashed in her eyes. "By the way, Roan, your mother is planning to take over the wedding."

Roan grunted.

"Don't worry. You know, your parents really aren't bad people, Roan. They just got caught up with the material trappings of life. I know for a fact they love you. If you look deeply enough into their eyes you'll see how ashamed they are of the past, and how much they need your approval."

Peeved with her assessment of his parents, Roan started for the steps, but she gently gripped his arm, stopping him.

"I know you believe in magic," she said softly, "but what you don't know is that most of its elements come from the heart. Roan, you're emotionally starting to reach out for your sister. Your parents deserve no less.

"Yes, your mother is being difficult, but you have it within you to bring out the woman she is so afraid to let surface."

"My mither isn't afraid o' anythin'."

"Ahh, you're wrong. Like your father, she's afraid of many things. Failure, for example."

Roan frowned. "O' wha'?"

She looked upward and sighed dreamily. "Of reaching for the stars and coming back empty-handed." She lowered her gaze to see a troubled look in Roan's eyes. "When your parents first wed, they were full of dreams for their future. Ironically, their goals were centered on the children they planned to bring into this world. But of course, Roan, like too many people, they lost sight of what was really important."

"Which was?"

"You and Taryn, of course, and each other. They became so wrapped up in providing the best the material world could offer, the family got lost. They always thought there would be time to make up for not attending school functions or having family gatherings, or to return for the son they had left behind while in search for a better social position in another country.

"They did plan to come back for you, Roan, once they had settled in the States. But by that time you had hardened your heart and wouldn't accept their phone calls or their letters."

"They didn't call! And it was years afore I received a letter!"

Blue sadly shook her head. "Your aunt adored you. It was in your mother's thoughts last night, whether Agnes had told you of her calls and letters."

"Aunt Aggie wouldn't have . . ." He sank his teeth into his bottom lip for a moment. He gulped back the emotions forming a ball inside his throat, then released a thready breath. "Damn me, could I have been wrong all these years?"

Blue tugged on his arm until he stepped close enough for her to reach out and place a hand to his left cheek. "Not wrong, and not right. Confused. Humans have easily created means to cross vast seas and the sky and land, but know so little about bridging rifts in the heart. Don't let this opportunity slip away from you, Roan. It may never come again."

A tenuous grin ticked at one corner of his mouth. "How does it feel to be so wise?"

"Boring."

He grinned in earnest, then released a purging sigh. "I guess 'tis easier to see the problems in ither's relationship, than one's own."

A light frown appeared on her brow.

"Blue, when you mentioned 'rift', I couldn't help but think o' the situation atween you and Reith."

A disparaging sound rattled in her throat. "No comparison," she dismissed with a wave of a hand.

"No?"

She eyed him peevishly before forcing herself not to submit to the bait. "Meet you at the drapes," she said. In the blink of an eye, she sprouted her wings and reduced her size to four inches. She darted down the steps and out of sight, leaving Roan to chuckle softly at her evasiveness.

"Maybe someone should use a bit o' magic on you," he murmured, then headed down the narrow stairway.

She was hovering by the drapes to the exit when he arrived, human-sized at five-foot-five, her wings causing a draft of cool air to circle in the immediate area. Roan had his arms behind her while her wings retracted and she began to drop. As he cradled her against his broad chest, she winked up at him.

"Don't drop me," she quipped.

Grinning, he asked as he passed through the drapes, "How much bacon is this going to cost me?"

"Lots. By the way, faeries believe in the exchange of gifts."

He started down the staircase. "I'm afraid to ask."

"I have a gift for you and Laura. A well-deserved gift, I might add." She smiled brightly. "So I'll consider some bacon a fair exchange."

"Oh?" He paused on the half landing and cocked an eyebrow. "Wha' kind o' gift?"

"You'll see. By the way, I understand congratulations are in order, *Daddy*. Deliah only told me because she's worried."

"Why worried?"

"All the stress you and Laura have been under. And I agree. We simply can't have the new laird and mistress stressed out, especially before the wedding."

"I'll warn you right now, Blue, I refuse to snort faerie dust."

The dining room door was open when they reached it. Roan carried Blue into the room, smiling in greeting to the faces turning in his direction. Laura, Beth, and Winston were placing platters of food on the table. Reith came through the kitchen door with a small tray of condiments. He gave a start at seeing his wife and, after passing the tray to Winston, hurried to meet Roan halfway to the table. Blue glowered at him when he held out his arms, his gaze locked with Roan's.

"Don't you dare—" she started to warn Roan, but she was in Reith's hold before she could finish. She looked up to see gloating laughter in her husband's eyes, and high color stole into her cheeks.

Roan walked to Laura, planted a kiss on her cheek, then told her he was going to fry up extra bacon for Blue. While this was going on, Reith, his back to those sitting at the table, said in a low voice to his wife, "Dinna mak a scene."

"Then be quick to find me a seat!" she demanded in a hoarse whisper, her eyes flashing, daring him to prolong their proximity.

"Do ye remember the last time ye were in my arms, *mo banrighrean?*"

Although his sensual tone made her blood stir with longing, her anger could not so easily be swayed. "I am not your queen," she whispered scathingly. "To be so, you would first have to be a faerie, which you're not. Nor are you considered human. You're but a nuisance trapped between my world and this."

A brief wounded look clouded Reith's features before he awarded her his most charming smile. "Were I but a wee nuisance and no' o' any world, would ye be tremblin' so tellingly in my arms?"

Before Blue could retaliate with a stinging portion of her magic, Lachlan appeared at Reith's side and smiled down at her. "Good morn, and wha' a grand one it is to have you wi' us for breakfast. Come along, lad."

Barely able to conceal his grin, Reith followed Lachlan to where he pulled out the chair at the end of the table, a seat which was normally his. Reith lowered Blue onto it, then caught up her left hand and bestowed a kiss on it before departing to help Roan in the kitchen.

Heat suffused Blue as she stared at the others sitting around the elongated table. She believed it would consume her, or worse, irrevocably melt away the facade she had perfected during her years amongst mortals. All eyes were on her, and if not for Deliah's look of sympathy she would have flown from the room and not cared who she shocked in the process.

Beth placed a calming hand on her shoulder. Looking up, Blue read understanding in the women's eyes and felt her insides cooling.

"I would like to introduce—"

"Blue," Blue interjected, realizing Beth was about to slip up and use her title. "My name is Blue."

"How unusual," Eilionoir commented in a dry tone.

The breakfast was going to be more of a challenge than Blue originally thought. She was considering excusing herself from the table when a plate was placed in front of her. Bacon. *Lots* of thick slices of bacon. The aroma filled her nostrils, and she found herself lulled into passivity. Dreamily, she gazed up at the server and smiled, not caring that it was Reith who received her silent gratitude. He filled her cup with steaming tea, set it down, then sat to her right.

Only half of her attention was given as Beth introduced her to the newcomers, and it was all she could do not to ignore them entirely and delve into the food she most cherished. But she did restrain herself until the others began to eat. She lifted one piece to her mouth, tore it in half with her teeth, then closed her eyes as she chewed and relished the divine flavor.

When she finished the last slice of bacon on her plate, her stomach was comfortably full and her craving satiated. She basked in contentment and glanced about the table. Some had finished their meals; others were nearly done. To her delight, Roan was listening to his father talk about his clothing store and the hardship of finding trustworthy employees. The boys were holding a conversation with their grandparents. Deliah and Winston were snuggled and staring into each other's eyes as if they couldn't wait to be alone again. Lachlan's arm was around Beth's shoulder as they, too, listened to Dugan Ingliss. Reith was staring at Laura, the sadness in his expression directing her attention back to the woman. Sure enough, although Laura appeared outwardly at ease she was nervous and tense, worrying how Roan's parents would take the news of her pregnancy.

Blue felt Reith's eyes shift to her and she swerved her gaze to him. It disturbed her that he did care about these people. It disturbed her because she preferred to believe him incapable of truly caring for anyone but himself. The truth, however, was there staring back at her.

Leaning toward her, he said low enough for only her to hear, "Canna ye do somethin' to ease her mind?"

"What do you suggest?" she asked coolly.

"If I knew, I would be doin' it. She told her faither, earlier. He didna say much. I think he's concerned how this will affect his grandsons."

"Okay, okay," she said with a scowl. "Back off. They both must do this in their own time."

Dealing his wife a sour look, Reith straightened in his chair and turned his profile to her, training his attention on the couple of his concern.

What did he expect her to do? Announce Laura's pregnancy for them? Blow a little faerie dust their way to perk up their courage?

Unexpectedly, Roan smiled and enfolded Laura's right hand with his left, then stood and coaxed her to her feet. He sucked in a breath as he glanced at the faces around the table, then began, "Laura and I— Darlin', do you want to tell them?"

Laura looked about ready to pass out. "Ah, no. You do it."

His smile wavered and he nodded as if needing a moment longer to gather his courage. "We are . . ." His smile bordered the ridiculous, something between sickly and euphoric. "Laura and I are goin' to have a baby."

At first, stunned silence prevailed. Blue was impressed to see the Bennetts reacting as if only just hearing the news. Even William conjured up an admirable glow on his lined face. Then the boys whooped with excitement, and clanged their utensils loudly on the table until their grandmother asked them nicely to please settle down. Their enthusiasm fortified Roan, and he looked into Laura's eyes with the pride of a peacock. Not just any peacock, but Braussaw, himself.

Of course, not everyone shared in the couple's good fortune. Eilionoir shakily rose to her feet, her face pale and taut, her eyes bugging out of her head as she stared at her son. Blue realized what was coming, but couldn't react before the woman exclaimed, "This wedding is a farce! First she traps you with her nephews, now this!"

"Enough!" Lachlan thundered, jumping to his feet and glowering at Eilionoir. "Womon, is there a *bloody* thing you do approve o' where your son is concerned?"

"Oh, shut up, you fool." Eilionoir shifted her gaze back to Roan. Oblivious to his pallid skin and the hollowness in his eyes as he stared at her, she lifted her chin defiantly. "Roan, this nonsense has to end. You're my son and, whether you to choose to believe this or not, I love you. Both your father and I love you! We want you to come home with us."

"And where would 'home' be?" he asked with a winter's bleakness.

"Rhode Island. Where else?" she huffed.

William Bennett slowly rose to his feet, his cheeks the color of a tomato. "Mrs. Ingliss, I resent your comment about my daughter."

"Resent it all you like," she clipped, sparing him but a brief contemptuous glance. "My concern is for my son."

Laura released a strangled sob, wrenched free of Roan's hand, and began to run for the door. Just as she would have passed Blue, the queen's hand shot out in a plea for her to stop. Laura slowed to a stagger and covered her face with her hands. Then Roan was drawing her into his arms and whispering in her ear, at the same time glaring at his parents as though the sight of them sickened him.

"Come to your senses!" Eilionoir cried.

The tension in the room ignited Blue's temper. "Come to yours!" she countered, her palms smacking down on the table at the same time.

"*You* stay out of this," Eilionoir warned, pointing a trembling finger at Blue. "I'll be damned if I listen to someone who has the gall to sit at a table and eat with her fingers in front of guests!"

"Och dìt," Reith muttered, looking askance at the fury building in his wife's eyes. Damn.

Deliah's eyes were wide with apprehension as she stared at the queen. Lachlan abruptly sat, as did William, although he wasn't sure why. Roan and Laura, locked in each other's arms, couldn't tear their gazes from Blue's face,

The boys gaped at Blue, then in unison looked at Eilionoir. Kevin quipped in a deep voice for a boy of eight, "You're in *big* trouble now."

The visual war between the queen and Roan's outraged mother lasted but a moment longer. Then Blue found her voice.

"Bacon is *always* eaten with the fingers. Regardless, in *my* world, I do as I damn please. In *this* world, I do as I damn please."

Eilionoir looked at her son. "Do you hear her, Roan? *Her* world, *this* world. These people are certifiable!"

In a heartbeat of time Blue's wings unfurled and she hovered above her end of the table. From Eilionoir's standpoint, the chandelier blocked out most of Blue, but she could see the lower part of the woman's gown, and the bare feet dangling beneath the hemline. Her jaw slack, Eilionoir dipped to one side. When she got a full view of the faerie queen she sat hard on her chair, her arms limp at her sides. Her husband blessed himself, twice. The Bennetts merely stared in amazement.

"Deliah," Blue said curtly.

Instantly, Deliah unbuttoned the front of her dress and pulled the back down enough to accommodate her own wings. Engaged, she flew up and away from her chair and came to hover alongside her queen. When Blue flew to a position next to Eilionoir, Deliah dutifully followed, hovering behind her queen..

Eilionoir could not bring herself to look up for several seconds. There was only the soft fluttering of wings to be heard in the room. When at last she forced herself to look into the faces of the two creatures, her expression was blank, her lips tightly compressed.

"Mrs. Ingliss, do you know the penalty for a mortal pissing off a faerie queen?" Blue asked in a deadly tone. *"Especially* a certifiable faerie queen?" asked Blue.

Eilionoir stiltedly shook her head. There was fear in her eyes now, and a mist of tears.

Blue gave a haughty flip of her head. "Fortunately for you, Mrs. Ingliss, I haven't been a queen long enough to have memorized the spells pertaining to insults and injury against royal personage. So if you're a smart woman—and I'm sure you are—you might first consider the possible consequences before you run off at the mouth again.

"Roan, Laura," Blue went on, her tone and demeanor calm now, "congratulations. I think the news is wonderful. Please accept my apology for losing my temper."

Roan managed a wan smile, and Laura nodded.

"Mrs. Ingliss," said Blue on a sigh, "you and I need to have a very long talk, but not today."

Eilionoir tried to look away from the faerie queen, but could not for fear she would somehow insult her by doing so.

"Tomorrow we need to get down to the business of settling the wedding plans," Blue went on, casting her gaze around the table before settling it on Roan. She smiled warmly at the still embracing couple. "Roan, I know you want your sister present for the ceremony, so in that, too, decisions must be made. Not now, though. We'll gather tomorrow. Your guests will need today to digest the fact that they will be attending a faerie wedding."

"I agree," said Lachlan with a fond look at Blue.

Everyone else in the room nodded in agreement.

"I'm sure you all are curious what a faerie ceremony entails, so this is what I propose," said Blue. "I will send six maidens to answer your questions and remain to watch over the children, including the twins, through the night," she said to Beth and Lachlan. "They will also keep the ghosts at bay, allowing the household to sleep soundly and undisturbed. The events of the past few days have taken a toll on each and every one of you, so please, allow me to do this. When tomorrow we gather, our hearts as well as our minds should be given to the planning of the wedding."

When nods were offered again, Blue flew around the table to Roan and Laura's side. "I have something slightly different planned for the two of you," she said, her eyes sparkling with mischief.

"Oh?" Laura murmured warily.

Blue grinned. "A chamber has been readied for you in Faerie. For the remainder of this day and all of the night, I promise you no interruptions or distractions. All you need to bring with you is the magic of your love. I've taken care of everything else."

His face aglow with elation, Roan asked, "All this for a plate o' bacon?"

She winked at him. "Imagine what a heaped platter would inspire in me."

Conversationally, Blue told Laura and Roan they would be reduced to the four-inch height of the faeries as they entered the invisible passage through the new oak, to accommodate the kingdom's dimensions. Laura wished she didn't know. It was all she could think about, although the furnishings and everything else lent the illusion that they were normal size. Blue gave them a brief tour of the main chambers, then instructed one of the male faeries to show them to their "special place".

Laura clung to Roan's arm as they followed the reticent male down several corridors. She was a bundle of raw nerves by the time he stopped in front of a mural. To her bewilderment he was smiling and gesturing to the artwork, as if she and Roan should understand what it meant. She didn't. And the puzzlement on Roan's face said he didn't, either.

The painting was of a large, arched, double set of wooden doors, similar to the entrances of ancient castles. Two iron rings were painted on each side, and a thicket of green and white ivy framed the doors and crept along sections of the aged wood. The detail was incredible, but nonetheless it was a painting. To break the silence, Laura said, "Very nice. It almost looks as if we could walk—"

With a gesture of one of the faerie's hands, the doors began to soundlessly part inward. Laura gripped Roan's arm with all her might, her eyes wide in disbelief and awe. She couldn't bring herself to look into Roan's face to see if he was as stunned by what stood before them, but from the rigidity of his body she strongly suspected he was.

"If you need anythin' more," said the faerie with a gracious bow of his head, "just call my name."

Roan frowned.

The young being smiled patiently. Blue must have introduced him, and yet neither Laura nor Roan could remember his name.

"Brandigan."

"Thank you, Brandigan," said Roan.

Brandigan gestured for them to enter the chamber beyond the threshhold. Roan hesitantly glanced into Laura's eyes, then heaved a sigh and led her into the room. Once the doors were cleared, they closed with the same soundlessness. The draft the momentum created told the couple they were now shut off from both worlds. It didn't matter. This getaway exceeded their expectations. Exceeded anything their imaginations could have conjured up.

It was spacious and round, with torches mounted on the walls approximately three feet apart. Alternately, the flames were aqua blue, purple, and fuchsia, and their glow bled across the room in iridescent wisps that swirled and ribboned through the air. There was no smoke, only a fragrance which strangely reminded them both of gardens and the sea and rich earth.

The most astounding feature of the chamber was the pool in the center, roughly forty feet in circumference. Its still water glowed with varying shades of purple luminescence, as if lights were mounted on the bottom.

Hand in hand, Roan and Laura stood atop a portion of the ivy that partly covered rocks bordering the pool and stared down through the deep crystal clear body of water to see there was only smooth rock on its floor. There appeared to be no origin to the lights.

A few feet from their position was a bed of large plump pillows within a gazebo built from woven roots and vines. Bowls of mystery treats and two pitchers of liquid adorned a table by the arch. A short stone path led to stone steps into the pool.

Laura looked up and released a sigh of sheer contentment. An illusion of stars winked in the dome-shaped ceiling. This combined with the swirling, ribboning mistlike colors in the air, made her feel as though she stood in the center of a galaxy in the process of birth. The enchantment of it all overwhelmed her, and she wept silent tears.

Roan drew her into his arms and held her for a time. Somewhere in the distance a soft orchestration of insect sounds reached them.

"This canna be real," he murmured, slipping back into the manner of speech he most favored. "Laura, pinch me. I need to know if I'm dreamin'."

A sound caught in his throat when she obligingly pinched his left buttock. Holding her away from him, he observed the impish gleam in her eyes, then laughed and threw his arms around her in a brief although bearish hug.

"Last one in!" he cried, jumped back and began to unbutton his shirt.

Laura arched one eyebrow, grinned, then dove into the pool. He was quick to follow. His head broke the surface a moment after hers. Face-to-face, paddling to stay afloat, they smiled into each other's eyes with the unspoken affirmation that this time was theirs to rekindle the carefreeness and abandonment of their youth, to make love within the womb of this magical place with no chance of interruption.

"How does the water feel to you?" she asked excitedly.

At first, Roan's mind couldn't formulate a proper description. Then he said, "Like rain water!" and laughed.

"It's so soft against my skin," said Laura wondrously, "it almost doesn't feel real. And it's delicious, Roan. Taste it."

He took some into his mouth, swished it around and swallowed it.

" 'Tis sweet."

Laura ducked beneath the surface. When she came up, she jettisoned a stream of water from her pursed lips, hitting him in the face. Thus began the splashing, dunking one another, and the challenges of laps across and around the perimeter of the pool. On all accounts Laura won—only she knew, because Roan deliberately held back. They frolicked for a long time and, although their muscles should have been aching with fatigue, they experienced quite the opposite. Both felt as if they were imbued with an endless source of energy.

Bobbing on the surface, his legs pumping to keep him afloat, Roan held out his arms. With a laugh, Laura glided through the water into his embrace. He led her into a rendition of a waltz. They swirled round and round and to and fro, and she wondered if he could dance so eloquently on a dry surface. He hummed a tune she didn't recognize, but discovered his voice was deep and melodic.

Unexpectedly, he pulled her against him and kissed her. They submerged, deeper and deeper, wrapped around each other, and settled on the bottom of the pool. The kiss went on for an indefinite time, and both were relatively sure their lungs should have forced them to resurface for more air. They separated and exchanged a look of puzzlement.

Roan opened his mouth. No air bubbles escaped, nor did the water enter the cavity. He inhaled and exhaled through his nostrils. It was if he were breathing air. He gestured for Laura to try and, after several moments, she widened her eyes in amazement.

For nearly another hour, they romped underwater like sea creatures, playing tag and pretending to have tails in lieu of legs, then somersaulting from one side of the pool to the other. Finally, hunger prompted Roan to leave the water and go to the gazebo. While eyeing the small banquet he stripped out of his clothes and placed them on the ground outside the arch, then took one of the bowls and returned to the edge of the pool.

"I'm starving," Laura said.

Roan glanced at her, then did a double take. He sat on the rock ledge and lowered his feet into the water. Laura was in the center of the pool, the upper part of her bare breasts bobbing in and out of the water. She, too, had removed her clothing. He didn't care where she'd tossed them. The water was so clear that he could make out every detail of her nakedness, as if she were standing directly in front of him. When he lowered the bowl to a rock next to him, she swam to where he sat and plucked one of the objects from the bowl. It was light brown and perfectly round. She bit into it, then rolled her eyes appreciatively. The texture was similar to the meat of a walnut, but was sweet and strangely juicy. Whatever it was, she ate half the bowl before grinning up at him.

"Try one. They're delicious."

"Wha' are they?"

"I have no idea, but they're really good."

He popped one into his mouth. Chewed. Swallowed. He repeated this three more times before commenting, "Hmm, they are good." Jumping to his feet, he went to the table and returned with two bowls containing different delights. They proved to be as succulent and as mysterious as the first.

When all three bowls were empty, Roan sighed with contentment and smiled lazily at Laura's upturned face. She had her crossed arms resting atop the rock by his left thigh, and her chin braced atop them. There was a dreamy, faraway look in her eyes, prompting him to ask, "Wha' are you thinkin' abou', love?"

"If it's possible we could make love at the bottom of the pool."

His eyebrows lifted. Since they could breathe this water, why not?

He dove in from his sitting position, broke the surface and gestured for her to follow him. Laura didn't hesitate. By the time she reached the bottom, he was sitting with his arms opened to her. She sat on his lap, facing him, bemused by the fact they weren't buoyant as they would be in ordinary water. This pool seemed to respond to their needs, and once again their lungs didn't demand air. Their bodies required nothing but the love they had for one another.

Their lovemaking began with a slow, penetrating kiss, then progressed with each exploring the other with their hands. The water caressed them. Coddled them. Awarded them the sensation of being submerged and sheathed in liquid tranquility, while freeing them to do what no other human being had experienced in this capacity. Their senses were heightened to only one another. Each stroke fired up nerve endings with unparalleled sensitivity. Two bodies of flesh and muscle and blood were as one. What Laura experienced, Roan shared. What Roan experienced, Laura shared, giving each a better understanding of what their lover preferred. They were of one mind. One soul. One embodiment.

Roan's mouth sought the rigid nipple of her left breast. The pleasure he normally felt was magnified when it was he who felt her sucking at his breast, while *she* experienced what should have been *his* sensory stimuli. This reversal of awareness and sensations brought a new and exciting element to their lovemaking and they lingered in their exploration, wanting to imbibe every nuance of sense-data now available to them.

Their legs entwined and their bodies stretched out against one another, they hovered horizontally above the bottom of the pool. The water gently rolled them round and round, obligingly utilizing their desire to feel as if they were atop solidity and in control of their movements. Curious to know what Roan felt when he entered her body, Laura positioned her legs about his hips, reached down and guided him into her, only it was her experience that she was encompassing a part of herself inside him. Roan, who had never thought about the woman's perspective of entry, was enraptured. In a most peculiar way, they felt as though they were making love to their own bodies, but reasoned this was how it was meant to be. The giving and receiving of pleasure, of physical love, was best when balanced.

Long after the spell had begun and they had satisfied one another in every imaginable and then some unimaginable ways, they left the pool and stretched out on the pillows. They lay wrapped in each other's arms, their legs entwined, and staring into each other's eyes with an unspoken vow that this time together was only their beginning. Whatever pain the past had dealt them, it was now irrelevant and held no purchase in their lives. There would never be fear of what awaited them in the future. Together they would walk each path, and meet every challenge as a team.

This magical chamber had bestowed on them a most precious gift.

A new appreciation of life.

* * *

Blue's eyelids were heavy, but she resisted sleep. Her chamber was as quiet and as still as a breezeless night on an uninhabited planet. The torches were out. She stared into the darkness, content in the knowing her gift to Roan and Laura had been well used. They were nice people. So were Lachlan and Beth, and Deliah's Winston. She'd long ago learned to mistrust humans, sure they were all inclined to be destructive creatures, as well as self-centered, blind to nature, and intolerant of their own.

That opinion had changed now. She not only considered these couples her friends, but knew the children would also become allies. So many kingdoms around the world had vanished. Without hope, magic waned. Without purpose, there was no hope. Mother Nature was a stickler for balance, and sometimes she found it necessary to end certain species. She had always favored her wee folk, but Blue understood that the time would come when even the faeries, too, would fade out of existence. No creature was excepted. It wasn't something she dwelled on. What would be the point?

Sighing, she folded her hands atop her chest and closed her eyes. Had other kingdoms discovered that faeries and certain humans could share a very rewarding co-existence? Deliah and Winston's child was proof there were changes unfolding within both worlds. She wished she knew MoNae's plan, but then also told herself she delighted in the mystery.

What would it be like to have a human lover?

The thought saddened her. Of course, she would never know. It was not her nature to deny the bond MoNae had created between her and Reith. A life of celibacy and loneliness was preferable to dishonoring herself. Pride was all she had left, and it would have to be enough. Unfortunately, there were ninety-nine years, forty weeks, and three days remaining to her reign. One hundred years now seemed an eternity to her, but it had always been the required term in all the kingdoms. It wasn't always easy to ignore her desire to isolate herself from faeries and humans alike. But that was simply too, too unqueenly.

Besides, she was actually enjoying herself since the kingdom's return to this land, thanks to Baird House. There was nothing normal in the stars for any of the occupants. They would cope, though, whatever the challenge, and she looked forward to observing them in the decades to come.

As for herself, after the long centuries of suffering the frustration and indignity of her virginity she had found a solution—for her frustration, anyway. Whenever the old feelings of love for Reith rose up to taunt her, or whenever her body ached to join with his, she now had a way to lift herself out of the morass.

Bacon.

She'd found her escape.

Love be damned.

CHAPTER 17

Lachlan wasn't sure what brought him to the tower until he saw red and gold streaks in the distance and realized the sun was creeping over the horizon. The air was already muggy and warm. Insects buzzed, and birds chirped. Peacocks perched atop the multiple levels of the rooftops on the mansion, geared up to voice their greeting of the new day. The peahens never left the ground, and were far quieter than their male counterparts.

One bird released a cry, inciting the others. Lachlan winced yet smiled, his gaze sweeping fondly over the creatures that had graced this land even before his arrival. He braced folded arms atop one of the higher sections of the crenelated wall and inhaled deeply. Above all else he smelled the rose gardens, the fragrance tantalizing his olfactory sense like a lover's seductive caress. Unbidden, tears misted his eyes.

"You're a damn fool, Lachlan Ian Baird," he murmured, his voice thick with emotion. He tried to will back the moisture, but a tear escaped down his cheek and he self-consciously swiped it away with the back of a hand.

He'd awakened several hours ago to the realization he'd

been having a nightmare. Although he had no memory of it, the aftermath haunted the periphery of his awareness. Granted, he was juggling a lot these days, with "the parents" trying to settle in, the lads overly active with all the new attention they were receiving, Taryn having absconded with the MacLachlan dirk, the faeries, and foremost, his stupidity in drawing the media to the estate once again. Any one item on that list was enough to make him restless. Combined, they chafed his idea of the man he'd believed himself to be once upon a time. The Lachlan of the nineteenth century no longer existed. In this time, his confidence took repeated blows. There was so much to learn and adjust to. Failure had never been in the old Lachlan's vocabulary, but these days the possibility of it shadowed his every waking minute.

A flutter of wings drew his attention to his right, and a smile turned up one corner of his mouth. "Good morn, my paughty friend," he said, reaching out to smooth a hand over the bird's extended head. "I thought I heard you caterwaulin' wi' the ithers."

Braussaw cocked his head before releasing a cry that made Lachlan clench his teeth and grimace. "I used 'paughty' affectionately." Gently lifting the peacock into the crook of his right arm, he chuffed an appreciative sound when Braussaw rubbed his head against Lachlan's bare chest and throat. "Weel, arena we a friendly lump o' feathers this morn?"

The bird fidgeted and Lachlan set him on the wall in front of him. Braussaw strutted in place, then fanned his tail for several moments before settling down so Lachlan could more thoroughly stroke his breast.

Lachlan's gaze shifted to view the sun's slow ascent. The brilliant orb filled him with a fey sense of renewal, one he couldn't define at the moment.

"Anither day," he said more to himself than the bird. He lowered his gaze to the peacock's steady perusal of him. "You were here afore me, and you'll be here when

I'm gone. I've always trusted you to watch over the ithers. Dinna let my absence sway you from your duties."

A choked sound escaped his control, and he rolled his eyes to the heavens. The humidity in the air clung to his bare skin, and he absently ran a palm over his chest and down the thigh of his black pants as he regarded the ancient peacock. When he had first begun building Baird House, Braussaw was there. Watching. Listening. Squawking his disapproval of what he considered a violation of *his* land. Although the bird was unusually aggressive for his species, he had also been quick to make friends with Lachlan, staying at his heels like a loyal puppy and craving attention for the duration of the construction of the house. After that, Braussaw was content to receive an occasional visit from the new master of the land.

"If I think o' myself as auld as dirt," Lachlan said humorously, "then you are as auld as the heavens."

The bird released a guttural sound, then cast off the tower and glided to the ground below, where he searched for breakfast amidst the greenery. The others followed in a flurry of colorful motion, their wings flapping and loosed feathers gently dotting the air in a slower descent to the earth.

Lachlan braced his forearms on the wall and absently watched the birds for a time before shifting his gaze to the sun inching its way into the sky. It was going to be a hot day, he decided. He told himself to make sure the grounds were watered more than usual, then corrected the mental notation when he remembered Reith would better know the grounds' needs.

"Aye, Reith is the better groundsmon," he said, unaware that he was speaking aloud and not mulling over his feelings in his mind. "Roan is the better laird, and Winston by far the best for the security o' this place. You've ou'stayed your usefulness, *auld* mon. 'Tis time to move on." He placed a hand over his racing heart, and willed back the pressure behind his eyes. Before the rest of the household awakened, he needed to rid himself of his melancholy, break the emotional chains tying him to his property.

A shifting of the air to his right jerked him around. At the sight of Beth standing within arm's reach he smiled, but it faded when it registered that her face was damp with tears. They shimmered in her eyes, brightening the blueness of her irises. She looked small and vulnerable in her pale yellow, linen nightgown, one of the thin straps about to slip over the curve of her shoulder.

She swallowed hard enough for him to hear, then forced a little smile. "I woke up and you were gone."

Lachlan pulled her into his arms and brushed his jawline across the soft curls covering her temple. He wasn't sure why she was upset, but somehow knew it was connected to him. "Bad dreams, love?"

He felt her mouth form a smile against the sensitized skin of his collarbone. Her arms wound about him, her fingers kneading his lower back. "No. I had to go to the bathroom."

Lachlan chuckled. "Then I willna ask if you were dreamin' o' me."

Tilting back her head, she searched the depths of his eyes. "I can't do this to you," she said, then shook her head as fresh tears brimmed her eyes. "Lachlan, I can't take you away from your home."

"Hush, darlin'," he said softly, and rubbed the tip of his nose to hers. "You're no' forcin' me to do anythin'."

He turned her to face the east and, standing behind her, slipped his arms beneath hers and linked his fingers against her middle. Resting the back of her head against his shoulder, she covered his hands with her own. She released a shuddering breath and said, "It's so beautiful here. You're part of the house and the land, Lachlan. We'll figure out a way to stay."

His heart flip-flopped, and his face glowed with elation. But reality was quick to reassert itself. "I do love it here. Sometimes, lass, I canna imagine bein' anywhere else. This land and I share a bond I dinna understand, and never questioned afore. Perhaps, 'tis o' my own makin'. My own imagination."

"I don't think so," she said miserably, then added in a lighter tone, "There are times I believe the house is a living entity."

"For a long time, these walls were my only family and friend."

"What about Braussaw?"

He frowned at the question, his face clearing when she explained, "I heard you say he was as old as the heavens. How long has he been here?"

"Afore me."

"Are the other peafowl as old?"

"No. Only Braussaw. He has a wee magic o' his own, and aye, I should have included him as my family and friend afore you came along."

"You fell asleep before me last night, and I was thinking."

"Uh-oh," he chuckled, and kissed her cheek. "Am I in trouble again?"

"No. I was thinking how we could stay here."

" 'Tis no' practical."

She nodded. "I could cut and color my hair, and wear plain lens glasses. A new identity would solve our—" She caught her breath when Lachlan spun her around to face him. She regarded his frown with amusement. "I could use an overhaul."

"Over my twice dead body."

"Aren't we overbearing this morning . . . Horatio?"

Lachlan threw back his head and laughed. When he again met her gaze, mischief sparkled in his dark eyes. "I'll no' stand for you changin' anythin' abou' you, lass."

"No? What if I want a drastic change?"

When he shook his head adamantly, she sobered and trailed her fingertips along the side of his face. Before she reached his chin he took the hand and planted a kiss on the smooth palm, then pressed it over his heart. For a long moment she stared at the placement of her hand, as if expecting his heart to leap into her grasp.

"Beth-lass," he said softly, and smiled adoringly when she looked up. "I may grumble and . . . weel, panic at times when I think o' leavin', but I swear on my honor I'll be happy wherever I go as long as I'm wi' you and our children."

Compressing her lips into a fine line, her eyes tearing again, she gave a shake of her head. "I've been such a bitch."

"*Ach!* Beth, since our return, you've had more'n your fair share o' emotions to juggle. Like me and my no' copin' when you needed me most, and tha' Cuttstone character usin' you."

"Using me? What are you talking about?"

His eyebrows arched in surprise. " 'Twas no' *you* hittin' and jabbin' me wi' the poker."

Beth jiggled her head in confusion. "I was there, remember? And I was in such a foul mood, I seriously considered running you through with that poker. Don't make excuses for my temper."

" 'Twas no' your temper," Lachlan laughed. "When you took the poker to me, I saw a ghostly mask o' Cuttstone appear in front o' your face. Beth, he was in your head compellin' you to hurt me. Tha' you didna succeed proves you were stronger than he."

A shudder coursed through her. "I vaguely remember hearing a voice whispering inside my head."

"Aye. 'Twas the bastard, all right."

"Can he do it again? I mean, can he get inside any one of us now?"

"No. He's an impotent spirit, more a nuisance than anythin'. He'll no' be here long. His ties to this world weaken by the day."

"Thank God," she murmured, then searched Lachlan's face, her eyes clouded with uncertainty. She ran her palms over the smooth, solid contours of his pectorals, then bestowed a reverent kiss between them. His skin was warm and moist from the rising temperature, and as familiar to her touch as was her own.

"Lachlan, let me do this for you." She met his gaze, her own pleading. "I know you won't be happy in the States."

"Have you ghosts there?"

Bewilderment flickered across her features. "I imagine so. Why?"

"Weel, maybe I'll acquaint myself wi' a few." He laughed at her horrified expression. " 'Tis a joke." He crossed his heart and lifted the hand above his shoulder. "I promise I've had my fill o' the dead."

"Thank God," she repeated, this time grinning ruefully.

"So put your mind to rest, love."

"I can't be that selfish. Dammit, Lachlan, this is your home. You'll be giving up everything you love for . . . for what? A mistake? You made a mistake letting that photographer take your picture, and for that you should be forced from your home? I don't think so. Not when there are alternatives."

Lachlan framed her face with his hands, kissed her, then lowered his hands to her waist and pressed his brow to hers.

"Aye, I love this place, my Beth, but I love you far more. I dinna know how many times I have to tell you afore you believe me, but 'tis no hardship sayin' so."

"What if you come to hate your life in the States? Or *me* for having you there?"

"Hate you, lass?" he said in a husky, incredulous tone, and lifted his head. "I could no more ever hate you than regret buildin' this grand house.

"Beth, I was lost for a long time, and you found me. I feared darkness, and you came and gave me light. I was hurtin' and cruel, but you came along and gave me hope."

He dipped back his head and closed his eyes for a moment. When he looked into her questioning eyes, he sighed from the core of his heart of hearts. "I love the way light reflects on your hair," he went on, smiling as he fingered one of her curls. "And I love every expression in your beautiful face and eyes." He kissed the tip of her nose and went on. "The feel o' you in my arms, the way you walk and the way you toss your hair when you're in a temper, and every blessed tone of your voice."

Tears slipped down her cheeks, and he caught one on his lips .

Tasting it, he continued, "Beth, I've been guilty of no' usin' a lick o' sense at times, but never have I doubted my love, or tha' we belong thegither. I'll never be sorry to live in your home or learn the ways o' Yanks. 'Twill be an adventure, one we'll share wi' our children.

"Now ask me if I canna leave here a whole mon, and begin anew in your country."

"Can you?" she choked out.

"Aye." He looked beyond her shoulder, then nodded. "Aye, I can," he said with conviction, then smiled down at her. "I was grateful when Taryn left and talk of the search came up, because it meant I would have more time here, more time in Scotland. But you've chased away my blues, lass. We can leave today if you want. I swear on my honor I'll no' look back."

"No." She shivered and pressed against him. "Too many plans have been made for the wedding."

"We dinna have to wait on Taryn. Roan will understand."

Beth lifted on tiptoe and lightly kissed his lower lip. Needing no further incentive, he fully encompassed her in his arms and kissed her properly from an infinite well of passion, conscious of only the feel, scent, and taste of her. When the kiss ended, Lachlan raked his fingers through his hair and moaned, "I'm o' a mind to have you here and now."

"With the sky watching us?"

"Have you no' heard o' a blushin' sky?"

"I'm not the exhibitionist you are," she teased.

Contentedly wrapping his arms about her waist, he asked, "Will you marry me, Beth, and promise to love me always, despite my flaws."

"Will you?" she breathed, her eyes radiating such happiness, love swelled behind his breast.

"Aye, love."

"Aye, love," she echoed, and kissed him deeply to seal their vows.

On the highest roof line, Braussaw was perched, quietly watching the couple on the tower. Were someone to look very closely, they might see approval in the bird's expression, in its dark eyes, a wisdom that went beyond the capabilities of its species.

Lachlan and Beth, hand in hand, headed for the exit to the servant quarters.

When they were out of sight, Braussaw released a sound that resembled a deep sigh of contentment. He glanced at the brilliant sun and puffed himself up.

The land and he had waited for Lachlan for centuries. With him had come hope, without which no magic could survive.

Time was on Braussaw's side now.